# PLA

# HOUSE

*Perfect families are just pretend*

# L.N. Lenon

Copyright © L.N. Lenon 2025
This book is sold subject to the condition that it shall not, by way of trade or otherwise, be lent, resold, hired out, or otherwise circulated without the publisher's prior consent in any form of binding or cover other than that in which it is published and without a similar condition including this condition being imposed on the subsequent publisher.
The moral right of L.N. Lenon has been asserted.

Charassein Books

ISBN: 978-1-0684105-0-5

# DEDICATION

*To you, my reader, and all the parts of yourself that keep you going and get you through. A special shout-out to the messy, badass ones. Respect.*

This novel is entirely a work of fiction although some of the historical details and characters are factual. Persons named within the script are fictional and are the product of the author's imagination. Apart from those in the public domain, any similarity to persons past or living is coincidental.

# CONTENTS

PROLOGUE ............................................................................................................. 1

PART 1
Chapter 1 ................................................................................................................ 2
Chapter 2 ................................................................................................................ 7
Chapter 3 .............................................................................................................. 11
Chapter 4 .............................................................................................................. 15
Chapter 5 .............................................................................................................. 20
Chapter 6 .............................................................................................................. 24
Chapter 7 .............................................................................................................. 30
Chapter 8 .............................................................................................................. 35
Chapter 9 .............................................................................................................. 40
Chapter 10 ............................................................................................................ 46
Chapter 11 ............................................................................................................ 51
Chapter 12 ............................................................................................................ 56
Chapter 13 ............................................................................................................ 61
Chapter 14 ............................................................................................................ 68
Chapter 15 ............................................................................................................ 74
Chapter 16 ............................................................................................................ 80
Chapter 17 ............................................................................................................ 87

PART 2
Chapter 18 ............................................................................................................ 94
Chapter 19 ............................................................................................................ 99
Chapter 20 .......................................................................................................... 106
Chapter 21 .......................................................................................................... 112
Chapter 22 .......................................................................................................... 117
Chapter 23 .......................................................................................................... 123
Chapter 24 .......................................................................................................... 128
Chapter 25 .......................................................................................................... 133
Chapter 26 .......................................................................................................... 138
Chapter 27 .......................................................................................................... 145
Chapter 28 .......................................................................................................... 150
Chapter 29 .......................................................................................................... 155
Chapter 30 .......................................................................................................... 161
Chapter 31 .......................................................................................................... 167
Chapter 32 .......................................................................................................... 173

## PART 3
- Chapter 33 .................................................................................................... 181
- Chapter 34 .................................................................................................... 186
- Chapter 35 .................................................................................................... 192
- Chapter 36 .................................................................................................... 198
- Chapter 37 .................................................................................................... 204
- Chapter 38 .................................................................................................... 210
- Chapter 39 .................................................................................................... 217
- Chapter 40 .................................................................................................... 223
- Chapter 41 .................................................................................................... 228
- Chapter 42 .................................................................................................... 234
- Chapter 43 .................................................................................................... 240
- Chapter 44 .................................................................................................... 246
- Chapter 45 .................................................................................................... 253
- Chapter 46 .................................................................................................... 260
- Chapter 47 .................................................................................................... 266

EPILOGUE ......................................................................................................... 272

ABOUT THE AUTHOR ..................................................................................... 277
ACKNOWLEDGEMENTS .................................................................................. 278

# PROLOGUE

## September 2023

*The three women stand outside Portsmouth Crown Court without speaking. After all this time, after everything, there is nothing left to say. The square, brown brick building is nondescript, utilitarian even. Two lines of windows reflect the outside world so that curious passers-by have no clue what transpires inside.*

*The women are familiar with the building. With the courtroom inside. Have seen the words emblazoned above the doors:* Courts of Justice.

*We'll see, they think.*

*They know where they will wait. Where they will sit. What they will say. The groundwork has been laid and all the preparation done. But still they pause. Preparation only takes you so far.*

*One reaches into the pocket of her grey jacket, fingers curling around a smooth, cool stone as she takes a deep, steadying breath. Another is restless, tapping out messages on her phone with long purple nails, shifting from one black-booted foot to the other. The youngest woman steps between them, linking their arms together like a cable chain.*

*"It's time," she says.*

*All three exchange a glance, looking first at each other, then at the steps which lead into the building.*

*"It is actually time," the woman with the stone replies, corralling the scattered parts of herself and calming their anxious chatter with a word. It is new, this ability to access quiet, inner space. The woman is grateful for it today.*

*"Well, then," says the one with the nails. "Why are we still hanging around out here? Enough with the waiting."*

*She tugs at the others. Arms still linked, they hurry up the steps and through the double wooden doors together.*

# PART 1

# Two years earlier

# Chapter 1

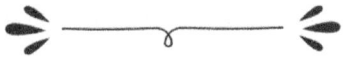

**Me**

*The Queen Mary's Dolls' House is the most famous doll's house in the world. When you are ten years old and already well acquainted with life's penchant for chaos, just standing in its presence on a school trip to Windsor Castle borders on magical. Built by Edwin Lutyens a century ago, it holds treasures from over 1,500 of the world's finest artists, craftsmen and manufacturers. It has a library of real miniature books by the top literary names of the time, a fully stocked wine cellar and a garden. It even has running hot and cold water, electricity and working lifts. Every room is fully and perfectly furnished...*

\*

It is one of those crisp, September days when the carefully woven threads of my existence begin to fray and unravel. You know the type... cool sunny mornings with air that draws out your breath in visible puffs and turns warm by lunchtime with the last dregs of summer. I am lucky John has an early start as I break all house rules by cranking up the central heating pre-mid-October and breathe in the smell of dusty radiators with an old sense of rebellion. John is very sensible about utility bills, and we've spent many a long winter locked in battle over the thermostat.

I am late getting started this morning, gritty-eyed and sluggish after another night of tossing and turning. I linger in the shower, step absently over John's discarded clothes, and stare unseeing into my wardrobe, unable to make a simple choice of outfit. It takes two cups of coffee from the Tassimo John bought as an anniversary gift before the day's tasks begin to order themselves before me.

The dishwasher has been emptied. The cat has been fed. Bright and on point from the moment he wakes, John possesses an early morning energy which is in equal measure endearing and deeply irritating. More so the latter as the years go by, and my own owlish rhythms jar, out of step with his, perpetuating my uneasy sense of less than. But this morning I am grateful for the tasks ticked. It is stock-taking day at the shop, and I am supposed to be opening early.

Upstairs, I collect my bag, tamping down the sudden swoop of emptiness as I hurry past Maddie's slightly ajar door, the room beyond empty and too neat. I resist the urge to bang on Will's door to double-check he has heard his alarm.

*Hope... leave him.*

John's voice, quietly admonishing. I am having trouble adjusting to being the mother of adult children. Or nearly-adult in Will's case. My role, donned like a comfortable old pair of shoes in the chaos of toddlerhood and the skinned-kneed innocence of primary years, is eluding me. How do we all fit together now?

I feel the faintest flutter of old panic emerging from a part of myself long buried under layers of family life. It is easily squashed. *No*, I tell myself, opening the front door and pulling my thin sleeves down against the morning chill.

*

Fran is already at the shop when I arrive, standing just inside the door like a sentinel. I sigh, already forming an apology for my lateness. Fran is a constant for me, ever since her brisk entry into the shop and our lives all those years ago. She is wearing her tweed skirt and practical shoes, her silvery brown bob swishing gently in the breeze as I hurry through the shop door. For as long as I can remember, she has worn her hair this way, with just a half-inch difference in length marking the exact six-week gap she leaves between cuts. I couldn't manage without her, a fixed point in the ebb and flow of student comings and goings. Her old-school exterior belies a delightful flair for creating the most wonderful miniature dolls' worlds. As well as a steady flow of locals passing through, collectors find their way to us from as far afield as Dorset and Hampshire to the West, and Kent to the East. I owe much to Fran.

"Sorry, sorry…" I say, pulling off my jacket and hastening towards my upstairs office. "So sorry I'm late."

I continue apologising as if seeking absolution from an unyielding entity. The effort sparks a flare of irritation, snuffed out before it fully forms. I have always been this way. Trying to measure up. Or make up for *not* measuring up. Fran puts a reassuring hand on my arm.

"Nothing to worry about," she says, pulling a plain blue face mask from her pocket and settling it over her features. "There's no harm done."

Teatime Miniatures was only a dream at first, fleeting and insubstantial. I knew better than to hope for good things. But an unexpected inheritance when John's mother died nearly ten years ago created a chink of possibility. A rare, vacant shop tucked away in the centre of Arundel nudged it towards reality. A few months later, I opened a combined doll's house shop and tea shop. Fran joined me soon after, followed by Spanish barista Carlos, whose chatty charm and full-bodied Espressos drew in a steady stream of customers. I could barely believe my luck. Still can't, nearly a decade later. I am literally living my dream.

*So, you should be happy.*

I shrug off the disapproving voice, busying myself with opening-up tasks. I *am* happy. It is just hard right now, that's all. Like it is for everyone after months of on-again, off-again lockdown, enforced closure and reliance on government grants to survive.

"Hope," Fran's voice pulls me into the moment. A smile tugs at her mouth as she reverently opens a delivery from the previous day. "The antique Georgian has arrived."

I turn to where Fran is standing. She lifts away the packaging to reveal Highbury House, a 16-room $1/12^{th}$ scale doll's house over five floors, standing nearly a metre and a half tall. Its top three rooms are nestled away in a lift-off roof, and it has a basement, with a walled patio. It is beautiful. The house will take pride of place in the bay window where we rotate working displays every few months. We are known for this. No expense spared as we renovate each room and hold workshops for local collectors, teaching them the art of creating perfect worlds in miniature.

As Carlos arrives with a cheerful *Hola!* and the scent of coffee wraps itself in tendrils around me, I shrug off the fatigue and misgivings which have settled over me like a sea mist. I lose myself alongside Fran and Carlos in the day-to-day business of the shop.

\*

It is only as I drive home later, navigating the pockets of traffic lining the A27 on irritated autopilot, that anxiety nestled all day just outside my awareness shifts and takes shape. I need to speak to Will. I just don't know if I have it in me right now. I picture the ground-out joint I found tucked round by the summer house earlier in the week, the smell of the charred weed casting me back to girlhood. I breathe in deeply against the memories, indicating to the right and veering around a camper van driving too slowly.

*Idiot.*

I glare at the errant driver as I pass.

It wasn't John's joint. I snort at the thought. It wasn't mine. Which leaves only Will, whose final year at school completing his A Levels is bumping dangerously up against his recent questionable choices and casually donned can't-be-arsed mantra. I don't know how to approach this. Don't want to upset the household's fine balance.

*Just leave it*, the voice inside me warns. *Forget it.*

The tie between me and my youngest child is strained at the best of times.

*You could have done better.*

I accelerate hard, as if to outrun the whispered accusation, but it is still there. Part of me.

It is past six pm when I pull into the drive of our Victorian end-of-terrace on the outskirts of Chichester. It stretches over three storeys, the loft conversion housing a tiny study and the master bedroom and ensuite which John and I share. I love our roof-top oasis, idly transformed in my mind into its miniature version many times over across years of wakeful nights.

John is home before me. His van is pressed up against the garage to make room for my car. It is a feature of our marriage. Me, the difficult one, taking up the most space. John, steady and yielding. His calm, safe presence both draws me to him and makes me want to kick out against him, like an angry toddler held too tight by its parent.

I let myself in and toss my keys on the shoe cupboard by the door. There are voices coming from the front room. John, yes. Not Will. I step forward curiously, listen, then freeze as the second voice grows suddenly clearer and laughs, yanking long-buried parts of me to the surface.

I step back, distancing myself, heart yammering. My fingers flutter against the silvery-striped flesh of my forearm.

*I need to leave. Now.*

But it is too late.

"Hope!" John calls out at the sound of the door, beckoning me in. "Come in. Look who's here."

As I struggle to catch my breath, resisting the powerful urge to flee, an old instinct cuts through the panic and quashes the wild beating of my heart with one swipe. It shakes into motion a person, Not Me, who walks stiffly through the door of the front room, a mouth that is Not Mine shaping itself into a smile. The Not Me pulls words from my mouth.

"Ros," Not Me says, reaching towards her, eyes skittering away from John's as I lean in for a stiff, unwanted embrace. "I can't believe it's you."

# Chapter 2

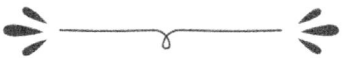

*Maddie*

Maddie wakes in the unfamiliar surroundings of her uni bedroom to the sound of her phone alarm. Setting the alarm is simply habit, as incongruous in the circadian rhythms peculiar to student life as she feels amongst her casually confident peers. She is an early morning person. Like her father. She feels a yearning tug of homesickness at the thought of him. Wonders if he is up yet and if it is too early to text. She sits up and decides against the message. She has to do this on her own.

*First step,* she coaxes herself, *coffee.*

The kitchen of the flat resembles the aftermath of a festival. Soiled pots, plates and cutlery are piled high in the sink, making it difficult to reach the tap to fill the kettle. The bin overflows with pizza boxes and beer cans, and the bottom of her slippers make a sticky sound on the vinyl floor as she picks her way to her cupboard. There is a stale smell in the air. Maddie stifles the urge to restore some sort of order, a habit deeply ingrained since childhood. Bed made, shoes lined up, clothes folded and put away. Will always moaned that their home was only acceptable when it looked like nobody lived there. Maddie would laugh along with him, glancing anxiously around, uneasy that Mum wouldn't get the joke.

Now she reaches for the coffee, balancing her mug on the edge of the worktop as she eases a heaped spoonful from the jar. She learned to like it strong from Carlos. She also learned the best Spanish swear words from him when she was young and still too wary to express strong feelings in her own language.

*Joder! Mierda! Gilipollas...*

Her mind flits back to the summers when she helped in her mother's shop, a small smile twitching her lips as she mutters the familiar words under her breath and imagines Carlos' creased-brow disapproval at the instant granules.

There is no milk. Maddie sighs. She only bought a pint yesterday. She has resisted the urge to label her food, not wanting to seem petty, trying to fit in. She takes the black coffee back to her room, legs curled beneath her on the bed, duvet across her lap to ward off the morning chill.

She has been here for just over a week. Eight days to be precise. She has even been able to attend a tutorial in person, though some of the big lectures remain online. The ground-floor flat is shared with five other students, three girls and two boys. One of the girls, Ella, keeps to herself. Maddie has only seen her two or three times, scurrying between her room and the front door like an anxious little mouse trying to stay invisible in a house full of cats. The rest of her flatmates are the opposite.

*Load of tosser 18-year-olds tasting freedom for the first time.*

Will's voice, passing judgement. Ironic, she thinks, sipping her too-hot coffee, as he is only 17. But Will is one of those people who has the ability – or arrogance – to present himself as an expert on just about any subject. Including exactly how Maddie should be approaching uni life. He is not even going to apply, she reminds herself, suddenly missing him, feeling the absence of their familiar sparring. She wouldn't want to be him when he tells Mum.

She gazes at her noticeboard, still mostly empty apart from generic information about the Wi-Fi code, pastoral support numbers and a poster detailing all the Freshers' Week events. It is circled in fairy lights, her mother's touch, along with the patterned cushions and a deep-red throw to brighten the bland student accommodation. Her mother thinks coordinated accessories are the answer to all of life's ills.

Tonight is movie night, then Student Mayhem at Pryzm. Two of Maddie's flatmates, Kate and Hannah, have persuaded her to go. Maddie checks her phone for her Covid pass, a daily ritual which has taken the place of compulsively monitoring infection levels. It is there. All in date. She is not sure about the mayhem part tonight, but knows she needs to break away from the safe and ordered confines of herself. She feels a small thrill at the idea, a pull of grown-up freedom which both excites and terrifies her.

She finishes her coffee. She will go for a run. Then to the library, maybe, to see if any of the books from her reading list are in. Maybe the others will be up by the time she gets back.

*

As one day merges into another, Maddie finds herself slowly relaxing. She is walking across the campus to Falmer Bar with Kate and Hannah, and another girl from Kate's course who has a shock of short pink hair and calls herself Herb. Giant oaks, beeches and sycamores mingle with red brick buildings. It is part of what attracted her to Sussex Uni. Hannah, a pixie-faced girl in oversized glasses, is trying to persuade Maddie to stay in Brighton for her 19th birthday.

"Come on," she cajoles, linking her arm through Maddie's. "Brighton is for turning nineteen. Not Chichester."

Maddie smiles, hesitating. She still has the faintest headache after last night's foam party. Who knew that was a thing? Mum is planning a family dinner for her birthday and will be gutted if she doesn't come home. It was always part of the plan. The prospect of an imminent reunion had eased the moment of parting nearly two weeks ago. The last of Maddie's belongings had been transported from car to room, the welcome pack thoroughly examined by Mum, and awkward introductions made with the new flatmates. Maddie and her parents had stood there together, uncertain how to negotiate this first separation. In the end it was Dad who spoke.

"Well. Time for us to give you some space," he said. "Let you settle in."

Maddie had felt a stab of anxiety mixed with a longing for the goodbyes to be behind her, wrapping promises to message every day in perfunctory hugs.

"Don't forget to check-in," Mum had said over her shoulder as Dad pulled her gently by the hand. "See you in three weeks!"

Maddie hadn't missed the catch in her mother's voice at that last sentence. Had steeled herself against it.

She checks her phone now, sees another message from Mum, and sighs.

"I don't know," she replies to Hannah. "I promised…"

"Madeleine!" Hannah is exasperated. "You can't go home two weeks after getting here."

"Everyone is going out on Saturday," Kate chimes in, manicured fingers tucking a long strand of blond hair behind a petite, silver-hooped ear.

Maddie is not sure who "everyone" is but feels her resolve slipping.

"Rob is having pre-drinks," Kate adds, like this is the clincher. "We're all invited."

Maddie vaguely remembers meeting Rob and a guy called Warren at last night's party. He is a tall third-year with floppy hair studying politics and living in a shared house near Brighton station. Kate was flirting with him all night. Maddie wishes she could be that confident. For now, just keeping up with who is who and what they are studying is enough. Apart from her flatmates, and a couple of people from her tutorial group, all the names and faces from the past two weeks are a blur.

She glances down at her phone, opens Mum's message and reads it.

*Everything ok?*

An emoji with a too-wide smile.

Maddie imagines the forced nonchalance in Mum's tone. She pockets her phone without texting back.

"Ok," she tells the girls. "I'll stay."

Maddie laughs as they whoop, savouring the warm flutter of acceptance as they head for the bar.

# Chapter 3

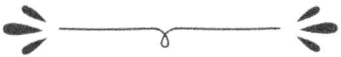

**Will**

Will surveys the cards in his hands, his face deadpan.

"I'll match you," he says, "and...raise you five." He pushes five matchsticks towards the small mound at the centre of the table.

The babble of the sixth-form common room fades into the background as he looks up and waits for Sam to make his move. Vijay and James folded two rounds ago and they are ribbing the pair still in the game.

"Winner takes all," Vijay dares, bouncing on his seat like an eager Jack Russell. "Loser brings the beer tonight."

Sam settles back in his chair, rests scuffed black shoes on the table and runs his hand through thick brown hair. He meets Will's eyes, pushes five more matchsticks into the pot and lays down his hand with a smirk. Three kings.

Will nods approvingly. "Nice," he concedes. "But not as nice as this."

He places a straight on the table, smiles, and sweeps the matchsticks towards him, laughing at Sam's glum expression.

"Guess drinks are on you, mate."

Sam rolls his eyes. "Knob."

The sound of the bell ringing stops any further chat. Study period is over, and Will has two hours of mechanics to get through. His heart sinks at the thought. Somewhere in the months of on-again, off-again lockdown, with its closed schools, cancelled exams and forced confinement to his bedroom, the desire to throw himself into life has abandoned him. Like a dream whose night-time shapes and colours disperse against the contours of a new day.

*What is the point?* His mind taunts him. *When everything changes anyway?*

He drags his feet, uncaring if he is late to class. It isn't that the work is too hard. Will aced his GCSEs.

*You mean the ones you never took, you pretender*, the critic inside him mocks.

Then he made the jump to A Levels with relative ease compared to the rest of his group. He is informal maths tutor to his friends when he can be bothered. But he is so bored. Bored of school. Bored of home. Bored of having no idea what he wants to do next. He bounces between wishing away this final year of school with its academic expectation hemming him in and feeling like he is being propelled from behind towards an uncertain future.

He doesn't want to be at home. Without Maddie around to run interference, all Mum's angst has been pointed in his direction. He's pretty sure she knows about the weed and he's bracing himself for the lecture. It is getting harder to ignore the daily silent tension in the house, grown more intense in recent months. Dad is the one who keeps the surface peace, gauging the mood and putting in checks here and balances there to keep things calm. Will prefers to stay out of the way.

But he can't leave, either. Not properly. The only way out that is remotely affordable is uni. Ha! At more than nine grand a year just for tuition. All to be stuck in another classroom for three, maybe four years. Will has no intention of applying despite predicted A*s. He can't bear the assumption that this is what he will do. From school. His parents. Even Maddie, newly emancipated over at Sussex.

*If you're going to leave, leave, he thinks. Go to Edinburgh, not bloody Brighton 20 miles down the road.*

He doesn't need everyone telling him what to do next. Fuck that. So, he is stuck, filled with an aimless lethargy that has settled over him like a thick layer of dust.

Beer helps. Drawing helps. Being around his equally clueless friends helps. And most recently the weed helps, enveloping him every time in a welcome fog which takes him outside his uneasy existence.

\*

Upstairs in his room later that evening, he is shoving a hoodie and fake ID into a backpack and working out the best way to slip out without a scene. He usually just has to flash the charm or go down the negotiation route, but tonight the mood in the house is weirder than usual. He was late home after hanging out with Sam after school, and instead of going on at him about communication and respect and *how am I supposed to know you're not dead in a ditch,* Mum popped out of her chair with a fake smile, plied him with questions about his day, and offered him tea. Will was too surprised to respond, glancing at Dad and only then seeing the spiky-haired woman with a tattoo snaking up the back of her neck sitting in their front room.

She is still here as he creeps down the stairs, sitting at the kitchen table with a bottle of beer, talking quietly to his parents. He pauses at the door, curious. She seems edgy. Jittery. Not his parents' usual type.

"Will." Dad stands up and beckons him in. "Come over here for a minute. I want to introduce you. This is Mum's –"

"Old friend," Mum interrupts, standing as well. "Ros. Ros... Will. Will... Ros."

Only Ros is still sitting. She nods in Will's direction, meeting his gaze with an air of appraisal. Her eyes are very blue, startling against the jet black of her hair. He is uncomfortable suddenly.

"Hi Will," she says, nodding in his direction. "Nice to meet you."

Her voice has a raspy quality, like she does gigs with a rock band or has smoked two packs a day her whole life. Will studies her with more interest.

"Hey," he replies.

There is a pause, a beat too long for comfort.

"Um..." he begins, breaking the silence. "I'm just off out for a bit. To Sam's?"

He slings the backpack over his shoulder, backing up and warding off the anticipated third degree which never comes.

"Yes of course," Mum says, whisking over and planting a peck on his cheek.

Will pulls a face and jerks his head back. Mum pretends not to notice and keeps smiling her fake smile.

"See you later. Have fun."

"Home by 11pm." His father. Acting more normal.

"Yeah... whatever." Will is keen to go. "See you later."

He replays the scene in his mind as he walks to the bus stop, passing a row of bungalows before taking a cut through to the main road. The hedges on either side draw in the early evening dusk. One of the streetlights isn't working, deepening the gathering gloom.

Mum is acting strange, Will thinks. Nothing new there, but... His mind turns to the woman. What was her name? Ros? He pictures her slight figure, fingers armoured in silver rings absently twirling the beer bottle as she turned to greet him. Something about her felt weird.

He shrugs and puts her out of his mind as he passes the Chinese take-away on his left, then the barber and a hospice charity shop. Finally, the Co-op, with deals plastered in the lit windows, evening shoppers trawling the aisles like robots. Will feels weird, too. Too smart for the rebels. Too bored for the smart kids. At home, he is maths not books. Parties not board games. Blond not dark. Indoors, not out. He doesn't have a clue what's next. Even Maddie studying for her what's-the-point English Lit degree has more purpose than him. Will can't imagine anything duller than reading all those old books and writing essays about them. He shudders. Give him numbers any day. They are either right or they are wrong. He knows where he is with numbers.

He arrives at the bus stop, waits ten minutes for the bus to get there, then climbs on, finds a seat and messages Sam that he'll be there soon. Reminds him not to forget the beer.

# Chapter 4

*John*

John carefully places the bulbs in holes he has prepared along the undulating edge of Mrs Myerson's flowerbed. Daffodils, Miniature Narcissi, Fritillaria, Crocus and Alliums nestle into their winter resting places, their papery brown packages holding the promise of a distant spring. He loves this most about his work. The relentless re-emergence of life in all its forms with each turn of the season. Most gardeners favour spring. John has always loved the slower pace of autumn when the golden remnants of summer lay down the last of their treasures and rest. He covers the bulbs with a practised hand, his intervention in this space complete for now.

He surveys the quiet earth as he rises to his feet, stretching out kinks in shoulders and back, and absently brushes soil from his hands. No matter how hard he scrubs, John's stubby nails always retain the faint outline of the day's work, much to Hope's chagrin. She no longer comments when he makes a pot of tea or lifts clean cutlery from the drawer with hands still rough and marked, but he sees the tension in the set of her jaw. Some days, he absorbs her coiled mood with arms wrapped round her from behind, chin resting lightly on her head in quiet solidarity. Others, he turns away, too weary to engage with the familiar rhythms of their marriage.

He is tired today. Normally he sleeps soundly, the physicality and fresh air of his days pulling him into unconsciousness within minutes of lying down. But last night, an uncomfortable sense of misstep had gathered in his chest after Ros left. A mix of childish dismay and stubborn defensiveness left him staring wakefully into the midnight darkness, carefully moderating his breathing so that Hope would not know he was awake.

"Why did you invite her?"

The fury of Hope's words earlier in the evening had caused his hackles to rise and then fall again as he made space for his established role as peacemaker.

"I didn't invite her." John had chosen his words, spoken slowly to lower the temperature of the exchange. "She came here."

"But you said she could *stay*!"

Hope had been incredulous.

John closes his eyes at the memory. Berates himself for the quick generosity which had offered Maddie's room to Ros without thought, moved by a nameless fragility shimmering just beneath her surface.

"It's just for a couple of weeks…" he'd trailed off, knowing that more words wouldn't help, but continuing anyway. "She's your sister."

Hope had turned on him then. Spitting out each word like a weapon. "She is *not* my sister."

John had walked away. Knowing there was nowhere else to go when Hope was like this.

This morning, he had left early, before Hope was awake, first checking his customer e-mails over a cup of tea and restoring a sense of inner balance as he made a mental note of the tasks which came with the change of seasons. Tidying borders and laying over a protective layer of mulch. Preparing lawns. Planting spring bulbs. Mrs Myerson wanted some new climbers while the soil was still warm from summer but carried the promise of moisture from the autumn rain. Far from damaging the business he had set up nearly 15 years' earlier, the 18 months of pandemic had boosted it, drawing well-heeled city dwellers from their frenetic and over-populated lives to quieter, more rural settings like osmosis. They needed a professional hand to bring their sprawling, neglected gardens into some kind of order while they conducted their business over Zoom.

Now John's list of customers is almost out of control. He loves being busy, feels most centred when his task list just surpasses the time available, but he is feeling the strain of his 52 years as he considers his growing workload. Maybe he will take someone on. Just for a couple of months.

He has finished the bulbs. Checks his watch. There is probably just enough time to clip the beech hedge marking the back of the property before he calls it a day.

\*

When John arrives home, Will is sprawled on the sofa tapping away on his laptop, headphones on, TV blaring in the background. His shoes, coat and bag have been abandoned without thought, creating stepping stones of debris across the room. John picks up the controls, takes the volume down a notch and catches Will's eye, indicating to take his headphones off. Will sighs and lifts one side up, eyebrows raised.

*What?*

John opts to smile pleasantly at his son.

"How was your day?"

"Fine?"

The single word holds an edge of defensiveness, like the question is ridiculous.

"Just fine?"

Will frowns. "Yeah?"

John nods, waits a moment to see if he will say something more, then concedes defeat.

"OK," John says, holding up a hand to delay Will as he lowers his headphones back into place. "Where's Mum?"

Will jabs a finger upwards, eyes already sliding back to his laptop, his father's voice muted.

John goes into the kitchen to make himself a mug of tea, delaying going upstairs for a few minutes more. He hesitates, then pours another mug for Hope, letting her tea brew extra strong. It is his move towards. A simple kindness to smooth the space between them after last night.

He finds her in the study on the top floor. It is not really a study, more a workshop, a retreat. He surveys the acrylic paints, wood stain and modelling varnish laid out across the shelves and desk, paintbrushes poking out from an array of containers amidst pieces of tiny furniture in various stages of completion.

Hope is working on a Victorian antique armoire, no more than four inches tall, with two panelled doors and one drawer each bearing tiny rosebud handles. John has seen this piece before. Hope has already sanded and treated the wood, has outlined the panels in gold-leaf paint, and is now painstakingly painting onto each of the panels a riot of flowers emerging from an exquisite gold vase. Each petal is so small that her hands are working beneath the main lens of the light-up magnifier, barely touching the tip of her paintbrush to the surface of the armoire as the design takes shape. Hope's concentration is complete and John thinks she hasn't heard his approach. Then she speaks.

"The trick," Hope says, not looking up or pausing from her work, "is patience. Not skimping on the preparation."

She tilts her head, examines with a critical eye the delicate lilac buds she is working on – Lisianthus maybe? "It's all very well rushing to the decoration, the bit that everyone sees. But it won't serve you in the end."

John suppresses a smile at Hope's lesson on patience, relieved that her softer self has settled back into place for the moment, eased in through the steady working of her hands. He is familiar with the calming effect of engaging wholly with the immediate physical task, when you are out of your own head and focused on the sight, the smell, the texture of creating. The tempo of the work grounds him on those days when he leaves the house mutely agitated and burdened on behalf of everyone else. He decides to raise the subject of Ros and Hope's extreme reaction last night into the relative calm of this space.

He places Hope's mug of tea on the desk beside her and rests a hand on the nape of her neck beneath the messy knot of dark hair. After a moment, he settles into the armchair in the corner. Fizz, their tabby cat curled up on the arm of the chair, stretches and purrs as he strokes her.

"I'm sorry I upset you last night," he begins, offering an apology as a prelude, choosing his words carefully. "I thought… well, I thought that after all these years, seeing Ros would be a good thing."

Nothing from Hope, apart from a barely perceptible shift in her seat and the set of her shoulders. She has paused her painting, the small brush held motionless in her right hand.

"She left so suddenly," John continues. "Has been gone for so long. You were devastated…" He trails off. Waits.

Hope lays down her brush now, switches off the LED light on her magnifier, and sighs, lifting her mug of tea and sipping it gingerly.

"It's not your fault," she says, swivelling her chair to face him, a stockinged toe reaching out to rest on his foot. "I'm sorry I shouted. It's just…

it took me by surprise, seeing her again."

John regards Hope. Sees how her thumb absently strokes the soft flesh of her forearm.

"But... it could be a good thing, no?" John continues. "That she's back?"

Hope shrugs.

"I wish you hadn't said she could stay."

John nods, concedes the point, but doesn't rescind his offer.

"I couldn't turn her away. I know it's been a long time. But she is basically family. She's in a tight spot."

Hope is mute, her toe still resting on John's foot, but her mind has retreated. She doesn't want to talk. John knows this go-to place and gives her a moment to come back. When she doesn't look up, he stands.

"It won't be for long," he says. "Just a week or two, until Maddie comes back."

Hope frowns and nods, as if convincing herself into agreement with John's position.

"Just a week or two," she repeats softly, swivelling back to her desk and settling her magnifier into place. "Until Maddie gets back."

# Chapter 5

**Me**

*Sylvanian Families is a 1980s nostalgic toy range based in a village where everyone loves nature and is part of a family. You can choose your favourite family of four from sets with whimsical names like Walnut Squirrel Family or Pookie Panda Family. There is a mum, a dad, a boy and a girl. Once your family is chosen, there is the question of where they will live. Will you go minimal with the Log Cabin or Sweet Raspberry Home, or more splash-the-cash with the Deluxe Celebration Home? If you're feeling adventurous, your perfect family of four can take a trip on the Sylvanian River Canal Boat or in the Family Campervan.*

*When your 18th birthday is approaching with no prospect of a special gift, and the longing for your very own Sylvanian Family has lived on well past the recommended play ages of three to eight, you might understand the delight surrounding the charity shop discovery of a vintage Sylvanian Mansion Doll's House. Complete with a Families Figure Bundle. For just £20.*

\*

The last time I spoke to Ros, nearly 18 years ago, I told her to fuck off and die. I can remember in sharp relief the expression of crumpled hurt on her face. How she stepped forward in mute appeal, one hand clutching at the sleeve of my jacket to anchor herself. I had shaken her off.

"I mean it," I said. "This is not my life anymore. You are not my life."

Days later, when the toughened steel which had covered my heart like armour had loosened its grip, the creep of grief and shame made its way through the chinks, rendering me bed-bound for a full month. The doctors found nothing wrong. Not even Maddie's year-old cries roused me from my stupor. John had taken over, holding the world at bay with an infant on his hip, coaxing me out of my darkness with endless cups of tea, day-to-day trivia and a steadiness authentic enough for parts of me to deem it safe to come out. But the darkness had done its work. I was fuzzy on detail, and when I told John that Ros had decided to leave for good this time, that I didn't know where she was, and that I missed her so much, it felt true.

I began to reconnect with my life as a new wife and mother, whiling away sultry afternoons on a blanket under the pergola, Maddie climbing across my lap sticky with sun cream and drool. I was not content exactly, more blankly at peace. Sustaining this state drained my reserves to such an extent that I was completely unaware of the growing existence of my second child. Until one day my morning coffee and boiled eggs made me vomit without warning in the kitchen sink. I was seven weeks' pregnant. How was that even possible? My own family of four was nearly complete.

*

I sit in Maddie's bedroom, outlining the bright yellow petals of the sunflower pattern on her duvet with a forefinger, soaking in the feel of her presence. Maddie inherited her father's love of nature and favoured the bold hopefulness of sunflowers over any other bloom. I remember the day she brought home the little pot from reception, a sticker on the side proudly bearing the spidery letters of her name. The delicate stem of the sunflower was hardly strong enough to carry the weight of its two tiny leaves.

"We have to look after it," Maddie declared solemnly. "So that it will grow."

She stroked one of the leaves with the heavy-handed gentleness of a five-year old.

"It needs the sun."

I think of Maddie now, barely 30 miles away, and feel a pang for the little girl that she was. I am uneasy that she is out in the world.

I can't remember how many sunflowers we nurtured after that. Maddie's grew to sturdy maturity along the sunny south-side of the summerhouse, heads drooping with the weight of a new crop of seeds. Will's didn't make it as far as outdoor planting, most often ending their days spindly and parched in the shade of his bedroom. The love of growing things had passed him by. Watching him stand outside the effortless father-daughter bond tugged at me over the years. I over-compensated and tried to make things easier for him.

I wonder now at the wisdom of this as I survey the calm orderliness of Maddie's room and try not to compare it with the muddled chaos of Will's space. I don't venture into his room these days. Not just to avoid the hostile stares he flings my way at such an outrageous breach. I can't bear the sight of empty drawers left haphazardly open, clothes piled high in crumpled heaps, empty drink bottles and crumbs of midnight snacks littering his floor. I don't even open his windows anymore. The ineffective bursts of fresh air don't stand a chance against the fug of late adolescence permeating the room.

I stand, decisive. I will change Maddie's bedding. The sunflowers belong to her and will be waiting when she comes home. Ros can have the guest bedding, a simple grey set. It is like a blank canvas with no context or story attached to it. It will set the tone for how this visit will go.

*

I am preparing a salmon pasta bake later that evening, absently stirring fresh basil and mascarpone into the bubbling white sauce. Will wanders into the kitchen, sniffing in the direction of the hob and asking when food will be ready.

"Maybe 45 minutes," I reply.

He groans. "I'm starving!"

He roots around in the cupboard, searching for something to have now. I resist warning him not so spoil his appetite.

"Where's Dad?" he asks, mouth stuffed full of bread.

"Still at work. He'll be home soon."

Instead of drifting back to his spot on the sofa, Will settles himself at the table, long legs sprawled in front of him, one big toe sticking out from a hole in his sock. He chews for a moment.

"Who was that woman?" he asks suddenly. "That... Ros?"

I tense and take a breath, still stirring as I lift the saucepan from the hob and pour it into the ovenproof dish, watching the pasta, salmon and broccoli disappear in its creamy depths.

"Ros is someone I knew a long time ago," I say finally.

"Yes, but, who *is* she?" Will persists. "How do you know her?"

His interest takes me by surprise. It has been a long time since a conversation between us has been more than a functional exchange, words edged with strain and the need to escape.

"We were in foster care together," I offer up finally, settling for the truth. "We ended up in the same group home."

I glance at Will. His eyebrows have shot up. He has stopped chewing for the moment as he contemplates this nugget of information mined from the closed-off ground of my past. My family knows about the foster homes, of course. They know about my father – or lack of one – and my mother, a bohemian free-spirit who bestowed on the infant-me the name of Juniper Hope in a haze of stoned and blissful new motherhood. But I have only shared the headlines with them. Even I can't access the full story.

"Why is she here now?" Will continues, his interest piqued.

*Good question. Why is she here now? Why has she come back, after all this time, after everything?*

"Things have been a bit difficult for her," I say carefully. "She's been travelling. She got stuck during Covid and, well... everything sort of fell apart."

"Yeah but... why is she *here*?" Will asks. "I've never heard you talk about her."

"She didn't have anywhere else to go," I reply, opening a bag of grated cheddar and sprinkling it on the pasta bake. "She's going to stay with us for a couple of weeks until Maddie is home."

Will's frown communicates his dissatisfaction at the missing pieces, the holes in my narrative obvious between us. He opens his mouth to ask more but is interrupted by the sound of the front door opening, then John's work boots clomping on the laminate floor as he shrugs out of his coat and hangs his keys on the rack.

"Something smells good!" he calls out, appearing at the kitchen door with a smile.

I smile back, glancing over at Will, who has shed his interest like a second skin. He slouches past his father with a grunt for a greeting.

# Chapter 6

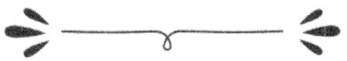

*Maddie*

Maddie feels the ache in her legs and the strain in her lungs begin to ease as she reaches the top of the slope bordering the Great Wood at Stanmer Park. The hum of early morning traffic along the A27 fades behind her as she continues running, past the church and tea rooms and into the village which borders the uni campus. She has nearly completed her morning circuit, and the endorphin rush of accomplishment clears her mind. It is her 19th birthday, and she feels like she can run forever.

She can hardly comprehend that just three weeks and 30 miles of separation from her old life has created so much fresh and unexplored space within her. It is more than just the new friends, a new course and a new place to live. Maddie starts each day with a sense of possibility that she has never experienced before. There is nobody else to consider. Nobody to please. She finds herself lingering in this inner place, content to rest amongst unmade choices, knowing any of them are hers for the taking.

She slows her pace to a brisk walk now, doubling back and cutting across the slope of the park towards the campus. Her flatmates won't be up for hours yet. Kate mocks Maddie for her dedication to early morning running, declaring her a traitor to slothful sisterhood and a disgrace to all freshwomen everywhere. She proclaims the latter in a faux-American twang, waving a cigarette in front of Maddie's face for emphasis. Maddie is learning to give as good as she gets, growing more confident in the repartee of the group, like she is one of them.

But the green shoot of belonging is still delicate, its roots barely anchored in this unrestricted version of herself. She thinks of Mum and the family WhatsApp exchange from the week before. Maddie should have said something sooner about staying at uni this weekend but she had put it off, knowing the response she would get. She thrust the easy excuses of a first essay due before her like a shield, but sharp stabs of guilt breached the flimsy defence.

*not going 2 make it home this wknd* she had tapped out, followed by a disappointed face emoji for extra effect.

Will was the first to respond.

*ur in trbl*

*shut up will*

Mum didn't see the exchange for another hour.

*What? No! Why?? Maddie it's your birthday.*

*essays - loads of work sry mum home soon*

*But what about your gifts? They're all here. I've booked Cassons.*

*i know sry*

Dad was slower to respond. He turned off his data during the day, so only saw messages when his phone picked up the Wi-Fi at home.

*We'll miss you Maddie. We'll bring your gifts over on Sunday. Grab a bite of lunch.*

*ok*

Maddie punctuated her response with an emoji blowing a kiss, muting the chat and her guilt and hurrying back to her friends.

\*

Kate and Herb are in her room while Maddie stands wrapped in a towel, carefully applying mascara. Hannah had to stay late in the lab. Kate is riffling through Maddie's clothes, muttering at her limited wardrobe.

"You are not wearing that," she says, pointing to the summery dress Maddie has laid out on her bed. Maddie glances at the pale blue garment. It is one of her favourites. Her dress sense has always been soft and unremarkable, allowing her to blend smoothly into the background without the drama of bold colours and audacious fabrics. From the time she was a little girl and the alarming, squalling bundle that was her brother took up permanent residence in her mother's arms, Maddie instinctively understood her contribution to the family. She would be a good girl. She wouldn't make a fuss.

Maddie turns back to the mirror, prising apart a clump of black lashes with the end of the brush.

"Why not?"

"So many reasons," Kate replies, her censure finding no words. "Hold on a sec…"

She dashes from the room, leaving Herb and Maddie alone for a moment. Maddie notices that Herb is not getting the same style advice, dressed in loose black jeans and a white shirt. Her only concession to Maddie's birthday celebrations is short hair dyed a more fluorescent shade of pink than usual.

Kate returns with a black dress, so short it looks to Maddie more like a long top than a complete garment. Kate thrusts it towards her.

"Try this."

Maddie pulls a face, dubious.

"Try it!"

She concedes, retreating to her ensuite to wriggle into the dress in privacy. When she eventually comes out and presents herself uncertainly before them, Herb nods her approval and Kate gives a proprietary cluck of satisfaction.

"Bitch!" she says. "That dress looks better on you than me!"

Maddie studies herself in the full-length mirror. A silver zip running from top to bottom of the dress pulls the black, ruched material taut against the smooth lines of her body, slender and toned from running. Maddie turns side-on to the mirror, then twists round to see the back of her dress, long dark hair swishing against bare skin. She resists the urge to tug the hem downwards and smiles at herself. She does look good. Kate dangles a pair of impossibly high heels from her finger as a finishing touch.

"I'll allow it as long as you don't get more attention than me," she says. "As it's your birthday."

Herb rolls her eyes and Maddie tosses a pillow at Kate, who has invited Rob, his weird flatmate Warren and some of their final year friends along for the evening. Kate has been obsessing over Rob all week, reeling him in with banter and suggestive texts. Maddie knows Kate is hoping to get off with him tonight.

She looks at the shoes in Kate's hand and draws a line.

"No," she says firmly, pulling her Doc Martens out from under the bed, laughing as Kate groans. She pulls them on to her feet. "There," she pronounces, tying the last lace tightly. "I'm ready."

*

Maddie lifts her arms above her head, swaying to the music, its deafening *thump thump thump* enveloping her in a wall of sound which both connects and holds her separate from the sea of bodies pressed in around her. She throws her head back and shimmies with the strobe of the lights, still visible through closed eyes.

*I am going to dance all night.*

It is not a conscious thought, more a melding into the moment. A release. She doesn't have to go anywhere or be anyone. Just here matters. Now. With the music.

Their group had expanded pied piper-like through the evening, gathering friends, acquaintances and nameless strangers as they moved from bar to bar, sipping cocktails and pints and stopping for chips. Pryzm is their last stop. Maddie can't keep track of who is still with them. Josh and Martin from the flat are here with a couple of their course mates, she thinks. Rob and his friends were propping up the bar last time she looked, Kate glued to Rob's side. Hannah and Herb are around somewhere.

*There.*

She sees Herb's pink hair bobbing up and down a few feet away, a fluorescent beacon in the smoky light. She doesn't know who all the others are. Doesn't care.

*Everyone can join.* She feels generous, expansive.

It took three cocktails for Maddie to relax into the evening and feel the first flush of pleasure at the appreciative comments and glances tossed her way. That was hours ago. Now she is dancing like she has never danced before. She doesn't want this moment to end. *Ever.*

"Hey, birthday girl!" A pair of arms snake their way around her waist. Maddie leans into the backwards embrace and smiles sensuously.

"Dance with me!" she says, twisting around and grabbing Hannah's hands, pulling her in.

"OK, party girl!" Hannah laughs, untangling herself from Maddie's grasp. "Calm down."

"Dance!" Maddie insists, raising her voice above the thrum of the music.

Hannah leans in close. "We're taking the party back to our place. Come on!"

"No…" Maddie dances away from her. "I'm staying here."

Hannah grabs her hands and tugs her to the edge of the room. "I don't think so, lovely," she insists, ignoring Maddie's protests. "Not in this state. You're coming with us. Herb!" She calls over. "I need back-up!"

Maddie allows the two girls to pull her along, scattering smiles and hellos liberally about her as faces she vaguely recognises blur by.

"Hokay…" she says. "Let's take the party home."

By the time they reach the flat, Maddie's cocktail high has dissipated into a sense of dozy wellbeing. She sits at the kitchen table munching on prawn crackers and scrolls through her phone. She barely remembers taking all the pictures on it from this evening. She will take a selfie to send home.

"Everyone come here!" she yells, boozy confidence lifting her voice above the babble of chatter. "Get in the picture!"

People shuffle around behind her as Maddie holds the phone aloft, angling it as best she can to fit everyone in. She doesn't know who half these people are. But who cares?

"One… two… three… smile!"

She pastes on a wide smile and takes a series of photos, lowering her phone to inspect them more closely. She picks one and shares it on the family group, with the caption *happy bday 2 MEEEEEEEEEE!!!!*

She looks up, squinting round the room.

"I need another drink," she says to nobody in particular.

Walking with exaggerated care to the cluttered worktop, Maddie searches for something she likes and pours herself a generous slosh of pink gin topped with lemonade. She weaves back through the clutter of bodies pressed into the kitchen and sets it behind her on the table before turning to Kate and laying her head on her shoulder.

"Love you…" she says.

"God, Maddie – you're pissed," Kate laughs. "Love you too, babe."

Maddie reaches round for her glass and takes a long swig, savouring the taste of the fruity gin, slaking her thirst.

\*

She is sooooo tired. Most people are still here, sitting round on sofas and chairs dragged into the common area. Someone has connected their playlist to a speaker and music fills the room. Josh, Martin and a couple of other guys are playing beer pong with Herb. Maddie waves at Josh and he blows a kiss in her direction. His blonde head blurs with Martin's dark one, like they are the same person.

*Beer pong... beer pond...*

Maddie snorts at her own joke, trying to tell Kate why it is so funny, but she can't see Kate and she loses the thread and her tongue feels fuzzy and too large in her mouth. She can't say the words. They swirl around and around in a thick fog. She is having trouble focusing.

"I need...gotobed..." she slurs to herself, stumbling to her feet and nearly toppling over. "Whooooooops."

She tips into the door frame, just catching herself. Nobody notices, either too pissed or engrossed in cheering on the beer pongers. Her legs feel like lead, the Doc Martens dead weights at the end of them.

"S'bed-time," she says to herself, inching along the corridor wall towards her room, leaning more heavily with each step. Where even is her room?

"Areyoumy room?" she asks as she reaches the first door on the left, leaning on its frame and banging on it until she hears the click of the lock as it opens. She falls into the darkened space with a thud.

"Owwww. Shit!" She is on her hands and knees.

She hears a groggy voice through a tunnel. "Who's that... Maddie?"

"Ella." Her eyelids are so heavy. "EllaEllaCinderella..."

Somewhere from her faraway early-evening self, the mocking words of the group briefly re-insert themselves into consciousness, then flash away. Maddie feels the pull of the floor beneath her. Then darkness.

# Chapter 7

**Will**

Will needs a cigarette. For the last hour of biology, he has tuned out the drone of Mr Packer's voice, allowing his mind to wander to less pointless places. He stretches his legs, kicking absently at the table. He knows all this shit, anyway.

Will used to love school when he was little. He remembers a time when the morning light filtering in through his curtains filled him with a sense of anticipation. He would pull on his uniform straight from the floor, cramming his bag with scraps of paper filled with important scribblings and Match Attax cards he'd saved to trade with Sam. He would take the stairs two at a time in his haste to begin the day. Mum would make him eat breakfast, fuelling his fizzing energy with a glass of apple juice and a piece of jam toast.

"Eat," she would say, then yell upstairs for Maddie, who was the late one back then. Will would bounce impatiently at the bottom of the stairs, resisting the urge to tell Maddie to hurry up, knowing this would make her take even longer.

Now Sam is jabbing him in the arm, opening his eyes wide and lifting two fingers to his pursed lips in the universal language for *smoke?* He has read Will's mind. Will gives a short nod. They will grab lunch and meet in the far corner of the field, just past the tennis courts. The boys' changing rooms mean they will be mostly out of sight of any teachers or jumped-up prefects.

The class springs up Pavlov dog-style when the bell rings out its familiar jangle of freedom. Will and Sam have already messaged their group with the plan and toss bulging backpacks over their shoulders as they make their way to the door. They ignore Mr Packer's raised voice reiterating tonight's homework.

A small group has gathered by the tennis courts. Will, Vijay, James, Sam and a guy called Josh, who Sam knows from sports science. Will doesn't like Josh much. He is one of those preachy, six-pack types who wears shirts a size too small and downs protein shakes for lunch. Will only tolerates his presence because Sam likes him for some reason. Will lifts his roll-up to his mouth, inhaling the untainted nicotine and blowing clouds of it in Josh's direction, smiling as Josh bats the smoke away with a frown. They are talking about Liam from Mrs Clarke's tutor group who tried to kill himself at the weekend.

"He hung himself," James says with grim relish. "Or tried to, anyway. In his garage. With climbing rope."

"How do you even know that?" Sam asks, re-lighting his roll-up, his hand curved protectively around the flame of the lighter as he inhales. "Nobody knows that."

The school had given only the sketchiest of information, swathed in heartfelt assurances about more lessons on mental health and an open invitation to talk, talk talk... *As if,* thinks Will, who finds it awkward making eye contact with teachers, let alone sharing his innermost thoughts with them. That level of real feels impossibly distant and grown-up, like having a mortgage or getting married. It fills Will with a breathless anxiety.

*Man up.*

He shrugs the voice away. The school's concern and open-door messages have clearly done bugger all for the poor sod who tried to hang himself.

"My sister knows his brother's girlfriend," James continues, smug and puffed-up with untold detail. "His dad found him. And only just in time, too. He'd kicked the chair over." James pokes his tongue out to one side, head lolling as he mimes hanging from a rope.

Will imagines finding someone like that. Wonders what Dad would think if it was him. He inhales deeply, holding the smoke in his lungs for three seconds, four... five... before releasing short puffs into the cool air. The thought of Liam stirs a raw discomfort in the pit of his stomach. He turns away from it, making space instead for aggression which fills his chest like an old friend.

"Why would you hang yourself?" Josh asks, curling one arm up and then down again, absently observing the pop of his biceps.

Will glares at him. "Why does anyone do anything? He obviously had a lot going on."

*Wanker*, he thinks to himself, stubbing out his roll-up and imagining it is Josh's head.

"Yeah, but why *hang* yourself," Josh persists. "I mean, if it was me," he pulls a face to make it clear that this would never be him, "I'd like, take a bottle of pills or something. Less drama. You know?"

"I think I'd jump off a bridge," James says. "That would get the job done, wouldn't it?"

"Shut up, James," Sam says, glancing towards Will.

"But it would, though, wouldn't it?" James turns to Vijay. "Wouldn't it? What would *you* do?"

"I wouldn't," says Vijay.

"Yeah, but if you *did*, what would you do?"

"I just wouldn't."

"Shut the fuck *up*, James." Will's tone creates a vacuum, sucking the air from the exchange.

They are quiet then, the spectre of Liam looping a rope into a noose, fixing it to the ceiling and making the conscious decision to step up onto the chair, one foot, and then the other, sitting uneasily amongst them.

*

Will is still thinking about it as he pushes dinner round his plate that evening. He has zoned out the adults around the table and only looks up when the shout of sudden silence snags his attention. He looks up. Mum, Dad and Ros are all staring at him.

"What?"

He is irritable. They never used to eat at the table every night. Maybe on Sundays or when friends came over, but that was it. Ever since Ros has been here Mum has insisted on this family mealtime charade. Force-feeding them all *edifying* family conversation. He misses sitting with a tray on his lap, tuning into whatever crap is on the TV so that he isn't required to engage.

"Ros asked you a question," Mum says with a pointed look.

*Be a perfect son. Play happy families,* Will interprets.

He is tempted to draw out the silence, making his own point.

*It's all bullshit.*

But curiosity prevails, so Will ignores Mum and switches his gaze to Ros, who is sitting at the end of the table nearest the door. She has been here for more than a week.

Ros gives a small smile, hands fluttering as though unacquainted with stillness. She fidgets in turn with her knife and fork, her empty wine glass, the saltshaker. Feathery rips shred the serviette on her plate.

"I just asked when you would be eighteen," Ros says in her gravelly voice. "If you were going to have a party."

She casts a glance in Mum's direction as she speaks, but it is Mum's turn to tune them all out. Dad keeps eating, one slow, steady bite at a time. Will can tell that he is listening, but he obviously doesn't feel the need to weigh in on the conversation.

"Um... 6th January?" Will replies. "It's ages away."

Ros gives a slow, thoughtful nod. Another glance in Mum's direction, but she is absently scraping old candlewax from the grooves in the table.

"Never too early to plan a party," Ros says lightly, reaching for the half-empty bottle of Malbec and offering a small smile to Will.

Will finds himself smiling back, not even caring when Mum suddenly re-joins the exchange, bringing up all his childhood parties like a badge of motherly honour.

*Do you remember this time, or that time, or the other time when...? Do you, John? Do you?*

Her voice swirls around them all, but Will is not paying attention. He is thinking about the party he will have when he turns 18 and the endless blank space after that. He wonders where Ros will be then.

\*

He spots her again from his bedroom window as he draws his curtains closed against the inky darkness of the early autumn sky. He takes a step closer to his window, partly shielded behind the curtain. His eyes adjust to the gloom and he makes out her shape in the chair next to the summerhouse. She is in his spot. As he watches, he sees the disembodied orange glow of a cigarette – *or is it weed?* – flare briefly and then fade out. He wishes he had the courage to join her.

The house feels different with her in it, even though Will has barely seen anyone over the past week. He is either at school, out with his mates or locked in his room and his head with noise-cancelling headphones, playing the hero in exotic Far Cry landscapes. Ros isn't much in evidence, either, as far as he can tell, drifting down for mealtimes and small talk, mostly with Dad. Other than that, she is holed up in Maddie's room with the contents of her oversized rucksack scattered haphazardly across the floor. Will couldn't resist peeking round the door once, when he knew she had gone downstairs, jerking his head back and feeling the creep of shame on his cheeks when he spotted a pair of lacy orange knickers tangled in the legs of her jeans.

*For fuck's sake – grow up,* he berated himself. *Don't be such a child.*

He watches her now from the safety of his darkened window, the hot glow and fade of her cigarette holding his gaze like a hypnotist's pendulum. Knowing she was with Mum in the foster home has awakened his curiosity. Ros feels like forbidden history pulled from the archives and ready to air.

# Chapter 8

*John*

The jingle of the bell announces John's arrival at Teatime Miniatures. His frame fills the doorway, and he stoops slightly as he steps into the shop, mindful of the uneven slope of the ceiling held aloft by pock-marked beams. The ebony-polished floorboards squeak beneath his work boots as though protesting his presence.

John helped Hope to refurbish the shop a decade earlier, maintaining the original features at the front whilst extending the original ground floor space to incorporate the bright and airy coffee shop out back. He spots Carlos pouring frothed milk into a cup and lifts a hand in greeting.

"Hola, John," Carlos calls out, nodding at him before returning his attention to the couple he is serving and regaling with one of his stories.

John goes to the bay window where Fran is working on a top-floor room of the latest display house, painstakingly measuring sheets of sage green wallpaper bearing a latticed design. She is being observed by a small group of collectors.

"The best place for the edges of the wallpaper to meet," she explains to the group, "is anywhere that is not a focal point in a room. So…" she points a sensibly-manicured finger, "not here where the fireplace stands, nor here near the picture window. Nowhere the eye will naturally fall in the first instance."

The members of the group nod earnestly, jotting down notes. John watches for a moment as she measures and cuts her sheet, applying a thin layer of wallpaper paste with a deft hand. She glances up at him.

"Hello, John," she smiles. "Hope is upstairs."

"Thanks, Fran."

John returns her smile, observes for a moment more, then moves through the array of dolls' houses on sale, towards the narrow staircase which twists up to the first floor.

He has spent the morning working in Mr and Mrs Benwell's rambling garden in nearby Binsted, lifting and dividing the perennials bunched and overcrowded after the abundance of summer. He had reached a natural break by noon and decided to surprise Hope with lunch by the river. He hopes the unexpected break from routine will soften the hard shell which has encased her in the two weeks since Ros arrived. What he would really like is for Hope to look up and see him. Really *see* him, not just point her eyes in his direction while her mind is distracted by long lists and endless inner battles. The unlikelihood of this happening is hard for John to acknowledge outright. Instead, he shrugs off his neediness like an unwelcome cloak and reminds himself that he's more than capable of fending for himself.

It takes him a moment to spot Hope, crouched down on the floor unloading a box of roof tiles and other items onto a shelf. She lifts first one, then the other of a pair of small chimney pots, examining each one with a critical eye before she senses John's presence and turns towards him.

"Hi." She is surprised to see him, scanning the space around him as if it will yield up the reason for his visit.

"Hi yourself." He steps towards her, bending down to plant a kiss on the top of her head. Dark curls have worked themselves loose from her hair band and tickle his nose. "Fancy a bit of lunch?"

He sees her do a quick recce of the unopened stock stacked next to her and mentally recalculate the order of the afternoon. Hope doesn't do well with sudden changes to her schedule.

"Um... lunch?" She stands and adjusts products on the shelf into regimented, equidistant rows while she talks. "I have to be back for two... there's a workshop."

John checks his watch. "I think we can manage that. I'll help move these boxes to the back," he adds, and Hope relents.

They cross over Tarrant Street and make their way downhill to the little café on River Road. It is still early, only just past noon, so there are plenty of empty tables outside. Hope selects one in the corner, its sun-trapped position softening the biting October chill. Still, she pulls her jacket more tightly around her.

"What will you have?" John asks.

Hope gives him an absent smile. "Anything is fine," she says. "Whatever you like."

John goes into the café, and orders two paninis, a pack of Pipers sea salt crisps, and two coffees. He watches Hope through the large plate glass window while he waits, wondering if their lunchtime escape will be worth the effort. Well, he thinks, shaking a packet of brown sugar into his coffee when it arrives, even if Hope can't relax, *he* needs the pause in the day.

When John first started the business, he could sustain the hard, physical labour of his work without stopping between dawn and dusk. By then, hard graft and obligation had become habitual, so deeply ingrained he could barely remember the carefree child he had once been. When John was just 15, his father had been eating his morning bowl of porridge, his hard hat and high vis jacket beside him, when he fell dead to the floor. A sudden clot to the brain excised him from the lives of his wife and two sons with the cold precision of a surgeon's blade. Friends and relatives had gathered round.

*You're the man of the house, now,* they said with well-meaning intent, swamping the bony jut of his shoulders with the ill-fitting mantle of responsibility. And then they were gone, leaving John to fill the man-sized hole that his father had left. He muted his own grief in deference to his mother and brother.

These days, he finds himself slowed by the ache in his knees and the bow of his shoulders after just a few hours of labour. It is getting harder to push through these physical limitations.

He focuses his attention on Hope, who is staring out across the river, narrow shoulders hunched against the cool air. He slides a coffee over to her before easing himself into his own seat. They sit quietly for a moment.

"Andy and Sue have invited us all for Sunday lunch," he says, pulling his phone from his pocket and tapping out his password with a forefinger. Where is the text from his brother? It came in while he was working this morning. His brow creases in concentration. *Ah – there.*

"Not this weekend. Next," he adds. "I've said we'll come."

Hope turns to face him.

"But what about Maddie?" she says. "Maybe she'll be home that weekend."

"Maybe," John says lightly. "If she is, she can come with us. The boys would love to see her."

Hope sighs, and John understands that sharing Maddie with the wider family is not part of the plan.

"We don't even know that she'll be back," he says. "She's obviously settled in. That's what we want, right?"

Hope doesn't answer at first.

"Right, Hope?"

"Right."

Her response is rote, skin deep.

The serving girl arrives with their paninis, melted mozzarella oozing out over a meagre salad.

"Thank you," says Hope, pulling the plate towards her.

Hope has been quieter than usual since Maddie's announcement that she will not be back for her birthday this weekend. She is disappointed. So is John. He misses Maddie's quiet presence, like ballast in a choppy sea.

Ros had picked up the scent of Maddie's extended absence with the instinct of a bloodhound, wondering aloud to Hope and John if it would be possible to stay for just a few days more.

"Until I've sorted a few bits out," she added. "And then I'll be off."

"Fine," Hope had replied, with an air of weary resignation before a surprised John had the chance to formulate the correct response.

To be honest, John has quite enjoyed Ros's presence in the house. The change in dynamic has shifted the focus from Maddie's absence and the brittle atmosphere at home. Most evenings, Hope takes herself upstairs to her workshop after dinner, Will disappears out or into his room, and John finds himself alone with Ros, drinking tea and reminiscing. Last night, their conversation had looped back more than two decades. Younger and more carefree then, John had been dismantling sets at the end of an August festival, work boots planted wide for balance while he wrestled to shift a heavy beam. It was hot work at the end of a long weekend, and all he could think about was putting his feet up and downing a cold beer back at his van. He had another job starting the following day and could do with the space. The sound of laughter and chattering voices caught his attention, and he paused his work, glancing over at the group passing by. He had seen Hope first, in grubby trainers and cut off shorts, picking her way across the field with long, tanned legs. As she walked, she lifted slender arms to tighten the messy knot of her hair, laughing at something one of the girls was saying. John couldn't take his eyes off her. He saw another girl, young and fragile as a bird, notice him first. Then Hope. John will never forget the first time Hope turned to him, meeting his gaze with a slow smile.

"We were just kids," Ros said last night, flipping her unlit cigarette over and over in her hands. "And you were so old."

"Steady on," John replied, taking a sip from his tea.

"You were over *thirty*," Ros continued, pulling a face. "Seriously old." She was silent a moment, lost in thought. "Hope didn't care, though."

*But you did.* The thought came unbidden to John's mind.

It was true. John was 31 when he met Hope, and Hope was not yet 20. Still a teenager. At 15, Ros had been her shadow, glued to Hope's side, sullen and watchful. It was months before she stopped treating John like an intrusion, and even then she had been sure to let him know where he stood in the pecking order. Hope first, Ros second. Then John. He had been OK with that, content to bide his time.

"Turned out OK, though, didn't it?" John said last night.

Ros smiled a small smile. Shrugged. "I suppose you've done OK for yourselves."

They fell silent then, the cosy warmth of the living room with its framed family photos on the hearth giving weight to her words.

John can still see the 19-year-old Hope in the face of his wife across from him. Her hair is still long and untamed, not even a strand of grey breaking its rich brown hue. The only concession to the passing of time are the fine lines that fan out from the sides of her eyes and the creases in her forehead which John longs to reach out and smooth. But her eyes are the same. Sometimes, when Hope goes to that distant place and shuts John out, he grounds them both with the memory of that first look, that first shared smile.

He reaches across the table to take Hope's hand now.

"Ready to go?" he asks.

She squeezes his fingers, nods.

"Yes," she replies. "Thank you for lunch."

The break has calmed her, and she smiles as she stands. "Time to get on now."

# Chapter 9

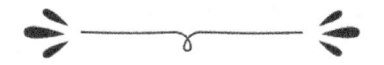

**Me**

*The intricacy of a fully-furnished doll's house is the first thing that draws you in. Each room holds undiscovered riches beyond that initial glance. The skeins of wool stacked in a basket tucked next to the armchair; the bread bin in the larder; the building blocks scattered over the floor of the nursery; the book and reading glasses resting on the bedside table. Acquiring this ready-made miniature world all for yourself is like finding treasure. You can't believe it is yours.*

*But after a while, settling for the world of another is like looking in from the outside. Life experience presents your otherness as truth. It whispers into your ear that this is all there is for you as you stand there, nose pressed longingly against happy family windows. The mere thought of something better feels dangerous. The perfection of the miniature world is unobtainable, but still you cling to it.*

I was still finding my footing on the precarious ground of new adulthood when John found me for the first time. His calm presence and dirty, calloused hands steadied me, even as part of me pushed against him, determined as I was to balance on the rocky ground of my life without help. But John was unfazed by my resistance and simply waited patiently for me to turn towards him. *John.* Even his name was solid. An unencumbered single syllable with no sharp edges or hidden corners. When we discovered that we shared the same birthday of November 1st, the fact of my existence underpinned by his, it seemed like a sign. I was only 19 years old when I first loved him, and he was entering his fourth decade. Somehow the distance in our ages and life experience created sufficient space to nurture within me something close to trust. I tasted its tender shoots like a timid mouse, ready to retreat at the slightest threat. All the while, Ros clung to me, brimming with watchful resentment.

I fell pregnant with Maddie as winter loosened into spring the following year, marrying John in the whirlwind of discovery and finding myself both wife and mother one month shy of my 21st birthday. In the photos, I am smiling a dazed smile through a sheen of exhaustion like any new mother, but for me there was more to it.

*This isn't for you,* the voice whispered, day and night. *You are not good enough for this.*

My attempts to tune out the voice and prove it wrong through feverish dedication to the creation of our first home built within me a terrible, pressure-cooker tension. It finally erupted one sleepless night while Maddie was cutting her first tooth.

"Shut up, shut up, *shut up!!*" I had screamed into the twilight darkness just before dawn. Maddie's tiny body was stiff with outrage as she reared back from my exposed breast and her wails intensified. "What is *wrong* with you?"

*No, what is wrong with YOU?* The voice was never far away. *I told you so!*

I started to shake her then, to stop her, to stop the voice.

"Hope... HOPE!" John's voice then. John's hands. Taking Maddie from me, rocking her gently back and forth to calm her desperate cries while I ran from the room. I crumpled to the floor, hands covering my shamed face.

*Not for you, not for you...* the voice taunted.

I knew. I had always known.

The next day, Maddie cooed in the arms of John's mother in the unseasonably warm April sunshine dappling our garden. I sat with John at the kitchen table, pale and mute with failure. My Nokia bleeped a text message from Ros.

*Fancy a cheeky birthday getaway?*

A getaway. Ros would be 18 soon. I had closed my eyes in longing. An impossible dream. Like climbing Everest. *No.* Like flying to the moon.

A second bleep.

*We've got Jazz's place the weekend of 25th.*

John must have spotted something in my face. A sign of life maybe.

"What is it, Hope?"

I handed the phone over to him and watched him read Ros's messages. He thought quietly for a moment. Then set everything in motion.

"A getaway may do you good," he said. "Go."

So, it was settled.

\*

Now Ros is 36 and that weekend getaway remains coiled between us like barbed wire. I am peeling potatoes, the mundane task tying me to the communal space of the kitchen. I long for my workshop in the eaves. Ros is at the table, doing a crossword.

"Twenty-three across," she says, chewing on the end of the pen. "Negligent."

"How many letters?" I ask, welcoming the safety of the simple exchange.

"Um… six," she says. "Last letter S."

I think for a moment, my mind circling the word, examining it from all angles. "Remiss," I say at last, plopping the potato into a bowl of cold water and picking up another.

Ros nods her approval. "Nice," she says. "How about this one? Pink flower with a yellow centre. Eleven letters. First letter P. There are a couple of Rs and Es – near the middle and one at the end."

I can't think, the set letters constraining me.

"I'm going over to Brighton tomorrow," Ros says suddenly, looking up from the crossword and laying the pen down.

I glance up at her.

"Oh?" I think of Maddie in Brighton. Quash the flare of longing in my chest.

"There are a couple of bedsits."

I raise my eyebrows, keep peeling, wondering how she will afford a bedsit, where she will find a deposit. *Not my problem,* I tell myself.

"They're probably crap," she continues. "But I may as well have a look."

"Why Brighton?" I ask mildly.

Ros tilts her head at me as though the answer is obvious.

"I'm not exactly Chichester material, am I?" she says.

I refuse to be drawn, shrug. Who knows what material Ros is? I don't say this, though. Conversations that venture beneath the surface are too risky. Instead, I ask Ros if she can pass me a saucepan from the cupboard next to her. I feel her looking at me for a long moment before she bends down to retrieve the pan, pushing it across the table towards me. After a moment of silence, she picks up the pen and repeats the last clue.

"Can you think of any pink flowers with a yellow centre?"

I shake my head no.

"Flowers are John's department," I reply. "You'll have to ask him. He knows everything."

Ros mutters something.

I freeze.

"What did you say?" I ask her, but Ros just shakes her head, flipping to the back of the book for the answer.

I tip the peeled potatoes into the saucepan, fill it with water and place it on the ceramic hob with a clatter.

"I'll be upstairs," I say, untying the apron and flinging it over the empty chair.

"Prairie Rose." Ros answers herself. "Who ever heard of a Prairie Rose?"

I ignore her and leave the room. I don't care about the stupid puzzle. Ros's mumbled words follow me up one flight of stairs, two, clinging to me like burrs even as I shut the door of my study against the rest of the world.

*But he doesn't know everything, does he?*

\*

Her words linger in the air as we eat dinner together later that evening, dangerous and untamed. I feel anxiety sitting high in my chest, unappeased even after an hour spent varnishing an oak balustrade for a Victorian house. I overcompensate by talking too much, filling the gaps so the words can't gain traction. Will has pushed his chair back as far as it will go while he shovels bites of cottage pie into his mouth, distancing himself from us. Still, I can't stop.

"I was thinking that we can all go to Brighton on Sunday," I babble. "You too, Will."

I don't include Ros. She is not one of us.

"We can bring her presents with us in the car, and maybe some more of her stuff. I wonder if she needs her bike in Brighton. John – do you think she needs her bike? Maybe you can put the bike rack on the car this weekend. I don't know if I should make a cake just for her or for her flatmates, too. How many of them are there again? Do you think she'll want a cake?"

I go on, not giving anyone space to respond, until Will finally interjects, pushing his empty plate away.

"Mum. Chill. Please."

I frown, stung. "I *am* chilled," I say.

Ros raises her eyebrows and Will snorts. John throws him a warning glance.

"I just want Sunday to be nice," I continue. "For Maddie."

"I'm busy on Sunday."

Will gets up from the table and adds his plate to the pile of dirty dishes next to the sink.

"For goodness' sake Will!" I snap, familiar irritation taking over. "The dishwasher is right there."

"All right! Calm down."

Will's response leaves me feeling wrong-footed, like he is the injured party and I am the irrational one. It is always this way. I feel the spring of coiled anger deep within me. I am tired of being the bad one. Weary with the effort of trying to get it right. Silence settles over us as Will stomps up the stairs, the sound of his footsteps echoing a protest around us.

"I'll wash up."

John offers the words like a gift, which angers me further. Why does he have to be so bloody reasonable all the time? Why can't he just lose his shit and get it wrong like the rest of us?

"I can manage the washing up, thanks."

The words are out of my mouth before I can stop them, and I see John's features contract. Ros looks up at him, offering silent solidarity in the face of the madwoman at the table.

I stand up, entrenched now.

"I'm not a complete fucking imbecile."

I pile up the rest of the soiled plates, casserole dishes and cutlery precariously. I push past Ros and John, who are frozen in place, before dropping everything into the sink and turning the tap on full. The force of the water propels bits of food from the dishes down the drain and the spray from the water soaks the front of my shirt. *I hope the sink clogs,* I think mutinously, reason abandoning me. *I hope it clogs and floods and explodes so that it can never, ever be fixed again.*

I stand at the sink, my back to the room, breathing deeply until Ros and

John make their escape. My rage diminishes, leaving in its aftermath a young, tearful part of myself that needs the warmth of a hug. But the old rage was too big, and I have frightened everyone away.

# Chapter 10

*Maddie*

The first thing Maddie notices through blurry, crusted eyes is the way the light falls into her room. The sun is shining full on her face. It is not supposed to be like that first thing in the morning. She turns her head to avoid the light and groans as a wave of pain shoots from the top of her head down her neck. Everything hurts, and there is a dull ache low in her belly. As consciousness creeps like tentacles around her, Maddie becomes aware of long strands of tangled hair sticking to her cheeks, of slick, sticky sweat covering her body, and a violent nausea that sends her springing to her feet. She barely makes it to her ensuite in time, hanging her head over the bowl of the toilet and emptying the contents of her stomach. Her head and body protest at the sudden movement, and she slumps on the cool tiles of the bathroom floor, too weak to move for the moment.

*How much did I drink last night?* she thinks, closing her eyes and breathing deeply against another rush of nausea and a cramping in her stomach. After a moment, the cool air of the room starts to chill her damp skin. She opens her eyes again, looks down. She is naked.

*Oh god,* she thinks, casting anxiously about for a memory of how she got here, but drawing a blank. *Where are my clothes?*

Maddie pulls the towel from the railing and runs it over her cooling skin, under the jut of her breasts and between her legs. She mops away the dampness and sour sweat before staggering to her feet like a new-born fawn.

She has a terrible thirst and runs the cold tap full blast, putting her lips to the stream of water and drinking it down in large gulps until the nausea threatens to overwhelm her again. She staggers back to bed, pulling the twisted duvet up over her body, shivering now, closing her eyes and falling once more into a deep, uneasy sleep.

When Maddie wakes again, the angle of the sun has changed once more. This time it barely creeps through the gap in her curtains and the suffused light in the room has a late afternoon feel to it. Maddie reaches out and tilts her phone towards her. Ten past five. In the afternoon. She takes a moment to compute that she has been asleep all day. All day. She can't remember ever doing that before. Gingerly, she lifts her head and shifts into a sitting position. Her mouth is fuzzy and dry, and there is a stale smell. She pulls the duvet up self-consciously, covering her breasts and taking a moment to look around her room. It is both familiar and alien against the black hole of the previous night. Kate's black, ruched dress lies crumpled on the floor, the long silver zip fully open. Both Doc Martens are abandoned near the foot of the bed, unlaced and tossed on their sides. She feels something with her toes and lifts the duvet to see the lacy edge of her knickers twisted into a tight knot at the edge of the mattress. Maddie squeezes her eyes closed, trying to recall arriving back in her room. Undressing. Going to bed. But it is like her memory has been swallowed whole. She remembers running yesterday in the morning, getting ready for the evening out with Kate and Herb and the others.

She focuses.

They went into Brighton. Had chips, some drinks. Back to the flat with everyone. Then... nothing. Maddie feels a pang of unease. She must have been completely smashed.

After a few moments, she picks her way to the shower, steadying herself against the tiles with outstretched arms, and allows a stream of hot water to run over her body, washing away the smell and stickiness. She stands until the water runs cold, but still the story of the previous night eludes her, its faint presence in her periphery dissolving under direct scrutiny.

It is getting dark by the time Maddie feels strong enough to pull on an old hoodie and jogging bottoms and venture into the shared kitchen. Music is playing and she hears voices chatting as she approaches. Josh and Martin are laughing at something on Martin's phone, and Kate and Hannah are sitting on the other side of the table. Kate looks as bad as Maddie feels, resting her chin on her hand as she listlessly scrolls through her social media. Hannah looks up at Maddie's approach.

"You're alive!" she cries, spreading her arms wide in dramatic welcome. Then, peering more closely at Maddie's wan face. "But are you, though?"

Maddie groans and slips into a seat next to Hannah.

"I feel like shit."

Hannah nods sagely, as if this is no surprise to her.

"Boys!" she says imperiously. "Tea. With plenty of sugar. And bread."

Josh looks up questioningly, and Hannah waves him towards the worktop where a large tub of Flora sits next to a Tiger loaf. Josh pulls himself to his feet and lumbers across the kitchen, pulling the bread towards him and rummaging round for a knife.

"When we couldn't wake you up this morning, we – as in me and the boys – bought a fresh loaf especially for you. This one…" Hannah leans over to give Kate a shove, "was nowhere to be seen."

Kate frowns at Hannah.

Maddie smiles weakly. Tries to frame her thoughts.

"I um… I've never felt this bad after a night out," she says to the room, while Josh slathers margarine on a wedge of bread. Maddie turns away, her stomach still unsettled. "I feel seriously ill."

"Well," Kate says, looking over at last. "You were packing it away last night. You deserve to feel a bit ill."

"Too right you were," Hannah chips in. She gestures to Josh. "Be a love and cut a slice for me," she adds.

"Fuck off," Josh says mildly, cutting her a slice anyway and tossing it in front of Hannah along with Maddie's tea and bread.

Maddie smiles her thanks up at Josh and chews half-heartedly, unable to shift the shroud of uneasiness that has enveloped her since she woke.

"What happened after we got home?" she asks. "It's a bit fuzzy."

This, Maddie thinks, is an understatement, her sense of last night more a vacuum than a blur.

"Well, you invited the whole world and his dog here for a start," Hannah says. "Hence this…" she sweeps an arm around the wreckage of the kitchen.

Maddie nods. This doesn't sound like her, but OK.

"You were taking pictures of everyone – check your phone," Hannah adds.

Kate looks up from her own phone. She isn't wearing make-up and looks tired. Her hair is pulled back in a messy ponytail.

"And then you made your dramatic exit," she says flatly.

"Dramatic exit?" Maddie feels untethered, like a balloon drifting helplessly skywards.

"You were hilarious," Martin says. Martin is the opposite to Josh – small, dark and wiry, like he is permanently poised to spring into action. "You sort of landed in Ella's room – flat out."

"What?"

"Yeah. You were out cold on her floor," Martin says, laughing. "It took two of us to get you to your room."

Maddie closes her eyes as she sips the sweet tea, trying to summon any memory of these events at all. Nothing. She turns to Kate and Hannah.

"Kate?"

"Hmmmm?" Kate is distracted, messaging someone, not looking up at Maddie.

"Did um… did you or Hannah, or Herb maybe, take off my – your – dress when you got me to my room?"

Kate frowns and continues texting.

Hannah looks up and pulls a face.

"Um.. *No*," Hannah replies. "That would be weird. We pulled off your boots, and tucked you in, dress and all. You are welcome," she adds with a gracious nod. "We even left the door propped open so we could check on you and make sure you didn't die of alcohol poisoning."

Maddie frowns. She doesn't remember the door being open when she got up. And she definitely wasn't wearing the dress.

"It's just," she hesitates, lowers her voice. "When I woke up, I wasn't wearing the dress."

Kate is still messaging. Maddie presses on.

"I wasn't wearing anything, actually. And the door was closed. So…"

Kate shrugs. "So what? Like I said, you were totally out of it. You probably got undressed and shut the door without realising."

"Yeah." Maddie tests this version of events against the black hole of the previous evening and finds it wanting. "Yeah… I guess."

She is weary of the company suddenly, too tired to stay awake.

"I need to go back to bed," she tells the others. "Sleep it off. See you all tomorrow."

She walks down the corridor to her door, her slippered feet padding softly on the laminate floor. As she opens her door, she hears a soft voice behind her. Ella.

"Maddie?" Ella takes a tentative step out into the corridor, one hand anchoring her to the door. Dark blonde hair frames her face and she wears an expression of concern. "Are you... are you OK?"

Maddie nods. "I'm fine," she says, more sharply than she intends. She feels a stab of shame at the image of herself flat out on Ella's floor. "Just a bit hungover. You missed a good party last night," she adds. "You should have come."

Ella nods, takes a step back to the sanctuary of her room.

"I'm not that much of a party person," she says with a smile. "But I'm glad it was a good night." She pauses. "I hope you're OK." She meets Maddie's gaze for a moment. "Really OK, I mean." Then she gives a nod, like she's said enough, and shuts her door.

Maddie feels tears well up behind her eyes and quickly blinks them away. *What is wrong with me?*

Back in her room, she stretches out on her bed, fully clothed and staring at the ceiling. As the pounding in her head abates, other aches and pains creep into awareness. She shifts uncomfortably onto her side to ease the ache in her belly, and gasps as she hits a tender spot on her hip. She props herself up on her elbow and lowers the waistband of her jogging bottoms. A purplish, black bruise is forming, stretching round to the front of her pelvis. Maddie flops back. She must have hurt herself when she fell in Ella's room.

*God! How humiliating.*

She really can't face her family coming here tomorrow. Maddie opens their group chat and sees the picture she sent in the early hours of this morning, momentarily unsettled at the sight of her grinning face, flanked by a sea of new friends and strangers. She can't remember taking the photo. Or sending it.

*sry guys* she messages to the family chat. *im not well cant do 2mrw*

Maddie doesn't have the energy to say any more and mutes the chat before anyone replies. She'll look at it tomorrow. Talk to them then. If she sleeps now, she might be up for a run in the morning. The thought centres her as she drifts off to sleep, comforted by the prospect of her old routine.

# Chapter 11

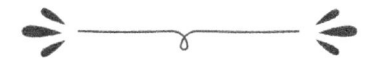

*Will*

It is the end of October and Dad has dragged Will out of bed on the final day of half-term. He wants help with the annual garden clear-up at Uncle Andy's place in Storrington. Today was supposed to be Will's last chance for a lie-in before going back to school. Resentment wraps itself round him, slowing his steps to a sluggish drag and reducing his words to sullen grunts. Nobody should be up this early on a Sunday, he thinks, tightening the strings on his hoodie so that it cinches closely around his face. He pulls the sleeves lower to cover cold fingers.

"Will!" Dad's voice drifts down from the top of a ladder where he is wielding a chainsaw and cutting away great chunks of green which fall to the ground in knee-high clumps. "Come on!"

Will sighs and rolls his eyes. He picks up the rake with weary resignation and half-heartedly pulls the clumps into bigger piles, ready to be collected and deposited in the compost heap.

Cutting back Uncle Andy's and Aunty Sue's garden every year ahead of bonfire night is one of those rituals that started before Will could remember. The first time Dad asked him to help, Will was just eleven. He still recalls his wide-eyed excitement, belted into the back of Dad's car, grinning and sticking out his tongue at Maddie. She just rolled her eyes at him and shrugged like it was no big deal that she wasn't getting Dad all to herself for a change.

"Loser," she mouthed, fixing headphones over her ears and staring out the window.

Will was not impressed with the teenage version of Maddie. At thirteen, she was snappy and moody. Impatience with her younger brother poured off her in waves, pushing him back whenever he ventured too close. But Will wouldn't let Maddie upset him that day. Dad wanted him, and he was going to make the most of it.

Now Will would give anything to swap places with Maddie, living away from them all, too busy to come home since she'd left nearly six weeks ago. And definitely not available for a day of slave labour with Dad. Even her messages on the family chat had slowed to almost nothing in the last couple of weeks.

Will should have just said no when Dad told him about today. He would be eighteen in a few months, and nobody would be able to tell him what to do then. But he could never quite shake off the eleven-year-old version of himself, chasing after approval from his father like a bloody dog.

He gives the rake an impatient tug, overbalancing slightly and catching himself on the base of the ladder.

"Careful, Will," Dad says, holding himself steady against the flat top of the hedge.

"Alright... calm down," Will mutters, using his hands to start piling the clippings into the wheelbarrow.

Will hears his uncle's voice and the high-pitched laughter of his youngest cousin as the family arrives home. Daniel, who is eight, comes tumbling out the back door with a football under his arm, unruly black curls framing a freckled face and a wide, toothy smile. Daniel waves as he nears them.

"Will!" he shouts. "Want to play?"

Will glances at Dad and smiles back. "In a minute, mate," he says, pointing at the rake. "I need to finish this first." He reaches out as Daniel draws near, pushing his cousin, laughing, into one of the piles.

Daniel's older brother Jake, lanky and self-conscious, ventures into the garden next. Only his eyes give away any interest at the prospect of a kickabout. Will tips his head at him, feeling an unexpected rush of solidarity with the older boy, more comfortable in the fringes than the spotlight.

"All right?" Will asks.

Jake nods, kicking at the leaves. "Want some help?"

"I thought you'd never ask."

Will tosses the rake to his cousin and heaves the full wheelbarrow to the end of the garden.

Working together, they finish the hedge quickly and break for a cup of tea and a plate of Aunty Sue's flapjacks. Will is on his second one, nudging the ball past a protesting Daniel to score in their makeshift goal of heaped jumpers, when he hears Dad mention Ros.

"No Maddie on Friday," he is saying, talking about their bonfire night get-together in a few days' time. "But we'll bring Ros along if that's OK."

"Still with you then?" Uncle Andy asks as Will dribbles the ball closer to listen. "I thought it was only for a week or two."

Dad shrugs. "She hasn't found a place yet."

Will sees Aunty Sue raise her eyebrows and make a harrumph sound at Dad. "I'll bet she hasn't."

"She's looking, Sue." Dad jumps to Ros's defence. "There's not much out there just now. She has a couple of job interviews coming up, so maybe after that…"

Will wonders what Aunty Sue has against Ros. What Mum has against her, for that matter. Ros is the only one who talks to him, and Will has found himself growing bolder and more confident in her presence. He knows she is somewhere in her thirties but she doesn't look it, and she treats Will like an equal, which is more than he can say about anyone else in his family. Earlier this week, after his parents went up to bed, he had lingered downstairs, hoping Ros would stay down too. He wasn't disappointed. She'd smiled at him and pulled a chair close to the open patio doors, nodding at him to join her. He'd dragged a second chair next to her. He could smell traces of her perfume, lingering in the cold air like a gift.

She had pulled a pack of cigarettes out of her pocket, placed one between her lips and held the packet out to him.

"Want one?"

Will looked around, checking his parents were nowhere in sight, before quickly taking one. He cursed himself for acting like a kid and switched to casual nonchalance.

Ros smiled and held the flame of her lighter towards him. Will inhaled, feeling the wave of the nicotine hit his system. He sat back in his chair, closed his eyes.

"So, William," Ros asked. "What's happening with you?"

Will hated it when his parents pried into his life, but coming from Ros, it was different. He felt grown-up, important when she spoke to him.

"School's shit," he said. "I'm so over it."

Ros gave a short laugh. "I hear you... it was never my scene either."

There was a brief silence as they both blew puffs of smoke out through the open doors. Will found himself wanting to tell her more. To hold her interest.

"There's this kid," he began, staring straight ahead. "Liam."

He pictured Liam, back at school now, set apart from his peers after last month's suicide attempt. Will found himself drawn to Liam. *What happened?* he wanted to ask. *How were you brave enough or desperate enough* – Will couldn't decide which it was – *to walk away from everything and actually try to end it all?*

"He tried to hang himself. In his garage."

Will glanced over at Ros to see her reaction, but she just nodded, looking out at the rain falling softly in the darkness.

"He's back now. At school." He paused. "I don't know how he can stand it. After doing that. After making that decision," he said. "To sit in a maths lesson and work out trigonometry problems like it's nothing when three weeks ago he wanted to be – tried to be – dead."

Ros glanced over at him then. "What else is he supposed to do?" she asked.

Will thought about that for a moment.

"I don't know," he said finally. "It's just weird."

Ros took another drag on her cigarette, then stubbed the end out in her empty mug.

"Sometimes," she said, "you just do the next thing because that is all you can do."

Will wondered if that was what Ros was doing. The next thing.

"My mum has scars on her arms," he said suddenly, thinking of the faint silvery lines laddering her forearms, kept hidden beneath long sleeves even in summer. All of them knew. None of them talked about it. Like always.

Ros gave a small smile and reached over to stroke his arm gently, fleetingly. Will felt a rush of heat and shifted in his seat.

"It's not the same," she said.

"But, did she ever...?" He couldn't form the words.

"It's not the same."

He didn't say anything more.

"Maybe," Ros said, "that is what kept her alive."

Will let the words settle, let them percolate down so they made sense. But he couldn't match the day-to-day picture of his mother, brim-full of busy efficiency, with this before version of herself, holding death at bay with a blade, marking out her intention to live one line after another.

"Why…" Will began, and Ros reached out and touched him again, making his words catch in his throat as he fought the sensations and drew back.

"Not now," said Ros.

Will wondered what she meant.

*

As he and Dad drive home from Uncle Andy's in the chilled Sunday twilight, wipers sweeping away a fine mist of rain that has started to fall, Will closes his eyes at the memory of Ros's touch, and lets it grow and evolve in his mind.

"Thanks for your help today," Dad says, glancing at him as he indicates left at a roundabout. "It was good to have you along."

Will feels a flush creeping up his cheeks as though Dad can read his thoughts. His response is more brusque than he intends.

"I didn't exactly have a choice," he says, regretting the words immediately as they settle between the two of them, creating a wall Will can't breach. He wants to take them back but doesn't know how.

"Well," says Dad mildly, squaring his shoulders like Will has seen him do with Mum when she's being difficult. "Thanks anyway."

Will shrugs, stuck in the habitual current of feigned indifference.

"Whatever," he says.

Dad doesn't say anything more, and they drive the rest of the way in silence.

# Chapter 12

***

**_John_**

John will always remember the day Will came into the world. He arrived two weeks early, in his own time and at his own pace, before everyone else was quite ready for him. Boxes of Christmas decorations were still stacked on the downstairs landing, waiting for John to hoist them into place on high garage shelves, and Hope's hospital bag was only half-packed. The forecasters had been predicting a winter storm for a week. The morning of Will's birth dawned muted and full of diffuse light, fat flakes of snow swirling from slate-grey skies and disappearing into the thick layer of white which blanketed everything.

"How will we get to the hospital?" Hope had panted, perched on the edge of the bed, legs braced, hands on knees as she breathed through a contraction. They were coming every ten minutes now, and John felt a twinge of anxiety as he surveyed the snow-covered road.

"I'll clear the drive," he said, shrugging a thick winter coat over his shoulders and laying a reassuring hand on Hope's shoulder. "St Richard's isn't far. We'll be OK."

"But Maddie!" Hope squeezed her eyes shut and tensed, forgetting for a moment to breathe. "Your mother can't come out in this weather."

John had already thought of that, had woken their neighbours early that morning. He didn't like to ask for help, but sometimes there was no choice.

"Next door will have her," he said gently. "It's all arranged."

By the time John had settled Maddie next door, and cleared enough of a pathway to navigate the car down the slope of the drive and into the road, Hope's contractions had grown so hard and close together that she struggled to place one foot in front of the other, the icy conditions causing both of them to slip and slide as they picked their way to the car.

"I... don't think... we're not going to...make it," Hope gasped, clinging to him.

"We are."

John spoke with an authority he didn't feel as he gently belted Hope into the front seat, slid into his own seat, and began driving as quickly as the treacherous conditions would allow. Getting to the hospital too late wasn't an option.

In the end, they arrived on the labour ward less than 20 minutes before Will made his noisy entrance into the world, outraged, it seemed to John, at the injustice of being expelled from the warm intimacy of his mother's womb into the cold January day. John remembers looking down at the angry red bundle placed in his arms and loving him fiercely from that first moment. His infant son kicked and pushed against him through the hospital blanket that swaddled him.

For Hope, the tie with Will seemed to come more easily than it had with Maddie. Will quieted more quickly in her arms than his father's, and it was she who was awarded his first gummy smile, who saw his first tentative step and who coaxed *mumma-mumma* from his toddler lips. John kept a watchful eye over both, mindful of the darkness just beneath Hope's surface. All the while, he took charge of Maddie's care and saw to the smooth running of home life. By the time Will was two, the family had settled into a way of being which felt like safety and allowed John to exhale.

*

It is Monday, and John has a rare break between a job which ended over the weekend and another which starts tomorrow. The unexpected time when everyone else in the household is busy feels like a gift. Before the list of half-completed tasks at home has a chance to reel him back, he is on the A286 speeding towards Harting Down. It is one of his favourite places. In the summer, this southern edge of the South Downs is awash with flowers and wildlife, attracting local ramblers and dog-walkers to its hill-top views and secluded valleys. Today is a grey, blustery November day, and it is quiet. As John strides out across the chalky grassland, still wet and slippery underfoot after the weekend's rain, he can see only one lone figure on the path climbing far ahead of him, a large black dog bounding back and forth between the figure and some other unseen point. Back and forth, back and forth, its exuberance evident even at this distance.

For as long as he can remember, John has wanted a dog. When he was a boy, his mother proclaimed it was too much trouble. After his father died, there was no time to think about a dog. By the time he had left home and started working, bringing a creature needing so much care and attention into his life simply wasn't practical. He had hoped that having a family of his own would finally provide the opportunity, but Hope had always wanted cats. When three-year-old Maddie crouched down in front of a litter of eight-week-old kittens, dimpled hands outstretched and face suffused with wonder, his own heart had melted. They had taken two home the next week. The tabby, Tiger, christened with a three-year-old's creativity, lived to fifteen and now has a memorial in the garden hand-painted only last year by a heart-broken Maddie. John smiles at the thought of his daughter, so attuned to life in all its forms she cannot even bear to squash a spider. Tiger's sister Fizz is still with them, but John wonders for how much longer. She barely goes outside and spends most of her time asleep under Maddie's bed.

John decides to call Maddie. They have barely spoken in the nearly two months since she moved to Brighton. Despite his regular assurances to Hope to *leave her be* and *this is how it is supposed to be*, a knot of worry has been tightening in his belly. They have always been close, and he hadn't expected this first separation to feel so final.

He pulls his phone from his pocket and checks the signal. Two bars. Good. That should be enough. It is ten o'clock, and if he's lucky, Maddie won't be in a lecture. He can't remember her timetable; is unsure if Maddie has even shared it with them.

He finds her number, presses the call icon, and lifts the phone to his ear, his steps slowing as he waits for her to pick up. He thinks she won't answer, and then, "Dad? Hello…?"

A smile creeps on to John's face.

"Maddie," he says. "It's so good to hear you."

"Is everything OK?"

There is an anxious catch to Maddie's voice, and John realises that his call on a Monday morning is unusual, has worried her.

"Yes, yes…" he says quickly, reassuring her. "Everything is fine. I just had a spare moment, was out for a walk. I thought I'd check in on you."

*It's been so long since we've spoken,* he wants to add, but doesn't want Maddie to feel reproached.

Maddie releases a slow breath.

"Oh," she says. "OK."

John shifts the phone to his other hand and resumes walking as he pushes it tightly against his ear to shut out the wind, bringing his daughter closer.

"How have you been?" he asks.

There is a pause, and John wonders if the connection has been lost.

"Maddie?"

"I'm fine, Dad. Everything's fine. Just... really busy, you know? There's so much reading to do. So many essays and stuff. I um... I haven't really had time to think about much else."

"No, of course. Of course. And your friends? Are you getting to know people?"

"Yeah." Maddie's voice is quiet. "Yeah, there's loads of people here."

Her tone is off, but John can't put his finger on it.

"Still running?" he asks instead.

"Yeah. Well, until this week anyway," says Maddie. "I haven't been feeling all that great. Just tired, I guess."

"Take care of yourself, Maddie, won't you?" John says, feeling a flutter of concern. Maddie hardly ever misses a day's running. "There are probably all sorts of bugs going around." He thinks of the Covid numbers, on the rise again. "You must look after yourself."

"Yeah, Dad. I will." Maddie changes tack suddenly. "How are you and Mum? And Will?"

They chat for a few minutes longer, John filling her in on the news from home. He tells her about Ros, and Sam's mum bringing Will home on Friday, too much beer slurring his words and softening his edges, about Mum's latest project sewing reems of doll-sized Roman blinds for the shop.

"We miss you, Maddie," he says finally. "It's not the same without you here."

He hears Maddie's breath catch. Her voice is tight like she is having trouble squeezing it out.

"I miss you too, Dad," she says. "Maybe I'll come back for a bit. Soon."

They end the call, and John feels the loneliness of the deserted Downs settle around him as he pulls his coat more tightly against the bitter chill of the wind.

*

When he relays the conversation to Hope as they get ready for bed later that night, wanting to connect in shared musings over their daughter and put words to his shapeless misgivings, Hope is irritated that Maddie has spoken to him and not to her.

"I've been trying to reach Maddie for two weeks now," Hope says. "Two weeks! She never picks up and she hasn't replied to any of my messages. Not properly, anyway."

John resists asking what a 'proper' response entails, snuffing out a flare of irritation.

"I just caught her at the right time," he says.

"Lucky for you," Hope mutters, pulling off her jeans and folding them neatly over the bed rail. "Apparently there is no right time for me."

John closes his eyes and breathes in deeply, weary despite the respite of a day off. He doesn't have the energy to soothe her tonight.

"Try again tomorrow," he says, laying down and turning towards the wall as he closes his eyes, blocking out further conversation. He feels the mattress shift as Hope slips under the covers next to him and turns out the light. When did they stop saying goodnight to each other, John wonders? He lets go of consciousness, drawing the tangle of his own thoughts around him like a web.

# Chapter 13

**Me**

*When most people think of dolls' houses, they think of the finished thing. An Edwardian mansion, chest-high, puffed out with intricate finery. A Victorian cottage, cosy and inviting, beckoning you to proclaim over each room. A Wild West shop, rustic with wrap-around deck and swinging doors. Turns out the real magic lies in a doll's house kit. Stacks of beige MDF hold the thrill of unrealised potential in their precision-cut edges, designed to slot smoothly together piece by piece. Until gradually, gradually, the plain wood takes on its three-dimensional shape, and the house begins to emerge. You think it is a blank slate, that the finished product is entirely down to you. That is a mistake. Even kits have instructions. And if you don't follow them just so, you are just as likely to end up with a useless pile of mismatched wood as you are the home of your dreams.*

\*

Ros has found a bedsit.

*Finally*, I think, as the prospect of her departure opens a window of space inside me. I am in the kitchen, trying to fit the Tesco shop into our crammed fridge. I grimace and pull out a cling-filmed bowl of pasta salad which is old and starting to smell.

"But not until the end of the month," Ros says, mouth stuffed full of cheese and onion crisps.

I try to ignore the sound of her chewing, telling myself that it's been six – no, *seven!* – weeks already, and another three hardly matters. At least she will be gone before Christmas.

"The only sticky part is finding the deposit," she goes on, licking each finger in turn and wiping them on her jeans.

I don't respond.

"I've got a job lined up. Well, probably," she says. "Just a pub job for now, but there's a chance I'll do more. The manager was impressed with all my experience."

Ros has spent years wandering from one country to another, picking up casual work and doing long shifts in bars and clubs in tourist hot-spots to support herself. She has been romanticising what was basically a vagrant lifestyle to a wide-eyed Will for weeks now. I hope he doesn't get any ideas.

"So, that should be good," she tails off finally when I still don't speak.

I look up.

"That's great, Ros," I say flatly.

She regards me for a moment.

"Well, don't overexcite yourself," she says. "God forbid we disturb all this 'happy family' shit with an actual emotional response."

I frown at her.

"What are you talking about? I'm glad for you, OK? What else am I supposed to say?"

"Glad for you, more like. You have been wanting me out since the day I got here."

I shut the fridge door and turn to face Ros, my arms crossed tightly across my chest.

"What did you expect?" I ask. "After all these years? After what you did?"

*After that weekend.*

Ros's eyes open wide, the memory of our final encounter clear between us.

"What I did?" she repeats. "I was on your side, Hope. I've always been on your side. I saw you drowning in your so-called family and pulled you out for a bit. Reminded you who you really were. I didn't hear you saying no. In fact, if memory serves correctly, you were an active participant."

Her words land like a punch to the chest. I have trouble catching my breath and my response disappears like wisps of smoke.

Ros leans back and crosses her arms.

"Oh for god's sake, Hope! It was forever ago. Move on."

I hold up my hand.

*No.*

I leave the rest of the shopping piled on the worktops, uncaring if the frozen food melts or if there are things to take upstairs. I need some space. I walk to the front door, pull on an old pair of garden trainers and a coat from the hook, and walk away from the house without looking back. I concentrate on taking deep breaths of cold November air.

*

I still remember the sweet, musky scent of spring blossom as I closed the front door behind me all those years ago, leaving 18-month-old Maddie at home with John. I ran lightly down the path to the car where Ros was waiting with a couple of older friends I didn't know. Tom-someone and his partner, bohemian and tanned, looking out of place in the fresh British spring. The previous night's rain had washed the world clean, and bright droplets clung to the petals and blades of newly cut grass.

*Go... go!* They seemed to cry, joining me in the rush of lightness I felt as I fled the impossible pressure of being the good wife, the good mother. I would never be those things. John had been understanding, so impossibly nice and supportive about my weekend away to celebrate Ros's 18th birthday. I found myself counterbalancing his patience with snappy responses, pushing him away and retreating to my safe, solitary self. I watched myself from the outside, hating the way I was with him, with Maddie. Longing to feel part of their cosy little circle, but not knowing the way in.

*I just need some space.*

The words reverberated through my head, leaked out of my mouth instead of an apology as John held me close against his chest with too-tight arms. He finally released me, and I sprang away, full of coiled energy.

"I'll be home in a couple of days," I assured him, backing away as I spoke.

John gave me a small smile, lifting a wriggling Maddie up into his arms as I eased myself out through the door and into the spring sunshine.

"I know," he said. "Enjoy yourself."

*

Ros's friend Jazz had rich parents with a holiday beach-front house in Bournemouth which was apparently all ours for the weekend. Jazz had invited a whole load of people to the house for the birthday party and Ros was buzzing at the prospect of all the attention coming her way. We drove west past Portsmouth and Southampton, then down through the New Forest and finally into Bournemouth. With each mile that passed, I felt the weight of my failure at normal life lighten on my shoulders bit by bit until I could breathe freely again.

We drove up a winding, single-track lane and finally reached our destination. Jazz, older than Ros by a few years and effortlessly elegant in the way rich people are, came out to meet us. I felt frumpy in comparison. Mumsy. Whatever that was.

"You made it!" she welcomed, cigarette held lightly in a manicured hand. "You're the last to arrive!"

Ros, initially struck dumb by the grandeur of the glass-fronted house before us, finally found her voice.

"This is *not* your house," she said.

"Not mine, exactly," Jazz replied, leading us through large double doors into an airy entrance hall, her wrap billowing out behind her. "The parents. Who happen to be out of the country until next weekend. So... my house for now, I suppose."

She led us up a winding staircase to a spacious landing and pushed open a door to a bedroom with a king-size bed, two large sofas and expansive views to the sea.

"Voila!" she said with a flourish. "Make yourselves at home."

She cast an eye in my direction. "You're OK to share, aren't you?"

I stepped into the room. A sense of disconnect between this reality and my life with John and Maddie settled over me, and I nodded as Jazz left in a cloud of expensive perfume.

"This is *amazing*!" Ros declared, flopping backwards onto the bed. "Can you believe this place?"

She sprang back to her feet and rummaged in her bag.

"Time to get this party started," she said, tossing a sealed Ziploc bag in my direction. It contained small multi-coloured tablets stamped with smiley faces. My chest tightened. I held it up and looked at Ros.

"What is *this*?" I asked, already knowing the answer.

"Happy pills, sis. And even though it is *my* birthday, I'm going to share with you."

"Don't be an idiot," I snapped, as images of my mother, stoned and volatile, surfaced and sloshed into the space between us. "You have no idea what's in this stuff."

Ros rolled her eyes and grabbed the bag back from me.

"Don't be such a bore, Hope," she said. "I thought you wanted to leave all the mum stuff behind for a weekend."

"I'm not being…" I stopped, containing a flare of temper. "I'm not taking that stuff. You shouldn't either. You have no idea what's in it. What it can do. Please."

I had spent years looking out for Ros, standing in the gap and making sure she was safe. I was still doing it. But she wasn't having any of it.

"Hope." She spoke like I was the child, the one who had something to learn. "It will be fine. Loosen up a bit, OK? It's not like I haven't tried it all before."

Before I could say another word, she popped a pill and left the room.

*

The party had been going on for hours, and I kept mostly to the sidelines, like my girlhood self, melting into the shadows of strangers burning hot and bright with intoxicated self-confidence. I found myself longing for the quiet of home, for John's calm presence and the weight of Maddie slumbering on my chest. I felt overwhelmed with a wave of sadness, an outsider looking into my own life. People like me didn't fit. Not there. Not here.

"Hope!" Ros's voice, breaking through my thoughts, words soft and slurred as she wrapped her arms around me. "What are you doing over here all by yourself?"

"I'm not really in the party mood."

I leaned into Ros despite my earlier anger, relaxing for a moment in the embrace of her warm familiarity.

"Come on. I've got something to put you in the mood." She tugged at my hand, pulling me to my feet.

"No, Ros," I protested weakly, following her despite myself. "I don't want any of that stuff."

Ros rolled her eyes and pulled me to the kitchen, all stainless steel and sleek design.

"I know, I know," she said, pouring me a generous glass of wine, turning away and giving it a swirl. "No hard drugs, you're scarred by your past, blah blah blah…"

I opened my mouth to speak as she placed her hand reassuringly on mine.

"But a glass of wine… and some food won't hurt."

She gestured at a table laden with plates of food. I realised I was starving.

"You can start," she said, lifting a brownie and putting it on a plate, "with birthday cake." She grinned and put a second on my plate, ignoring my protests. "Here. Have two."

*

It is dark and frosty-cold when I make my way back to the house. I let myself in quietly, creeping upstairs to avoid conversation with John, with Ros, with anyone. The memories of that night, of the morning after, so potent with shame and regret, live in a locked box buried deep with the others beneath 19 years of carefully constructed family life. Ros's presence in our home has prised open the box with a crowbar.

The realisation, too late, that the wine, the brownies were drugged. Outrage replaced by disconnected euphoria. Tension melting from my body. A sense of well-being and belonging creeping in, subtly at first and then overpowering.

*At last…*

Dancing, laughing, at one with everyone in the room, minds melding, bodies meeting. Slipping off clothes and inhibitions along with my sense of 'less-than', of being damaged goods.

When I woke the following morning, late, sluggish and sick, Ros was sleeping on one of our sofas. Others were on the floor, tangled in blankets and cushions forming makeshift beds, and I was in the big king-size bed, naked, a stranger next to me. A man whose name I still don't know.

I close my eyes against the nausea that rises with the memory, regret and self-loathing filling my chest like lead. The weight of my own stupidity and Ros's betrayal pins me down.

*Why did you give them to me?*

*You took them. You drank the wine. You ate the brownies. Come on... A part of you knew what was in them!*

*I didn't! I would never.*

*I didn't see you complaining last night. You were the one wanting out of your fake life. You were gagging for it.*

*I was NOT.*

*Well, you are welcome. I only hope you used protection. You can't trust men to be the responsible ones.*

I packed my bag. Flung myself out the front door. Fled from what happened at that glass house on the beach. I ran blindly to the road and left my last words to Ros behind me.

*This is not my life anymore. You are not my life. Fuck off and die, Ros.*

But no matter how fast I ran, how hard I tried to shake away her words and what happened that night, shame coated me like oil on feathers, slick and deadly, impossible to shake off.

# Chapter 14

*Maddie*

Maddie has escaped her flat and is sitting in the library, staring at her laptop, fingers poised to add notes to the essay which is due on Tuesday. *What role does misogyny play in Taming of the Shrew?* Maddie tries to summon up images of the soft-spoken and unassuming early Bianca, to look beneath the surface and tease out Shakespeare's intentions as her character develops. But her mind is blank, and she is struggling to keep her focus trained on the task. She tells herself it is because she has never been a die-hard Shakespeare fan, is firmly in the camp that his plays were written to be watched, not read. But the truth is, Maddie has been struggling to focus for weeks now. Her early enthusiasm for the course and her eagerness to do well in this new world has dulled like a faded blanket left too long in the sun. She has even stopped running, unable to summon up her usual early morning energy and preferring to linger in bed until it is time for morning lectures.

She doesn't allow the flutter of alarm at this unwelcome shift so early in her first year to land and gain traction. It feels safer that way. She is still settling in, that's all. Moving out of home and starting a new, independent life isn't supposed to be easy.

But Maddie can't help but compare her now-self with the self that laughed and partied and bantered with the rest of them in those first weeks at uni. Where has that version of herself gone? Maddie likes that girl better than the quieter, moodier, lazier self that has taken her place. Her flatmates have commented on the change.

"Cheer up, you miserable old cow," Hannah said earlier this week, when Maddie had simply shrugged in response to an invite to go into town for the evening. She was pretending to read a tattered copy of Jane Eyre.

"This..." Hannah said, whipping the book from Maddie's hands, "is not how we have fun."

"I'm not in the mood for fun," Maddie said, reaching out for the book, and keeping her hand out until Hannah finally gave it back.

"Just leave her," Kate muttered from the corner of the room.

"Suit yourself," Hannah said, dismissing Maddie. "If you change your mind, Kate and I are meeting Rob and Warren and a load of their mates in the Druid's Head at eight. Then maybe we'll catch a late film or something."

"Cool," Maddie replied, eyes sliding back to the book.

She hadn't wanted to go out with Rob and Warren and their crowd again. He and Kate had hooked up a couple of weeks ago and now they were always here, lounging around and making themselves at home. Last week while Maddie, Hannah, Josh, Martin and Herb were sitting in the kitchen, Rob had kissed Kate full on the mouth in front of them all. He wrapped his scarf round Kate's neck and pulled it tighter and tighter until she had finally pushed him away, laughing warily.

"Don't be a knob," Kate said, massaging her neck and giving him the finger, even while she grinned and wrapped her leg around his.

"Yeah, don't be a knob, Rob," Warren had echoed, laughing at his rhyme.

Maddie had pretended to be washing up, uncomfortable, but felt Warren's eyes on her back as she scrubbed at the dried lumps of concrete-like porridge stuck to a bowl. She felt awkward and clumsy in his presence and wasn't overly enamoured with Rob, either. He had a possessive quality that made Maddie feel ill at ease. Kate was more tetchy with her friends when they were around.

"All right there, Mads?" Rob had called over easily, running a hand up and down Kate's back as he spoke.

"Fine," she'd replied, leaving the bowl to soak and gathering her things from the table. "I've got work to do."

But work is barely holding her attention. She has to get 3,000 words written, not to mention magicking up an impressive-looking bibliography in the next couple of days. She forces her attention back to her laptop.

*Come on, Maddie. Focus.*

She eases her mind back to *Taming of the Shrew*, encouraging her thoughts to settle. If you looked at his protagonists, Shakespeare's view on women was actually very advanced and contemporary for his time. She tapped out a few sentences to this effect, settling at last into the rhythm of the work.

"Hi Maddie."

The voice interrupts her half an hour later, and Maddie looks up, fingers still fleshing out her next thought on the keyboard. She sees Ella standing there, large purple backpack slung over her shoulder, its size making her appear even smaller and more childlike. But the smile on her face is warm and genuine, and Maddie finds herself responding.

"Oh hi," she replies, gesturing for Ella to sit down on the chair opposite.

Since the night of Maddie's party, she and Ella have crossed paths on several occasions, mostly early in the morning when Maddie was still running each day, and Ella was on her way out to wherever she went. Maddie found the quieter girl's presence unexpectedly soothing and surprised herself by actively seeking out her company in the flat.

As Ella shrugs the backpack from her shoulders and eases into the hard wooden seat at the library table, Maddie feels a sudden pull of exhaustion, followed by a faint nausea. She closes her eyes.

"Are you OK?" Ella asks.

Maddie doesn't open her eyes and just nods, breathing in deeply through her nose and out through her mouth until the nausea ebbs away.

"Just tired, that's all," she says finally. "I'm never going to finish this bloody essay."

"Yeah." Ella, who is studying History of Art, pulls out her laptop and powers it up. "I've got a presentation comparing and contrasting Art Nouveau and Art Deco styles to give on Monday," she says. "I know the stuff, but the thought of presenting in front of everybody..." She tails off, shuddering and peers more closely at Maddie.

"Are you sure you're OK? You look a little pale."

Maddie realises that actually she isn't OK. She hasn't been OK for weeks now, and she is starting to worry. Ever since her birthday when she let herself get so smashed that she couldn't remember anything, a sense of unease has been growing inside her, intangible yet impossible to ignore. She has never felt so tired and her appetite has dwindled to nothing. Even her usual go-to of running it off has failed her.

"I don't know," she replies to Ella. "I haven't felt right for a while."

Ella is silent for a moment.

"Maybe you should see a doctor."

Maddie scrunches up her nose. She doesn't want to be dramatic. She is still adjusting to these new surroundings and should give herself some time.

"Seriously, Maddie. What do you have to lose? Maybe you have a vitamin deficiency or something."

"Maybe."

The girls settle to their various tasks and Maddie finds herself pondering on Ella's words. She decides she will book an appointment as soon as she has finished for the afternoon.

\*

The following week, Maddie is looking listlessly in her cupboard for something to eat. It is nearly 5pm on a rainy Wednesday afternoon. The flat is noisy and over-warm, full of Martin's mates playing a game of Trivial Pursuit. Maddie is half-listening as they toss the questions to each other, trading good-humoured insults when they get the answers wrong. *Philadelphia isn't a state, you idiot.*

Hannah is out somewhere. Herb is here and Kate is around with Rob and Warren in tow, as per usual. Ella, who usually makes herself scarce with this many people about, is heating something in the microwave to take back to her room.

"What are you having, Ella?" Warren calls out, sniffing appreciatively. "Want to share?" He raises his eyebrows suggestively and laughs as Ella flushes, saying nothing.

"Oh come on Ells…" Warren gets to his feet, wandering over to Ella and leaning his head on the back of her shoulder.

Ella flinches and slides away from his touch.

"Leave her alone, wanker," says Herb mildly.

"Alright, alright!" he says, raising his hands and backing away from Ella. "You and your food are safe from me."

Maddie catches Ella's eye and smiles as the other girl leaves the room, the ready meal balanced on a plate and a can of Pepsi in her hand. The waft of food curdles in Maddie's stomach.

Herb shakes her head at Maddie and turns to face Kate.

"Kate," Herb says, carefully peeling away the dimpled skin of a satsuma.

"Your boyfriend and his friend need taming."

Maddie's phone vibrates in her pocket. She pulls it out to see who is calling.

*Doctor.*

Maddie frowns. She had made the appointment like Ella said. The GP made her go for a blood test the next day to check her iron levels or something. The doctor thought maybe she was anaemic. She wasn't expecting to hear back so soon. Maddie had convinced herself that she was wasting his time. She hated making a fuss, more comfortable below the radar.

She walks swiftly from the room into the relative quiet of the corridor, accepting the call and placing the phone to her ear.

"Hello?"

"Madeleine Graham?" the voice at the end asks.

"Yes. That's me."

"Hi Madeleine." The voice loses its formal edge, softening around the casual greeting. "Do you have a quiet space to talk?"

"Um… Yeah. Hold on."

She walks quickly to the end of the corridor, fumbling with her key as she opens the door to her room. Her heart thumps in her chest. Why is the doctor calling her? Does he have some kind of bad news? She is pretty sure that anaemia is no big deal. Just up your iron and then everything will be fine.

"OK." She hears a quaver in her voice and fights to steady her breath.

"The results of your blood test have come in," the doctor continues, "and we'd like you to come into the surgery."

Maddie's mouth is dry and she feels her phone tremble against her ear.

"Ok. Fine… Why, though?"

"We need to schedule in a check-up with the nurse, and you might want an opportunity to talk through your options."

"Options?" Maddie repeats.

"Can you tell me the date of your last period?"

"What?" Maddie isn't following the thread of the conversation. "Why? How come you need to know that?" She is trying to calculate the date as she speaks but can't remember her last period. She's been so busy and tired… maybe the anaemia has affected her more than she thought. "I don't really know…" she trails off, feeling foolish.

"Not to worry," the doctor continues soothingly. "You can talk more about it with the nurse when you come in."

"Talk about what?"

"Your blood tests show that you are pregnant, Madeleine. We need to get you in as soon as possible to…"

But Maddie doesn't hear any more. His words are making no sense.

"What?"

"You're pregnant."

"That's not possible," Maddie says, sitting heavily on her unmade bed. "I don't even have a boyfriend. There must be some mistake."

The doctor is quiet for a moment.

"No mistake, I'm afraid," he says. "The test results are clear and they show that you are pregnant."

# Chapter 15

***Will***

Will surveys himself critically in the bathroom mirror, turning his head first this way, then that. He rubs his fingers over his chin, trying to feel if the faint outline of his beard is getting any thicker. He can't tell. His blond hair makes it difficult to see and his face feels soft beneath his fingertips. Unlike Sam, who has been shaving every day since he was 16, Will only runs a razor over his face every week or so. He sighs. At least he's not short.

He hears Mum calling up the stairs.

"Will – Dad and I are leaving now!"

He opens the bathroom door a crack.

"OK!"

"There's some chilli on the hob – enough for you and Ros. We won't be late."

"Yeah. Thanks."

Him and Ros. Will feels a thrum of pleasure hearing their names paired and finds himself anticipating dinner, just the two of them. He has blown off Sam and the others to make sure he's around tonight. Maybe they can watch a movie on Netflix or something. Will pulls out his phone and opens the app, looking for something to suggest over dinner.

His phone bleeps as he heads back to his room, and a message from Sam pops up on their group chat. There is a picture of him and James necking bottles of Amstel. Josh is behind them, flexing.

*ur missing the fun*

Will snorts.

*wot hanging out with u losers?*

*ur loss m8*

Will silences the chat and tosses the phone on his bed. He wants to go downstairs and heat up the chilli. See if there are any Doritos around. He wonders if Dad will notice if he has a beer.

Lately, Will has been feeling better about life, less bothered about not knowing what is next, and not so furious with everyone around him. Even his parents have noticed and commented, tempting Will to reel in this happier, more relaxed version of himself just to annoy them. But he doesn't. Can't be arsed – but in a good way.

"Are you feeling OK, son?" Dad had asked when Will washed up the breakfast things without being asked earlier in the week.

"Funny," Will had replied, waiting for the familiar surge of irritation to envelop him. Instead, he reached out a hand, gesturing for his dad's empty mug. "Drink up, old man, or you'll miss your chance."

Dad had chuckled.

"I'm not one to turn down a golden opportunity like this," Dad said, handing over the cup, and resting a hand on Will's shoulder before heading to work.

Now Will turns on the hob and stirs the chilli with a wooden spoon, dabbing his finger into the mixture to check the temperature. Still cold. He turns the heat up and listens for the sound of Ros's footsteps coming down the stairs.

Ros doesn't have any qualifications but she has lived a more exciting life than anyone he knows, working in Barcelona, then Lanzarote, then Croatia and most recently in Greece. Sleeping in late and going to the beach in the day and serving drinks and partying until the early hours of the morning.

"Didn't earn all that much," Ros told him. "But I made it work. There were always others like me around, and we found ways to make do."

Will had been rapt, thinking of himself shrugging off the spectre of more study or a boring nine-to-five job, unformed and already stifling, and imagining himself a free spirit, hanging out with people like Ros. He felt something akin to hope for the first time in months.

"Why did you come back?" He didn't get how Ros could prefer living in their uptight house to being free in another country, far away from everything.

Ros stubbed out her cigarette and shrugged.

"Brexit," she said without elaborating. "Covid. You know."

Will nodded wisely, like he did know. He got Covid of course. The pandemic that shut down everything with dizzying speed, locking him in the house with his sister and parents. The once solid world changing shape. But if he was Ros, he would have stayed trapped in Greece. It had to be better than being here. Will could hardly bear to think about the weeks and months of lockdown. The only decent thing to come out of it was his drawing.

A couple of months into the first lockdown, bored out of his head and staving off the anxiety that had taken residence in his gut, Will had pulled out a sketchbook from under his bed. A present from Uncle Andy and Aunty Sue from a million years ago. He'd dug out a pencil and, sitting in his room, began to sketch out caricatures of each family member, laughing to himself as he exaggerated their features and added speech bubbles and words he decided they would say. He was so absorbed in his work that he didn't look up for a couple of hours, only becoming aware of his surroundings when Mum barged through his door and told him dinner was ready.

"Knock!" Will had shouted, irritated to be pulled back to normal life.

"I did knock," Mum said.

"Yeah... well, it defeats the point if you come in without waiting for me to answer."

The argument was familiar, a smoothed and well-worn path between them.

"Fine, OK," Mum had said, like he was being awkward. She caught sight of his sketchpad and peered over his shoulder for a closer look before he could close it.

"Did you do these?" she said, reaching over and pulling it closer.

"Yeah?" Will was dismissive. Why couldn't she go away?

"They're really good, Will."

Mum picked up a sketch of Dad, glasses balanced on the end of his nose, frowning as he swung his gaze between the mobile phone in his hand and a grandfather's clock beside him.

*when dads dont get tik tok* the caption read.

He felt a flush of pleasure at the compliment, but stuffed it down, pushing the sketchbook away and closing it.

"What's for dinner?" he said, changing the subject, and leading Mum out of his room.

*

He sits at the table now, hoping the chilli doesn't burn while he's waiting for Ros to come down, and absently sketches her image into a notebook. He still has the pen in his hand when she comes into the kitchen a few minutes later, smiling and pulling up a seat next to him. Will's heart thuds in his chest at her nearness and he finds himself smiling back, resting his hand lightly over the sketch to cover it up. Ros tips her head, meets his eyes and pushes his hand away, her purple polished nails brushing his skin. Will catches his breath.

"Is that me?" Ros says, pulling the notebook towards her and studying the image of herself, trademark hair spiked and messy, wearing a wrap-around sarong, a bikini top and sandals. She is leaning languidly on a beach bar, gazing into the distance.

*no limits,* says the caption

Will flushes and tries to pull the notebook back.

"It's just a stupid drawing," he says.

"Ah ah ah..." Ros stops his hand with silver-ringed fingers, and keeps hold of the picture, examining it from every angle.

"It's just... your life sounded so cool," Will says lamely, rushing to fill the silence. "It's how I imagine you – imagined what life must have been like for you – that's all," he finishes.

Ros smiles at him.

"You're good," she says simply, and Will feels something in his chest expand at the compliment.

"Word of advice from me," she adds, pulling a cigarette from the pack. "Never explain yourself to anyone else. Just do what you do."

Will thinks about this.

"Like you...?"

Ros gives a short, clipped laugh, and Will can't tell what she's thinking. "Maybe not like me," she replies, lighting the cigarette and gesturing for Will to open the patio doors. "Just learn from my mistakes."

Will wants to ask Ros about her mistakes, but the smell of burning starts to permeate the air around them, and Will jumps to his feet, cross with himself.

"Shit!" he says, stirring and scraping a layer of hardened chilli from the bottom of the pan with the wooden spoon. "Shit. Sorry. Lost track of time."

Ros points the end of her cigarette at him. "Will."

He likes the rough sound of his name coming from her mouth.

"Never explain yourself."

\*

A couple of hours later, the chilli bowls are soaking in the sink, and Will and Ros are watching *Red Notice* on Netflix. Will has been looking forward to seeing the film, but he is finding it hard to concentrate. While Ros ran upstairs for some thick socks, Will piled a whole load of stuff on the smaller sofa, which means that now, he and Ros are sitting together on the three-seater, lights turned low. They shovel mouthfuls of Doritos and sip beers. He glances sideways at her as she laughs at Ryan Reynolds running rings around The Rock. Will laughs too, inching closer under the blanket Ros has thrown over them both to ward off the chill.

*This is good*, he thinks. *Ros is good.*

During the bull-fighting scene, they both laugh out loud, turning to each other in the same moment, faces just inches apart. Will doesn't think. He leans in and kisses Ros full on the mouth, skin hot, blood pounding. He barely takes in the softness of her lips and the moment he has been imagining for weeks now when Ros wrenches backwards. She jumps up, scattering Doritos all over the floor.

"What the fuck, Will?" she says, flipping on the overhead light and exposing his flushed face, igniting his shame.

"I just... I thought..." Will is on his feet now too, fumbling with his words like a dumb schoolkid. "You said..."

"I said *what*?" She is looking at Will like he is disgusting, like something on the bottom of her shoe.

"You said," Will gulps, gut clenched, "you said never explain yourself. You said that!"

He is horrified to hear his voice crack as he speaks, and he takes a step backwards, close to tears. What a fucking loser he is!

Ros takes a breath and her expression softens. "Will," she says more gently now. "You're a child."

He shakes his head and continues his retreat to the door.

"A child... I would never..." She closes her eyes, breathes in. "Your mum is my sister. You're like... my nephew."

Hearing the words, standing here in the unforgiving bright light, Will feels young, exposed, a complete fool. The old rage rises in him, blanketing his vulnerability. He swipes traitor tears from his eyes.

"I'm nearly eighteen!" he yells, tripping and catching himself on the door. "In like, two months! And you..." he jabs a finger in her direction. "You are not my mother's sister. No wonder she doesn't want you here!"

Will's breath is jagged now, humiliation tightening around his chest like a vice. He runs to his room, grabs blindly for his coat and backpack, and takes the steps back down two at a time.

"Will."

Ros stands in front of him, but he pushes past her, pausing for a moment as she falls into the wall, and then he makes for the front door. As he flings it open, he sees his parents coming up the path, keys at the ready.

"Will!" His father's voice now, alarmed at the sight of Will bolting from the house, Ros pale-faced against the wall. "Will!" he repeats.

But Will doesn't answer him. Doesn't slow his pace as he escapes from the house and disappears into the night.

# Chapter 16

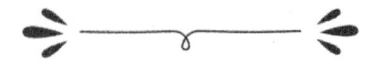

*John*

John can barely make out Will's twisted features in the damp, evening darkness as his son rushes past him and down the front path. But he doesn't miss the unshed tears glinting in his eyes in the sickly light of the streetlamp. He and Hope have to step quickly aside to make sure they are not knocked over in his single-minded intent to escape.

"Will!" he calls out, moving towards the retreating back of his son. "Will!"

John starts to follow, picking up his pace as he reaches the end of the path, but is distracted by the raised voices coming from the house.

"What have you done?" Hope is saying, rushing over to a white-faced Ros. "What's wrong with Will?"

Ros gathers herself, pushing away from the wall where she has been leaning, and drawing herself up to her full height, which is still shorter than Hope.

"What do you mean what have *I* done?" Ros shouts back, shrugging away from Hope, putting distance between them.

"Well, something has obviously happened!" Hope continues, pursuing Ros into the living room.

"And of course *I* must have done something," Ros retorts. "Anything that goes wrong is obviously down to me."

With a last look down the dark road after Will, John reluctantly retraces his steps and goes into the house, pulling the front door closed behind him. He takes a deep breath and enters the lounge. Hope and Ros are squared off in the middle of the room. A crumpled blanket and upturned bowl of Doritos litter the floor, and John resists the urge to crouch down and start tidying up before his wife and Ros grind them into the beige carpet with their feet.

"Who is the adult here, Ros?" Hope is saying, jabbing a finger in her sister's direction.

John steps in and lays a gentle hand on Hope's shoulder, hoping his touch will pull his wife into a calmer space and give them all a chance to talk. Like the adults they are. She shrugs off his hand and tosses a glare in his direction.

"Something has clearly happened," she says defensively, then turns back to Ros. "And I want to know what."

"Can we all just take a breath?" says John, stepping forward with two hands outstretched like he has the power to hold them apart with his will alone.

*May the force be with you.*

The thought drifts inappropriately through his mind, bringing forth memories of garden light-sabre fights with a younger version of Will.

"Let's just sit down and get to the bottom of what has happened."

When the two women still do not move, John adds: "Will is the important one here."

The rage slips from Hope's features, and she steps back one step, then two, slumping onto the sofa. Ros shifts a bunch of stuff from the two-seater and sits down as well, back straight and unyielding, eyes darting to John, then Hope, and back to John again. She is uncharacteristically tense.

John joins Hope on the larger sofa, leaning forward with forearms resting on his knees, and says gently:

"Ros. Something has clearly happened, and Will is obviously upset. Can you tell us anything?"

Ros closes her eyes for a moment and takes a deep breath. When she opens them again, she looks calmer and looks only at John.

"I swear I didn't know what was going on in his head," she says earnestly, willing him to believe her. "I mean, we've been talking. Loads. Of course we have. He is trying to find out who he is in the world, and he doesn't have anyone else to talk to. If I'd realised…"

John reaches across and puts a restraining hand on Hope's arm as he senses his wife opening her mouth to say more.

"Realised what, Ros?"

"If I'd realised he had a… a *crush* on me, I'd have put a stop to it! I am *not* like that."

"*What?*"

Hope is back on her feet and Ros looks at her pleadingly.

"I didn't know!" she protests. "I thought we were mates. I wasn't thinking."

"You never think. Never! That is your problem," says Hope, her face flushed and angry. "God, Ros," she continues, as if what Ros has said is only just sinking in. "He is a child. *My* child. What did you do? What did you say?"

John's mind hitches on Hope's words, *my child*, but he pushes down the irritation at his wife's casual removal of his place in this scenario. Instead, he stands up, encouraging her to sit back down and give Ros a chance to say more. She shrugs him off again, but perches back on the sofa.

"Well?" she challenges Ros.

Ros takes a deep breath. "We had dinner. We chatted like always. You've seen how we chat, right?" she asks, beseeching John to take her side.

He gives a short nod, encouraging her to continue.

"We were having a chat, and then watching a movie. It was funny, we were laughing." Ros is gazing inwards now, replaying the scene in her mind.

"And then, out of nowhere, he... he kissed me!"

Hope is on her feet again, mouth open.

"*What?*" she repeats.

"I didn't kiss him back!" Ros counters. "I pushed him off. God. I would never... never!"

But Hope isn't listening, eyes wide with disbelief. "You kissed Will?"

"Will kissed me!"

"What's the difference?"

"Enough. ENOUGH!"

John is standing now too. This time putting hands on both women's shoulders, holding them apart, trying to process himself what Ros has just told them. His raised voice, so rare, quiets them both for a moment.

John breathes into the moment and speaks.

"Ros? What happened after that? Why did Will run out like that?"

"Because I pushed him off. I told him no. I think I really upset him, John."

"OK." John holds up a hand to hold back any more words from Hope, who is about to interject in the face of his acquiescence.

"Did Will say where he was going?"

"No," Ros replies miserably. "No. He just shouted at me, pushed me aside, and ran."

John looks down at his watch. Nine pm. Where would he go? He looks at Hope, eyebrows raised in question.

"Sam?" says Hope, her thoughts mirroring his own.

Sam. Of course he will be there.

John nods, and Hope digs in her bag for her phone.

"You try Will. I'll call Sam," she says, throwing a blistering glare in Ros's direction as she stalks into the kitchen to make the call.

*

Will's phone goes straight to voicemail, and John leaves a message, asking his son to call back as soon as he picks it up. He briefly considers calling again straightaway, but he doesn't want to push Will away any further, and it is unlikely that he has come to any harm. John can hear Hope's voice talking quietly in the kitchen and goes in to join her. Ros has retreated to her room.

She turns to him.

"He's not there."

John reaches out and pulls Hope into his arms, her soft curls tickling his chin as he gently strokes her back.

"He'll be OK," he soothes. "He's embarrassed, that's all. He just needs to blow off a bit of steam."

Hope nods her head against his chest, circling her arms round him more tightly.

"He hasn't even had a girlfriend," she says, her voice muffled by their closeness. "Hasn't even had a first kiss."

John smiles.

"I'm not sure we know that."

He thinks of how little his mother had known about his life when he was seventeen, not that he'd had much time for fun and getting up to no good. Still, his mother hadn't been his first port of call for sensitive information, and he doubted that he and Hope were the first port of call for Will, either.

"He'll get over it," says John. "This will all fade away."

"I want Ros to leave," Hope says. "I want her to leave now."

John continues to stroke Hope's back, her hair, warding off the return of Angry Hope, to keep this gentle and vulnerable version a bit longer.

"She'll be gone soon enough," he says. "I don't think she meant anything by it."

Hope sniffs.

"She never does."

By midnight, John can't hold his worry in check any longer. Hope has arranged for Sam to call her if Will shows up at his place, but by 11.30pm he still hasn't arrived at his closest friend's house. Sam said he was heading to bed but would text if he heard from Will. When the old clock that had once belonged to his own father dongs twelve times on the landing, John decides that he's had enough waiting around. He is going to get into the car and go looking for his son. Despite his assurances to Hope, he is concerned, the stricken look on Will's face lingering in his mind like an afterimage.

As he is starting up the engine, he sees the front door fling open, and Hope come running out, waving her phone at him like a beacon. John cuts the engine and opens the door.

"What is it?" he asks, hope and dread coursing through him simultaneously.

"It's Maddie," Hope says, pausing to catch her breath.

"Maddie?" John doesn't understand.

Hope shakes her head, holding her hand up so that she can explain.

"Will is with Maddie," says Hope. "He's just turned up at her place."

*

John drives to Brighton the following morning. Hope wanted to join him, but Fran isn't well, and Hope has had to pick up two fully booked sessions with customers at the shop today.

"We'll be back this evening," John reassures her.

He can see from her face that she can hardly bear the thought of him going to Brighton without her.

"We haven't even been to see Maddie yet," she says, frowning. "I can't believe we haven't visited."

John agrees. More than two months have passed since their daughter left for university, and he had never imagined that she would settle in and disappear from their day to day lives so easily. But Maddie has been consistent in her reticence about coming home, or inviting them to see her, and John has tried hard to respect her wishes, pushing aside his own hurt.

Now that the sharp anxiety about Will's safety has dulled to a more amorphous worry about how he is doing in the wake of Ros's rejection, John allows himself a flush of pleasure at the thought of seeing his daughter again in her new life. If he's honest with himself, he is pleased that he is going alone. He can enjoy the peace of the drive along the south coast and have his children all to himself for a bit. His steps are almost buoyant and he feels a lightness inside as he parks at the university campus and follows the path to Maddie's student accommodation. The route is still etched in his mind from when they dropped her off in September.

He buzzes her flat from outside and waits for her voice to come over the intercom.

"Come up!" A disembodied voice, not Maddie's, echoes tinnily through the speaker, followed by the buzz of the door release.

John makes his way up to the first floor, finding the door to Maddie's flat. Flat 12. He knocks. A tall blonde boy in jeans and a green hoodie answers the door and nods. John can hear music thumping from somewhere behind him.

"Maddie's dad?" he asks.

John nods, trying to decide whether to hold out a hand to shake. He opts against it, pushing his hands into his own pockets instead.

"She's through there. In her room," the boy says, opening the door more widely in invitation.

"Thanks," says John, stepping in.

The music grows louder as John walks down the corridor. He sees a group of girls and a couple of guys lounging at the table and on the sofas in the shared kitchen. Will is sitting there with them, a mug of tea cradled in his hands. He meets John's eyes, expression inscrutable. John lifts a hand in greeting and gives Will a quiet nod. He won't embarrass him in front of Maddie's friends. He nods his head in the vague direction of Maddie's room, indicating to Will that he is going to see her. A ghost of a smile flits across his son's face, unspoken gratitude at his discretion.

John walks towards Maddie's room, stops at her closed door and knocks. He feels a wide smile gather on his face as he hears her steps approach and the door opens. He steps forward and his smile freezes at the sight of his daughter. She is pale and too thin, her usually lustrous dark hair hanging limply down her back. She wears black leggings and a baggy, oversized jumper. Her face is blotched and red, eyes puffy with tears.

"Mads?"

John reaches out towards her, and after the briefest of pauses, Maddie flings herself into his arms.

"Daddy," she sobs, unable to say another word.

# Chapter 17

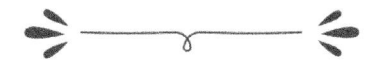

**Me**

*Five mistakes to avoid when building a doll's house:*
1. *Starting too big. A four-storey Victorian mansion might sing to your heart, but if you don't know what you are doing, beware. The bigger the house, the greater the pain when it all goes wrong.*
2. *Building your house on the cheap. Throwing a house together on a budget may seem like a good idea at first, but real treasure is worth waiting for.*
3. *Using a glue gun. Impossible to control. Despite your best efforts, you will end up with a quickly cooling, sticky mess.*
4. *Putting up baseboards before the wallpaper. No matter how beautiful the wallpaper, it won't look right unless you work from the bottom up.*
5. *Using the wrong tools. Creating a perfectly formed doll's house is an art, and you will only be successful if you start with the right tools. Blagging it will catch you out in the end.*

\*

The lighting in the shop is soft and warm against the slate-grey backdrop of the chilly November day. Fairy lights adorn the dark beams above us. Music, the clinking of forks against plates, and the rich smell of Carlos' coffee spirals up the staircase to where I am sitting with a group of six other women. It is a regular group which meets every Thursday to continue work on a themed project. For the past two weeks, they have been fine-stitching tiny tapestries for an array of doll's house furnishings including fire screens, footstools, bellpulls, cushions and stair carpets. I am working on an intricate leaf pattern on a dining-room chair cover. I feel the pull of concentration across my brow.

"Shit."

The word is involuntary as my needle slips and pierces the tender skin of my thumb.

"Sorry."

"Fiddly little buggers," says Janet beside me, a neat and contained octogenarian, patiently unpicking a knot from her own festive table runner.

"You can say that again," adds Lucy. She is young, enjoying the freedom of an afternoon without her children, and the others nod their agreement.

Normally this setting would imbue in me a deep peace, the warmth and relaxed creativity of the shop wrapping themselves around me like a soft blanket. On any other day I would have jumped at the chance to stand in for Fran at the last minute, favouring the contained and well-trodden routines of the shop over the muddle of options at home. This confusion around doing the right thing and taking the correct path through the tangle of domestic life is not new to me. When John and I first married and Maddie was born so soon into our new life together, the combination of wifehood and motherhood was so overwhelming that I froze on the spot, mute and paralysed. Until I wasn't. Until I dashed headlong to the other extreme on Ros's 18th birthday, blind and reckless as a lemming flinging itself over a cliff edge. Unlike a lemming, I didn't perish, and from the outside you could almost believe that nothing had happened. Yet deep down, in the dark places of myself where nobody, not even me, have ever dared to venture, something had shifted and taken shape during that weekend with Ros. It set in motion a chain of events that nudged and pushed against my well-defended surface.

Today I am distracted, sitting like a mannequin amongst the group, fixed smile masquerading as my real self, which is miles away with my family in Brighton. Has John spoken to Will yet? Seen Maddie?

"Hope?"

Lucy's voice pulls me into the present moment, my thoughts lagging behind my gaze which settles unseeingly on the completed tapestry she is holding out for me to inspect.

"What do you think?"

I make a show of taking the tiny tapestry from her hands, turning it one way then another, and bringing it close to inspect each fine stitch.

"It's beautiful," I say, handing it back.

Lucy flushes and inspects it herself.

"Do you really think so?"

The others lean in and comment, and I feel the buzz of my phone in my pocket, its vibration pulling me to my feet and away from the group.

John.

I fumble to answer.

"Hello?" I say, holding one finger to my ear and moving to the relative quiet of my office. "John?"

I can hear music in the background and press my phone closer to my ear, as if I can block out the sound that way.

"Hope, it's John," he half-shouts down the phone.

"Is everything OK?" I ask, anxiety creeping into my voice. "Have you found Will?"

"Yes... yes, Will's fine," he replies. "I'm bringing Maddie back with us."

I stand up straighter.

"Maddie's coming home?" I feel a surge of anticipation at the prospect of seeing my daughter again after two months.

"Yes. Just wanted to let you know. So you can get her room ready. Be prepared. She's not herself." I hear the concern in John's voice. "She needs her mum, I think. A bit of TLC perhaps."

A smile tugs at the corners of my mouth, and I am already gathering my things from the office, my bag, my raincoat. The group can manage without me. Maddie is coming home. And Will is OK. For the first time in weeks, I feel the welcome pull of home and family, drawing me to them like gravity.

*

I have texted ahead to Ros to warn her. To let her know that Maddie is coming and that she will have to make space. Sleep on the couch tonight. Whatever. Where Ros sleeps – where she goes at all – is no longer my concern. I was her protector, her defender, sacrificing myself for her all through our teenage years and look where that left me. Look how she repaid me. All I care about now is my family being all together again. Safe. Ros is not part of that picture.

As I pull into our drive, I see the yellow glow of lights spilling out from inside, the warmth of the house beckoning me from the gathering gloom. I toss my keys on the cupboard and kick off my wet shoes, discarding my raincoat and bag as I make my way to the stairs up to Maddie's room.

"Ros!" I shout as I climb the stairs. "Are you here?"

"In here," she calls out from Maddie's room.

I reach the door. Stop in surprise as I see that Ros has already stripped the old sheets off the bed and made it up with Maddie's sunflower set. She is smoothing the cover down with her hand. Her own backpack is sitting open on the floor next to the bed, clothes crammed in haphazardly, sleeves and bra-straps escaping over the edges and trailing on the floor. Ros swipes her hand across her face, still turned slightly away from me.

"Oh," I say, at a loss. "You've made the bed. And tidied up."

"Yeah?" Ros gives a sniff, leans down and sweeps the last of her clothes into her pack. "Of course."

I continue to look at her.

"Maddie's coming home," Ros says simply. "This is her space."

She looks up at me. She has been crying. I feel something shift inside, my cold resolve to hate her and cut her off softening and loosening even as I reach after it, like grasping for a scarf caught in a gust of wind. But it eludes me, and an unexpected surge of emotion rises. I take a step closer.

"Ros," I say again. Softly this time.

She smiles her crooked smile.

"It's OK, sis," she says, "I know my place."

I am not sure how to respond to this. Both of us understand that she is telling the truth.

"Come downstairs?" I offer. "For a cup of tea?"

Ros considers this.

"Why not?" she replies, hefting her bag over her shoulder and surveying Maddie's room for a final time before stepping out the door.

\*

We sit in the kitchen, cradling steaming mugs of tea in our hands. A fragile peace surrounds us like a bubble, and I am loath to move, even to breathe too quickly for fear of bursting it. The antipathy of the past few weeks may have faded in this moment, but both of us know it is ready to rush in and fill all the empty spaces at the slightest provocation.

"I need a smoke," Ros says.

"Not in the house." My response is automatic.

Ros fixes me with a look.

"Obviously," she replies, squinting out through the darkening windows to see if it is still raining. It seems to have stopped for now.

"Come on," she says, nodding towards the patio doors and holding out a cigarette for me to take.

I pull a face.

"Oh, come *on,* Hope," she says, pulling at my arm.

I allow myself to be led to the door and we step into the chill of the garden, picking our way down the path towards the summer house, closed and locked up for winter. Ros lights up her cigarette and then holds the lighter out to me. After a moment's hesitation, I lean in and inhale, cupping the end of the cigarette with my left hand.

"I'm sorry about Will," says Ros, so softly that I'm not sure I've heard her correctly at first.

"I mean it, Hope," she says. "I didn't mean to upset him like that. To give him the wrong idea. God no…"

She pulls a face, her discomfort at what happened evident in the twist of her features.

I believe her and am relieved that I do. Perhaps made easier knowing that Will is safe, that John has him, and that Maddie, John and Will are going to be arriving home any minute. Perhaps we'll have a takeaway. Sit in front of a movie wrapped in blankets like old times.

"Ros…" I begin, feeling expansive, thinking I will invite her to stay for the evening. To sleep on the sofa for a couple more days until her Brighton bedsit is ready.

Ros is talking again now. I don't pay much attention, content in the moment. Nodding absently along and drawing the nicotine deep into my lungs. Thinking I will need to brush my teeth before the others get back. Change my top and hope the smell of smoke doesn't linger in my hair. Ros pauses for a long moment, then speaks again.

"Have you ever wondered about Will?" she asks me.

I freeze. It is a moment before I find my voice.

"Wondered what?" I carefully reply, dropping the cigarette and grounding it out with the toe of my boot.

She just looks at me.

"About Will and that night," she says. "I'm not stupid. I've done the maths."

I draw in a breath and look up at the dark sky, stars hidden behind the thick cloud.

"Hope, I think you should tell him."

Still, I say nothing. I feel the jab of the Not Me like an elbow in the ribs.

"You should tell him," she repeats. "Tell *them*."

It is so cold. I cross my arms tightly across my chest and shiver. The Not Me pulls me towards the back door, putting distance between me and Ros and those words.

"It's not fair, Hope," she says, moving towards me, but I stumble away from her, losing my balance and steadying myself against the wall, clinging so tightly to its solid surface that I can feel the rough grooves of the bricks against my palm. The Not Me is covering my ears, keeping Ros at bay, but still her words break through.

"The secret is killing you. You know it is. And they have a right to know."

Her words cut through the thudding of my heart, and I feel a panicked rage course through me, pushing furious words from my mouth.

"You don't know what you're talking about! You don't!"

But she does know.

And so do I. I have always known. But after a lifetime of practice, I am so skilled at pushing painful truth down, down, down into the depths that I had almost *unknown* it. Almost.

"Hope," she says.

"Shut up!" I yell, squeezing my eyes closed, my hands clenching into fists and slamming into the sides of my head. "SHUT UP!"

Ros reaches me in two steps and wraps her arms around me. I start to cry.

"OK. OK, Hope. I'm sorry," she says, holding me close.

"John can't know," I sob. "He can *never* know. Never!"

My voice rises in distress until I am all I can hear, blotting out the sounds of the early evening city. Words never spoken come loose. Wild and unfettered.

"He can't know!" I repeat.

"I know… I know," Ros soothes. "I'm sorry."

"He adores Will. *ADORES* him!" I continue. "And John is the only father Will has ever known."

"Shhhh…. Shhhh." I am dimly aware of Ros's hand on my back, patting out a rhythm, holding me together.

"They can NEVER know!"

"Shhh!" I feel Ros's arms tighten, her body stiffening, like she has only just realised how important it is that this whole thing stays buried, a secret for all time.

"If John knew that Will wasn't his, it would kill him – it would kill *both of them!*" I wail.

"Hope! Be quiet!" Ros says sharply, pulling away from me suddenly.

Through the blur of tears, I see that she is no longer looking at me, but beyond me, through the door, into the kitchen.

My body responds first, the racing beat in my chest coming to a painful, thudding halt before resuming like a death knell, steady and inevitable. My mind creeps in next, understanding now what Ros is looking at, *who* she is looking at. I meet Ros's eyes, see my own distress reflected there, and turn slowly around.

John, Will and Maddie stand mutely in the open doorway, faces white against the darkness, greetings frozen on their lips. I look beseechingly at John and take a step towards him, but he backs away, hands held up in front of him like a shield.

"No," he says in a voice I don't recognise. "Don't."

Will turns and flees back towards the front door, and Maddie just stands there, looking at me like she's never seen me before.

# PART 2

# Chapter 18

**Ros**

Ros was six years old when she was taken to her first foster home. She is fuzzy on detail but can still feel the cool satin edge of the blanket clutched between her fingers and smell the stale odour of her jumper hanging soiled and frayed to her knees. She remembers the feet of the grown-ups lined up on the doorstep of her temporary new home. Then waiting, still as a statue and quiet as a mouse so that bad things wouldn't happen.

She had been found by a neighbour. He caught her rooting in a bin for scraps of food and saw her scurry away at his booming, *Who's there?* Exactly 24 days had passed since her mother had closed the door of their house and never come back. Ros wasn't fast enough, though. The neighbour caught hold of her as she ran, grasping her bird-like wrist in an impossibly large hand and asking, more gently, *Are you OK? Where is your mummy, child?*

But Ros's words were stuck and frozen deep in her belly, so the man had taken her back to her house and when he couldn't find her mummy, he called the other grown-ups instead. They asked more questions. Asking and asking until their strange-voiced words swirled round and round in her head and Ros felt sick and vomited all over her bedroom floor. Everything happened very quickly after that. Ros, mute with terror that she would be in trouble for making a mess, only had time to snatch up her little pink blanket, turned soft with use and age, before the strange grown-ups took her away from her house forever.

The blanket stayed with Ros for years, well past the time Hope came into her world, but somewhere along the line she had moved on without it.

Even now, Ros feels a twinge of raw, unprocessed grief at the loss of this one tiny piece of her history, frayed and used as it was.

*

Ros's first instinct is to make herself scarce and hide away behind closed doors during those first hours after Hope's wailed words created a shock wave which enveloped and flattened everyone in its path. Will had vanished as quickly as he had appeared, the bang of the front door reverberating across the stunned silence, and Maddie had simply stood there, mute and pale as a ghost. John had backed away from Hope like a magnet repelled from its polar opposite, stumbling backwards and catching his hip on the kitchen worktop. His arms were outstretched, an invisible barrier keeping everyone away.

*No... don't.*

Disbelief contracted his strong, gentle features into something unrecognisable. It was this expression, foreign and frightening, and his immediate retreat that made Ros question what she had started this evening. Maybe she shouldn't have raised the subject of Will. Never have encouraged Hope to face the truth and make her family do the same. She is not quite sure why she did it – because it was for the best? Because this family – everything she had ever wanted and never had – was strong enough to deal with the truth? Or something darker... less noble? Ros stifles the sense of remorse which rises in her, squeezing the breath from it until it is still and silent. She has been dealing with hard truths and their consequences since before she had the words to describe them. And she has found a way through. Secrets lead to nothing good. She should know.

Ros suspected about Will from the beginning. After that terrible weekend of her 18th birthday, when Hope had abandoned her like everyone else in her life, Ros had gathered her things and chased after her foster sister. She sofa-surfed with people she knew and skulked in the shadowed edges of Hope's cosy family circle, desperately looking for a way back in. But Hope didn't show her face, hiding away for weeks on end behind the fortified walls of the little house she shared with John and Maddie. And when Ros finally did catch a glimpse of her months later, leaning on John's arm as he pushed Maddie's buggy through the stifling summer heat, she barely recognised the

Hope she saw. Her dark, curly hair was pulled tightly back from her face, her long arms and legs too thin and pale despite the endless blue sky. And then the unmistakable bulge of life growing beneath her light yellow, floral dress.

Ros swears that Hope looked directly at her that day. That she saw Ros standing, awkward and flushed, on the other side of the road before fixing her gaze straight ahead, away from Ros. Walking by.

In that moment, the small part of Ros that held hope of something different, something good in life, crumbled to dust, and a different version of herself emerged. This version blew the dust inside away, into the deepest corners of herself, and then she turned away just as deliberately as Hope and walked in the other direction without a backward glance.

*

Despite the great distance that stood between them like a giant, steel wedge for the best part of two decades, Ros could never quite disown Hope in the way that Hope had disowned her. She owed her too much, both loving Hope for being the only one who had ever stood up for her and hating her for the endless sense of indebtedness that marked their relationship.

Which is why Ros is standing beside Hope now, hand resting tentatively on her shuddering back, voice whispering for the second time tonight, *Shhhhhh.... Shhhhhh.* But Hope is beyond Ros's small comforts, eyes squeezed closed against the world, head buried in folded arms.

Ros is expecting John to come down. To scoop up Hope like he always does, exchanging rolled-eye solidarity with Ros that here he is again, carefully skirting Hope's sharp edges and covering them over with care. She realises that like Hope, she too has been safer and steadier in John's presence. Feeling adrift when he doesn't show up. As far as Ros is aware, John is still in the house, but unlike Maddie, who uttered a muffled *go away* in response to her tentative knock, John gave no response at all, the silence on the other side of the bedroom door heavy and visceral.

When he doesn't reappear, Ros decides to act. Spurning her earlier instinct to run and hide with the rest of them, she picks up her bag and puts it next to the sofa in the empty living room, a temporary space for tonight at least. Then she returns to the kitchen and sits herself down. Hope still hasn't moved, quiet now.

"Hope?" Ros begins tentatively. "Hope I'm going to make us a cup of tea. And then a bite to eat. Maybe some beans on toast or something?"

Silence.

"Hope...?" she tries.

Hope mutters something, but Ros doesn't catch her words.

"Sorry, Hope, what did you say?"

"Not hungry," Hope says again, more clearly this time, her shoulders slumping further as though the effort of speaking has drained the last of her energy.

Despite Hope's disinterest, Ros busies herself with preparing a meal for the two of them, not sure what to do about the others. She spoons a large portion of baked beans over buttered wholemeal toast on her plate and Hope's, then grates cheese over both before carrying them to the table. She slides the plate towards Hope.

"Eat," she says when Hope fails to lift her head from her arms.

Ros pushes the plate, so it nudges Hope's forearm.

*"Eat,"* she says again, shaking Hope by the shoulder until she lifts her head, cheeks flushed, eyes distant and unfocused.

"Starving yourself isn't going to help, Hope," says Ros.

Normally Hope would bite at Ros's sweeping statement, but today she gives an infinitesimal nod as she looks down at the plate of food, hand absently twiddling at her fork.

"What have I done?" she says – to herself or to Ros, Ros cannot tell. She is still staring at the food in front of her, the fork in her hand now, scraping beans into little piles on the toast, making no attempt to lift any of it to her mouth.

"You told the truth," Ros says firmly.

"Truth?" Hope echoes weakly. She looks at Ros now. "What is so good about the truth?"

Hope has a point, Ros thinks. The truth is dangerous and unpredictable. Like a wild animal, cornered and intent on escape.

"They will be OK, Hope," says Ros. "They just need a bit of time."

Tears form in Hope's eyes and spill over, slowly at first, then in rivulets down flushed cheeks.

"I don't know if they will, Ros," she says in a broken tone. "This might be too much."

Ros feels a rush of warmth towards Hope, this foster sister who was always her idol, her defender before everything went so wrong between them. She straightens in her seat, squaring her shoulders and reaching out gently to rub Hope's back.

"Try not to worry," she says. "They'll come around. And in the meantime," Ros takes a deep breath, "you have me."

Hope doesn't respond. Just keeps pushing the beans around her plate, staring vacantly ahead.

"I won't leave you, Hope," Ros says, knowing her purpose here. "I will *never* leave you."

# Chapter 19

*Maddie*

Maddie cannot process what she has just heard. Cannot add it to the turmoil which is already her constant companion. At first, she just stares at Mum, and the spiky-haired woman next to Mum. Her dad and brother melt away. Then she is gripped by a wave of nausea so powerful that she turns and runs to the bathroom, slamming the door shut and locking it. She vomits lunch into the bowl of the toilet, gasping as her mind tries to grasp what is happening. Nausea rises again. *What did Mum just say?*

*If John knew that Will wasn't his, it would kill him – it would kill both of them.* She continues to kneel on the bathroom floor, her face resting on the cool porcelain of the bath. Vaguely she hears someone banging on the door.

"Go away," she calls out weakly, retching again. Hoping they can't hear her.

When the nausea retreats enough for Maddie to find her feet, and when everything is quiet in the house, she carefully opens the door and tiptoes to her room. Her bed, freshly made with the sunflower quilt, is a welcome retreat. She climbs into it fully clothed, pulling the covers up over her head. All she wants to do is sleep. And rewind. Rewind to two months ago when her family was normal and she had choices and freedom ahead of her. But even as she drifts off to sleep, her fanciful wishes take on a dreamlike quality, wisping around and away from her like early morning mist.

\*

Mum wants Maddie to stay. Begs her the next morning when Maddie stumbles downstairs, dressed and carrying her packed bag, looking for some dry toast, anything to ease the queasy roil in her belly. Mum looks dreadful. Almost as bad as Maddie. There are deep shadows under her eyes and her dark curls are springing more wildly than usual from her head.

"Please don't go straight back, Mads," Mum pleads, reaching out and grabbing her hand.

Maddie nibbles on a piece of wholemeal toast, swallowing miniscule bites and carefully washing them down with cold water. She can't contemplate juice. Or coffee. The thought alone makes her insides rise up and rebel. She lets her hand rest in her mother's for a moment, feeling bad for Mum despite herself.

"Is it true?" she whispers.

Hesitation, then a quick nod from Mum. Maddie's nausea grows stronger.

"What happened?" she asks softly. "What did you do?"

For a minute, she doesn't think Mum is going to tell her, but then Mum squeezes her hand tightly and talks.

"It was a long time ago," she says.

*Obviously*, thinks Maddie, wanting to pull her hand away, but not wanting to upset Mum any further. *Eighteen years is a long time.*

"I was at a party."

Mum glances at Ros now, then back to Maddie.

"Life was... hard," she says. "I wasn't coping."

Maddie frowns. How old was she when Mum wasn't coping? Not even one. She is not sure what to do with this information.

"I drank too much." Another glance at Ros. "Smoked some weed. Took something else. I don't know what."

"*You?*" Maddie breaks in. Mum has always been so preachy about drugs.

"I didn't realise – "

"Didn't realise?" Maddie interrupts. "How could you not realise?"

Ros reaches out a hand and lays it on Maddie's arm. Maddie snatches it away.

"And what?" she goes on. "You just... slept with somebody else? Because it was a hard day? Because you wanted to party?"

Maddie pulls back. Unfamiliar hot rage courses though her. She shouldn't have started this. She can't deal with it.

"Stay. Please. We can talk." Mum is leaning forward with her elbows on the kitchen table, arms outstretched while Maddie stands.

"I don't want to talk," Maddie says, backing away. "I've called an Uber."

"Please, Maddie."

"Mum!" Maddie's words stop Hope. "I can't talk right now, OK? I have enough going on."

She hardens her resolve as Hope's face crumples.

Then she is at the front door and is gone.

*

On Saturday morning, Maddie lays flat on her uni bed, hands resting lightly on her chest, taking in deep, rhythmic breaths.

*In, two, three, four... Out, two, three four... In, two, three four... Out, two, three, four...*

Her hands rise and fall with each breath. She has read somewhere that focusing on your breathing is a good way to fight the nausea. Some days she is sick, which is better. Other days she waits to be sick, trapped in a sea of queasiness like a moth in water. The sickness has been worse since her disastrous visit home, losing its early ebb and flow quality and wrapping itself permanently around her like a clammy second skin.

Focusing in on her breath and the feeling of her body stretched out flat on her bed doesn't just ease the sickness. It helps to empty her mind. To shrink the clamouring thoughts inside her head, down, down, down, until they are miniscule dots, distant and inconsequential.

Maddie's phone bleeps beside her, shattering her concentration and breaking the fragile nothingness. The reality of her situation rushes in to fill the space, and she feels her heart race and the sickness worsen.

*How did I get here?*

Those words, or variations of them, have been swirling around her for days now, adding to her sense of unreality. She is stuck in some alternate existence, is an entirely other Maddie who has a past that is a mystery, a present that is impossible, and a future she hasn't planned.

*How can I possibly be pregnant?*

At first, Maddie assumed the doctor who called her had made a big mistake. Had called the wrong person or looked at the wrong results. Not normally given to dramatic emotion, Maddie was surprised at the rage she had felt at the error, deciding on the spot to make an official complaint.

But the tiredness, the sense of things being out of kilter, and then the nausea... After the call, Maddie had furiously thrown on her coat and trainers and walked briskly out of her flat and onto campus, ignoring the rain blowing sideways into her face. Had bought a test. To prove to that doctor that what he had said couldn't possibly be true.

*You have to actually have sex to be pregnant!* Maddie had fumed. *Birds and Bees 101. Bloody, incompetent, useless GP!*

But the test was positive. And the second one. And the third.

Maddie had felt something deep inside of her come unmoored, setting her adrift in rough, unfamiliar seas as the hows and whys and sheer impossibility of it all bobbed around her in the unrelenting swell.

*How. Could. This. Be?*

But even as she asked herself this question, turning it over and over in her mind and examining it from every possible angle, a tiny shoot of awful possibility nudged at her. That night she couldn't remember. Her birthday. The party. The dress, unzipped and crumpled on the floor. Her knickers, kicked to the end of the bed in a tight ball. The ache in her body and bruises on her hips. The complete black hole of nothingness that enveloped that night. The way things changed for her after that. Like her own instincts were trying to tell her something. Something she couldn't bear to hear.

But Maddie knew. Even as she asked the question, and her mind and body clamped down on the nameless dread forming into words, she knew. Now that knowledge sits within her like a cold weight. Impossible to unknow. Impossible to let in. She focuses on her breathing once more. Her heartrate gradually slows as she lies in her room, curtains drawn against the light outside, phone face down to shut out the world. She is not Maddie. She is not here.

*

She hasn't left her room since she arrived back in Brighton, surviving on cream crackers and sips of tepid water. Herb poked her head around the door last night, eyes widening at the dishevelled sight of her, and she and Hannah had gone into tag-team caretaker mode.

"Poor you," Herb said when Maddie explained that she had a particularly bad stomach bug. "What do you need?"

*I need this not to be happening,* Maddie thought silently, feeling tears gathering and closing her eyes against them. *I need to go back to before. I need my family back.*

But she simply smiled weakly at Herb, and asked her for more water, rolling away with her back to the door to convey that she wanted to be alone.

\*

When Will turned up on her doorstep late at night a few days ago, saying that he needed to get out of that fucking house and could he crash here for a couple of days, Maddie had surprised herself by being pleased to see him. He was normality. Her life before everything had turned upside down and inside out.

But Will refused to tell her anything, saying only that home was messed up and he never wanted to go back. She'd talked him into letting her message their parents, and when Dad called her straight back, his familiar deep tones brought buried tears to the surface. Dad was coming. He would know what to do. She was going home.

At first, seeing him, feeling his arms wrapped around her and smelling the familiar scent of earth and outdoors, had settled her. Given her a glimmer of light in this nightmare. She should have gone home sooner. Touched base with everything familiar the moment she knew something was so terribly wrong. Except home turned out to be the worst place of all. That rush of belonging, that scent of all things familiar and safe as she stepped through the front door, wrapped round her like a soft blanket, only to be ripped away moments later by Mum's words. Words so foreign and incomprehensible that they are still running amok in Maddie's head, impossible to capture or place.

*What the hell is going on?*

She has tried texting Will. Calling him, even though Will hates speaking on the phone, but he hasn't responded. Hasn't even seen her texts as far as Maddie can tell. Even Dad has gone AWOL.

*How? How? How?*

The world has lost its shape like flattened clay, and no matter how hard she tries, Maddie can't form it back into what it was.

\*

After another day, she forces herself to get up from her tousled bed, to have a shower and to venture into the kitchen. Herb has been in to see her a couple more times, concern etched on her face, fingers swiping through her bleached hair as she perches on a chair near Maddie's bed. Today she is sitting in the kitchen with Ella. Maddie is surprised. She didn't know they were friends.

"Maddie!" Ella's face lights up as Maddie pads in, duvet wrapped tightly around her shoulders to ward off the chill in the air. The heating is rubbish here. "You're up!"

Maddie gives a wan smile and plops down into a chair at the table, the movement aggravating the dull ache behind her temples.

"I'm up," she agrees.

"Let me get you some tea," says Ella, springing to her feet and reaching for the kettle.

Maddie is about to say no but realises she would love something hot to drink.

"Thanks, Ella. Weak and black, please." Milk makes her want to heave. She rubs her hands across her forehead to ease the pain, and senses Herb's eyes on her.

"Are you sure you should be up and about, Maddie?" she asks. "You look like shit."

Maddie gives a mirthless laugh. "Thanks."

"You do," Herbs says.

"I have a headache, that's all," Maddie replies, laying her head on her arms, and willing the kettle to boil. She definitely needs that drink.

"Have you taken anything?" Herb asks. She riffles in her bag, pulling out a crumpled box of Paracetamol. "Damn. Empty."

"It's OK..." Maddie replies, except her head really is killing her. "Actually," she says to Herb, "I've got some in my room. In the bathroom cabinet." She pushes her room key towards Herb. "Would you mind...?"

"Course not." Herb grabs Maddie's key and goes out.

"Here you are." Ella brings a steaming mug to Maddie and puts two more out for her and Herb.

"Thanks, Ell," says Maddie. "You're a star."

She cradles the mug in her chilled hands and they are silent for a moment. Ella is easy to be around. Someone who doesn't mind just being quiet. Dad is like that too. Maddie feels a twist of pain at the thought of Dad and pushes it away. She is just about to ask Ella how she and Herb became friends when Herb comes back into the room, a frown lining her forehead, eyes serious.

"Maddie," she says quietly.

Maddie and Ella turn towards her, and Maddie feels her heart drop like a dead weight. Herb is holding up one of Maddie's pregnancy tests. Even from here, the double blue line is obvious.

"What the hell...?" Herb can't finish the sentence.

Maddie leaps to her feet and crosses the room in one smooth movement, snatching the test from Herb's hand.

"What are you doing with that?" she shouts, tears of anger and shame gathering in her voice. "That's *private!*"

"I dropped the box of tablets," Herb protests. "It fell in your bin, so I went to get it out and..." She holds out both hands. "I saw it, OK? I'm sorry. I didn't mean to pry."

Maddie slumps back into her seat, head in hands. She feels Ella's hand on her back and senses Herb sitting down on the other side of her.

"What's going on, Maddie?" Herb asks, gently now.

Maddie's shoulders start to shake as everything she has tried to contain and hold inside bursts out. She can't believe she is making such a scene, but she can't help it.

"I don't know, I don't *know*..." she squeezes out between sobs, leaning her head on Herb's shoulder. "I don't *know!*" She is overwhelmed with the hopelessness of it all, with the dizzying effects of her upturned world.

"What the hell am I going to do?" she asks, crying more softly now, allowing Herb and Ella to shuffle in close to her. She hears the front door opening and closing. Voices approaching. Kate's voice. And Josh's. Not Rob's or Warren's, thank God. Maddie can't face all of them right now. Without a word, she gets to her feet, wipes her face and goes back to her room before the rest of her friends arrive.

# Chapter 20

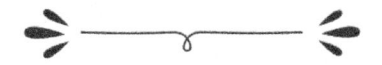

*Will*

Will doesn't remember deciding to leave. Doesn't remember his feet walking the familiar route to Sam's, one step and then another. Onto the number fifty bus and then off again. More steps and then more until he blinks and finds himself on Sam's doorstep, wiping the damp hair from his face, barely aware that it has started raining again. He is holding the backpack he picked up when he left the house in a haze of shame and anger the day before. It hangs limply from one hand as he raises the other to knock on the door. After a moment, Sam's mum Sally opens it, drying her hands on a tea-towel, her surprised expression melting into concern at the sight of him.

"Will?" she says. "Are you OK?"

When he doesn't answer, she opens the door wider and gestures for him to come in.

Sam appears in joggers and a T-shirt as his mum closes the front door behind Will.

"Mate?" he says, raising his eyebrows at the sight of his friend, and flicking his gaze to his mum and back again. "What's going on?"

But Will's words, muddled and muddied, are locked somewhere inside, so he just shakes his head, kicks off his trainers and points up the stairs before heading up to the boyhood familiarity of Sam's room. Sam shrugs his shoulders at his mum and follows Will upstairs.

\*

It is late the next morning; Sam has gone to school. His mum left for work ages ago, and Will is alone in the house. He is lying sprawled on the sofa in Sam's room, long legs poking out from the end of the tangled blanket Sally gave him last night. He can feel the chill in the gap between his sock and his jogging bottoms, which have hitched up just below his knee after a night of tossing and turning. He pulls his legs back into the warmth of the blanket like a cocoon, shifting awkwardly onto his side and staring unseeingly at Sam's rumpled bed.

Earlier this morning, when the bustle of the house drew him out of uneasy slumber, Will had wanted only to be left alone. Sam had been questioning him since the moment he arrived, only stopping when Will feigned sleep, and had resumed his interrogation this morning.

"What do you mean you're not coming in today?" Sam had asked, picking up a jumper from the floor and sniffing at the armpits before shrugging it on over his shoulders. "We've got that maths test... Packer will go mental."

When Will doesn't reply, Sam shrugs, kicking clothes out of the way until he locates his bag.

"Are you ill?"

"No."

Will's voice sounds strange in his own ears, hoarse and croaky, like it has been hibernating through a long winter.

"You look ill."

In response, Will had turned over, letting his silence do the talking.

Now, though, the quiet of the house and the absence of people around him feel like a weight pressing down on him. He doesn't want to move, but the urge to push back the oppressive silence is suddenly overwhelming and Will sits up, breathing hard. His heart is racing. The sense of disconnect which brought him here the previous day is slipping away, giving way to a rising anxiety and the creep of cold anger.

He snatches up his phone, scrolling down the screen. Missed calls from Maddie and Mum. Last night and today. One from Ros.

*Fucking Ros.*

Nothing from Dad.

*Dad.*

Will allows the anger to steady him. To plug the hole that threatens to open at the core of him and swallow him whole.

Fuck. *Fuck.* FUCK!!!

He stands up and hurls his phone against the wall, barely registering as it cracks and breaks, the glow of its screen and his connection to his family and everyone else going dead.

*

By the time Sam comes home later that day, Will has helped himself to bread and cheese from the kitchen and downed a bottle of Pepsi Max he found in the fridge. He has retreated to Sam's room to ward off any third degree from Sally, who will be home any minute. He is leaning out the open window smoking weed, oblivious to the chill of the room.

Sam clatters in and stops short at the sight of him.

"Will! What the hell are you doing?"

Will turns his head slightly, acknowledging Sam's presence with a wave of his hand.

"Living my best life, mate," he replies, drawing deeply on the joint, and closing his eyes in quiet appreciation of the wave of chemical wellbeing that takes him away... away...

"What the...!" Sam lunges at him, grabbing at Will's hand, but Will holds it easily out of his reach. Sam has always been a short ass.

"Put it out!" Sam hisses. "My mum will kill us."

Will laughs. "She's not even here. Relax."

"Well, it's a bloody good thing," Sam says, pushing past Will and opening the window wider. "You can smell the weed as soon as you walk through the door."

He leaves the room and proceeds to open all the upstairs windows, fanning ineffectively at the scent of the weed and glaring at Will.

"Mate! Put it out."

Will stretches, eyes Sam as he takes a last, deep drag, then stubs the joint out on his plate.

"OK," he says as Sam stands guard like a bulldog. "Relax. It's out."

He holds up the blackened stub to prove it, and Sam's shoulders relax as he shrugs off his coat and drops his bag.

"What is wrong with you?" Sam says now, the urgency leaving his voice. "You're being a knob."

Will laughs shortly and slumps back on the sofa, the blanket bunched uncomfortably beneath him. He shifts slightly and shrugs.

"Nothing is wrong," he replies flatly.

Sam raises his eyebrows and just looks at him. They have been friends forever, and even in his stoned state, Will knows he won't get off that easily.

"I just need to get away for a bit," he says at last. "Home is shit."

Sam nods.

"OK...," he says slowly. "Is it something to do with that woman, Ros?"

Will feels his lip curl at the sound of her name, forces his features into a neutral expression, and shrugs, like he doesn't give a fuck. He. Doesn't. Give. A. Fuck.

"Amongst other things."

Sam waits but gives up after a few moments when it becomes clear that Will isn't going to offer anything else. He notices the cracked phone laying on his bed.

"What happened to your phone?"

Will shrugs.

"Smashed it."

\*

When Sally gets home later, hurrying into the house with brisk efficiency, Sam spins a story about Maddie having Covid and Will needing a place to stay out of the house for a few days. Will holds back, letting Sam do the talking, feeling awkward and ill-placed. He can see from Sally's face that she isn't fooled, but he is relieved that she seems willing to go along with it, for now.

"Fine," she relents, when Sam has finished. "Stay for a few days. Sam can clear the boxes and washing from the spare room and you can sleep there, but..." she raises a finger to quash Sam's protest, "only on the condition that you let your mum know you're here."

"Well, she knows," Sam breaks in. "Maddie has Covid and Will..."

Sally breaks in. "That's my condition," she says quietly, and Will nods.

"Now what shall we have for dinner. Chinese?"

While they are waiting for the takeaway, Sam rings Will's mum, as Will's phone is toast. Will can't hear her end of the conversation but can tell by Sam's face that he is getting grilled. Sally follows up with a text.

*Rather them than me,* Will thinks, plugging headphones into Sam's laptop and watching YouTube videos of rollercoasters, zoning his dysfunctional family out. As he watches, his mind keeps veering towards what he heard Mum say like the rollercoasters on the video, plunging helplessly down, around, upside down, their cargos screaming in terrified delight, arms raised high. Except Will feels no delight. Cannot raise his arms and surrender to this ride's destination. He is clinging to the bar, eyes closed tight. None of this is happening.

\*

On Monday, Sally makes Will go to school with Sam. She stands in the kitchen, arms crossed, determination emanating from all five feet of her. Sally has raised Sam single-handedly. It has always been just the two of them.

"You're not lying around here doing nothing all day, William Graham. I don't know what has happened and why you have run off from home." She shushes Sam's protests about Covid and staying well for their mock exams with one outstretched hand. Her gaze never leaves Will. "But while you are under my roof, you're going to school. Understood?"

Will nods, and Sally smiles.

"Good."

So now Will is sitting in a biology lab, Sam on one side, and stupid Josh on the other side of Sam. They want Will to go to the gym with them after school, and they're mucking about like idiots.

"Fuck off," Will says dully, in response to the invitation.

"Come on, Will," Sam says, still trying to persuade him.

They are dissecting locusts. They each have a board with a decapitated locust pinned to it, nerve endings still firing enough to make their jointed legs jerk and twitch on the board. Will watches in detached fascination, clipping first one leg, then another from his specimen until only the stumps are twitching. Will is vaguely aware of some of the girls screaming at the task before them, and nerdy Mr Willis, usually mild-mannered, shouting at them in frustration.

"You know you want to."

Still the gym thing.

Josh joins in.

"Come on, mate." He pulls up his sleeve and flexes his biceps, bulging veins snaking disgustingly across his arm. "You don't get this without a bit of effort."

Will feels the cold rage rising through his chest and neck, and up into his head until his vision blurs. His pulse is pounding.

"I. Fucking. Said. NO!" Will shouts, standing suddenly and sweeping his board with the pinned locust across the work bench. It skids and smashes into Sam's board and then Josh's, knocking them upside down onto the floor and squashing the twitching corpses of the locusts beneath them.

Will is vaguely aware of Mr Willis shouting his name and rushing into the melee, of Sam's incredulous face and Josh's brainless one gaping wordlessly at him, but he is somewhere else, far away from the normal life of double biology on Monday morning. He grabs his bag and runs from the classroom, rage driving him down the corridor and out the front door of the school. Will is running, running, running until even the rage can't keep up and he doubles over, gasping for air and wanting only to escape from his messed-up life.

# Chapter 21

***

***John***

In the first moments after those words spill from Hope's mouth, John feels the years roll away from him. He is not 52 years old. He is not John, husband and father, running a successful gardening business, holding everyone up and together. He is not standing in his own house, with his son and his daughter beside him, looking out into the darkness where his wife and Ros now stand, gazing at him in dismay.

He is 14 years old. He has just learned that his mother cheated on his father, the intensity of the lowered-voice confrontation drawing him to the stairs of his family's small home. He heard his mother's quiet sobs, his father's pained disbelief.

*It was only the once, Bill. Just once. Please... I beg you!*

But he never heard his father's reply. Had backed hastily up the stairs as his father grabbed his jacket and left the house, returning late in the night. Nobody spoke of it again. At least not in John's presence.

And then John was 15 and became the man of the house overnight when his father dropped dead in front of them all. John was not a man given to grudges, but that night, the night his father left them for good, a small, cold nugget of doubt lodged itself deep in his belly, wondering if things would have been different. If only.

As Hope reaches out to him now, wordless, beseeching, the boy inside crumbles and backs away, Hope's face blurring with his mother's.

*No... Don't.*

He takes the only option open to him. Retreat.

He goes to the room he has shared with Hope for two decades. Locking the door behind him, he sits mutely, throw neatly smoothed over the foot of the bed, cushions piled just so at the headboard. Even when he hears knocking at the door, Ros's voice calling out *John? John?* and notes the rattle of the door handle, he doesn't answer. Can't answer. The boy inside has always known that the world outside is not kind and does not play fair. That it can change shape and implode without a moment's notice. The boy reminds him of this now, and John cannot argue with him.

*

He doesn't unlock the door that night, cannot bear to see Hope, to hear any more of the words from her mouth. In the midst of the disbelief, the meaning and consequences of her words not yet fully formed in his mind, he feels an odd sort of freedom. Since the day he first met her, his whole reason for being has been to hold Hope up, to hold her together, to be the strong one for the family. He had taken on this role gladly, without thought, wearing it like a comfortable old jacket. Being the steady one, the one who weathers all the storms on behalf of everyone else had given him meaning, had kept him going and held his own demons at bay.

But just lately, that old jacket had become less comfortable, its fit less moulded to his form. Perhaps his back became more stooped as he entered his sixth decade, his strong arms more tired and stiff. Perhaps it was time for a new coat. But old clothes are hard to shed, and John's deeply ingrained instincts never allowed him to try another for size.

Until now.

In the wake of Hope's revelation – John can't bring himself to think too deeply on it just now – he feels free to shrug off that old coat, and to roll and stretch his tired shoulders, testing out how the world feels when it isn't all resting on him.

*

He creeps out early the next morning, before it is fully light. Hope, Ros, Maddie and Will are nowhere to be seen, and John is relieved. He doesn't want to face any of them right now.

The rain has cleared and the temperature has dropped overnight. There is a light frost sparkling in the streetlight. John fumbles about in the glove compartment of his van for the scraper, pulling it out from the tangle of insurance documents, torches, pens and a half-eaten pack of polos that he doesn't remember buying. He scrapes the windows and side mirrors of the van quickly, without turning on the engine, wanting to complete the task and make his escape without waking anyone up. When he is finished, he climbs into the driver's seat and feels relief wash over him as he backs, unchallenged, out of the drive. The air is frigid, puffs of his breath still visible in the darkness.

His first job is in Wisborough Green. A 40-minute drive if traffic conditions are good. There are a few cars out on the road this Friday morning, but it is still quiet. He will be too early, so he detours to a truckers café he knows just outside of Pulborough, ordering a steaming mug of tea and a bacon roll. He chews quietly, weathered hands cradling the steaming mug, mind blank. When he is finished, the sun has risen higher in the sky, a welcome change to the previous day's rain. It is a good day to be outside.

His day is taken up with clearing borders, revealing the chipped and weathered trellises and fencing which is grey and bare without its summer colour and foliage. He is grateful for the dry weather which allows him to treat the wood, preparing it for spring. The work absorbs him, the blank peace and strange lightness enveloping him as the hours pass until the light begins to fade. He has left his phone in the van. Switched off. Silent.

But the oasis the physical labour provides is illusory and short-lived, and as he packs his tools into the van and stretches the chilled kinks from his body, the raw pain he has been holding at bay all day worms its way in.

*Will.*

*Maddie.*

Will. His son. His gut twists at those two words. A fact. A given. Woven into his life. Now pulled out like a loose thread, the fabric left behind unravelling.

Maddie. The pallor of her face. The dark shadows seeping down from troubled eyes. Something is wrong.

He fumbles for his phone. Tries Maddie first – this call is easier – but there is no reply. He leaves a message. Asks her to call. Then Will. He takes a deep breath and presses the call icon. The phone just rings and rings. There is no option to leave a message, so he texts.

*Will. It's dad.*

John feels a twist of pain. Deletes the last word. Changes it to *It's me –*

*Call me.* The urge to connect with his son, with Will, is suddenly overpowering, and he starts the van and drives home.

When he arrives at the house, he takes a deep breath, waiting a moment before turning off the engine, then opens the van door and goes to the house. He puts his key in the front door and sees Hope's familiar shape through the frosted glass, hurrying to meet him as he opens the door.

"John!"

She looks terrible, her anxiety palpable and her need hitting him like a blast wave.

"I've been so worried. I'm so sorry. Thank goodness you're home."

Her words babble past him like a stream in flood, but John looks beyond her, searching for either of his children. He cuts through Hope's words.

"Where is Will?" he asks, and she stutters to a halt.

"Will? He's... he's with Sam. Staying there for a few days. Sam just called..."

John's heart thuds painfully. He needs to see Will.

"And Maddie?" he asks.

Hope looks broken.

"She's gone back... back to uni. This morning. She wouldn't stay."

John takes a deep breath and, without removing his coat or boots, turns abruptly and heads back for the front door.

"John? John! Where are you going?" Hope is pleading now. Just like his mother. He doesn't respond, just closes the door and climbs back into his van.

When he arrives at Sam's, warm light spills out from around the front windows, the curtains inside closed tightly against the cold darkness. John knocks softly at the front door and waits a few moments before Sally opens the door and smiles a welcome at him.

"John, hello," she says.

John smiles back but has no energy for niceties.

"Is Will here?" he asks. "I'd like to see him."

"Oh... yes," says Sally. "He came last night. The boys are upstairs watching a film. I'll just go and get him. Come in."

John steps into the small hallway, his height and the scent of cold winter air pouring from him and filling the space. A moment or two passes, then Sally comes back down the stairs, looking uncomfortable.

"Um. John, I'm so sorry, but Will says he doesn't want to see you."

John feels the words like a punch to the gut.

"You could go up… if you like."

John shakes his head, already backing away.

"No. It's OK. I'll come back. Just tell him to call when he's ready."

Sally gives a quick nod and smiles sympathetically.

"You know what boys this age are like," she says, reaching out and touching his arm. "I'm sure he doesn't mean it."

"No. Thanks, Sally."

John goes back to his car. Checks his phone for messages from either Maddie or Will. Nothing. He deletes the missed calls from Hope. Wonders what to do now. The thought of home fills him with an emptiness he cannot face right now, so he gets in the van and drives until he finds a pub where he can eat, somewhere with welcoming lights and people who are strangers.

Much later, when he arrives home, he slips quietly through the front door, ungreeted by Hope this time. He carefully removes his boots and jacket, laying his keys silently on the cupboard by the door before padding quietly upstairs and into Will's room. He picks his way through the mess on the floor, inhaling the stale fug of unwashed clothes and body spray before slipping out of his work clothes, climbing into the unmade bed and wrapping Will's covers around him as tightly as he can.

# Chapter 22

***Me***

*Imagine, if you will, a tiny house. The house has eight rooms. Three on the ground floor, two upstairs, and three in the attic. The rooms have no doors, and the front of the house can be opened so that from your giant's perspective, you can see everything that is happening in each room at the same time. A nanny with the children in the nursery. A cook in the kitchen preparing the evening meal. The ladies of the house gathered in the music room. The men gathered round the billiard table. A maid polishing the silver. At first sight, it appears that all is well. Everyone is doing what they are supposed to be doing. But bring your head in more closely and observe for a moment... Each room is separate. One does not lead to the other. The little dolls are faithfully living out the roles assigned to them, but they cannot connect with one another. They are trapped in their own space. Stuck in perpetual activity with no sense that anything else is possible.*

\*

I was 14 years old when I went into foster care, closed off and dragging my feet behind the social worker that first day. She prattled on with grating cheeriness as we crossed the threshold into the group home, handing me over to strangers, her steady flow of words filling all the anxious space until she left and I was alone. Nobody wanted to take on a silent, moody adolescent more accustomed to crack dens than youth clubs, and my presence felt extraneous and unwieldy from that first day. Like the simple fact of my existence took up too much space.

I made myself as small as possible, and was grateful that the second bed in the room they gave me was empty. The only good thing about the place was the downstairs study, where bookshelves groaned under the weight of their treasures. I found solace in the imaginary worlds contained in the pages of those books, whiling away many a day and night staring off into the distance, my mind taking the stories and weaving them into something more, a place where life was ordered and kind.

Ros arrived a few weeks after me. An impossibly small waif-like girl, thin and pale with eyes too big for her face. She was 11 years old. They put her in my room, where we sat that first night, staring at each other from our respective beds. Ros spoke first, in a high-pitched voice with a defiant world-weariness that belied her childlike features.

"I give it one month," she said, kicking off her shoes and flopping back on to her pillows.

"Give what one month?" I asked, taking the bait.

"This..." she spread her arms to indicate the room we were sharing. "Being stuck here."

"Stuck in this room?" I said, slow to understand.

Ros laughed at me, stretching her arms behind her head and closing her eyes.

"Um... No," she said, words heavy with disdain at my obtuseness. "Stuck here. In this house. With these people."

I learned that this was Ros's fifth foster home in as many years. That as soon as she approached anything close to settled, she would kick off and make life so difficult that nobody could handle her. Apparently, this place was known for managing the tough kids, or the ones too old to place with normal families. Ros viewed this as a personal challenge.

"How do you even know this stuff?" I asked her one day, learning early on that despite her diminutive size and childlike manner, Ros was the streetwise one. The one to go to if you wanted to know things.

Ros shrugged. "Just do."

Nothing fazed her, and I found myself drawn to her, attracted by her tough courage which I could never harness for myself. Over the weeks and then months, we became inseparable, and for the first time in a long time, I felt a chink of light creep into my lonely soul.

Then Jeremy arrived. The home's new manager. And everything changed.

\*

In the days following my terrible, uttered words and the scattering of my family, I feel a sense of numbness snake over me, welcome and comforting as an old blanket. I retreat outwardly to my room in the loft, which John vacated in favour of Will's empty room days ago, and inwardly to a safe place within, where feelings are simply words that other people experience.

At some point during the retreat, I find it in myself to phone Fran, to plead a bad dose of flu and ask her to see to the shop, to call in one of our seasonal staff to help, perhaps. Fran is instantly sympathetic, the warm tones of her voice reaching out through the phone and threatening to breach the new walls of my safe place.

"Oh, poor you," she says gently, and I feel a response rising up, catching in the tightness of my throat. I want to lean into her, to rest my head on her shoulder. Maybe she can make everything right again. But even as the thought forms in my mind, a vicious voice inside swipes it away.

*Nobody can help you, you silly bitch. You are on your own. This is all your fault. What would Fran think if she knew about you?*

I retreat further. The voice is right. It's true. This is all my fault and I am finally getting what I deserve.

"Is there anything I can do?" Fran asks. "Do you need anything?"

I hear her words dimly and force a response from my mouth.

"No," I whisper. "No thank you Fran. I just need to rest, that's all."

"Of course, dear," she says. "You take all the time you need to feel better. We can manage here."

I end the call, turning my phone face down. At some point I have stopped checking for messages, for texts, for the familiar ping of connection from the family WhatsApp group. It has been silent, empty, like the family who populated it has just disappeared.

At first, I could not be parted from the phone, my only tangible link to the others. The first call came from Sam, followed by a message from his mother, Sally, who texted to say that Will was staying with them for a few days and that he was safe. I thanked her, then immediately texted Will and sent a WhatsApp message as a follow-up, signalling through every means at my disposal that I was here for him.

*Please call. Please message. Please...*

The two ticks never turned blue. No dots on the screen telling me he was tapping out his words at the other end. Will wasn't even picking up my messages, let alone responding to them.

I tried Maddie. She answered, at least, but had been short, distant. I overcompensated with too many words.

"*Mum.*"

The word was quiet, forceful, halting me in my tracks like a parent grabbing a wayward child careening towards a busy road.

"I can't deal with this right now."

I was silent, holding back the urge to cling to her, to draw her back to me, nodding into the phone.

"Mum."

Gentler this time.

"I have my own stuff going on. You just... you just have to deal with this yourself. I'm sorry. OK?"

Her words made something shrink inside me. She was right. Of course, she was right. It wasn't fair I was putting all of this on her. Not just when her life was beginning. When she was starting out in a way that I never could.

"OK."

I would leave her alone. But I couldn't stop the nagging pull of more words.

"You're OK, though, right? *We're* OK?"

There was a pause. Silence on Maddie's end of the line.

"I have to go, Mum."

And that was it. All I had heard from my children in days.

The loss is too much. Like always. But for the past two decades, when the familiar weight of *too much* threatened to close in, there had always been John. Strong, reliable, solid John. Even when I was at my worst, when the parts of me that held all the rage and injustice of what came before revolted and threw everything at him, even when he retreated to his plants, or drew a deep, steadying breath the way that he did and placed a gentle boundary between him and the worst parts of me, he was still there.

Until now.

That first night, I couldn't go to him. Couldn't even bang on our locked bedroom door the way Ros had. The second night, I was so desperate to speak to him, to make things right, that I ambushed him at the door when he came in after work. I didn't recognise the look in his eyes. He didn't even see me. I was invisible. I felt something collapse inside, the broken shards of my perfect family, my perfect home driving into the buried parts of myself that had always known that it wasn't real, that I couldn't do it.

*I told you so... I told you so...*

So tonight, I climb slowly up the stairs to the top floor that John built. I carefully close the door behind me and walk to my workshop, shrugging off the bulky cable knit cardigan that can't keep out this particular chill, and rest my arms on the workbench. I push up the sleeve of my jumper and survey the silvery-striped flesh like it belongs to someone else. I had started to believe that it did. To the Not Me. But it turns out that I have been the Not Me all along.

I search carefully through the pots of brushes and tools that I use to craft my perfect little accessories in my perfect little world until I find what I am looking for. A Stanley knife, its blade carefully sheathed in yellow plastic. I press the button on the side and ease the blade up, surveying it from somewhere far away.

Then I put the knife to my forearm, press the tip into the flesh, just far enough, and pull it up and across.

Up and across.

Up and across.

Until three long cuts overlay the old scars with new lines of bright, red blood, oozing pain I understand. I welcome it, closing my eyes and making space for the numbness to come in and do its job.

*

It takes a full day before Ros stops waiting for me to respond to her repeated knocking on the bedroom door and just comes in. I am in bed, staring dully through the skylight, blurred and grey with rain which has returned after a brief respite in the weather. I haven't showered or dressed, but I have covered the fresh wounds on both arms with rolls of bandages. I found them buried in the back of the bathroom cupboard, behind a stack of cleaning cloths which were crisp and stiff with age. This is familiar territory.

The Not Me is in charge now.

*Everything will be fine now,* the Not Me says. *Just leave it to me.*

Ros steps up the stairs and into the room and stands observing me for a moment before she speaks. Then, with movements as deft and practised as a finely choreographed dance, she teams up with the Not Me, just like the old days.

"Don't worry, Hope," she says, climbing onto the bed and wrapping her arms round me from behind. Her slim body fits against mine like a lost puzzle piece slotting into place.

"I'm here now. Everything is going to be OK."

# Chapter 23

### *Ros*

Everybody underestimates Ros. Without fail. It started when she was six years old, weeks into her first foster placement. The family – she can't remember their names now, they've blurred and faded along with all the others – assumed she was a lovely, lost little girl, who would feel better if they gave her a pretty bedroom filled with dollies and spoke to her in oh-so-sweet voices. Well, Ros showed them. Pulling the heads off those dollies and stuffing them in the toilet until it blocked and overflowed, flooding the bathroom floor. Wetting her bed and smearing her own filth over her pink-painted bedroom walls until she gagged. Ros wasn't stupid. She knew that grown-ups couldn't be trusted. That sooner or later they would leave, and she was right. By the time she was seven, that first family had given her away. By the time she was eight, she had lived in three different places, and by the time she was eleven, she didn't even unpack her meagre belongings when she arrived somewhere new. Leaving was easier every time. The trick was to beat everyone else to it.

When she first met Hope, curled up with a book, pale face hidden behind a curtain of long curls that fell past her shoulders and halfway down her back, Ros was prepared to hold her at arm's length, like everyone else. She sheltered behind this version of herself, hurling inflammatory words and behaviour before her like cannonballs, curious to see the craters they created when they landed. But far from hiding away, or angrily asserting herself like all the stupid foster parents, Hope seemed to unfurl in Ros's presence, laughing with admiration at Ros's antics. Ros wasn't used to being liked, and Hope's unexpected warmth cut through all her defences and touched a part of her heart that had been frozen for a very long time. Ros thought that perhaps, this time, she would stay. Just for a little while.

When Jeremy arrived a few months after Hope and Ros became foster-sisters, Ros was immediately on alert.

"He's a dickhead," she warned Hope. "Stay away from him."

"What are you talking about?"

Hope was carefully sellotaping together the ripped pages of a book she'd found in the study and wasn't really listening.

"Jeremy. The dickhead. He's trouble."

Hope looked up briefly and shrugged.

"I didn't notice anything."

But Hope should have listened to Ros. Whenever he was near Ros, dickhead stood too close and smiled in that creepy way which set all her alarm bells ringing. She went out of her way to avoid him. But one Saturday morning, when she was lounging in the study waiting for Hope to come back from her paper round, dickhead found her there, pinned her against a wall and put his sick, disgusting hands all over her. Without conscious thought, Ros bit him, hard, kicking out and dashing to the door, nearly knocking the returning Hope over in her need to get out, to get away.

"Ros!" Hope called after her, but Ros couldn't hear her past the roaring in her head, wasn't thinking about Hope as the study door slammed shut, leaving Hope alone in the room with dickhead.

*

*Hope needs me to save her now. Just like she saved me.*

Ros feels, rather than hears these words deep within her. She is here for a reason. To save Hope from going back to that dark place. To be the person who never leaves. Who is always there, no matter what. Which is more than she can say for Hope's family right now. John is living in the house, but you wouldn't know it. Maddie has disappeared back to uni without a proper word to any of them. And who knows what is going on with Will. She went to knock on his friend Sam's door the other day, to tell him to stop behaving like a spoiled child and to come home, but she hesitated at the last minute and retraced her steps. Maybe Hope was better off without everyone crowding into her space. Ros feels a flicker of discomfort at the memory of her last encounter with Will, but quickly extinguishes it. That was all Will, just being the kid that he was. In the end, Ros realises, it is her and Hope against the world. Like always.

When the letting agent contacts Ros to let her know that she has a moving date of 4th December for the bedsit in Brighton, Ros e-mails her back and says her circumstances have changed. That she won't be needing that bedsit anymore. It was a dive anyway. So what if she loses the holding fee that she gave that shark of a landlord? Hope is what is important now. Ros will stay here, in Maddie's room, where she is needed.

She falls easily into a daily routine, finding a surprising sense of solace in the domestic rhythms of the day. No wonder Hope has turned into such a housewife. Boring has its benefits. Waiting for John to leave before getting up, throwing open the curtains and bustling around the kitchen, clearing up dishes from the previous night, putting on the kettle, checking the cupboard to see if they need anything for dinner tonight. Taking a steaming mug of tea up to Hope, coaxing her into a sitting position while Hope stares blankly ahead. Running a bath, foamy with half a bottle of bubble bath, and encouraging Hope to ease herself in after gently unrolling the bandages that cover her arms. Noting any fresh cuts, and nodding in satisfaction when Hope is submerged, her pale face the only part of her visible above the bubbles.

"I'll make us some boiled eggs on toast," she tells Hope, like Hope is interested in food. She stands guard outside the open bathroom door until she hears that Hope is safely washed and out of the water.

John doesn't come home for dinner most nights. He leaves early, before the household is up, and returns long after dark, the sound of his boots stamping on the porch outside heralding his arrival. Mostly Ros shuts herself in Maddie's room or curls up beside Hope watching TV, but tonight Ros meets John as he comes through the door, his eyes weary and shoulders slumped. His face, usually weather-beaten and glowing after a day outside, is pale and drawn.

His eyes meet Ros's for a brief moment, and he gives a quick nod before walking past her into the kitchen and putting the kettle on. Ros follows him, not quite sure why.

"Well?" she says, hands on hips. "Are you going to live like this forever? Coming and going like a ghost? Not talking to anyone?"

John sighs slowly, pulling a mug and the jar of teabags from the cupboard.

"Not now, Ros," he replies, his back to her.

"When then?" She feels the familiar antagonising spirit rise in her, wanting to jab and poke until she gets a reaction. "Tomorrow? The day after? When? You can't keep this..." she waves a hand at him, "...whatever this is, up. It's not fair on Hope."

He goes still, then turns to look at Ros, spots of colour appearing on his cheeks, eyes sparking.

"Not fair on *Hope*?"

His words are quiet but carry a weight that nearly pushes Ros back a step. She holds her ground.

"Yeah. That's what I said. She's in a terrible state. You would know if you'd bothered to check."

Ros watches John as he presses his lips together, as if struggling to hold back the torrent of words he wants to throw at her.

*Yes. This is more like it.*

Ros feels a flare of old energy as battlelines are drawn.

John is breathing hard, and he jabs a finger in her direction as he speaks.

"Whatever terrible state she is in is her own making. Her own making. And quite frankly, for the first time in a long, long time, I don't care how she is. I really don't!"

He turns and sloshes water from the kettle into the mug, swearing as the scalding liquid splashes onto his hand. Ros sees that it is shaking, and John speaks more quietly now.

"I care about Will. I care about Maddie. How could Hope...? How could she do this to our family?"

"She didn't do this to your family, John," Ros replies coolly. "This isn't about you."

"Isn't about...?" John can't finish the sentence. "How is this not about me? I don't even know if Will is my son!"

There. It is out there. Those terrible words. That terrible new truth which has splintered this family apart as effectively as a stick of dynamite.

John's breaths are coming quickly and he is looking inwards like he is weighing up his next words.

"Who is he?" he finally asks Ros, his voice quiet again.

Ros is momentarily confused. "Who is *Will*?"

"No, not *Will*!" John spits out. "Who is he? Will's … This other man?"

Ros hesitates for a moment.

"I don't know," she replies at last. "I don't think Hope knows either."

John's eyes widen at this, his knuckles turning white as he clenches the hot mug in his hands.

"She doesn't *know*?" He is incredulous. "She risked everything but doesn't know? How can she not know?"

Ros sees him thinking it through.

"My God, Ros. How did it happen? When?"

Ros simply shrugs her shoulders, her silence encouraging his own mind to carry him further and further away.

"And you *knew*?"

She shrugs again, claiming her own territory over Hope's life.

"There is a lot I know about Hope, John. Stuff that you don't."

She watches John's face close and crumple in on itself as he backs away, then he turns and treads heavily up the stairs to Will's room.

Ros makes two more cups of tea and makes her way up to Hope's room, dark apart from the flickering images from the TV playing across Hope's face. She is sitting up and turns her head towards Ros as she enters the room.

"Was that John?" she asks, her voice croaky with underuse. "Is he home?"

"Yup." Ros sets the tea down next to Hope.

Hope pulls herself up with a sudden surge of energy.

"I need to speak to him, Ros. To explain…"

Ros stops her with a hand on her arm.

"He doesn't want to see you."

The flicker of light fades from Hope's eyes, but she tries one more time.

"No. I just need to –"

"He doesn't want to see you, Hope."

Ros says it more firmly this time, pushing her back against the pillows. Ros wipes at the tears falling down Hope's face, then holds both her hands in her own.

"I'm sorry, Hope, I know this is hard…" She squeezes. "But I am here for you. I'll look after you."

# Chapter 24

*Maddie*

Maddie cannot think, let alone plan or make any kind of decision which will transport her out of this mess and back to her old life. The fact of this pregnancy is unfathomable enough. She still can't associate herself with that word. But the whos and the hows swirling around her ever-present reality have tightened around her like a net, holding her captive. Even thoughts of escape to the once safe space of her family have become as insubstantial as a desert mirage.

Herb and Ella have not left her alone since they found out. Maddie has begged them not to tell anyone else. She can't cope with the whole world knowing what is going on when she can't understand it herself. Hannah has been busy with work anyway, and Kate has been acting off with her and has retreated with Rob and Warren and their friends. Maddie hasn't got space to worry about Kate right now. Martin was easily brushed off when he asked her if she was OK, and Josh isn't really the type to pry. Maddie is grateful for that at least.

She has gone over and over it. First in her own mind, and then with Herb and Ella. The only way, *the only way* this could have happened without Maddie knowing is if, somehow, someone spiked her drink and then… then… Maddie's mind goes as blank as her memory, refusing to take her any further. She can't think about it.

"It was your birthday," Herb says again a few days later as the three girls sit in Maddie's room, fairy lights throwing off warm light but leaving the edges of the room in shadow. This suits Maddie. She doesn't want to be seen. Herb runs a hand through her hair, outrage on Maddie's behalf etched on her face. "It had to be your birthday."

Ella is quiet, holding tightly to Maddie's hand.

"You went to bed…" begins Herb.

"Had to be *carried* to bed," Maddie interjects bitterly.

"You went to bed," Herb repeats more forcefully, trying and failing to capture Maddie's gaze, "and we left the door propped open so we could check on you."

Maddie looks up.

"Did you?" she asks. "Check on me?"

"Yes." Ella now, speaking quietly and giving Maddie's hand a squeeze. "I couldn't really see you under the covers, but you were sleeping. You were OK."

Her voice catches on those last words, and Maddie squeezes her hand back.

"It's not your fault, Ells," she says quietly.

It isn't Ella's fault. Maddie knows that with 100% certainty. It isn't Ella's fault because it is all Maddie's fault.

"I was so out of my head that night," she says dully. "I don't usually do that. I haven't done it again. But it was such a good night. I just wanted to have fun."

Maddie buries her face in her hands, disgusted with herself. "If I hadn't worn that ridiculous dress, if I hadn't had so much to drink…"

Her words trail off and Herb jumps in.

"No, Maddie," she says. "Don't you dare."

She leans over and shakes Maddie's arm until her friend looks up.

"This is not *your* fault either. You are *not* to blame."

Maddie hears the words coming from Herb's mouth and registers their meaning and intent, but still knows without a doubt that if she hadn't been so weak and stupid, then she wouldn't be trapped here now. She listens dully as Herb keeps talking.

"Some absolute shit-for-brains tosser *coward* spiked your drink that night, waited until you were alone and out of it, then let himself into your room and… and…"

Even Herb can't finish the sentence. Ella does it for her.

"Raped you," she says, the word feeling big and more powerful coming from Ella's gentle mouth.

Maddie shakes her head, whether to refute Herb's and Ella's words, or to deny that any of this is happening at all she can't tell. All she knows is that saying it out loud isn't helping at all. Nor is talking endlessly about who *he* is, trying and failing to remember who was there that night, pausing to speculate over this person and that and ending up back in the same place they had started.

"We're not going to let him get away with it," Herb says, unable to sit helpless with the mystery of it all. "He has to pay for what he did to you."

Maddie doesn't bother to argue that you can't make someone pay if you don't know who they are. For now, at least, there is a more pressing problem. Whoever *he* is, and whatever happened that night, she has been left with a person growing inside her. A person that she never wanted and never asked for. The hopelessness of the situation hits her afresh.

"*What* am I going to do?"

Her hand drifts to her belly, even flatter than usual after weeks of nausea. She could almost believe that none of this was real. But Maddie knows the truth. She is home to another life. Another human being.

Herb springs into action.

"Hold on," she says, jumping up from the bed and going out the door. She returns a moment later with her laptop and squeezes herself between Maddie and Ella, waking up the screen and navigating to an open tab. Maddie peers down at the screen.

*MSI Reproductive Choices*

"What's that?" she asks.

"They offer all sorts of stuff," Herb replies, clicking on a few links until she finds the page she's looking for.

*I'm pregnant. What are my options?*

She quickly scrolls down.

*One in three women in the UK will have an abortion by the time they're forty-five*, Maddie reads.

"Hold on." Herb scrolls down a bit further. "Here you are." She pushes the laptop towards Maddie.

*What are my options?* Maddie reads, feeling like she is in someone else's skin.

*Continue with the pregnancy and raise a child.*

*Continue with the pregnancy and consider adoption or fostering.*

*End the pregnancy.*

Maddie can't focus, but Herb grabs the laptop and continues to scroll down.

"You can have something called a medical abortion or a surgical abortion," she says. "I didn't even know those were a thing. I thought an abortion was an abortion. But a medical abortion…" She pauses as she opens another tab and finds what she is looking for. "Sometimes you don't even have to go into the clinic. You can just take a couple of pills at home. Job done. That's if you're less than ten weeks pregnant. Which…" she does a quick calculation in her head, "…you are, I think. Just. We at least know the exact day you got pregnant. So, you shouldn't have to face any of that horrible vacuum or forceps stuff." She grimaces. "Hopefully you'll hardly notice it's happening."

Herb looks up, then goes silent as she sees Maddie's face, which has paled while Herb has been talking.

"What's wrong?" she asks, looking from Ella to Maddie as if to glean clues.

Maddie shakes her head and pushes the laptop away. She is afraid she is going to vomit.

"I think maybe I just need a bit of time alone," she tells her friends, unable to put into words the sense of panic and dread which has leached into her system. She looks first at Herb, then at Ella. "Thank you. I'm sorry. It's just…"

"It's OK," Herb says.

And Ella nods and puts a hand on Maddie's arm.

"We'll give you some space, OK? But we're here if you need us."

"Thanks." Maddie is grateful for their concern, but right now needs nothing more than to be by herself and to put the endless questions, possibilities and harsh realities as far away from herself as possible.

\*

Over the next few days, Maddie forces herself through the motions of student life, attending lectures and tutorials, going to the library, buying food from the campus shop and locking herself away in her room with books and papers to try and catch up on the assignments she has allowed to lapse. She resists all attempts by Hannah and the guys to coax her out clubbing, drinking or even to the cinema, preferring the safety and control of her own four walls and locked door. Maddie notices that they are starting to ask her less, and she is relieved about that. Herb and Ella check in on her regularly and, when she can, she tries to walk with them when she leaves the building, feeling more secure in their company than when she is alone. When she is by herself, she imagines everyone's eyes on her, knowing her secrets and laughing. Maybe even *his* eyes are on her. The thought causes her heart to hammer uncomfortably in her chest.

But as much as the normal routines help pull a sense of superficial calm around her, allowing her to get up in the morning and put one foot in front of the other until the end of the day when she falls, exhausted into bed, they do not even begin to touch what is happening inside. Maddie knows that the clock is ticking.

She finally yields to the sense of urgency that has been growing inside. One chilly Thursday afternoon, when the rest of her flatmates are out and about and she is guaranteed no interruptions, Maddie pulls her own laptop towards her and googles MSI Reproductive Choices.

*We're here to support you through your decision about a pregnancy and talk to you about the options available to you.*

Maddie reads on, opening each option in turn and reading it through, unable to place herself in any scenario. But she has no choice. This pregnancy is here no matter how much she pretends it isn't. And it is not going to go away by itself. Her hand slips again to her lower belly. Maddie imagines the life there, clinging to her like a limpet, tries to imagine that life as a baby, as a child, playing outside, going to school, waking up at the crack of dawn on Christmas Day. Her child. And – her mind closes off at the thought – *his*.

She can't. *She can't*. It is too much. Too unreal. She is not ready for this.

*Call our advice lines to discuss your needs.*

There is a number.

Maddie takes a deep breath, pulls out her phone and taps in the digits, lifting the phone to her ear as she waits for the call to connect.

# Chapter 25

*Will*

Will has discovered that Liam can get ecstasy. He finds out by chance when they are both sitting outside the head's office. Bloody Mr Willis had reported his disappearing act from Monday's biology lesson. After talking to Will's other teachers, he has worked out that Will has been in school for precisely one day all week, give or take a few hours. Will doesn't give a toss. He will be 18 in a month's time. Old enough to get out of this shit-hole and do his own thing.

*And do what? And go where?*

He squashes the nagging, anxious voice, preferring instead to entertain vague fantasies of freedom and no responsibility or expectation somewhere far away and sunny. Like Ros. Except he can't think about Ros without a hot flush of shame enveloping him. So, he has been doing the next best thing: bunking off school with his sketchpad and pens, and hanging out anywhere except where he is supposed to be.

He is perching, mutinous and uncomfortable, on a chair outside Mrs Whelan's office when Liam shuffles over and slumps onto a chair two seats away. He looks dishevelled and overgrown in every way. Long, lanky limbs and messy brown hair flopping over hooded eyes. Will looks at him sideways, curious despite himself about why the other boy is here. Everyone knows what he did at the beginning of term.

"Fucking waste of time," Will offers by way of introduction, nodding his head towards Mrs Whelan's door.

Liam glances over at Will from beneath the wave of his fringe, nods briefly, then looks down again at his lap. He is picking at his thumbnail, engrossed as he pulls at the skin down the side.

"What are you here for?" Will asks. Shouldn't Liam be going to see the head of house or something for some kind of pastoral support? So he isn't pushed over the edge again?

Liam looks flatly at Will.

"Drugs," he says.

Will nods slowly.

"What kind of drugs?" he asks.

Liam shrugs his shoulders and reels off a list. "Weed. Mushrooms. MDMA. Prescription crap," he says dully. "Whatever I get my hands on."

"What, like, for you? Or..." Will lets the sentence hang.

"Yeah," Liam says. "And anyone else who is interested."

"Fuck," says Will. "And they found out?" He jabs his head towards the closed door of the office.

"Yeah."

Will is pretty sure the school has a zero-tolerance policy about drugs but wonders if Liam will get special treatment because of what happened.

Liam looks over at Will. "I can get you whatever you want," he says. "For a price."

*

Over the weekend, Will considers Liam's offer. His account is nearly empty after he replaced his old phone with a cheap new one during the week, deliberately getting a new number so he could maintain the distance between him and his family. He has some cash stashed at home. He just has to go there and get it. The thought of it makes his gut clench with anxiety. He doesn't want to see any of them. Not Mum. Not Dad. And not bloody Ros. With any luck he can pitch up in the middle of the day, and Mum will be out at the shop, Dad will be working as usual, and Ros will be doing God knows what. Will doesn't care. He needs more of his stuff, anyway.

He heads towards home, stopping in the park on the way to roll a joint and light up. Will inhales slowly until the familiar high of the weed conjures up a false bravado and confidence. He navigates the last few streets before he is standing in front of his house. He hasn't been here for over a week, and it feels all at once familiar and alien. Will knows every nook and cranny, every creaking floorboard and every bit of chipped paint. But the people inside feel like strangers in the familiar space, and he is the worst intruder of all.

*If John knew that Will wasn't his, it would kill him – it would kill both of them!*

His mother's words and the implications of what lay beyond them knock hard against Will as he stands outside his family's home, but he won't grant them entry. He won't. Instead, he puffs himself up on the dregs of his high, lifts his head and lets himself in through the front door.

At first there is no sign of anyone, and Will feels a cautious relief. But then he hears footsteps and Ros appears at the kitchen door, wearing his mum's apron and wiping her hands on a tea towel like she bloody owns the place. Will's heart gives a painful thump at the sight of her before a sneer creeps across his face and he turns his back on her, heading up the stairs to his room. He can get out of here in five minutes flat.

"Will!" Ros calls after him and pursues him up the stairs.

*For fuck's sake!*

"Will, you're back," Ros says, following him to his room and standing in the doorway, blocking his way out.

Will ignores her, going to the built-in cupboard and pulling clothes and shoes out of it to stuff in an empty duffle bag. He opens the wooden box from his uncle on his desk and takes the cash out. His room feels different. His bed is made, and stuff that isn't his is stacked on the windowsill and draped over his game chair. *What the…?* It is like he has already been chucked out.

Ros sees him looking at the stuff, and says, "It's your dad's. He's been sleeping in here."

*My dad*, he thinks bitterly, casting a look in Ros's direction like this is all her fault. It is in a way. Things were fine, well, not *fine* exactly, but normal at least before she turned up and ruined everything.

Will hears footsteps on the stairs from his parents' loft room. He moves more quickly, wanting more than anything to get out of here. He is unplugging his games console when his mum pushes past Ros in the doorway, wrapped in a dressing gown. Her hair is all flat and bunched up on the side where she has presumably been dossing about in bed all morning. He can't help comparing her to Sam's mum, Sally – neat and efficient and normal.

"Will?"

He can't bear the pleading note in his mother's voice.

"Will?" she repeats, taking a step towards him.

Will backs away.

Mum drops her hand and says simply, "You're back."

"I'm not *back*," Will snaps, shaking his head and indicating his packed duffle bag and the games console, now wrapped in its lead and resting on top. "I just need some stuff."

Mum nods, tightening the belt of her dressing gown and folding her arms across her chest. Will sees Ros step forward and put a hand on Mum's back, like Mum is her family, not his.

"OK," Mum says, like she is expecting this. "So, um… when will you be home? It's good of Sally to put you up, but, well, you can't really stay there forever. You belong here."

Will hoists his bag onto his shoulder, tucks the console under his arm and squares up to both Mum and Ros, the weed fuelling his courage and anger.

"When will you tell me who my real father is?" he spits out at them, his face just inches from Mum's. "You can't keep it from me forever, like you were obviously planning on doing. And…" he jabs a finger towards the two women for emphasis, "… quite clearly, I do *not* belong here. And you know it. You *always* knew it. But you thought you would lie to me my whole life and pretend that I did."

He pushes past Mum and Ros, shaking now and infuriatingly close to tears.

"Nice one, Mum," he says, taking the stairs two at a time and escaping out of the door before the tears have a chance to gather and fall.

He makes his way back to Sam's and stashes his stuff in the spare room. He pulls his phone out and sends a text to Liam.

*i have ££*, he taps out. *where do u want 2 meet?*

\*

Even after getting grilled by Mrs Whelan, Will doesn't go back to school the next week. He can't. His whole world has morphed and reshaped itself around him and he can't find his footing in this new landscape. Doing all his usual stuff like nothing has changed just makes him feel worse. He can't stay at Sam's, though. Sally can detect him bunking off like a sniffer dog, so he has to find somewhere else to go each day. Today he has taken the train down to

Portsmouth. After buying five ecstasy tablets from Liam for nearly £100 and paying for the train to get down here, he is skint, so he is sitting on the harbour wall, smoking and watching the ferries coming and going. Maybe he'll go and get some chips in a minute. He pulls out a tattered sketchpad from his backpack and sketches the big ships on the choppy water, imagining himself into the picture, sailing away to somewhere else. Anywhere else.

The little bag of pills is in the front zipped pocket of his bag. He has been thinking about them all day. Wondering what it will feel like to take one. He might not be able to sail away on an actual ship, but maybe he can sail away in his mind. He looks around him, checking to see if anyone is nearby. There are people milling about, but nobody who is interested in him. He slips a hand into his backpack and riffles around until his fingers find the small plastic bag. He opens it and takes out one little pill, examining it in his hand. It is small and orange, with a happy face on it, smiling at him. Will looks out to sea again, and before he can overthink it, pops the pill in his mouth.

# Chapter 26

***John***

In those first weeks and months after his father's death, John's transition to man of the house, with all its unrelenting responsibility, demanded every moment of his time and attention. John welcomed it at the time. The weight and importance of the task filled him with purpose, keeping him busy and exhausted, and covering over the yawning great hole left by the loss of his father. After a while, John didn't even remember that he hadn't always been this way, that once he had been a child, with childish dreams and pursuits.

When Hope crossed his path, her quiet beauty and fierce independence pulled him in. But even more than that, he was drawn to the vulnerability he sensed beneath. Hope was like a broken vessel, glued together and beautiful as a kintsugi vase, but fragile along seams which might shatter under pressure. She stirred up all of John's protective instincts which had already saved him once.

Then came Maddie, sweet Maddie, so like him in many ways with her love of the outdoors and all things living, so gentle and easy to love. Such a contrast to her bright and quick-witted brother, who challenged them all from day one with a different way of seeing and interacting with the world. But even though Will was just as likely to leave John exasperated and wordless as anything else, his son's spirit also triggered a deep-seated love and something like admiration in John.

*My boy*, John found himself thinking over and over in the weeks following Hope's revelation. *My boy*.

\*

After two weeks of sleeping in Will's room and acting like a stranger in his own house, John has had enough. He won't play games anymore. That has always been Hope's department. It has been easy enough to avoid Hope until now. Between his self-imposed long hours at work, Hope's retreat to her own inner world upstairs, and Ros's newly donned role of running interference whenever he is in the house, a chasm has appeared between him and his wife. This has suited him. Now, though, John finds himself standing on his side of the chasm and wondering how best to navigate his way across, if only to have a conversation. To get some answers. He deserves that at least. This new truth of Hope's past, of Will's parentage, has stripped away his role, his very place and purpose in this family, finding fault-lines in his foundations which are threatening to shift and split apart beneath him.

For reasons he does not fully understand, John pretends to leave for work one dark Friday morning two weeks after that awful night, but instead of continuing out of Chichester and on to the A27, he pulls over at the side of the road in his van, his house just visible in his rear-view mirrors. He heard Ros say last night that she was going shopping in the morning. After half an hour or so, Ros appears at the front door, Sainsburys bag looped over her arm. She turns left and heads on foot to the supermarket half a mile away. John wonders what happened to Ros's bedsit in Brighton. She was supposed to be moving out but hasn't said another word about it. So here she still is, ever present and taking over the household tasks that normally fall to Hope. John starts the engine of his van, swings round in a quick three-point turn and drives the short distance back home.

He finds Hope upstairs as expected, out of bed, but still in her dressing gown, sitting at her worktable, hands empty before her. Despite himself, John's heart hitches and squeezes at the sight of her, familiar as the air he breathes.

"Hope," he says quietly, and she starts, turning quickly to face him.

"John!" She is on her feet now, cinching the dressing gown more tightly and reaching up a hand to calm the wild curls of her hair. "I thought you were Ros."

"Ros has gone out," he says. "And we need to talk."

Hope nods her head before speaking. "Yes," she agrees. "We do."

John sees the need in her eyes, a longing. Instead of drawing him in, he finds himself stepping backwards and away.

"Not here. You need to get showered and dressed," he says shortly. "Dress warmly. And bring a good pair of shoes. When you're ready, we'll walk."

Half an hour later, Hope is downstairs, and John leads her by the arm to his van, keen to be away before Ros makes a reappearance and becomes part of the discussion.

"Where are we going?" she asks, buckling herself into the front passenger seat.

"Harting Down," says John.

It is his place. Where he belongs. And this time he is calling the shots.

\*

There is an icy wind blowing across the Downs as John and Hope walk side by side along the bridleway leading down the steep hill towards the trig point. Churned mud has frozen into ridges, so they have to pick their way down carefully. It is December, and the chill in the air has turned Hope's pale cheeks a bright, bitten red. Normally John would wrap a strong arm round her shoulders, pulling her close and inhaling the scent of her hair, smiling with pleasure at their closeness. Today they don't touch, each navigating the downward path alone.

They didn't speak in the van, and the silence between them now is heavy with their anticipated conversation. John waits until they reach the firmer ground of the valley, and then speaks.

"What happened, Hope?" he asks quietly, the wind swiping at his words and swirling them round in harsh, wintery eddies.

She is silent for so long he wonders if she has even heard him.

"I wasn't coping, you know that, John," she replies at last, a pleading note to her tone which sets his teeth on edge.

"And?" *What's new?* The angry voice inside him adds, thinking of all the times in their lives when Hope hasn't coped.

"And I wasn't thinking straight, OK? I just… I made a mistake."

Hope glances over at him, sees his face and adds, "A *big* mistake. I get that. And I'm sorry. But I've worked so hard, *so* hard to make things right, to make sure that you and the kids have a lovely home and a *safe* place to be."

She emphasises the word 'safe', and John recognises the familiar ground of their disagreements over the years.

"I never had that John, *never*. You don't understand what that's like. What that's left me with."

He breathes in deeply, thinking of the broken parts of his own family, the betrayal of his mother and the devastating loss of his father, how his job was to hold all the different parts together.

Hope is still talking, careening down her well-trodden pathway of defence.

"I was alone by the time I was fourteen. Alone long before that, actually! How many kids have to start all over again in a foster home like I did? I didn't have anyone, except maybe Ros and that doesn't count. Do you have the faintest idea what that is like, John?"

He is tempted to shake his head wordlessly, to be dragged along down Hope's path like usual. She always does this. If John's words hold so much as a hint of criticism, if she sniffs out the slightest sense that he is challenging her or implying that she may actually hold some accountability, Hope either goes on the attack, finding something that he, John, has done wrong, or opens up the tragedy of her neglected and unprotected past, parading it before him as incontrovertible evidence that she cannot possibly be wrong now. Either way, it has the same result: obliterating the original challenge with an avalanche of words, leaving John and Hope stranded on either side of the heap, unable to cross it or reach one another.

But not this time. This time Hope needs to hear *him*. He steps in front of her, blocking her path with his physical presence, and takes hold of her arms, forcing her to stop and look at him.

"No, Hope," he says. "This has nothing to do with all of that."

She goes to open her mouth, but John doesn't give her a chance to speak.

"You are not the only one who lost a parent. Whose childhood was ruined by a tragedy that you had no control over."

"I know your dad died and you –"

"You don't know," John interrupts. "You don't know what it was like to live my story, and I don't know what it was like to live yours. I am sorry for everything you faced. Your mum, the crack-heads she hung out with. Ending up in foster care without a family to call your own."

Hope's face closes at the mention of foster care. She doesn't like talking about it. Has never said what it was like, living there, apart from the barest details. John continues, not wanting to lose her now.

"But none of that made you do whatever it is that you did. None of that is responsible for you... *having sex* with someone else! And then, then... lying to me. To our whole family. Letting me believe that Will is my son. That I am his father."

John's voice cracks at the last sentence.

"Nobody made you do that," he says.

Hope is mute now, almost limp as he lets go of her arms.

"You need to tell me what happened," he says. "And you need to tell me now."

Hope's shoulders slump. She starts walking forwards again, and John falls into step beside her. And she tells him. About that weekend. About Ros. About the drugs Ros fed her and about wanting to escape her new life, terrified of its security. About the night she spent with the other man. About waking up to the horrifying reality of what she'd done. About coming home and shutting down. Closing out the whole world. All apart from John and Maddie, and the new life growing inside her.

"You know the rest," she says, and John remembers how scared he was by her retreat, how he'd spent every moment he could with her and Maddie, holding Hope up until she could stand again by herself. He'd thought that losing Ros had triggered everything, that she was missing her foster sister and struggling with new motherhood and all the responsibilities it carried. But it turned out that wasn't the reason at all. John had stood by her, had loved her back to health. She had given herself to another man without thought. Nameless and unknown, but forever imprinted in his boy. His Will.

"How do you know he isn't mine?"

His words, barely more than a whisper, hold physical pain. "You can't know for sure, can you?"

He sees Hope's face tighten with pain.

"Because I lied," she says. So quietly that he has to tilt his head towards her to hear them.

"Lied about what?" he asks.

"My due date."

John wrinkles his forehead, not understanding.

Hope draws a deep breath.

"When I first suspected I was pregnant," she explains, resigned now, "we hadn't had sex for weeks, months. I knew it couldn't be yours."

She glances up at John, then quickly back down. John looks straight ahead.

"I panicked. Realised what I had done. Thought about maybe having an abortion."

John's heart squeezes at the thought. Will.

"But I couldn't. I couldn't do that. So instead…"

Hope pauses, struggling to form the next words. John feels nausea rising within him, willing her to stop talking now that he knows what is coming. She takes a deep breath.

"So instead, I… I…"

"Seduced me." John finishes her sentence, remembering the flush of pleasure, the spring of hope within when Hope had emerged from her state of collapse, frail and beautiful and *seeing* him, *actually seeing him*, and drawing him back to their bed. It had been so long, and he had thought he had lost her.

"Not seduced you!" Hope protests.

"What would you call it then?" John asks bitterly. "Used me? To cover up what you'd done?"

His voice rises now as the hurt and outrage take deeper root. "For God's sake, Hope!" he says. "I thought you loved me. I thought you needed me. I thought you were coming *back to me*!"

"I did!" Hope replies. "I was. I was…"

But what she says is meaningless. John's mind loops back to her earlier words.

"You said you lied."

Hope nods quickly.

"About my due date."

"Will came early," John says, remembering the frigid January day, driving through the snowstorm to get to the hospital on time.

"Will came late," Hope corrects. "He was due in December."

"How did you… How did I…?" John can't form the words, unable to grasp the full extent of Hope's betrayal.

Hope is silent, allowing the truth to sink in, to permeate the very core of him with its bitter roots. Suddenly John wants nothing more than to be away from her and to be alone. He cannot process what he has just heard. He only knows that he can't be in her presence for a moment longer. He stops and turns abruptly, lengthening his stride so that Hope has to stumble and half-run in his wake. When they reach the steep hill back, she cannot keep up, and he strides upwards, ahead of her, the distance widening with every step.

# Chapter 27

**Me**

*When you unearth a vintage doll's house from the back of an old antique shop, it rarely comes beautiful and fully formed. Perhaps its roof tiles are missing, or the chimney pot is askew. Maybe it has a broken window or two. Almost certainly its damask wallpaper has faded or peeled away from walls warped and spotted with damp. The grand central staircase may have come loose, with missing newel posts and spindles, the floors rotted away. But beneath these things there is beauty. You have seen its true value. So, the restoration begins. The first thing you must do is disassemble all that came before. Wood that is beyond repair is replaced, but most can be salvaged with a bit of cleaning, scraping and sanding. Stripped back walls are primed and floors replaced. Exteriors and interiors are painted and papered with carefully matched hues and patterns true to the original. Finally, the reassembly begins, and once it is done, everyone can see the beauty you knew was there all along.*

\*

The first time Jeremy touched me, I froze, confused and uncertain about what was happening. He had always been so nice to me, and I didn't want to upset him or be rude. It started with a soft hand on my face the day Ros ran out of the study, leaving me and Jeremy alone. It was nice, being seen, and his hand on my face sent shivers down my arms. Then his hand slipped to my neck and then to my breasts, where it lingered for one moment, then two. I couldn't move and wasn't sure how to feel about the strange sensations coursing through my body. I wanted to run, to make sense of what had just happened, but my legs wouldn't move. Not until Jeremy straightened and stepped back, patting me on the cheek like a little child and sending me away small and shamed with a curt *off you go*.

After that first time, Jeremy would seek me out, cornering me when nobody was there, summoning me to his office, even visiting me in the room I shared with Ros. He silenced us both with his warnings.

"It's you or Ros," he said to me with each stroke of his hand.

"One word and you're out," he said to Ros the first time she protested, after backhanding her and pressing hard on her neck until her face turned red and her eyes bulged. After that, she turned away from us to face the wall, eyes closed and headphones on until it was done.

The worst thing was not what he did or how he hurt me, especially at first. The worst thing was that part of me was glad I had been chosen. That out of all the others, even Ros, I had been noticed. For three years, I let him do whatever he wanted to me, whenever he wanted, even seeking him out on occasion like the disgusting, terrible person that I was. When I made the very first cut on my arm at 15 years old, the sharp blade of the knife was a relief compared to the darkness I carried inside.

\*

John moves out the day after the walk on Harting Down. He drags out a suitcase from under the bed and silently pulls clothes out of the wardrobe and chest of drawers that we share, folding each item carefully as he places it in the open case. When he has finished, he closes the lid, zips up the case and heaves it from the bed. I watch from the shadows of my work room, saying nothing, waiting for the bottom of my world to crack and come loose, for it to hurtle into the endless space beneath it, with me tumbling helplessly after. Instead, I feel oddly calm as John turns and faces me, a mixture of sadness and resolve etched across his oh-so-familiar features. I want to reach out and touch him, to stroke his face and wrap my arms around the solid set of his shoulders, but I do not move.

"I'll let you know where I am," he says into the space between us.

And then he is gone.

I turn my head to look at the Stanley knife sitting on my workbench, its blade wiped clean and safely sheathed. I reach out towards it, the gesture instinctive as breathing. Then I stop and pull my hand back. The urge to pick it up, to give way to the Not Me and cut until the pain transfers into something I can endure is not there like it usually is. My hand drops back into my lap, and I wait for it to hit me like an incoming wave. John has left. *John has left*, I tell myself. I am alone. Again.

But the wave never arrives. Everything is quiet. There is a numbness in and around me. No… not numbness – that's not it. A stillness. A space. I am not familiar with this feeling, am not sure what to make of it, but it is not unwelcome. Tentatively I get to my feet. I will have a shower. I will go downstairs.

Ros is in the kitchen, washing up last night's dishes and listening to the radio, singing along with Taylor Swift.

*"It feels like a perfect night, to dress up like hipsters and make fun of our exes, ah-ah, ah-ahhhh,"* she sings, swinging her hips to the music as she scrubs at something stuck to the bottom of the saucepan she is holding.

She senses my presence and turns, putting a hand to her chest and splashing foamy water on the floor. She is surprised to see me.

"You scared me!" she exclaims, wiping her hands on her jeans and taking a deep breath. She arranges her features into a look of concern and takes a step towards me.

"Are you OK, Hope?" she asks, reaching out. "I saw John with his suitcase, putting it in the van. He wouldn't say anything to me."

"He's moving out," I say simply, going to the cupboard and pulling it open, looking for a mug.

"What? No! I can't believe that. He wouldn't do that to you."

I shrug, putting the mug on the side and picking up the kettle to fill it.

"Bloody hell," Ros says. "You can't even trust the good ones."

I frown, her words jarring.

"I told him about that weekend," I say. "About the other man."

Ros jumps immediately to my defence. "You were out of your head!" she says indignantly. "It was forever ago. It wasn't your fault."

"It was."

"This is too much for you, Hope," Ros continues, as though I haven't spoken. "Too much! It's not fair for John to just up and leave like this, knowing what it will do to you."

"I pretended Will was his," I say. "For 18 years."

Steam pours from the kettle as the water boils. It shakes on its base like an impending explosion, then switches itself off.

"Well, what else were you supposed to do?"

The belligerence in Ros's voice reminds me of her younger self. That self who wasn't fazed by anyone or anything. Until Jeremy came along and silenced her. Silenced us both.

"Tell him the truth, perhaps?" I suggest as I lift the kettle and pour, watching the swirl of brown from the teabag expand and darken until I can no longer see the bottom of the mug.

Ros snorts as though the idea is ridiculous, then hurries over to give me a hug, leading me to the living room like an invalid, arm tight around my shoulders.

\*

In the days that follow, I continue to wait for the despairing hopelessness, the blanket of numbness to find me in the empty space following John's departure. Even when I get his text saying that he is staying with his brother in Storrington for a couple of nights, when I walk through the rooms of my house and feel the wrench of pain at their emptiness, and share each meal of the day alone with Ros, it doesn't come. Instead that same, eerie sense of calm filters through me, and I realise that rather than sinking further after the spectacular mess I have made of everything, I am feeling a little bit lighter than I have in some time. Full of grief and regret, yes, but present. I have been holding secrets for as long as I can remember. They have weighed me down like blocks of concrete. I have been so proficient at denying their presence that I almost convinced myself they were not there. Almost. But this one secret, lodged in the pit of my belly like a tumour, has finally been excised, laid out for better or for worse just as it is. I realise I am relieved to have it out of me.

I phone Fran the weekend after John leaves and tell her I will be back at work on Monday.

\*

It is towards the end of my first week back when Maddie calls me. Fran and I have worked hard all week to decorate not just the shop with Christmas greenery and warm, twinkling lights, but also the dolls' houses on display, each heralding the festive season in their own unique way. Customers draw close, *oohing* and *aahing* at the intricate detail. I usually love the lead-up to Christmas, the warm sights, the scents of cinnamon and pine needles, the sounds of carols heightening my desire to tuck myself away with the people who matter the most. This year the familiar festive routines fill me with sadness and bring tears to my eyes. Fran sees me wiping my eyes with a tissue and takes the box of doll's house figures from my hands, inviting me to join her for a cup of tea at one of the corner tables in the café. She reaches out and grips my hand, her own hand cool and papery in mine.

"John has moved out," I sniff, laying a tentative piece of my secret before her.

"Oh Hope," says Fran, squeezing my hand. "I'm sorry."

"It's my fault," I say.

She does not rush to fill the space with words. She neither questions me nor reassures. I find her silence oddly comforting.

"I…" I hesitate over the next words, not wanting Fran to hate me too.

"I cheated on him," I say, offering tentative truth, to see what it will do. "A long time ago, but still…"

Fran simply squeezes my hand more tightly. I look up, expecting to see disappointment or disgust. It's what I deserve. But her grey-eyed gaze is steady, and her eyes are full of compassion.

"I'm so sorry," she says. "This must be so terribly hard for you."

I let the tears fall, the gentle acceptance in her words overwhelming. Fran simply sits with me, shooing Carlos and his second cup of coffee away, letting me be as I am until my tears slow and dry and we are interrupted by the ringing vibration of my phone. I glance down at the screen, my heart skipping a beat when I see who is calling.

"I'll be upstairs," Fran says gently, leaving me alone.

"Maddie?" I say after accepting the call.

"Mum!" The word comes out as a sob, and I push the phone more tightly to my ear, heart thumping painfully now at the sound of her voice.

"Maddie, are you OK?" I hear my voice rise and force myself to take a breath, to lower my tone. "What is it?"

"Mum?" she says again. "Something has happened. Please will you come and get me?"

# Chapter 28

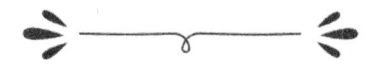

**Ros**

Ros didn't ask Hope to save her from the dickhead. Didn't expect it. It just happened, like everything did. And once he had fixated on Hope like some sicko, there wasn't much she could do about it. She tried, once. But the dickhead was stronger than Ros, and when he was strangling her, he whispered past the roaring in her ears that if she kicked off again, she would be leaving in a box. Ros didn't tell Hope that part, holding the threat inside until it worked its way through her body, coating her insides like grease. After that, she closed her eyes and pretended that he did not exist.

In the years that followed, there were times when Ros was so drawn to Hope that the feelings inside her swelled painfully into what Ros could only imagine as love. Was love like this? Not wanting to be with anyone else? Wanting to spend every moment of every day being near someone? When Hope started cutting, Ros helped her clean and wrap the angry, oozing wounds. She might not be able to save Hope from the dickhead, but she could be there to pick up the pieces. Other times Ros hated Hope. Hated her for opening something soft and needy in Ros, for mattering. Forcing Ros to owe something to another human being.

Three years after the dickhead came into their lives, when Hope was 17 and Ros 14, and Ros had watched Hope wither away and harden all at the same time, Hope ran away.

"I'm done," she whispered into Ros's ear one night, lying down next to Ros in the narrow bed and wrapping her arms round her. "I have to go."

Ros's eyes had widened in the darkness.

"No!" she cried out, wrenching herself from Hope's arms and into a sitting position. *"No!"*

"I'll come back for you," Hope said desperately, "once I've found somewhere. I'll be 18 in a couple of months and then I'll be able to get a job, to earn some money and look after us both."

"Take me now!" Ros begged, unable to bear the thought of being parted from Hope. "I can help!"

But Hope had gently loosened Ros's arms from her own. She stepped back and left her, cold and shivering on the bed.

"I can't, Ros," she said softly. "They'll find us. I can't look after both of us yet. I just can't."

Ros felt parts of herself battening down and hiding away from yet another person leaving her all alone. She pulled her worn covers over her head and turned her back on Hope.

"I promise I'll be back, Ros," she said. Then she left.

Hope did keep her promise. But by the time she came back for Ros, a whole year had passed, and the part of her heart that had softened for Hope was now cold and solid as a rock.

*

After John leaves, it is just Ros and Hope in the house. Just how little Ros had always imagined life would be until Hope left her for the first time, and then left her again. During those times, Ros imagined shaking free of Hope, cutting her loose like every other human in her life. Free from caring. For the longest time she had done it. She lived the life of a nomad, connecting with fellow nomads in different places for days, maybe even weeks or months at a time, but never deeply, never for real. With Hope it had been real. And Hope always drew her back in the end.

So here she is again. Playing housewife in Hope's house, filling the space that John and the children have left behind. She keeps busy and imagines that this time things will be different.

When Hope goes back to work, Ros packs away John's things, left behind and scattered around the house like flags marking territory. She gathers everything together and shoves them in bags which she stuffs under Maddie's bed. She doesn't want to put them in Hope's room, doesn't want Hope stumbling on them and thinking about what she has lost. It's bad enough that she has gone back to the shop, shrugging away Ros's concerned questioning about timing, about being strong enough, about being sure she can cope, with an irritated *I'm FINE, Ros*. Ros has taken on the role of being indispensable, so that Hope can never leave her again.

She finds the note from John when she is straightening the shoes in the hallway, lining them up in size order like Hope does. Lodged down the side of the cupboard is an envelope. Curiously, Ros pulls it out and recognises John's scrawled handwriting.

*Hope* the envelope says.

Ros narrows her eyes. *Where has this come from?* She looks over at the front door. It couldn't have come through the letter box. It is too far away. Has John been back then? No, she shakes her head. Not possible. She, Ros has been here every day since he left. The only thing that could have happened is that John has left it propped on the cupboard and it has slipped down the side, out of sight.

Ros carries the envelope into the living room and lowers herself slowly onto the sofa. She turns the letter over and over in her hands. Hesitating, she takes a deep breath, slides a long, painted nail under the flap of the envelope and carefully opens it. Pulling out the single sheet of folded paper, she reads.

*Hope,* the letter begins.

*I don't have the words right now, or the energy to try and understand why you did what you did. I only know that finding out that you have betrayed me like you have and that Will is not my son is too much for me to bear right now. You sleeping with somebody else while we were married isn't even the hardest thing. It's bad enough, but it's not the worst. The worst thing is that you chose to lie to me. You chose to pretend for all those years that you didn't do what you did, and that Will was mine. Your decision to do that has broken something. I don't know if it can ever be repaired.*

Ros takes a deep breath, brings the letter in closer and continues reading.

*But I also can't pretend that the last twenty years haven't happened,* John writes. Ros feels her heart squeeze in her chest.

*I can't pretend that you and Maddie and Will haven't been the biggest and most important things in my life. I can't just switch that off. Honestly, I wish I could, but I can't. So, for now I am taking some space. I can't think when we are under the same roof, and I need time to think. I need time to understand what has happened. To decide what happens next.*

*I am not sure where I am going, or how long I will be gone. I am not sure*

*I can come back. I can't reach out to you right now, Hope. I just can't. I've been reaching out to you all our life together. But if, after a while, you want to reach out to me, then we'll see. I will text you when I have found somewhere to stay and we'll take it from there.*

*John*

Ros finishes the letter. Her breaths come quickly. Agitation forces her to her feet, and she paces the room to dispel the nervous energy that has gathered inside. It doesn't work.

Why is John being so *reasonable*? Ros asks herself furiously. Why can't he just bugger off like a normal person in the face of his wife's bad behaviour? If John comes back, if he and Hope have a chance to talk things out... well. There will be no place here for Ros. Maybe at first there will be, but not in the long-term. Not once they realise they are better off without her.

Well, Ros won't let that happen. She makes a decision. Marching to the kitchen, she rummages through the drawers until she finds what she needs. A box of cook's matches. She folds John's letter in two and tosses it in the kitchen sink along with the envelope. Then, lighting the match, she carefully holds it to each corner of the folded letter and watches as it flares, brightly at first, then dimmer as the flames take hold. She watches as the paper curls into the heat, thinning and blackening until it falls away as ash. When the flames extinguish themselves, Ros turns on the tap and washes the soggy grey mess down the drain.

\*

The headlights of Hope's car shine bright beams through the living room window when she gets home from work, early by Ros's reckoning. The nights are drawing in by 4.30pm and Ros hasn't yet drawn the curtains. She can see as soon as Hope comes flying through the door that something has happened.

"I'm going to get Maddie," she says, breathless and purposeful. "She needs me."

"What?" Ros asks, feeling a tug of disappointment that Maddie is coming back early. "Why? Is she OK?"

"I don't know," Hope says, taking the stairs up to Maddie's room two at a time. Ros hasn't seen Hope so energetic for weeks. "I'm just popping home first because Maddie wants me to bring her bags to pack her stuff. We took them home after we dropped her off."

"Pack her stuff?" Ros asks. "Why does she need to pack? How long is she staying?"

Hope tosses Ros a look that pushes her back, to the outside.

"She *lives* here Ros," Hope says. "She is staying as long as she wants."

Hope looks under Maddie's bed for the bags. Ros remembers John's things are there and heads her off.

"I'll get them," she says.

"Fine. Thank you."

Ros finds the bags pushed against the wall under the bed and pulls them out, handing them to Hope.

"Are you sure you are up to the drive?" Ros asks. "You haven't been well, remember," she adds, indicating Hope's arms and the bandages still wrapped around them. "I could come with you?"

"I'm fine," Hope replies. "Thank you. But no. This is a family thing."

The words knock painfully together in Ros's chest. She folds her arms tightly. Hope glances over and realises what she has said.

"Sorry, Ros. I don't mean it like that. It's just…"

"It's fine," Ros says. "I'm fine." She doesn't want to hear Hope's excuses.

"Just go and do what you need to do."

Hope smiles at Ros and heads downstairs to the front door. "Don't wait up," she calls back. "I might be late. Oh, and Ros…?"

Ros follows her and leans on the wall, eyebrow raised in question.

"You couldn't just move your stuff out of Maddie's room, could you? And maybe make up the bed with fresh bedclothes and towels? She is going to need her room back."

Hope slams the door behind her and is gone.

# Chapter 29

*Maddie*

Maddie sits in the clinic with Herb on one side and Ella on the other. She wasn't sure they would be allowed to come with her with all the talk of rising Covid cases and threats of more lockdowns. Maddie can't let her mind contemplate the possibility of all that and is simply grateful she isn't here alone. She pulls her face mask higher, thankful for the sense of anonymity it offers. She wishes she could cover the whole of herself, or even better still, disappear. She stares straight ahead, dimly reading the motivational quotes printed on the wall of the waiting room.

*You are stronger than you know… don't forget that.*

*Believe in yourself when nobody else does…*

If she was here for any other reason, she would roll her eyes and have a laugh with Herb at the cliched words, but today she is only just holding it together. Talking to her friend like everything is normal feels too risky. She is in a box, and nothing can touch her.

When Maddie made the phone call to the clinic a week ago, she was hazy about the date of her last period. Maybe just before she moved to uni? She couldn't remember.

"But I know when it happened," she whispered into the phone, shame clogging her throat.

If the person at the end of the phone was surprised by this, she didn't let on.

"OK," she said. "Well, let's start there. When did it happen?" she asks, echoing Maddie's words.

Maddie cleared her throat.

"It was, um… my birthday, 5th October. Nearly nine weeks ago."

"OK That would probably make you around…" Maddie heard the other person tapping at the end of the phone. "...eleven weeks now."

"No!" Maddie's voice came out louder than she had intended. "No... not eleven weeks. Nine weeks," she corrects, feeling the beat of her heart accelerate.

"You conceived nine weeks ago," the voice agrees, "but the length of your pregnancy began on the first day of your last period," she adds. "Which is most likely eleven weeks ago."

"But... no," Maddie said, thinking of everything she had read. You had to be less than ten weeks pregnant if you wanted the kind of abortion you do yourself at home. She didn't want to go anywhere or see anyone. If she just took a couple of pills in the privacy of her own room, she could pretend that none of this was real.

The voice at the other end of the line was gentle.

"Maddie. Let's get you in for a scan first, and we can work out your exact dates. We'll take things from there."

They'd booked Maddie in two days later and confirmed that she was too far along for an at-home medical abortion. Somebody came and talked to her about her options, asked if she would like some counselling either now or afterwards. Maddie didn't. Talking would make everything real. They offered her tests for STIs, and Maddie numbly accepted. She could not believe this was her life. At the end of the appointment Maddie signed a consent form and booked an appointment in for the following week. She would have a surgical abortion.

"You'll be in and out in a few hours," the nurse reassured her, putting an arm round her shoulders. "We'll look after you. Make sure you bring somebody with you. For afterwards."

Now she is back here, and as Maddie waits, Herb and Ella on either side, the nurse from the scan last week steps into the waiting room and calls her name.

"Maddie?" she says, smiling warmly and inviting Maddie to stand. "Come on through."

Herb gives her hand a squeeze as she stands, and Maddie walks forward stiffly, following the nurse through a frosted door.

*

When Maddie was very little, her favourite thing was working with her dad in the garden, shadowing him and mimicking his every move. She would plunge dirty fingers into the moist earth, clearing away old weeds and willing the green shoots emerging from the rich earth to bloom. She would sit sometimes, watching and waiting, oblivious to the chill lingering in the air. She imagined that if she was patient enough and stayed very still, nature would hurry itself up just for her benefit. It never did, but the anticipation of the new life emerging still held her there.

She remembers a sunny day in April, or maybe May, when Dad called her name softly, beckoning her over to the summer house in the garden. He lifted her up so that her eyes were level with the overhanging eaves.

"Look, Mads," Dad said gently, leaning in so that she had a better view. "A house sparrow's nest. And there are eggs in it."

Maddie's eyes had widened, and a soft *oooh* slid from her lips. She wanted to reach out and touch the tiny eggs, but Dad stopped her, covering her small hand with his large one.

"Don't touch them, Mads," he said gently. "We don't want to frighten their mummy away."

Maddie shook her head solemnly and drew her hand back. They waited one more week, watching from a distance, and then the first egg hatched, then the next two. One evening, just before bed, Dad lifted her up to see the grey-feathered nestlings, impossibly small and bunched together in the nest, wide yellow mouths pointing upwards and begging for food. Maddie had never seen anything so beautiful in her whole life.

*

As she follows the nurse down the corridor and into a treatment room around the corner, Maddie remembers those tiny birds. How their high-pitched cheeps broke the stillness in the air when the mother sparrow returned with a beak stuffed full of food. The delight she felt when enough time had passed for them to wobble uncertainly at the edge of the nest before flying away. She lets her memory settle into the happiness of that time, so that the reality of the treatment bed in front of her, clinical and cold, and the dread at the contents of the trolley next to it, do not have any space to settle and become real.

She is 12 weeks pregnant. Twelve. That is when most people tell their friends and family about the baby they are expecting. When, she read online after last week's scan, the first trimester ends and the baby is 7.5cm long, with lungs and kidneys and a liver. When it has arms and legs, fingers and toes developed enough that you can count each one. If you want to.

Maddie slips out of her clothes and into a gown at the instruction of the nurse. Although the gown drops to mid-calf and is big enough to pull tightly across her front, she feels chilled and exposed in the treatment room. When she is asked to step onto the table, her legs do not move. The pregnancy inside her is no longer an embryo, she had read online, no longer a mass of cells that her mind can brush away as something medical, something to be fixed. It is a foetus. An actual life, clinging to her like a limpet. And this foetus is right now, right in this moment, curled up inside her, big as a plum, with a heart beating alongside her own.

"I can't do it," she whispers, her voice barely audible.

The nurse steps closer and reaches out to touch Maddie's arm.

"Maddie?" she asks quietly. "Are you OK?"

Maddie feels something within her shift and shakes her head. Then she looks up and meets the eyes of the nurse.

"I can't do it," she repeats, more loudly this time. "I can't."

"It's your decision, Maddie," the nurse replies, squeezing her arm. "It is not too late to change your mind. If that's what you want."

Tears have filled Maddie's eyes and are spilling down over her cheeks. She doesn't want this. She hasn't asked for any of it. But, like finding the horizon in stormy seas, the thought forms itself into words and holds steady. She doesn't want *this*.

She can't do it.

Maddie takes a deep breath and wipes her cheeks.

"Please can I have my clothes?" she asks, holding her hand out to the nurse. "I need to leave now."

\*

Herb and Ella are surprised to see Maddie emerging from the clinical area so soon after going through, pulling on her coat, cheeks tearstained. She clutches leaflets and numbers from the nurse, given to her in case she wants any further support. Maddie doesn't. She just wants to leave. Herb leaps to her feet, Ella rises more slowly.

"Mads?" Herb says. "What's happened? I haven't had a chance to call the Uber..." She fumbles for her phone, but Ella stops her with an outstretched hand.

"You didn't go through with it," she says simply, and Maddie shakes her head.

"No."

Ella nods and pulls on her own coat, shushing Herb and putting out an arm for Maddie to take.

"Let's walk back," she says.

Maddie is settled in her room later that afternoon, tucked under her duvet and curled into a ball. There is an empty mug next to her, the remains of the hot chocolate that Ella had made for her crusting and drying just below the rim. Despite the nausea which remains her constant companion, the sweet drink has soothed Maddie, and she is feeling drowsy.

The girls have been lovely, concerned, holding the other flatmates at bay. Kate and Hannah were in the kitchen with Rob and Warren and some of their friends when they arrived back, but Maddie ignored them, and Herb and Ella had hurried her into her room. Despite their kindness, Maddie is relieved they have finally left her alone. It has been a long day, and she hasn't got the energy to talk. Herb especially had been horrified at her decision.

"You can't keep it," she said, ignoring Ella's warning look. "You can't keep some... *rapist's* baby!"

"Herb!" Ella rarely raised her voice.

"What?" Herb responded. "She can't!" She turned back towards Maddie. "You can't," she said more softly now. "I know it must be so awful to go through an abortion but think about it for a moment, Maddie. This is *your life*. Why should you have to put it on hold for... for..." She struggles to find the words. "For a baby that you didn't ask for, by a man – no, a *sociopath* – who raped you? For God's sake, Maddie, you don't even know who he is!"

"I know," Maddie replied. "Do you think I don't know all of that?"

Herb was silent, face pinched with concern for her friend.

"I know you don't understand. I don't expect you to. *I* don't understand." Maddie struggled to find words she hadn't fully explored herself. "I just know that in that moment, in that place, I couldn't go through with it. I couldn't. And I won't."

Exhaustion was tugging at Maddie's vision and blurring her words, so Herb and Ella finally left her.

It is late and she is curled in the warmth of her bed, drifting towards sleep. There is one more thing she needs to do. She snakes a hand from under the covers, grabs her phone, and selects 'Mum' from her favourites. The phone rings once, twice before Mum picks up.

The sound of her voice at the other end, even after everything, releases something in Maddie.

"Mum?" Maddie sobs, feeling the tears from earlier rising again.

"Maddie, are you OK? What is it?"

"Mum?" she says it again, as if to reassure herself that Mum is really there, yearning to be a little girl again. "Something has happened. Please will you come and get me?"

# Chapter 30

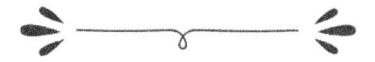

**Will**

Will has managed to steer clear of school for another week. It turns out Liam was suspended after getting hauled in by the Head. The school clearly has no clue that he is an actual dealer, or he would be out by now. Will has found himself gravitating to the other boy. Not just because Liam has access to a steady supply of weed and ecstasy, which is the one bright spot in Will's life right now. Will can talk to Liam. About real stuff. Not just the mindless shit that Vijay, James and Josh spout on about. Will has finally gathered the courage to ask Liam about trying to hang himself. Every time he sees Liam, he thinks about it. Wonders why.

They are smoking weed in the park, sitting on swings and watching the lights of passing headlights cut through the gathering dusk. Will inhales deeply, holding the sweet smoke in his lungs for as long as he can, squeezing out every bit of the rush. He ran out of ecstasy a few days ago and is already missing the feelings that go with it. Feeling good and relaxed, like he can do anything he wants. Ha. What a joke. It scares him a little that he can only get near those feelings when he takes the tablets, that the comedown is worse every time, taking him deeper into the pit that made him take the pills in the first place. He wonders how he can find the money to get more. He is completely skint, and there isn't exactly anyone around to ask.

"Why did you do it?" Will comes right out and asks Liam. "You know… hang yourself?"

Liam gives no indication he has heard bar a slight narrowing of the eyes and a deep drag on the joint he is holding. His shoulders are hunched and bowed forward like they know the swing wasn't made for him as he pushes himself backwards and forwards with the scruffy toe of his trainers.

Will feels awkward, and shuffles uncomfortably on his own swing.

"Sorry, mate," he says. "I didn't mean to –"

"Because I couldn't think of any other way out," Liam says. "Because it made sense at the time."

Will thinks about that for a moment.

"Way out of what?" he asks finally.

Liam gestures around.

"Out of all this," he says, and then taps his head sharply, "and away from this."

"But it didn't work," Will adds.

Liam gives a mirthless laugh.

"No," he says. "It didn't work."

He stubs out the joint and stands up. "Turns out getting out isn't as easy as it sounds. And I'm as shit at that as everything else."

Will wants to ask more. Why a rope? What was going through his head at the time? How did his family react? But Liam's face has closed in on itself. He wants Will to back off.

*

The next morning, Sally doesn't go to work as early as usual and is clattering about in the kitchen downstairs. Will is pretty sure she suspects he hasn't been holding up his side of the bargain and going to school, so he reluctantly hauls himself out of bed and into the shower after Sam is finished. When he comes out of the spare room, dressed and with his backpack slung over one shoulder, Sam raises an eyebrow at him.

"Feel like coming in today?" he asks sarcastically.

There is a distance between Will and Sam that has never been there before. Something inside of Will wants to reach out to him, to smack him on the arm and laugh and jostle their way downstairs, behave like they used to. To wind the clock back to when they were kids and life was so much simpler. But Will can tell that Sam has had enough of him. Enough of the weed, enough of covering for him about school, enough of Will's dark moods. So, Will just nods and says, "Yeah," like Sam's question is out of line.

Sam shrugs and heads downstairs.

"Whatever," he says. "You do you, mate."

*You do you.*

The phrase throws Will back to an earlier time. Before this year. Before all the lockdown shit. When Sam, Vijay and James were lying out on the school field in the heat of a summer's afternoon, mocking the nameless masses whose social media posts were spattered with *u ok huns?*, *luv u babes!!*, filtered photos and public conversations.

*Shoot for the moon. Even if you miss, you'll land among the stars!*

*Don't worry! Be happy!*

*Don't march to someone else's beat. You do you...*

He watches Sam's departing back, hears the front door slam as he pulls on his shoes, and squashes down the bloom of regret in his chest.

Sally is standing in the kitchen as he walks to the front door, arms crossed and gaze steady.

"Everything OK between you two?" she asks.

Will shrugs and opens the door.

"Fine," he says shortly as he leaves the house. He can tell Sally doesn't believe him.

He walks in the direction of school, raw pain in his chest. His feet take him down the familiar paths without conscious thought. It is only as he approaches the school gates that he realises where he is and stops abruptly. He doesn't belong here anymore. He doesn't belong anywhere. As groups of students jostle past him and through the gates, laughing and talking about pointless shit, Will can't make his legs move.

"Will."

The voice comes from behind and startles him. Heart pounding, Will hoists his backpack higher on his shoulder and slowly turns around.

Dad is there, leaning on his van parked on the side of the road. Like he has been waiting. Will says nothing as Dad straightens up and walks towards him.

"I was hoping to catch you," he says. "You haven't been picking up my messages."

Will shrugs. Doesn't tell Dad that he has a new number. That he hasn't been picking up anyone's messages. That this is exactly how he wants it.

"I wanted to see how you are, son," Dad says.

Will flinches, feels the rawness inside him flare like a wound doused in salt. He forces his features into bored sullenness.

"Well, now you've seen," he replies. "I've got to go to school."

"Will…" Dad reaches out to him, and Will steps back, almost stumbling on the curb in his haste to maintain distance between them. "Son."

That word again.

"I know you must have so many questions. So do I. I want to be here for you. To help."

Will sneers. Hardens his heart against the expression on Dad's face. Thinks about the empty bag of pills. About the only thing that helps right now.

"If you want to help," he says, "you can give me some money. I'm totally skint."

Dad sighs and hesitates long enough for Will to know that he's on to a loser.

"Will. I meant I want to talk about this. To be here for you."

Will shakes his head in mock disappointment and turns away towards the school gates, empty now apart from a few last-minute stragglers hurrying in before the bell.

"Forget it, John," he says, tossing the words like a grenade. "Thanks for nothing."

He walks away before he can see his dad's face, the burning inside almost too much too bear.

*

Will doesn't go to class. He doesn't go anywhere. Just wanders the streets without direction. He is trapped. Even his sketchbook isn't helping today. He texted Liam last night and asked for more pills.

*i'll bring cash*

Will loops back towards Sally and Sam's house. She should be at work by now. And he knows where Sam has a stash of cash, tips from his Saturday café job. He will just borrow it. He'll pay him back.

When he reaches the house, he opens the front door, listening carefully. Sally's car isn't in the drive and the house feels empty. He hurries upstairs and into Sam's room, pulling open the bottom drawer of Sam's bedside table. There. In an old tin. A jumble of notes and coins that Sam refers to as his stash. Before he can talk himself out of it, Will stuffs a handful of notes into his pocket and slams the drawer shut. He hears footsteps on the stairs and stumbles hurriedly to his feet.

*Fuck.*

Sally pushes Sam's door open and steps into the room.

"What are you doing, Will?" she asks quietly.

"I... um..." Will can't find the words, the borrowed money heavy in his pockets.

"Why aren't you in school?" she continues.

"I just..." His protestations drop into a hole between them.

Sally sighs, like she is sad. Or disappointed maybe. Will wishes she would just be angry, so that he could be angry right back. Instead of feeling hopeless and awful and worthless like he does.

"Will," she begins, and Will knows what is coming. "This isn't really working, is it?"

Sally waits for a moment and then when Will doesn't speak, continues.

"I know that you haven't been going to school."

*Bloody Sam.*

"And before you think of laying this on Sam," she says, like she can read his mind, "he hasn't said anything. I wasn't born yesterday, Will. I know there is something going on, and I want you to go home and deal with whatever it is. You can't stay here any longer. I'm going to let your mum know and I want you to go home tonight. Do you understand?"

He can't go home. He can never go home. He doesn't belong there anymore. Will feels something inside him snuff out. He is numb. Deadened.

He nods. Finds his voice.

"Yeah, OK," he mumbles, stuffing his hands in his pockets and pushing past Sally to leave. "I'll pick up my stuff tonight."

\*

But Will has no intention of picking his stuff up tonight. Or any night for that matter. He has no intention of going to school. Not anymore. All he can think of are the pills. The pills and the escape they offer from all of this.

He meets Liam as planned, exchanges most of Sam's money for another little bag of pills, then uses what is left to get on the train to Portsmouth. He wants to sit on the beach. To watch the ships going in and out and pretend that he is on them. To smoke a spliff and wash the whole bag of pills down with a beer. Will closes his eyes and imagines the euphoria, the lightness and the energy he will feel, magnified ten times over, and then the nothingness. He gets it now. Why Liam did what he did. Because right now, right at this moment, the thought of nothingness is the only thing that brings Will any peace.

# Chapter 31

*John*

John noticed the scars on Hope's arms the first week he knew her. The festival had ended, the noise and the bustle of crowds and nameless faces had faded away to the edges, and it was just the two of them. They were sitting together in a pub garden, sipping pints and talking, offering snippets of themselves to one another, testing the ground. The air was warm in the afternoon sun, and as Hope raised her arm to capture the attention of the barman, the long sleeves she wore slipped back to her elbow, leaving her forearm exposed. She saw John noticing. The smile slipped from her face as she lowered her arm to her lap, tugging the sleeve down over her fingers, drawing inwards.

But rather than creating distance between them, Hope's retreat drew John closer. He reached his hands towards her, resting them on the table, palms up.

An invitation.

Hope hesitated, eyes lowered, skittish as a rabbit, and John wondered if she would dart away. Instead, she took a breath and looked at him, offering him first one hand and then the other. John let them rest there for a moment before gently turning her arms over and slowly pushing the sleeve of her top up, leaving the soft skin of her forearm exposed. He stroked the ladder of pale, silvery scars with the rough pad of his thumb, waiting as the tension slowly left Hope's body.

"It's just something I used to do," she told him. "Before."

He raised his eyebrows, inviting more.

"Before?"

"Yes," she said softly. "Before I got out. Before this."

She smiled at John then, eyes sad, and he waited.

"I was in care for a few years," she offered. "It wasn't great."

He sensed understatement in her words but did not press.

"Where was your family?" he asked.

She gave a short laugh, sharp with old bitterness.

"What family? No idea who my father was. Some loser crack-head who offered my mother a fix maybe. Who knows?"

"And your mum?"

"Gone," said Hope shortly. "Dead. Ros is the only family I have now."

John felt the empathic pull of connection, the caretaker part of himself resurfacing and reaching out to Hope.

"I'm so sorry," he said. "That must have been hard for you."

Hope gave a sharp nod and pulled back. She wrapped her arms tightly around herself as she held his gaze watchfully.

"It's fine," she said shortly.

Taking a deep breath, she shook back her curls and reached for her drink. She smiled at him, slow and lazy. "I'm good now."

Throughout the years of their marriage, Hope never wanted to talk about her past, and John didn't push her. Apart from the dark weeks following Ros's 18th birthday weekend when she locked herself away and cut again for a brief time, she seemed settled. Driven and highly strung, yes, but focused on John and the children, on their wellbeing and safety, and later, when the children didn't need her every hour of the day, on making her shop a success. As his own history retreated and faded with the death of his mother a decade ago, and amidst the clamouring responsibilities of work and family life, John had been content to let the unspoken past loosen and fall away. The present was all that mattered. He didn't realise that the present – his family's current reality – rested so precariously on the secrets of the past.

\*

The sound of his phone ringing in the darkness wakes John from uneasy sleep. Despite the exhaustion that clings to him like a shadow, it had taken him hours to drift off. Will's words earlier that day circled him in the darkness until the ache in his eyes and his head matched the pain in his heart.

*Forget it, John. Thanks for nothing.*

At first, the ringing sound merges with his dreams, the school bell pulling Will away from him and out of his reach, gates clanging shut as his son retreats, away, away from John. But as the subconscious scene changes shape and pace, the ringing continues, persistent and jarring until John's eyes snap open and he fumbles in the unfamiliar darkness for his phone.

"John?" Hope's voice, sharp with panic, brings him fully awake.

He sits up, swinging his legs to the floor, neck stiff and sore from folding himself for another night into his brother's too-small spare bed.

"Hope?" He can hear the ragged sound of her breathing mixed with the muffled sound of traffic and an unsteady signal. "Hope – what is it? What's wrong?"

There is a pause, and the sound of Hope talking to somebody else, then: "John, it's Will."

A sense of foreboding fills his chest like lead. His heart beats in a painful staccato rhythm.

"Tell me," he says.

Hope is crying now, and he strains to hear her words.

"...in the Queen Alexandra..." she says, voice fading in and out. "...taken an overdose..."

"What?" John's hand tightens around the phone. He is on his feet now, fumbling for his clothes from the previous day.

"He's been taken to hospital, John." Hope's words are momentarily clear. "He's taken an overdose. You need to come."

John moves forward on autopilot, barely aware of his surroundings as he gives a mumbled explanation to his brother and Sue who have emerged, blinking in the glare of the hallway light. He dashes down the stairs, pulling on his coat as he leaves the house. He does not see the trees and darkened houses hurtling past as he speeds through Amberley, up the hill to Houghton, then on to Slindon before turning onto the A27. He presses his foot down on the familiar dual carriageway, cursing each roundabout that slows his progress. He is intent on one thing only – to get to Will. To get to his son.

He arrives at the hospital's emergency department shortly after 2am, his heart pounding as he pushes through the glass doors, locating the reception area and hurrying over.

"My son is here," he says to the woman behind the desk, his voice muffled behind his hastily donned mask. "William Graham."

"John!"

He turns to see Hope hurrying towards him, followed closely by Ros and Maddie.

"Daddy!"

Maddie flings herself at him, and John wraps his arms tightly around her, his eyes meeting Hope's over his trembling daughter's head.

Hope takes a breath, steadying herself. He sees Ros put an arm round Hope's shoulder, pulling her close. John ignores her.

"What happened?" he asks Hope, anxiety giving his words a rough edge. "How is he?"

Hope shakes her head.

"I don't know, I don't know..." she says. "Sally called me during the evening. To say that Will was coming home. But he didn't come home... I didn't know what to do. Then the hospital called me – just after midnight. He came in an ambulance. Someone found him, on the beach in Portsmouth –"

"In Portsmouth? What was he doing in Portsmouth? In the middle of the night?"

"I don't know!" Hope repeats. "I don't know what he was doing there."

"What have the doctors said?"

Hope is crying harder now, and John waits for her to find her words, holding impatience in check.

"They think he's taken an overdose. The person who found him. They said Will was out of it. There were empty beer bottles around him. A bag with some pills in his pocket. He had his wallet on him, with his student ID... They're working on him now." Hope's voice raises a notch. "Oh John, what if he's not OK? What if –"

"Stop, Hope!" John says, stroking Maddie's hair and taking a breath. "Just stop."

He loosens Maddie's arms from around him, vaguely registering the pallor of her face and the dark shadows beneath her eyes. He leads the way to the bank of chairs where they have been told to wait. Numbly, he lowers himself onto the unyielding plastic, stretching out his cramped legs. Old loss gnaws round the edge of his awareness and thoughts of Will, alone and unconscious, open like a black hole before him. He takes a deep breath. Not today. Not like this.

Minutes pass. Then one hour and another as they wait silently for news.

Just when John thinks he can bear the quiet stillness no longer, a doctor – young enough to be his son, John thinks – approaches them. Hope is on her feet in front of him in an instant, John and Maddie following more slowly. Ros doesn't move, anxiously chewing a nail as she watches them.

The doctor looks tired beneath his mask, stethoscope hanging round his neck like a portent, his thick blonde hair mussed and ruffled like he has been running anxious fingers through it.

"Mr and Mrs Graham?" he says in a voice deeper than John expects.

John nods and Hope responds with a breathless, "Yes?"

"William is stable," he says, gesturing towards the chairs and inviting them to sit. His expression is serious as he waits for them to settle. "He's lucky. If he hadn't been found when he was… Well. It could have been a very different story."

Hope's hand is clasped to her mouth. With her other hand, she reaches over to John. He is still as stone. The doctor goes on to tell them that they've done full bloodwork, that Will has taken an overdose of MDMA or ecstasy, combined with alcohol – a potentially lethal combination. By the time he arrived at the hospital, he had lost consciousness, was experiencing an erratic heartbeat and his blood pressure and temperature were dangerously high. John listens to the catalogue of frightening symptoms as though he is somebody else. He can't connect these words, this situation, with his son. It isn't possible.

The doctor is still speaking. "What has happened tonight is very serious. Although he is stable right now, we need to monitor him here in the hospital for the next few days. But the physical care is only a part of the picture. Once he is strong enough, the consultant psychiatrist will need to see him and talk through his ongoing care and support."

The words are flowing around John like a river, relentless, impossible to stop.

"Mr Graham… Mrs Graham…?" he continues. "Can you think of any reason why your son would want to take his own life?"

John glances over at his wife, at Maddie and Ros sitting still and silent beside her.

"It's been… difficult, lately," he manages at last, emotion clogging his throat. "But… to take his own life…" John breaks off, unable to continue, shaking his head.

The doctor reaches out and lays a hand on John's arm.

"He's in good hands now, Mr Graham," he says. "We'll get him the help that he needs."

They are only allowed to see Will one at a time. He is sedated, and looks pale and young, hooked up to an intimidating array of monitors and machines. They are informed that only one adult will be permitted to stay with him through what remains of the night. Hope moves to step forward, a mother assuming her natural role, but John places a hand on her shoulder.

"No," he says, his voice soft, firm. "Take Maddie home. I will stay with Will tonight."

He thinks Hope will argue, but instead she gives a quick nod, linking her arm through Maddie's and gesturing to Ros.

"I'll be back in the morning," she manages. "You'll call me…"

"Yes," John answers. "If there's any change, I'll call."

He plants a kiss on Maddie's head, nods briefly at Ros and then they are gone.

There is a chair near Will's bed. John drags it closer and settles his large frame as comfortably as he is able, laying a weathered hand on his son's. Tears course silently down his cheeks as he wills him back. To health. To the boy he once was. To John.

# Chapter 32

**_Me_**

*If you want, you can buy complete doll's house families with no features at all. A box of wooden pegs. Oversized chess pawns to place in your house as you will. Two and a half inches tall for adult family members. One and a half inches for children. Mix and match them to your heart's content. You are meant to paint them, of course. To bring them to life with colourful clothes, hair, two eyes, two ears, a nose and mouths forever smiling. Or frowning or curious or blank. But once painted, they cannot change. Their personalities are frozen in time with a stroke of the brush. There was a time when this is exactly what you wanted. Perfect control. Perfect clarity. A perfect family in each of their perfect places. But as you go on, you realise that your wooden family is not really a family at all. That staying perfectly frozen in time simply isn't possible. Because emotions and responses and personalities must have the freedom to change and grow and fit together in a whole new way. Then your family might have a chance.*

\*

Leaving the home just weeks before my 18th birthday with little more than the clothes I could stuff in a backpack was like running off the edge of a cliff. Gathering speed, heart accelerating as the drop approached until I couldn't stop if I wanted to. Then, leaping over the edge, arms flung wide, eyes shut at first and then open again as the exhilaration of falling kicked in and took over. Each second taking me further from all that lay behind. Wondering if the parachute would open, would slow my fall into this new terrain. Not really caring one way or the other.

The parachute did open. At first, I found myself on the streets, still preferable to Jeremy and the care home, then in a squat, then sofa surfing with some new friends who had found themselves a bedsit to rent. I never touched the drugs that got everyone else through the long days and nights, preferring to stay alert and in control. Safe.

Instead, I found a job. Cash in hand to clean a bakery after-hours, then another shop along the parade – a shop that sold dolls' houses and drew me in, in ways I could not explain. Then another until one day I was earning enough to rent my own room in a shared house. Not much, but mine. I was 18 years old, an adult, and it was time to find Ros.

I couldn't bring myself to go anywhere near the home, so I stalked the places Ros went, outside the school gates, in the park where she hung out when she bunked off. Finally, I saw her, small and thin in her school uniform, trudging down the road, eyes fixed on the ground.

"Ros!" I called out expectantly, hurrying towards her. "Ros!" I repeated when she didn't turn immediately. I caught up quickly and reached out to grab her arm. She stopped and turned slowly towards me.

"Ros," I said, smiling. "It's me… Hope."

Ros looked at me, mouth pulling itself into a tight smile that didn't reach the dull blue of her eyes.

"Hope." She spoke my name flatly, looking me up and down as if checking I was real. "You came back."

\*

Ros and I are sitting at the kitchen table early the next morning, waiting for John to call with an update, inviting me to return to the hospital, when Maddie shuffles into the kitchen. I take in her exhausted appearance and pull out the chair next to me.

"There's coffee in the pot," I say, getting up to find a mug.

Maddie pales noticeably and shakes her head.

"No thanks," she says, turning on the tap and filling a glass with water. "This will do."

We haven't had a chance to talk since I drove to Brighton to get her. Maddie slept in the car on the way home, and rising concern about Will's non-appearance after Sally's call demanded all my attention as the evening wore on. This morning, I am jittery, every sense on alert for the sound of my phone and further news of Will, but something in Maddie's demeanour snags at me.

"Mads?" I say gently, reaching out to lay my hand on hers. "What's going on?"

A single tear rolls down Maddie's cheek, and I catch Ros's eye across the table. Maddie glances over at Ros, then back at me. I forget that Maddie doesn't really know Ros. Hasn't been here with us these past months.

"I've got some stuff to sort out," Ros says, getting to her feet.

When she has left, I squeeze Maddie's hand.

"Well?"

Maddie raises her eyes, then looks at me and takes a deep breath. Her hand is cold and clammy. A dart of anxiety shoots through my chest.

"I'm pregnant, Mum."

The words don't register at first. I stare at her. Of all the things I'd expected her to say, this wasn't it.

"What?" I draw back.

"I'm pregnant. Just over 12 weeks."

"But..." I am trying to process what she is saying. "But... how?" I realise how ridiculous the question sounds. "Who? I didn't even know you had a boyfriend!"

I am thinking that I don't even know the names of her friends at university, when I register her earlier words like the delayed sound after a rifle shot.

Twelve weeks.

"So, you got pregnant..." My mind struggles with the maths. "...in September? Just after you got there?"

Maddie's hands cover her face.

"Hope..." Ros speaks from the door. She has been listening. "Let her speak."

"Yes..." I reply, reaching for Maddie again. "Yes... sorry. I'm so sorry, Maddie. I'm just... surprised. That's all. Please... talk to me."

There is a long pause. Then Maddie talks.

About the night of her birthday. About being out with her friends. With girls called Kate and Hannah and Herb. About dancing and drinking too much. About everyone crowding back to the flat and the picture she took. I think of our WhatsApp group and remember seeing it. Missing her so much but glad Maddie had found so many friends. She hesitates now, gathering herself.

"I don't remember after that," she says. "I've tried. But there's nothing. And when I woke up the next morning. It had happened. I think. I mean, I… know."

"How much did you drink?" I ask, and immediately regret the question as Maddie's face flushes and Ros throws me a look. She has re-joined us at the table.

"A lot," she says, voice small and ashamed. "But… I remember everything else, and then nothing for, I don't know, 12 hours at least so –"

"Someone spiked your drink," Ros says.

Maddie nods tightly. "I think so," she whispers.

"Who was he?" I ask sharply.

"I don't *know*, Mum," Maddie replies, her voice rising. "That's the whole point! Don't you get it? I don't know what happened and I don't know who did it, and if I hadn't been drinking in the first place, none of this would have happened, and now it's all my fault!"

For a moment, I am frozen. How can this have happened to Maddie? How? After everything I have done to keep her safe. To make sure the world was kinder to her than it had been to me.

"No, Maddie." Ros reaches out to her. "No. This isn't on you."

"It *is!*" she insists. "I let it happen! I was stupid. So stupid. And now…" Her hand drops to her belly, hidden beneath a long shirt. "Now I'm pregnant. And there's nothing I can do. I tried to get rid of it, but… I couldn't. I just couldn't. I'm stuck. My whole life is ruined."

"No." I force my body to move, to shake off the icy stillness. I think of Will lying in a hospital bed 20 miles away. "You weren't stupid," I tell her. "You didn't ask for this to happen. You were just having fun on a night out. That doesn't make this your fault. This is all on him. Whoever he is."

Maddie's head is shaking as I speak. She raises her gaze to meet mine.

"Is that," she asks, voice quiet now, "what you tell yourself? About Will?"

I sit back, her words like a punch.

"That was different," I say.

"Yeah," Maddie's voice is weary now, drained of emotion. "Of course it was."

I hear the ping of a text and drag my eyes down to my phone. It is from John.

*Will is awake. You can come now. But only one visitor at a time. So come alone. Text when you're here and I'll come down.*

I look at the phone, then at Maddie, then Ros.

"You have to go," Maddie's voice is monotone. "It's fine. I get it. Just go."

"I'll stay with Maddie," Ros says, and I hesitate. I should be with Maddie. Not Ros. But I have to go to Will. To John.

"Go, Mum," says Maddie. "I'll be fine. I'm knackered anyway. I'm going back to bed."

I nod. "OK," I agree. "OK." I plant a kiss on Maddie's head, taking in the smell of sleep and sweat and wanting to pull her into a tight hug. "I'll be back as soon as I can. And then we'll talk."

"Sure." Maddie is already standing and leaving the room. "Whatever."

"We'll find out who did this," I say to her retreating back. "We won't let him get away with it."

My words follow Maddie up the stairs, but she doesn't reply.

\*

When I arrive at the hospital, mind full of Maddie, I text John from the car park. He comes down after ten minutes and slides into the passenger seat next to me. His face is drawn and there are shadows beneath his eyes. I want to reach out and touch him. To stroke his stubbled cheek until the colour and scent of the outdoors returns. Instead, I clasp my hands together in my lap, the usual order of things reversed. I feel the pang of loss that reaching out to him, vital and familiar as my own heartbeat, is no longer open to me. I think for a moment that I will tell him about Maddie, but my mouth clamps down on her story, a dark echo of my own. Not today.

"How is he?" I ask.

He shakes his head.

"Awake," he says. "Alive."

His voice cracks on the last word, and I see the sheen of tears in his eyes. My heart twists with love and pain for him.

"How did it come to this, Hope?" he asks. "How did our boy reach a point where this... *this*... was his only choice?"

Our boy.

I hang onto those words.

"I don't know," I say. "I didn't see it. Didn't see... *him*."

As I say the words, I realise they are true. In all the mess of the past few weeks – even months, or was it years? – I had been so caught up in my own pain, that everyone else had slipped beneath my radar. And this is what happened.

"It's my fault," I whisper. "I should have seen it."

The old John would have reached out, drawn me in, soothing my demons away. But this John makes no move towards me.

"No," he says. "No, Hope."

I look at him, confused.

"This is not about you," he says, turning to look at me. "And it's not about me. Let's not make this about us. This is about Will. Only Will."

I stare at him, feeling the pull of opposing parts of myself. One part shrinking with shame at his words, the other surging towards him ready for a fight. For once, though, I don't allow them into the driving seat. Instead, I take a deep, steadying breath and agree.

"You're right," I say quietly. "Will needs us both right now."

When I enter Will's hospital room a few minutes later, I have to calm myself once again. His eyes are closed, his hands resting lightly on the neatly folded sheets of his bed. The machines around him bleep out a comforting rhythm, monitoring his every heartbeat, each breath. I am grateful for their sleepless vigil.

As I pull a chair close to his bed, his eyes flutter open.

"Will?"

I lean in, grasping his hand in mine. He turns his head to look at me.

"It's Mum," I say. "I'm here."

At first, I think he hasn't heard me, but then his mouth speaks words, and I lean in closer so that I can hear him better.

"What did you say?" I ask.

He speaks again, more clearly this time.

"Well... duh," he says, chapped lips pulling themselves into the ghost of a smile.

Despite myself, despite where we are and everything that is such a mess, I laugh.

I spend the rest of the day with Will. John will come back this evening to take over, and I want to make the most of our time. I have spoken again to the young doctor from the previous night, who has told me again that Will is lucky, that this has been a close shave. He tells me the consultant psychiatrist will come and see Will in the next day or two, when he is stronger.

"What will he do?" I ask in whispered tones away from Will.

"He'll talk to Will. Assess his mental state," says the doctor. "We want to make sure that Will has appropriate support when he leaves us and has good safety plans in place."

I nod, wondering if planning to be safe makes any difference. But I say nothing.

As the late afternoon fades into darkness, I talk to Will in tones too bright, trying to convey a sense of hope and optimism for what will come next.

"I'll get your room all ready," I say, words tumbling over one another. "We are going to decorate the house for Christmas," I continue, unable to stop myself. When Will doesn't respond, I hurry on. "Or we can wait until you're back. You can help us choose the tree, put up the lights…"

"Mum."

I lean in.

"I'm not coming home."

I don't understand.

"What?"

He clears his throat, raspy after last night's treatments.

"I'm not coming home, Mum," he repeats.

"But… where will you go?" I ask, grappling with what he is saying. "Of course you'll come home. All your things are there. I can look after you. And… and it's Christmas," I add weakly. "You have to be home for Christmas."

I feel tears gathering in my throat and fight to hold them down, clenching my hands into fists on my lap.

"I'm going to stay with Dad," he says.

"Dad?"

"We've talked about it. When I get out of here, Dad and I are staying at Uncle Andy's."

I am a bystander watching my perfectly imperfect family break apart and tumble away in opposite directions.

"Don't stress, Mum," Will says, closing his eyes again, exhausted by the conversation.

Will is sleeping when John texts to say he has arrived to take over. I meet him just outside the entrance, the chill dark of the winter's night covering us like a shroud. Our words are sharp and brittle as the frigid air.

"How is he?" John asks.

"Fine," I say, both of us knowing this isn't true.

"Good."

He gives a brisk nod, and hurries through the doors to Will. I stand alone, huddled in the darkness, hands pushed deep into coat pockets reaching for warmth that isn't there.

# PART 3

# Chapter 33

### *Ros*

Ros was 16 when she finally escaped the home. One day, a few weeks after Hope found her, she packed her bag for school and walked out the front door without looking back. At first, she stayed with Hope in her rented room, her heart cold and hard as the floor where she slept. Opening up, softening, would allow that year alone with dickhead and the terror of abandonment to wreak internal havoc. Ros was too smart to let that happen. She was simply playing her cards right. A life under the radar with Hope and her new friends was the best option open to her and she was going to take it.

But little by little, as Ros graduated to the sofa of the shared house, earning cash in hand from odd jobs here and there, smoking pot and snorting molly whenever she could wangle it, she created a fragile bubble of peace around herself. As time passed and she remained unmolested and safe with transient people just like her, she began to relax on the outside and came as close to happiness as she ever had. But a part of her knew it would never last, a part that took great pleasure in parading this inevitability before her.

When Hope first saw John that hot summer day at the festival, Ros trailing in her wake, that part's gleeful *I told you so!* echoed so loudly in her head that Ros turned to see who had spoken. But there was nobody there. And when she turned back to see if Hope had heard the strange voice too, Hope was already out of reach. Laughing and touching the arm of the tall, dark-haired man in dirty work clothes, like Ros wasn't even there.

*

The Christmas and New Year following Will's overdose reminds Ros of that time after dickhead and before John, when the world was just her and Hope and nothing else mattered. Of course, Maddie is in the picture now, but unlike 19 years ago, when Maddie was born and took Hope away, Ros actually enjoys having the younger woman around. She has used the time to forge a bond with her that almost feels real. With Hope busy at the shop and travelling to Storrington to see Will recovering at his uncle's with John, there has been plenty of time for the two of them to find common ground.

"Oh my God," Maddie says when Ros lets slip about her year with dickhead a few days after Christmas. They are sitting in the living room picking through a half-eaten tin of Quality Street, the coloured lights of the tree twinkling through the afternoon gloom. Hope is back at work with Fran, readying the shop for next week's sales, and Ros and Maddie haven't moved from the sofa all day.

"Why didn't you tell anyone?" she asks. "I mean, surely someone would have done *something*."

Ros carefully selects one of the toffee logs from the tin, untwisting first one end of the gold wrapper, then the other.

"Unlikely," is all she says, thinking of everyone who made sure they didn't notice what was happening to her.

Maddie nods. "I guess things were different then."

They sit in silence for a bit, and Ros wonders about telling Maddie more.

"Does Mum know? About what he did to you?" Maddie asks at last.

Ros shrugs. After Ros left the home, she and Hope never spoke about what happened there. Tacit understanding between them drew a line between past and present. But even the best-laid boundaries have their vulnerable points. And the past has a way of finding and breaching them with military precision.

*Does Hope know?* And if she doesn't actually know in a facts and details kind of way, Ros is pretty sure that Hope isn't naïve or stupid enough to imagine that Ros was safe after Hope left her. Logically, Ros knows that what happened with dickhead was not Hope's responsibility. That was on him. One hundred percent. But deep down, where the logical voice never ventures, a much younger version of herself tells her that it is, in fact, all Hope's fault.

"Let's see what's on," Ros says, picking up the TV controls and ending the conversation.

*

New Years' Day comes and goes, creeping up on the household like an intruder. With each passing day, the colour returns to Maddie's cheeks and Ros imagines the swell of her belly beneath her baggy clothes. It reminds her of Hope, pregnant with Maddie a lifetime ago. Starting her real family. But Maddie isn't Hope. She doesn't have a John and a fake life all lined up, and as far as Ros can tell, she doesn't have the slightest idea what to do next. Unlike Ros, who can see the path ahead for Maddie like a runway outlined with guiding lights, visible from miles away.

"We need to find him," she says to Maddie one morning after breakfast. Hope is in the shower, and Ros and Maddie are sitting at the kitchen table, cradling mugs of steaming tea. The certainty that whoever did this to Maddie cannot be allowed to get away with it has grown so large inside her that she can't contain it anymore.

"Who?" Maddie is distracted, scrolling through her phone and stirring her tea, teaspoon clinking against the side of the mug.

"Him!" Ros answers, gesturing at Maddie. "The guy who did this to you!"

Maddie sighs, like they have had this conversation a million times, but it is the first time Ros has said it out loud.

"I don't know who *he* is," she says to Ros. "I'll never know who he is. And even if I did –"

"What?" Ros challenges, daring her to say it.

"Even if I did, what would be the point?"

"The point," says Ros, grabbing Maddie's hand and squeezing it for emphasis, "is to hold him accountable. To make him pay for what he did to you."

The words feel good in Ros's mouth. Like they have been stuck inside for a lifetime and have finally come out. As she says them, she realises with absolute certainty that this is why she is here. This is why she has come back. To help Maddie. To make sure that what happened to Maddie never happens to anyone else. She gazes at Maddie, willing her to get onboard with Ros's plan.

But Maddie simply stares into her teacup, quiet for so long that Ros wonders if she has even heard her.

"What did you do?" Maddie asks. "About that dickhead guy? Did you make him pay?"

Ros sits back, dropping her hands in her lap.

"That was different," she says.

"Why?" Maddie has lifted eyes just like Hope's to look directly at Ros.

Ros thinks for a moment, her mind skirting round the reality of the year after Hope left. She focuses instead on the rage and disdain which live just below the surface, guarding her from the memories.

"Unlike you," Ros says, trying not to let the bitterness creep into her voice, "I didn't have anyone to help me. My only choice was to move on and not give dickhead another thought."

Maddie sighs and her eyes fill with tears. "Well, maybe that is what I want to do, too," she says. "Maybe I don't want to go back to that night, to know what actually happened. I was out of my head. Wearing this tiny little dress... Dancing with *strangers*."

"No," says Ros. "Stop doing that."

"Doing what?" asks Maddie. "Facing the truth? That if I hadn't put myself in that position, *none of this would have happened.*"

"Stop blaming yourself," Ros says. "You did not do this. *He* did."

"Well," says Maddie, pulling herself up from the table and taking her mug to the dishwasher at the sound of her mother coming down the stairs, "we don't know who *he* is. So I am the only one around here to blame."

She pushes past Hope who has appeared at the kitchen door and disappears up the stairs.

Hope looks at Ros, eyebrows raised like a question mark.

Ros just shrugs, considering her next move. She is not going to give up that easily. She's going to help Maddie if it's the last thing she does.

\*

For the next few days, Ros formulates a plan. Maddie's friend Herb is coming over for a couple of days before both girls head back to uni. According to Maddie, Herb was there that night and is one of the only friends who knows that Maddie is pregnant. Apparently, Herb is as outraged about the whole situation as Ros, and Ros figures that together, they can convince Maddie to share her secret with some of the other people who were around that night. Between them they will put the pieces together. Somebody must know something. And it's not like Maddie can keep the secret forever. Her pregnancy is growing with every passing day, and it won't be long before people start noticing. It makes total sense to Ros to get ahead of the game.

Tentatively, she tests the idea out on Hope, who surprises her by agreeing. They need to do something. Hope is less moody and distracted these days, as if the reality of John gone and both her children in crisis has sharpened her focus, cutting away the fuzzy edges. Ros is afraid that if Hope is thinking too clearly, she will cut Ros away, too. She has noticed that Hope is no longer cutting herself and is facing up to each new day like a duel at dawn.

"Does John know about Maddie?" Ros asks Hope casually. Hope is peeling potatoes at the sink, briskly slicing away the skin like it offends her.

"No," Hope replies.

"Why not?" Ros asks.

Hope runs the peeled potato under a stream of cold water and tosses it into a bowl, then shrugs, picking up another.

"I guess it's up to Maddie to tell him," she says carefully. "And he hasn't exactly been around much lately."

It is true. Apart from coming over to grab a few bags of Will's stuff the day before Will was discharged from hospital, John hasn't been to the house once. Not even over Christmas. Hope, Maddie and Ros went to Storrington on Christmas Day, arms loaded with gifts and food for an awkward day with John's brother and his wife. Maddie barely ate a thing and Will had withdrawn to his own world. The moment to tell all hadn't really presented itself. The three of them had made their excuses and left not long after lunch, Hope hugging a listless Will tightly to her before retreating to the car.

"I'm here when you want to talk," Ros had heard her whisper to Will, who shrugged and stepped away.

"I guess John really doesn't want to hear from you," Ros says, pretending not to notice Hope's shoulders stiffening.

Ros thinks about John not coming to the house, not knowing what is going on with his own daughter. She thinks about the letter he wrote to Hope, remembering its black curling edges as she burnt away his invitation to reach out when Hope is ready. She wonders how he feels as each day passes with no word from Hope. How he would handle knowing there is yet another secret taking root in this house. Yet another thing Hope is not telling him.

# Chapter 34

***Maddie***

Maddie sits in an armchair wrapped in a fleece blanket. She has angled it so that it faces the patio doors looking out onto their garden. It is too cold and damp to sit outside for any length of time, so Maddie stretches out her feet from under the blanket to bask in the square of weak January sunshine which lies on the carpet like a gift. Fizz is sharing the meagre warmth with her, and Maddie tucks her toes under the cat's soft belly for extra heat. Fizz stretches, mouth opening in a sharp-toothed yawn before resting her head on her paws and falling back to sleep. Even in the sunshine, the garden outside has a drab quality to it, like hunkering down for winter is all it knows.

Even so, Maddie finds the peace of the moment soothing. She cannot remember when she last felt quiet inside and is savouring this brief respite from the storm all around her. Ros has gone shopping and Mum is upstairs cleaning. Maddie has found living at home these past few weeks oddly comforting. The unusual rhythms of this all-female house are so different from the home she left back in September, it is like this unexpected version of herself fits somehow. She is no longer the compliant child Maddie, forever scanning the family dynamics for any unusual peaks or troughs to determine the least obtrusive place within them. She hasn't got the headspace for that right now. Couldn't blend into the background even if she wanted to. And despite everything, it is a relief. She needs her mum and she needs Ros. Ros is showing all the fight that Maddie knows she should be harnessing for herself, unwavering in her determination to discover who *he* is. Even though Maddie's natural response is to hide herself away, hoping it will all go away, a part of her is shaking itself into life and gearing up for battle.

Her thoughts drift to Will and Dad, living up in Storrington. She has only seen Will once since that terrible night in the hospital when she thought she might lose him. Her brother does her head in and has always been a live wire, full of restless energy, but the prospect of life without Will had jolted Maddie so badly she felt it like a physical punch. She had absorbed it that night, and the following day, knowing she had to tell Mum about the baby, about what had happened. But once that was done, the aftershocks of Will's overdose stayed with her.

"What were you thinking, you idiot?" were the first words out of her mouth over Christmas. And then she hugged him. Tight. The thing that made her cry was that he let her. She wanted him to push her off, to screw up his face in disgust like he usually would, to tell her to *get out of my personal space, weirdo*. He didn't do any of these things.

"Don't ever do that again," she'd said, drawing a smile from him. "Or you'll have me to answer to."

"Scary," Will replied, his voice hoarse. He'd smiled a little, and Maddie let her shoulders relax.

"You don't even know what scary is," she said, shoving him and walking away.

Dad hadn't been home once since then. Maddie tried and failed not to feel hurt by his absence. She got it that he and Mum were messed up right now, that they needed some space from each other to work things out, but what was any of that to do with her? She missed their easy connection, the way they didn't even have to talk to get each other. She hates that she is carrying this secret, this awful thing, and he doesn't even know.

She pulls her toes back under the blanket as the patch of sun shrinks and retreats. Fizz doesn't move. Maddie hears a key in the door and thinks it is Ros coming back with the shopping.

"I hope you remembered fresh bread," Maddie calls out, her appetite making a return appearance these past few days after weeks of nausea.

"Sorry. No bread."

Maddie spins round at the sound of her father's voice, wondering if her lonely thoughts have somehow summoned him here in person.

"Dad?"

She leaps up, the blanket falling away, and hurries over to him, leaning in for a hug and sighing deeply as his arms wrap tightly round her, his chin resting on her hair.

"What are you doing here?" she asks, voice muffled against his chest. "Is Will with you?"

"Will is with Uncle Andy," he says. "I'm here because of this."

He holds up his phone, a long text on the screen. It is from Ros. Maddie takes the phone from his hands and reads it, scrolling down until she reaches the end. Tears gather in her eyes, blurring the words, but she can't look up. Shame coils in her belly, pulling everything inwards. *I thought you should know*, Ros ends. *She's your daughter.*

Maddie keeps her gaze fixed on her feet. Dad reaches out and gently cups her chin, raising her head until their eyes meet. The look on his face is both tender and fierce, and for the first time in a long time, Maddie thinks she might be OK.

"Why didn't you tell me, Mads?" he asks gently. "About all of this?"

She sees his gaze fall to her belly, hidden under Will's giant hoodie which she has stolen from his room.

"I tried…" Maddie said. "I couldn't. I'm… I'm so sorry!" It comes out in a rush. She is in such a mess.

He pulls her in for another hug, more tightly this time.

"Don't you apologise," he says to her. "Never apologise."

They stand like this for a moment until Maddie feels Dad tense and pull away. Mum has come down the stairs. Is standing there with a bottle of bleach and an old towel in her hands. Maddie can't bear to see the hope in her face, which falls away as soon as Dad speaks.

"How could you keep this from me?" he asks her, his voice low and vibrating with angry energy.

Maddie pulls in a deep breath and wraps her arms round her middle.

"After everything that has happened. How could you keep this a secret?"

Maddie waits for Mum to crumble, for Dad to reach out and hold her up, like always, but her mother's voice is calm when she speaks.

"It was not my story to tell," she says simply.

The words are like an accelerant, fueling something in Dad and propelling him towards Mum. He stops just in front of her, his face inches away.

"Not your story to tell?" he asks. Maddie sees his fists clench at his sides. Her heart pounds in her chest.

"Dad!"

He doesn't hear her.

"Not your story to tell, like *our son* being high on drugs every day and slowly losing his mind isn't your story to tell? Or you forgetting you were married, with a baby daughter and buggering off with another man not being your story to tell? Or is it the bit where you kept the truth about Will from me for 18 years?"

Mum is silent. Bright spots of colour have appeared on her cheeks. Maddie wants to reach out to her but is frozen in place.

"Exactly which part of the story," Dad continues, eyes flashing, "were you planning on telling me, Hope?"

"I'm sorry," she says quietly.

Maddie is not sure which bit Mum is sorry about exactly, but the words make Dad stand back and unclench his fists.

"You're sorry," he says flatly. "Well then. That makes everything OK, doesn't it?"

He turns to Maddie as if remembering why he is here.

"Get your coat and boots," he says to her. "We're going for a walk and then for some lunch. We have a lot to talk about."

Maddie casts an apologetic look in Mum's direction, then follows Dad out of the room.

\*

Spending time with Dad, just knowing that he is there for her and is standing by whatever she decides to do, has fortified something in Maddie. In the days since his visit, and before she returns to uni for the spring semester, she feels her head lift a little. Her shoulders begin to stretch and straighten out of the shamed hunch they have adopted. Her path is no clearer, and she still has another human growing inside her, but she feels less alone and less vulnerable than before.

Herb notices the difference as soon as she sees her. She has come to stay with them in Chichester for a few days before they travel back to uni together in Herb's beat up Corsa. The car belonged to Herb's grandmother until she died last summer, and now Herb is almost reverent with the temperamental old car, keeping it clean and clucking over bald tyres and spots of rust like a mother hen. Maddie and the girls laugh at her for being so un-Herb with the car, pooh-poohing its impact on the environment and the money it is costing her. Herb just waves them off.

"Shhhh," she would say fiercely. "You'll upset her."

After she finishes hugging Maddie, she holds her at arm's length, eyeing her up and down like a concerned physician.

"I see you still have the sprog," she notes, eyes meeting Maddie's as she shakes her head disapprovingly. "Against doctor's orders, but... your choice. Other than that..." she continues, before Maddie can speak, "I would say that you are looking better. Well, even. *Good.*"

She gives a brisk nod and follows Maddie into the house. Maddie introduces her to Ros and says that Mum will be back later that day, after the shop has closed. Ros and Herb greet each other and join forces that first evening, kindred spirits intent on getting Maddie to find her attacker and put a battle plan in place.

"First step," says Herb, sitting in Maddie's room with her. Ros is there and Mum is standing in the doorway. "Photos. Hand over your phone."

Maddie pulls out her phone and gives it to Herb, trying not to look skeptical.

"I've looked at all the pictures from that night," she says. "It makes no difference. I don't remember anything."

"Looking at the pictures is one thing," says Herb, forwarding them all to her own phone. "But properly examining them and going through the process of elimination is another."

Maddie waits for Herb to transfer all the pictures, then takes her phone back.

"Is there a printer in this house?" Herb asks.

"For what?" Maddie isn't following.

"To print the pictures, obviously," she says, nodding in approval as Ros gets up and hurries downstairs to check the printer has paper. Mum is quiet, watching from the doorway.

"Print the pictures?" Maddie asks. "What is this, 1995?"

Herb ignores her and, connecting to the printer, begins to print off every image from the night of Maddie's birthday on both their phones. There are more than Maddie remembers and, despite herself, she is curious as she flicks through the growing pile. There is Kate, clinging on to Rob, with Warren not far away. Then Josh and Martin with friends from their courses. Maddie can't remember all their names but has seen them around loads since then. Hannah is laughing in almost every picture with her in it, obviously having a good time. And, thinks Maddie, not too out of her head to know what is going on.

*Stop it.*

She hears her own voice, speaking to the part of herself that wields the big stick and tells her what a loser she is for getting into this position. For once, that part listens and stands back. Maddie takes a deep breath, feeling the extra space inside that it leaves in its wake.

Herb stands up with the pictures and begins sticking them to Maddie's bedroom wall, like a crime scene board on TV. All she needs now, thinks Maddie, is a see-through screen and a black marker to use for scribbling her timelines and detective notes.

"Right," says Herb. "Let's get started."

# Chapter 35

### *Will*

Will chews the end of his pencil and tips his head to get a better view of the cartoon-version of Uncle Andy and Aunty Sue that he has drawn. She is oversized and red in the face, stirring a vast number of pots and pans and covered in billows of steam, while Uncle Andy sits smoking a pipe, giant dirty work boots propped up on the table.

*Accident waiting to happen,* Will scribbles beneath the drawing.

He has tucked himself away in Jake's room for the afternoon, away from the endless bustle downstairs. Jake has moved in with his younger brother Daniel to make room for Will as Dad already has the spare room. Will feels bad about Jake but is grateful for his own space.

It has been a month since he left hospital, more than a month since he has been home, and a month since he was last in school. Will knows that he won't be able to stay in this bubble forever, that eventually he will have to think about the *what's next*, but for now, he feels something close to peace floating along inside its fragile walls, letting the wind take him this way and that.

He hears the hurried thump of Daniel tumbling up the stairs and waits for him to come barreling through the door. Seconds later, he bursts in and stops short as his mother's repeated instructions to *knock first, Daniel* catch up with him. He steps back behind the door, leaving just his dark, tousled hair peering round the edge.

"Hi Will! Sorry." he says, voice breathless. "Can I come in?"

Will nods at his younger cousin.

"Yeah – come in. No worries." He pats the space on the bed beside him.

Daniel leaps on to the bed, scattering Will's pens, and leans over to see what Will is drawing.

"Is that Mum and Dad?" he asks in wide-eyed wonder. "Cool! Mum looks like she is about to explode!"

He mimics an explosion and falls sideways. Will remembers being as energetic and as full of life as Daniel once. He wonders where that enthusiastic boy has gone.

"Can you draw me?"

"Sure." Will picks up a pen and starts sketching.

Daniel and Jake don't know why Will was in the hospital. Just that he was poorly and needed the doctors' help. On the one hand, Will is happy that his cousins do not know the truth. He is not really up for their questions when he doesn't have the answers himself. On the other hand, it makes him feel a bit like a dirty secret. Apart from squeezing him extra tight when he arrived at their house before Christmas, Uncle Andy and Aunty Sue haven't mentioned his overdose at all and are continuing with life like nothing happened.

That night is blurry and indistinct, as were the days that followed in the hospital. As well as making sure that he was going to be OK physically, the consultant psychiatrist had come to see him, asking him all kinds of questions and giving him emergency numbers and an app called Staying Alive. Will had downloaded it and looked at it once, but shut it down again just as quickly. The thought of how close he had come to dying or doing himself serious damage makes him feel sick and scared.

"It's not that I wanted to *die*," he tried to explain to the psychiatrist. "I just didn't want to be here anymore. To deal with stuff."

The psychiatrist had nodded, like this made perfect sense to him. Will found his unruffled response comforting. A relief from the 24-7 concerned vigilance from all the other adults around him. Even Maddie had been weird with him, one minute silent and sad, and the next hugging him and crying. He had had two follow-up appointments with the mental health team after leaving hospital, which were fine, but Will didn't feel like talking. It didn't change anything. No matter what they said, the world was still a crazy place – pandemics and wars possible at any moment, school still shit, and his family still messed up.

He forces himself to relax his grip on the pen. To put the finishing touches on the cartoon drawing of Daniel. He sketches in a cape, and a giant

D on Daniel's cartoon-chest.

"I'm a super-hero!" Daniel exclaims, delighted. "What am I called?"

"That," says Will, tearing out the page from his notebook and handing it to Daniel, "is up to you."

"Really?" Daniel asks, like Will has given him a gift.

"Really."

"Cool!" Daniel jumps up from the bed and is halfway down the stairs before yelling back his thanks. "Mum... MUM! Look what Will drew for me! I have superpowers..." His voice fades as he runs.

Will smiles, remembering he and Sam assigning each other powers, battling out their differences with toy light-sabers, certain they could conquer any baddie foolish enough to cross their paths. He feels a sudden longing for Sam and the days when they really believed that anything was possible. But Will knows you can't go back. And even if you could, that boyhood innocence, elusive as smoke in the wind, cannot be recaptured.

*

Mum comes to see him a few days later. She and Will go out for coffee and cake in a little teashop in Storrington. Will chooses the table in the furthest corner, and, after the briefest of hesitations, Mum joins him. A girl with long, dark hair pulled back in a messy ponytail to reveal a shaved hairline at the nape of her neck and around her ears takes their order. Her name badge says *Freya*. Will notices the delicate silver cuffs laddering her ears, the gentle curve of her neck where a tattoo peeps out just above her collar. A flower maybe? Or a butterfly wing? She catches him looking, her brown-eyed gaze amused. Will drops his eyes with a flush. *Shit.* What if she thinks he is some creepy stalker? In the next thought he wonders why he cares.

She brings their food and drink a few minutes later, and Will is careful not to look at her. Mum thanks her, and the girl checks if they need anything else. She is not from around here, the shape of her words from somewhere up north. After she leaves, he and Mum are quiet for a while. Will fiddles with his fork, scraping the cream away from his cake and trying to voice the question which is lodged in his throat like a bone. He finally speaks.

"Who is my dad?" he asks.

Mum is very still and for a minute he thinks she won't answer, or will do that mum-thing where she over-explains without answering anything at all. But she surprises him, laying down her fork with a sigh and meeting his eyes.

"I don't know," she says simply. "I don't know who he is."

Will feels a flare of disappointed anger at her words. He is not sure what he was expecting, but not that.

"How can you not know?" he asks. "It should be pretty simple, right? You met some other guy, fucked him, and bam! Suddenly you are stuck with me and have to pretend that I am part of this family."

Mum flinches at his words, then reaches out her hands to take his. Will pulls them away, not ready to accept her touch or give any impression of forgiveness.

"You have always been a part of this family," Mum says. "From the moment we knew you were there. As much as Maddie. As much as me. As much as Dad."

Will hears her, but her words bounce away, like there is a forcefield all around him protecting him from enemy attacks.

"Dad has always been your dad."

Will is shaking his head before the words have left her mouth.

"Except that he's not, though," he mutters, crushing the cake into crumbs. He feels loss form in his stomach like a black hole and is horrified as tears spring up. He swipes them away angrily, surreptitiously checking to make sure that the girl, Freya, isn't looking. She is busy at a table on the other side of the café, her back to them.

Mum reaches out to him again. This time he doesn't pull away, letting his hands rest, passive and limp in hers.

"I'll tell you what happened," she says, squeezing his hands and waiting until he looks up to continue. "So that you are not left wondering. But know this Will. What happened is on me. All of it. You... you were something good that came out of it. And me and Dad..." Mum's voice catches at this point, and Will shifts uncomfortably in his seat, "...Dad and I love you so much."

And she tells him. No bullshit. All the details. Will tries not to retreat into himself at the thought of his mother being so off her head that she ended up in bed with some random guy while Dad and Maddie were at home. Tries not to feel sick that some coke-head, some fuzzy nobody from his mother's stoned memory, is his biological father. He can't equate that picture with the word Dad. That guy is not his Dad. He is nothing to do with him.

"Why didn't you tell Dad?" he asks. "Or me? Why didn't you let us know the truth?"

Mum thinks about this before replying.

"At first it was because I wasn't in any state to be honest with anyone. Not even myself. I was carrying a lot of... crap. Going through the motions. This was just one more secret to carry."

Will wonders what she means. What other secrets she has. But he doesn't interrupt. Doesn't want to risk Mum stopping. Not now that she is actually talking to him like an adult. Like what he thinks and knows matters.

"After a while, things settled down, and then I couldn't risk losing him," she says. "I was so afraid he would leave if he knew. And I didn't think I would survive that."

"But you are," says Will. "Surviving."

Mum thinks about that and nods with a sad little smile that tugs at Will despite himself.

"Yes," she says simply. "And then you came along. You came into our lives like a little whirlwind, stirring up the surface and making sure we all knew that you were there."

Will thinks of all the stories his parents have told him. Family folklore. About the baby who didn't eat, didn't sleep, wasn't content just to sit and observe, but wanted to be right there in the thick of the action, whether it was convenient for everyone else or not.

"Your dad loved you from the second he saw you," Mum continues. "You should have seen him when he held you for the very first time. *My boy,* he said."

Will's heart thumps. He knows how that sounds. Heard him saying those very words when Dad thought he was sleeping in the hospital.

*My boy.*

"By then, I couldn't tell him," Mum goes on. "I couldn't destroy all of that. I thought I was the only one to know. And I buried it so deep that after a while I almost didn't know anymore. I didn't realise Ros had worked it out. I thought I could keep it buried forever."

When she puts it that way, Will can almost get it. Each decision and fear and rationale piled one on top of the other until it was a mountain so big and so heavy that it squashed what had really happened into something flat and unreal. Except that what really happened did happen. And his dad is not his dad. And his cousins are not his cousins. Even Maddie is only his half-sister. Dad is all hers. Like she has full rights as a family shareholder, and he is lucky to have a place at the table. Mum is the only one who is really and truly his family. How fair is that?

"I'm sorry, Will," Mum says. "Really and truly sorry."

Will wonders if this is the first time Mum has been completely honest with him. Maybe, maybe not. All he knows is that after 18 years of living in a world that wasn't quite real, perpetuated by the person he should have been able to trust more than anyone, he's not quite ready to let her in. He simply nods, acknowledging her apology but not knowing what else to say. He straightens and leans back, tucking his hands on his lap and wondering if Freya is going to bring the bill soon.

# Chapter 36

***John***

John stands at his brother's kitchen sink, stooping down to scrub at a stubborn burnt spot on the casserole dish from tonight's dinner. The hot, soapy water reaches midway up his forearms, and John lingers there, comforted by the warmth. He looks out the window, seeing only his reflection staring back at him in the dark glass. He has been here for too long. His brother and Sue assure him he can stay for as long as he needs, that Will can stay too, but John knows that their presence is putting pressure on the family. They are taking up too much space. It is uncomfortable for John to acknowledge this. He is the provider, the caretaker, the person in the room who sees everyone else and who moderates and calms. He knows that man. This new surplus man, the one who exists in this space, is none of those things. He is big and unwieldy and doesn't fit. John has been going out of his way to make himself useful, seeing to the frozen garden as much as he can, cleaning when Sue doesn't shoo him away, washing up after home-cooked meals. Like tonight.

He reaches for another pan, submerges it, then looks up, sensing movement behind him. He sees Will's reflection, insubstantial as a ghost. He is leaning on the kitchen door, hesitating like he is about to cross the threshold into an unknown land. Since Will left the hospital, they have been careful around one another, mentally weighing every word and interaction before committing. Will's ghost eyes meet John's in the window and he steps into the kitchen.

"Want a hand?" he asks casually.

John nods and gestures to the tea-towel hanging on the oven handle.

"Thanks," Will replies.

They work in silence for a bit.

"I saw Mum today," says Will, glancing over at John. "I asked her who my dad was – my biological dad."

John steadies his breathing, slowly and deliberately releasing the tension gathered in his shoulders and back.

"Turns out she doesn't even know who he was. Just some loser stoner passing through."

John thinks about Will and the drugs. The revelations in hospital that he has been smoking weed and taking ecstasy for months. That none of them spotted the escalation. He feels bad about lashing out at Hope about Will. About her not knowing. He didn't notice either.

"You're not like him," says John, voice low and steady.

Will gives a short laugh. "But how do you know? You don't know him."

"I know you. And you're not like him."

Will gives a deep sigh, his breath hitching as he speaks.

"But I'm not like you, either," he says.

John thinks about Will during his growing up years, so different from Maddie, and yes, from him too, bursting with impatient energy and ideas, uncertain of his path in life but beating one out anyway.

"Will," he says gently, turning to him now. Looking at the real boy, not just the reflection in the window. His blonde hair is mussed, a flush of red across his cheeks. John realises that even with his shoulders stooped as they are now, Will is nearly as tall as him. "You are like you. And that is good enough for me."

Will looks down, screwing up his face to contain his emotion, reminding John of the little boy who tried not to cry after falling over, of the 12-year-old confused by his own frustration when thwarted, of the young man battling fears and anxieties during lockdown. John places a hand on Will's shoulder.

"You are like you," he repeats.

Will leans into him, wrapping his arms around his father's back and holding tight.

*

After another week, John messages Hope. He will pick her up from the shop after work so they can talk – about the kids, about what's next. Wherever he and Hope are, Maddie and Will need them both now. Maddie has just gone back to university, a thought that fills John with angry unease. If he ever lays hands on that bastard, God help him. Will seems a bit better, joining the rest of the family more, taking his drawing stuff to the café in the village and getting out of the house for hours on end. John tries not to worry when Will is out of sight, to remind himself that he needs the space. This is normal. But John has learned afresh what life might take away. There is a fragile, new connection growing between them, and John fears that any sudden move could snap it. He can't bear to think of Will drifting away, untethered.

John has held out for as long as he can, waiting for Hope to respond to his written invitation to talk. He needed her to reach out this time. To be the one to make the first move. But after seven weeks, there has been nothing. No move on Hope's part. It is always down to him to build bridges. To repair the rifts. He is tired of it. Done. The well which has nourished everyone else since he was 15 years old has run dry.

Light rain is falling as Hope leaves the shop. John is waiting outside, collar pulled up against the cold, unwilling to go inside and face light conversation with Fran and Carlos. Despite his anger with Hope, his heart gives a leap at the sight of her, like it hasn't caught up with life as it is now. Apart from the air of sadness clinging to her like a fine mist, she looks well. He is not sure how he feels about this. He does not hold out an arm out for her to hold, and they walk side by side to the restaurant he's booked, hurrying through the darkness.

Once they are seated, their meals ordered and drinks delivered, Hope tells him about Ros and a pink-haired girl called Herb gathering round Maddie, trying to jog her memory and find clues about who attacked her. Maddie is showing more interest than she did at first, wanting answers now. John is constantly amazed at the quiet strength of his daughter, walking this unwanted path, returning to university with shoulders squared to face whatever awaits.

"I'm worried for her," John confides, and Hope reaches a hand towards him, thinks better of it and pulls back.

"Yes," she responds. "Me too."

"That bastard is still out there."

He tries to soothe the hot pit of anger which has been roiling in his belly since he found out what happened to Maddie. His mind stops short of picturing what that... animal... did to her. His gentle, kind-hearted daughter. John isn't accustomed to rage and isn't quite sure what to do with it. It is like a wild thing, held in check by a flimsy chain, and it frightens him to think what might happen if the thing breaks loose.

John thinks of Will instead, calming himself with the thought of his son's gradual return to life. He tells Hope about his drawing, how Will is with his cousins – kind, funny, like he sees in them younger versions of himself. He is a quieter, more thoughtful Will just now, and whilst one part of John is heartened by this change, another part misses that old spark, the combative Will who challenged him at every opportunity. This Now-Will exists in a space somewhere between his old life and whatever comes next, and John knows he can't stay there forever.

"Have you spoken to the school again?" he asks. Hope nods. At the beginning, just after it happened, they let the school know he would be away. As Will has grown stronger, the question of when he will return, or even if he will return, is looming larger.

"They're sending through some work – stuff he can do to catch up," says Hope. "But with how he was before all this, and now after everything, he's pretty far behind."

John nods, tension gathering in his gut. It is not what he wants for Will. He wants him to have all the freedom and opportunities out there, to have the education to back him, but here they are. In the worst place possible for his final year.

*Not the worst place*, he reminds himself, thinking of Will, bruised eyes closed against translucent skin, bound to indifferent machines in the hospital. John closes his own eyes for a moment, mentally recalibrating. School and what's next would fall into place when the time was right.

"John." Hope is speaking again and something in her tone of voice makes him tense. He puts down his fork, facing her. It is hard to feel anything as he regards her troubled face.

"There is something I need to tell you."

John sighs, brow furrowing, wild thing stirring. He shifts in his seat. He is not sure he has room for another revelation. Another secret. He says nothing. Hope gathers herself before speaking.

"When I was in foster care... when I was 14, there was this man," she says. "His name was Jeremy."

John frowns, wondering where this is going.

Hope takes a deep breath and continues. "He was the one in charge. And. Well... he took a liking to me."

*No.*

*Heat rising.*

"He um... well, he sexually abused me," says Hope. "Raped me, actually. For three years. Until I ran away."

She is stroking her arm now, tracing old scars as she speaks.

John cannot speak. Holding the heat and the wild thing inside is taking everything and he is afraid to open his mouth. His mind flashes to a young Hope. A vulnerable Hope younger than Maddie at the mercy of some other sick bastard. Oh God! He hasn't got any space for this new piece of history. Not in this moment. Hope is looking at him anxiously, wringing her hands on the table across from him.

"Why?" he manages.

"I don't know," Hope says flushing. "I know I should have stopped it but..."

"No."

John holds out a hand, shaking his head. His face is flushed and he needs some air.

"Why are you telling me this now?"

It is Hope's turn to be silent.

"All these years..."

Hope's voice is small when she speaks. "I just... I just wanted to forget," she says. "To put that life behind me. To forget who I was then."

"And now?" John doesn't know how to feel, thoughts of Maddie pregnant with the child of some twisted chancer, Will barely hanging on, Hope... Hope at 14, at 15, at 16... He can't think about it.

"Now I need to stop pretending," says Hope. "Stop pretending that this didn't happen to me. I'm getting some help. Have booked an appointment to see a counsellor..." She trails off when John says nothing. "I just thought you should know."

John pulls his coffee towards him, drawing in its warmth as he circles the mug with his hands. He pushes what Hope has told him away from him. Out of reach.

"I asked you to call," he tells her. "I asked you to reach out."

"What?" Hope looks startled by the change of topic.

"When I left. I wrote in the letter that it was up to you to get in touch. To be the one to come to me. For once."

He knows his timing is off. That this thing Hope has shared is big. Bigger than his mind can grasp just now. But he hasn't got anything to give her.

Hope looks confused.

"What letter?"

"Oh for God's sake, Hope!" The heat inside rises, and John feels the rumble of the wild thing's growl. A part of him is dismayed to see Hope flinch, but the wild thing swipes it away. "I left you a bloody letter when I left, and even after everything, after all your secrets ruined our family, you are playing the ignorant card. You still can't find it in you to think about what I need. To reach out to me."

"John," Hope's voice filters through the heat which is shimmering before him now like a mirage. "I never saw any letter. I didn't know."

"You didn't know," he repeats flatly. "You couldn't tell me. You can't cope. It's not you…" He is on his feet now. He has got to get out of here. "I can't do this anymore, Hope. I just can't."

He senses eyes on him as he pulls his coat from the back of his chair, toppling it in his haste to get out. The only thing he can think of is escape. Getting out of here before the rage bubbles up and spills over like lava.

Once outside, he leans on the damp brick wall of the restaurant, drawing in deep breaths, heart pounding. But the frigid January air does little to cool the heat inside. He straightens and pulls on his coat, then turns and walks briskly away.

Enough.

# Chapter 37

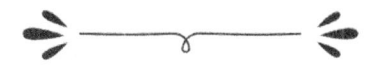

**Me**

*What is more exciting than an old, forgotten doll's house, lovingly restored to its original glory? I'll tell you what. An old, forgotten, lovingly restored to its original glory doll's house that has a secret room. The painstaking hours of creation that strain the eyes and crook the back are worth every uncomfortable minute. Behold! A sliding door masquerading as a bookcase in the master bedroom! Behind it, a room full of secrets that only you can see. Only you know that the room is there. And only you have the key to gain entry.*

\*

I was 14 years old when everything ended just like I knew it would. As I arrived home from school one bright May day – that is 'home' in the loosest possible sense – the scent of late spring drifting on the sun-warmed breeze met the creeping smell of death like wave interference. They flowed through and into each other until they were the same thing. To this day, I cannot bear the scent of lilac, its sickly sweetness conjuring the sight and smell of my mother, lying wide-eyed and pale as alabaster in a pool of her own vomit. Strands of long dark hair stuck to her face like weeds, the paraphernalia of the drugs that killed her scattered all around.

I felt nothing for the longest time after I found her. I simply stared at the lifeless person who had been my mother as the inevitability of the moment laid its reassuring arm across my shoulders.

*Look, Juniper Hope*, it reasoned. *Now you have nothing to fear.*

It had a point. My whole life up until then had been lived somewhere between watchful uncertainty and full-blown high alert. I was never sure how I would find my mother. Glassy-eyed and high, oblivious to all but her inner demons. Or trying on the role of adult for size, dancing and laughing and serving up beans on toast for tea, coaxing me to join her with a red, laughing mouth and a *Come on, Juniper Hope!* When I was little, I would run to her, not yet cognisant that this was an illusion, that come the morning I would be back in a world where I was ill-equipped and in charge. By the time I started secondary school, wariness and resentment had kicked in, and I was fully aware that my life was on a different trajectory to those of my classmates. I learned to keep them and everyone else at arm's length. But even then, the little girl me, who was far too small to keep her balance on these ever-shifting sands, still longed for the safe arms of her mummy and never stopped trying to reach her.

The irony of it all as I shed my mother's choice of the name Juniper that May day and shuffled wearily into the ill-fitting title of Hope, is that the voice of reassuring inevitability was wrong. I had everything left to fear.

*

I am so off balance at John's sudden departure, red-faced, blundering, and a different version of the man I have always known, that it takes me a full 15 minutes to gather my thoughts and ask for the bill. I tap my card on the server's machine, not even noting the price of the meal or adding a tip, and gather my things, mind racing.

*What letter?*

I am drawing a blank. Even in my terrible state during those days after everyone but Ros left me, I would have remembered a letter. All I had wanted was for John to come to me. To reach out like he always had. But he never came.

A thought creeps into my consciousness as I hurry back to the shop, to the small parking bay beside it where I have left my car.

*Everyone but Ros.*

The only person who might have seen the letter was Ros. Nobody else was in the house. Surely not... But then I think back to the scene between us, two weeks earlier when John had turned up at the house, a tell-all text from Ros held aloft in his hand like proof.

"What were you thinking?" I had shouted as Ros came through the door later that day, arms laden with food shopping. "You had no right!"

Ros had defended herself. Of course she had. Maddie needed her dad, she couldn't tell him, so Ros had stepped in like her bloody saviour, *blah blah blah*... But now this. Had Ros somehow intercepted the letter? Kept it from me? As I grapple with the possibilities, hands clenched on the steering wheel, wipers groaning out their back-and-forth creak in the light rain, I realise with growing certainty that Ros has been at the centre of everything that has gone wrong. All these secrets, the things I kept hidden under lock and key for survival, had only started to emerge when Ros turned up. That kissing thing with Will, the revelation that John was not his biological father, the message that John didn't want to see me, to leave him be... It was for the best, Ros had said. Then spilling the beans about Maddie. On a mission now to help Maddie – what is *that* really about?

I am pressing my foot down on the accelerator, driving too close to the cars in front, weaving impatiently behind them until there is space to pass, reckless in the rain-blurred darkness. I need to talk to Ros.

Light is pouring out through every window of the house like a beacon when I pull into the drive, as though Ros is inhabiting every room at once. I take a moment to slow down and breathe before leaving the car and letting myself inside. The radio is playing in the empty kitchen. Ros is perched on the corner of the living room sofa watching something on Netflix. She is drinking a glass of wine. She glances up as I kick off my shoes and come into the room.

"Hi," she says, glancing over briefly before turning back to the TV.

"Hi."

Now that I'm here, I'm not sure how to start. I wait a few minutes, then pick up the remote and switch off the TV.

"Hey!" says Ros, voice indignant.

"I need to talk to you."

"Well, can it wait? I was enjoying that."

Her long nails – bright yellow today – are tapping the side of her wine glass in irritation. She sees my face and sits up straighter.

"Is it Maddie? Or Will?" she asks. "What's happened?"

"Ros," I begin. "After John left, did you find a letter?"

Her face hardens with a defiance reminiscent of her 11-year-old self and tells me all I need to know before she opens her mouth. She gives an exaggerated sigh and leans back, crossing her arms.

"So what if I did?" she replies.

I tamp down my anger and keep my voice level.

"So what if you did?" I repeat. "Is that all you have to say?"

"Look, Hope," Ros says, like she is speaking to someone who is particularly dense. "You were in no fit state to read a letter from John. He had just walked out, and you weren't coping. You know how you get when you're like that. I was protecting you. Making sure you didn't get any worse, OK?"

She presents this like she is the rational one and I am the one who is unbalanced. I shake my head and shrug off her skewed reframing of what happened.

"You had no right," I say, "to make that decision for me."

A thought strikes me.

"Did you read it?"

Ros is unrepentant. She shrugs.

"For fuck's sake, Ros," I say. "Where is it now?"

"I burned it."

I have no words for a moment. To hide the letter is one thing. To read it and burn it – removing me from the process entirely – well, that is something else.

"And you texted John about Maddie."

Ros rolls her eyes. "We've already been through that. John needed to know. Maddie needed him to know and she is doing better since she spoke to him about what happened."

"That's not the point!" Despite my earlier intentions, I am struggling not to shout.

"What *is* the point then, Hope?"

"The point is that ever since you got here things have been going wrong."

Her eyes widen and she is about to respond, but I hold up my hand and continue.

"You have interfered in everything," I say. "With Will – what was *that* about – with breaking confidences on one hand and hiding information on another." As I speak, the downward spiral of my family takes on a new shape, twisting and turning in ever-descending circles with Ros right there at the centre. "And now you've hooked into Maddie and are manipulating her too."

Ros sits forward, eyes flashing. "I am not manipulating Maddie," she says. "I *care* about Maddie."

"You barely know Maddie!"

"I know her well enough. I know how she feels."

"She is *nothing like you*," I hiss back, wanting to separate Ros and her toxic meddling as far as possible from my daughter.

Ros stares at me, features frozen.

"I didn't make any of this happen," she says. "You got pregnant by some random asshole. You chose to keep it a secret. You built your family on all of that. You, Hope. Not me."

The truth of it settles in my chest like a swarm of bees, angry and unsettled.

I stand up.

"I think it is time for you to leave now, Ros."

"Oh for God's sake, Hope."

"I mean it."

The knowledge that this is what needs to happen is as clear to me as spring air after rain. "You've been here long enough, and I want you to leave. You have until the end of the week to sort yourself out."

Then I leave the room and climb the stairs to my empty bedroom in my empty house.

\*

Ros leaves two days later. I don't know where she goes. At this point in time, I don't particularly care, though despite myself my heart squeezes at the sight of her waiting at the end of the drive for a taxi with her backpack and bags. I think of the small 11-year-old I first met, acting out and moving from one foster home to another. Angry, defiant, vulnerable, impossible. Ros will never settle.

*She is not my responsibility*, I tell myself, concentrating hard to make the words feel like truth.

I have other things to think about now. I have booked the first appointment with a counsellor for this afternoon. I have almost cancelled it ten times over.

*What the hell are you doing?*

The voice inside berates me, but I am used to its bullying, and I shrug it away. I decide to walk into Chichester, trying to calm the bees in my chest which have not stilled since the confrontation with Ros. Their buzzing has taken on a different tone now – less angry, more agitated.

*Risky, risky, risky...* they are saying.

I ignore them too.

I am fortunate that the counsellor is local. Somehow it feels safer, staying on home territory. As I approach the blue door that is number four, Barnabas Lane, I feel all the Russian doll layers of myself shift uneasily, stirring up the dust of my past into the hopeless mess of my present. Anxiety kicks to the surface, leaving me breathless and sick, palms moist. I hesitate, scanning the quiet lane around me, taking in the terraced cottages stretching away to the right and to the left, the stonework solid, centuries old. I close my eyes and focus on the distant cathedral bells chiming, my fingers moving absently to the lines of silvery scars on my inner arm, stroking them gently.

*Breathe,* I tell myself. *Just breathe...You can do this.*

I square my shoulders, bid the anxious voice to *shhhh*, just for now, just for a minute, and ring the bell.

# Chapter 38

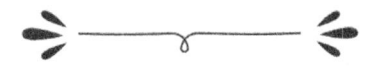

**Ros**

If there is one thing that Ros can do, it is to run. To leave. To shake the dust from her feet and find a new place. She never looks back. Never. In her distant past, where memories are more fantasy than fact, fading away under direct scrutiny like shapes in the darkness, Ros sometimes feels the presence of the little girl who stayed. And waited. And waited. And waited. Until the strange people took her away to a place where her mummy would never find her.

*That is what happens when you stay,* Ros would tell the little girl, shushing her and pushing her back into the darkness. *Bad things happen.*

*

Ros can feel that little girl in her right now. Flooding her whole body with unbearable pain and longing. Crying and telling her to *stay… stay… stay…*

*Shut up!* Ros says, more desperate than angry. She tries to kick the little girl to the ground, to press a hob-nailed boot into her frail chest until she is silent, panting and gasping for air. But the anger is diminished and doesn't have the power to hold her down. Ros turns her face away from the little girl's wide-eyed plea and climbs into the taxi taking her away from Hope and the house in Chichester that feels like home. The girl follows her into the taxi, tugging Ros's arm.

*Don't go.*

Ros shrugs her off, taking in deep breaths of air so she can speak.

"Chichester station," she tells the driver.

She will get on a train and go to Brighton. She knows people there. Had a job lined up not so long ago. She'll see if they've got anything casual going now. And Maddie is in Brighton. As the taxi weaves through the traffic to the station, Ros tries to harness the rage which has always kept her standing. She thinks of Hope, blaming Ros for everything, scrolls back through the years she was on her own without anyone, remembers dickhead and being left with him while Hope made her break for freedom. But the rage is elusive as a wild horse, ducking and diving just out of reach. Without it, Ros feels something collapse inside, and a grey sadness envelops her.

*

When she arrives in Brighton, she goes into automatic pilot. Running away consumed with anger might be her weapon of choice, but it has nothing on her capacity to survive. Within a week, Ros has tapped up Harriet, a dreadlocked, bohemian acquaintance from her travel days, convinced her to let Ros sleep on the sofa – just for a couple of weeks until she finds her feet – and has picked up some casual shifts at a bar on the outskirts of the city centre. It isn't exactly glamorous but it will do for now. Just being in Brighton helps Ros breathe more easily. She should have come here sooner. She stayed too long in the claustrophobic confines of middle-class Chichester.

Even when the blustery February winds are frothing and stirring up steel-grey waves, barely distinguishable from the glowering, heavy skies, and the stony beaches are empty apart from dog-walkers, heads bowed and hoods pulled tight around their faces, Ros finds solace here. She fits. Maybe it is the buzz of constant activity filling the streets like electricity once you leave the winter quiet of the seafront. Or the eclectic mix of people milling in the bars and clubs after-hours. Nobody stops and nobody looks twice at you in Brighton. Ros is good with that.

After two weeks, an anxious restlessness joins the sadness which is her constant companion and Ros find herself longing for connection. With no word from Hope, she reaches out to Maddie.

*How are things?*

Ros taps out the message, hesitates for a moment, then presses send.

Maddie replies half an hour later.

*yeah ok*

*Want to grab a coffee some time?*

Maddie's response is faster this time.

*Ok,* and then: *where r u*

Ros tells Maddie she is living in Brighton now, has been here for a couple of weeks. She is just reaching out to Maddie to check in. She has some time this afternoon if Maddie wants to meet her.

*cant today*, Maddie replies, *lectures*

Ros feels disappointment rise like the tide.

*2mrw?* Maddie adds.

*Sounds good,* Ros replies.

They arrange to meet in a coffee shop in the Lanes tomorrow at noon, and when they have finished messaging, Ros mutes her phone and shoves it in her bag, wondering how she will fill the afternoon until her shift that evening.

The next day, Ros arrives early to bag a table by the window. When Maddie comes through the door Ros barely recognises her. Her long dark hair has been cropped to her chin and a rough fringe cut in, framing Maddie's face and highlighting her dark eyes rimmed with thick black eyeliner. She is wearing a long coat – almost to her ankles, black Doc Martens just showing, and is carrying a bright orange satchel that bumps just below her hip as she walks. She spots Ros and waves, weaving past the other tables and squeezing herself into the space Ros has saved for her.

Ros stares at her in surprise.

"You look…" she fishes around for the right words, "…different."

Maddie raises her eyebrows and picks up a menu with a small smile.

"Good different," Ros adds, realising she means it. Like the new hair and bold make-up are presenting a tougher version of Maddie. Ros approves.

"That was the point," says Maddie, running her eyes over the menu. "Are we eating?"

Over lunch, Ros fills Maddie in on the past two weeks. The bit about her moving anyway, not the confrontation between her and Hope. Maddie already knows she is no longer living at the house in Chichester. *Of course Hope told her,* Ros thinks, wondering what else Hope has said. But Maddie didn't know Ros had moved to Brighton.

"I have friends here," Ros says.

'Friends' is perhaps overstating it. She thinks of Harriet, smoking a roll-up and asking questions this morning about Ros finding her own bedsit, or a room she can rent maybe. *Space is a bit tight, you know, so…* Ros put her off with a casual *Yeah, yeah… nearly sorted*, then dipped out of the flat under the guise of picking up an extra shift.

Ros waits for Maddie to finish her toastie before asking how she is *really* doing, and how the search is going for the guy who did this. She doesn't mention Maddie's baby, still under wraps from the world's eyes and hidden from sight under her bulky clothes. Hope was wrong about Ros wanting to manipulate Maddie for her own purposes. She is here to help Maddie. To fight for her, like nobody ever did for Ros.

Maddie stirs the ice at the bottom of her drink with a straw, thinking about her answer.

"Honestly?" she says. "I don't know how I am. Every day I get up, I shower, I have breakfast, I go to the library or lectures, I work my ass off and I come back. I hang out with people on my course, and with Herb and Ella. Kate is off in her own world, and you never know when Hannah is going to be around."

She sighs, and Ros waits for her to continue.

"But I'm better than I was," she says. "God knows why."

"But what about finding this guy?" Ros asks, unable to hold the question back. "How is that going?"

"Between you and Herb…" Maddie sighs, not finishing her sentence and making a decision. "Look. Why don't you pop over to the flat tonight? Herb and Ella will be there. We'll grab a pizza and talk."

*

Maddie's flat is heaving with people when Ros arrives later that evening. Herb lets her in and leads her by the hand through groups of students laughing and drinking in the hallway, past the open kitchen door and into a room at the end of the corridor. She knocks. Maddie pulls the door open a couple of inches and, seeing who is there, she walks in, then re-locks the door after Ros. A petite girl with fine blond hair pulled back into a knot at the back of her head is perched on Maddie's bed like a vigilant meerkat. A desk lamp and fairy lights throw soft light into the room.

"It's Martin's birthday," Maddie says, gesturing at the door and all the people on the other side. "Half his course is here, so…"

"We thought we'd find a quiet space," continues the girl with blonde hair. She holds out a hand to Ros. "I'm Ella by the way."

Ros nods a greeting and finds a seat.

"So," she says, getting straight to the point. "Where are we with all of this?"

"Maddie's got her suspicions," Herb says, looking over at Maddie and shrugging a *What?* when Maddie frowns at her.

Herb explains that they have gone over and over Maddie's birthday. Have gathered all the pictures and worked out pretty much everyone who passed through the flat that night. She holds out her hand to Maddie, and Maddie reaches behind her bed and pulls out a folder. In the folder are the printed pictures from a few weeks ago. Only now, there are more and they are sorted into two groups. Some with red crosses through them and others with question marks. Ros takes the red-crossed pile and slowly sorts through them. She holds up the first one.

"That's Josh," says Maddie. "He's harmless. A friend. It's not him."

"OK..." Ros doesn't say what she's thinking. That you can't assume anyone is harmless. She picks up the next one marked with a cross, and the next.

"Martin," says Herb, "and one of Martin's maths-geek friends. Also not them."

"Because they're maths geeks?"

"Because it's *Martin*," says Herb, and Maddie nods in agreement.

"It's not him."

Ros quickly shuffles through the others with a cross, not bothering to challenge the girls' flimsy selection criteria for the moment, instead shifting her focus to the handful of pictures marked with question marks. She peers at the one on top. She can barely see who it is – just his eyes and the blonde top of his head visible at the back of a group selfie. She raises her eyebrows at Maddie, who shrugs.

"We can't work out who he is," she says. "So I don't know."

There are three or four more like this, and another of two guys with a girl. The taller of the two has an arm draped loosely around the blonde girl.

"That's Kate," Herb offers. "She lives here. That guy," she points to the one with his arm around her, "is Rob, and that guy is his wanker friend, Warren."

There are question marks over Rob's and Warren's faces. Ros raises her eyebrows at Maddie, who shakes her head.

"Tell her, Maddie," urges Ella.

"But I don't know," Maddie is agitated, cropped hair mussed and sticking out where she has run her hands through it.

"You might not know here," says Ella, pointing to Maddie's head, "but you know here." She places a hand on her own chest.

"But that's just the point. I *don't* know," Maddie says, taking back the pictures and piling them together. "I know they're both idiots, but Rob is with Kate – they're practically joined at the hip – so it's unlikely to be him. Warren gives me the creeps if I'm anywhere near him, but he gives everyone the creeps."

"Because he's a tosser," Herb adds, speaking to Ros.

"The truth is, I might have a gut reaction, but I can't be sure. For all I know it was a random stranger passing through."

"It wasn't a random stranger passing through," says Herb. She takes back the picture of Kate, Rob and Warren, and jabs a finger at Warren's face framed in the crook of the red question mark. "I'd put money on it being him."

"Well, I won't do that," says Maddie.

They talk some more but go round in circles, so they order pizza and allow the conversation to drift away from the turbulent whos and whys to blander topics in calmer waters. The party outside is still going full swing, and laughter and the *thump thump thump* of the music surrounds the room like a heartbeat.

Ros is tired after the previous night's late shift at the bar, so she stands up, ready to go. Maddie and Ella are watching something on Maddie's laptop, and Maddie gives her a small wave, engrossed in the show. Herb stands up with her.

"I need to go, too," she says. "I've got a tutorial in the morning."

They push their way through all the people milling around, unable to talk over the thrum of sound enveloping them. Ros can see how someone could get away with spiking a drink, then creeping in through an open door at the other end of the corridor without anyone noticing. People only see what they want to, she thinks, dickhead's face coming unbidden to mind, along with all the other faces turned the other way. When she and Ros push through the door to stand in front of the building, the sudden quiet and the crisp, fresh air are startling.

Ros pulls a cigarette from her bag and lights it, a barely perceptible tremble in her hand. The flare of the match briefly lights the space between them. Ros extinguishes the match with a quick shake.

"Can you send me that picture?" she asks Herb.

Herb nods and doesn't bother asking which one.

# Chapter 39

*Maddie*

Maddie gazes into the mirror of the ladies' toilets outside her seminar room, her mind still occupied with the group's discussion about Victorian women finding their voices through poetry. She turns her head first to the left and then to the right. Lifting a hand to her hair, she runs her fingers roughly through it, breaking up its smooth shine and leaving something messier in its place. She leans forward and carefully applies red lipstick, dabbing her lips with a tissue and smiling at her reflection.

Better.

She cut off her hair last week, putting distance between her now-self and the shadow-self that barely made it through last term. Roughly at first, with a pair of scissors in her room. Then again at the hairdresser, at Herb's insistence.

"I'm all for this badass version of you," she said, hands on Maddie's shoulders as she critically surveyed the jagged edges framing her face. "But it is possible to do badass with a little bit of style."

Hannah had clapped in admiration at her first sight of this new Maddie, and Kate had pulled a face, absently stroking her own long, straightened hair.

"Each to their own, I suppose," she said before turning her attention back to her phone.

Maddie was surprised to find that she didn't care what anyone else thought.

Except, she thinks now, standing alone in front of the mirror, maybe Dad who has always loved her long hair. She hasn't told him yet, a part of her still wanting to be his little girl with all the world before her. But the serious woman staring back at her from the mirror isn't a little girl anymore, and Maddie is tired of secrets. She has witnessed their wrecking-ball power firsthand. Making a decision, she takes a picture of herself and sends it to the family group with the caption *new me*.

It is still difficult for Maddie to grasp how completely her life has changed in six short months, her mind lagging behind everything that has happened like a tired toddler who is grizzling and dragging its feet. Last summer, the most stressful thing she had to think about were her A Level results and which uni she would attend. A little anxiety over leaving home and being thrust into a whole new post-Covid world perhaps, but that was *good* anxiety. A sign that life was moving on, exactly as it should be. Today, she is like a traveller in a foreign landscape. Nearly losing Will. Learning he is her half-brother. She feels a pang at the thought of the more tenuous connection between them. Dad leaving. Mum falling apart. Ros coming into their lives. Then that night. The big black hole of *him*. Of what he did. She glances down at her belly, still masked from friends and tutors by her winter clothes. Out of nowhere, a life growing inside that she never wanted but can't turn away. The who and the why has infiltrated her secret thoughts and her conversations with Herb and Ella like a raging pandemic.

"You know Ros is stalking Warren," Herb said to her as they hurried across the campus together earlier that day. A strong wind whipped around them with an icy edge, chasing students into faculty buildings and living accommodation.

"What?" Maddie didn't really want to think about what this meant.

"She knows who he is now and she's following him."

"Why?" The thought plucked at her breath and her heartbeat quickened. Herb shrugged.

"To catch him out," she said. "To make sure he can never do this again."

Maddie sighed and wished she'd never said anything to Herb and Ella when she'd first looked at that picture of Kate, Rob and Warren. In that unguarded moment weeks ago, something inside had shifted in wordless recognition, intangible as a sixth sense. Herb had seen her confusion, her hesitation, and pounced.

"It's him!" she'd shouted. "I *knew* it!"

But putting such bold words to the unease deep in her gut had only served to push her visceral reaction into the wings. Her rational self took over.

*I can't possibly know. I was unconscious. I've never liked Rob and Warren. Can barely get near Kate because of them. I hate the way Rob treats her with such patronising arrogance. Of course, seeing pictures of them that night is going to cause a reaction. It doesn't mean anything.*

And on and on in her mind. And now Ros is on the case, with Herb standing on the sidelines encouraging her. It is all starting to feel out of control.

Maddie's phone pings. There is a reply to the picture she sent to the family group. From Will.

*sick*

Maddie smiles and messages back.

*i know right?*

\*

A few days later, she feels the baby move for the first time. As subtle as a bubble pop or the flutter of a butterfly's wings. At first, she thinks she is imagining it, the movement too feather-light to grasp. She is stretched out on her bed, a well-thumbed copy of *Tess of the D'Urbervilles* in her hand. She stops reading for a moment, closes her eyes and waits. Nothing. It is all in her head. She picks up the book again, and just as she is losing herself in Angel Clare's betrayal, she feels it again.

*Pop. Pop. Pop.*

Maddie lays completely still, willing the feeling to come again, holding her breath so she doesn't miss it.

*Swirl.*

She can definitely feel that. Something inside of her – a part of her, yet separate.

Maddie lays a hand gently on her belly and tears spring to her eyes. A new self, small and uncertain as a field mouse, reaches out and connects with the tiny life growing inside. Despite everything, Maddie smiles.

When she can no longer feel the swish of life in her belly, she leaps to her feet, hurries from her room and bangs on Ella's door.

"I felt it!" she bursts out to Ella the moment the door opens. She pushes past her into the room. Books are piled high on the desk and Ella's laptop is open where she is working.

Ella smiles back at Maddie, confused.

"Felt what?"

"The baby!" Maddie replies, laying her hand on the place she'd felt the movement. "I felt it move. Just now."

The smile falters and slips a little from Ella's face before she catches herself.

"What?" Maddie asks.

"Nothing," says Ella, always keen to please, to see Maddie's side of things. "It's just…"

"Just what?" Maddie repeats, feeling the creep of shame like an ink blot on paper.

"What are you going to do with a baby, Maddie?" she asks gently. "You're 19. You have your whole life ahead of you. If you have the baby, what about your degree? And I just think… I just think that it will always remind you of what happened. How will you cope with that? I just don't think getting excited about it is going to help. I think it is going to make everything worse."

Ella flushes as she speaks, uncomfortable with so many frank words. They pop the little bubble of wonder that has inflated Maddie's chest, leaving a vacuum behind. She takes a step back as Ella moves towards her, hand outstretched.

"No – it's fine," Maddie says, waving her off and straightening her back. "I'm not stupid. I know those things. Don't you think I haven't been thinking them every minute of every day?"

Ella tries to speak, face stricken. Maddie cuts her off.

"It was just a moment, OK? Aren't I allowed a moment?"

"Of course, I…"

"I'm going to go, OK, Ella? We can talk later."

Maddie leaves. Too agitated to sit alone in her own room, she goes to the kitchen to make tea and toast, stepping inside and realising too late who is there. Kate is at the table eating a portion of chips, grinning as Rob stands behind her, sliding his hands down her shoulders and tapping out a drumbeat on the top of her breasts. His eyes meet Maddie's. Warren, sprawled out next to Kate, jumps to his feet and grabs his jacket.

"We're off," he says to Kate, sauntering towards the kitchen door. Maddie hurries past him, heart accelerating, trying not to let Warren see the effect he has on her. Nausea rises from the pit of her stomach. Rob pulls himself from Kate reluctantly. Passing close to Maddie, he lifts his hand to touch her cropped hair and pulls the mussed strands towards his face for the briefest moment. Maddie jerks back.

"Nice do," he says winking, then follows Warren out the door.

Maddie is rooted to the spot, staring after them.

"Why do you always do that?"

Kate's voice pulls her back into the moment, and Maddie struggles to focus.

"What?"

"I said, why do you always do that?"

"Do what?" Maddie is clenching and unclenching her fists as she tries to calm down.

"Act so stand-offish," Kate replies, "like you're better than everyone else?"

"What?" Maddie doesn't understand.

"Rob's my boyfriend, OK?" Kate says, voice rising a notch. "He doesn't like you. He feels sorry for you."

This conversation is like being in an alternate universe.

"I don't like *Rob*," Maddie replies. "Literally. I don't like him."

"Of course you don't," Kate says. "That's why you come in here with this Goth thing – what is *that* about by the way – and swish your new hair in front of Rob's face, like he is even into that look."

Maddie can't find any words, and Kate goes on.

"That's why you're always giving him looks and hanging around, and that's why you came on to him the night of your party when you knew I liked him. *In my dress, for fuck's sake!*"

"I didn't come on to him!" Maddie's mind is struggling to grasp what Kate is saying.

"I saw you, Maddie," Kate says, shaking her head in disbelief. "Flirting with everyone there and then staggering off to your room like a helpless damsel in distress. That is an old look, by the way. Welcome to the 21st century. You needed everyone to notice you and check that you were OK. I saw Rob coming out of your room, OK? You may as well admit it."

Kate pauses as Maddie feels her face blanche. Her hands fumble for the solid worktop behind her, legs suddenly weak.

"That's right," Kate says, misinterpreting Maddie's reaction. "I know you were so off your head that you came on to him. Tried to get off with him. But Rob wasn't interested in you. He was just being a gentleman. Looking out for you. He's told me the whole story."

Maddie's thoughts will not form themselves into a coherent response, and Kate stands, tossing a triumphant glance in her direction.

"That's right," she goes on. "I know what really happened, so no need to play the innocent party with me. Just back off, OK?"

Kate leaves the kitchen, and Maddie closes her eyes as her breath comes in shallow gasps. She slides to the kitchen floor and rests her head in her hands, waiting for the sickness and dizziness to pass. The words in her head are stuck on repeat, like they are etching themselves into her very core.

*Not Warren.*
*Rob.*
*Not Warren.*
*Rob.*
*Not Warren.*
*Rob.*
*Not Warren.*
*Rob...*

She sits like that with her head in her hands until she is cold and stiff. The chill of the floor creeps ever upwards, past the swirl of life in her belly, up and around her heart and into her head. It slows the frantic race of her thoughts until they are still, like hapless creatures encased in ice.

# Chapter 40

***Will***

Will is sitting at a corner table in the café with his laptop, his back against the wall and his legs stretched out in front of him. He takes a sip from his third coffee of the afternoon and scrolls down the page to read the maths assignment due in by the weekend. School has been sending stuff through for a few weeks now. Engaging his brain has been a bit like jump-starting a temperamental old car that has been stuck in the garage all winter. It is frustrating because he has always been quick to grasp complicated concepts and presumed this was the norm. Now that he is not quite firing on all cylinders, he regrets this casual assumption.

He casts a furtive glance towards the till where Freya is taking orders from the first in a long line of customers. It is a crisp, sunny day, and the bright weather has drawn the locals out of their centrally heated homes and into the shops and cafés. Mostly mums with young kids leaving for the school run now or old people who don't have anything better to do.

*Like you have something better to do?*

The voice inside is familiar, throwing out its usual insults, but half-heartedly now, like it is not quite sure of its purpose anymore.

*Join the club,* Will tells the voice. He feels a spark of kinship with it in the place of the usual antagonism, both trying to find their way.

Freya is holding out a card reader now, and a dour, grey-haired man is fumbling in his pocket for a wallet. He is complaining loudly about the long wait for his food. She listens patiently and, looking up, catches Will's eye. She raises her eyebrow with a small smile. He ducks his head down quickly, cursing the traitorous flush creeping up from under his collar, and pretends to study his laptop.

*Idiot,* the voice says mildly.

He reaches into his bag and pulls out his sketchbook and pens, closing his laptop and pushing it aside for now. It is hard enough concentrating on schoolwork without his brain fixating on Freya.

He has been coming to the café most days for the past couple of weeks. Hardly his usual scene, and, apart from Freya, nobody his age in sight, but it is out of the house and by himself. Will has found this new routine oddly soothing. Today is the third time he has been here when Freya is working. He ordered his coffee from her, words clunky in her presence. Then some chips when he got hungry, nodding mutely when she asked if he wanted any sauces, but other than that has not said a word to her.

He bends low over his sketchbook and scribbles away furiously until a figure forms on the page and his insides feel calm and steady. Freya – arresting even as a two-dimensional line drawing – is spinning plates and smiling serenely while her octopus arms serve a roomful of customers all at once. He captions the image.

*How may I be the brunt of your life's shortcomings today?*

He is so engrossed in his work that he doesn't notice Freya's approach until she is standing right beside him, head tilted as she takes in the drawing. He looks up quickly and, too late, tries to cover the page.

Freya reaches out and pulls the sketchpad from under his arm, a frown creasing her forehead as she takes a closer look.

"Is that supposed to be me?" she asks.

"Um. Well…"

*Speak, idiot.*

He shrugs the voice aside like an irritating friend who can't read the room.

"Yeah," he says finally. "I guess."

She glances over at the till, which is quiet for the moment after the school run rush, and sets down the tray, taking the seat next to him, still looking at the drawing. Will sits up straighter, holding his breath.

Her brown eyes are the first part of her face to smile, crinkling softly around the edges. Then her eyebrows rise, her lips twitch, and finally a laugh, lovely as pebbles tossed in water.

"This is epic," she says, voice low and amused. "You're good."

"Um. Yeah. I mean, thanks!" Will says, hoping the heat in his cheeks is not visible.

She stands, picking up his empty cup and placing it on her tray.

"Want another coffee?" she asks.

"Oh... no," says Will, stuffing his things into his backpack and standing up. "Probably I'd better go. You know. Homework and stuff."

The voice inside doesn't speak, but Will feels it rolling its figurative eyes. He waves it away.

"But... maybe tomorrow?"

Freya rests the tray on one hip, standing just close enough for Will to see the tattoo on her neck clearly from his taller vantage point. Definitely a butterfly. She smells like spring.

"Or a drink tonight?" she asks, like a dare.

"A drink? Tonight? With, um... *you*?"

Freya gives him a look.

"Yes, with me, idiot. The Anchor? Eight o'clock?"

Will feels something like happiness bloom in his chest and finds himself smiling at her as he swings his backpack over his shoulder.

"Yes," he says. "Eight o'clock."

\*

As nervous as Will feels when he walks to the Anchor later that evening, conversation with Freya comes easily, like an old friend. She left school last summer and is working as many jobs as she can so that she can go travelling next year. Will feels a longing inside for the freedom she is describing.

"The world is going to open up, Will," she tells him over their second drink. "I know it. People are starting to move again, and I for one am not going to let this Covid shit set me back anymore."

Will finds himself leaning in and drinking in every word that Freya says, possibility inching into his soul as she describes the countries she will visit and the things she will do. After two long years of doors closing and his world shrinking down to nothing, her dreams are like a drug more potent than anything he's ever taken.

"You should come..." she says, reaching out and holding his hand in both of hers.

Even as his mind leaps at the idea and his body responds to her nearness and physical touch, he feels the fragile possibility within stutter to an uncertain halt.

"I can't," he says, his response automatic. Feeling trapped is all he knows, and there is a certain safety in its stifling familiarity.

Freya leans back and stretches out her legs until both her feet rest on his.

"You can," she says.

Freya is an only child and lives alone with her mum. Her dad *buggered off when I was two feet high,* leaving just the two of them to do life together. Freya has no issue standing out from the crowd and seems immune to all the expectations piled on kids their age. Will envies her confidence and the easy relationship she has with her mother. He tells Freya about his own family. About the state they're in. Dad told him about Maddie after going to see her at home, and Will is still struggling to take it in. Drug-raped on her birthday. God. That's so messed up. His thoughts touch on Mum and what she did, then scurry back like the receding tide. He feels so guilty that Maddie went through all of that on her own, yet he was the idiot who ended up in hospital after an overdose. The psychologist guy who saw him in the hospital told him that beating himself up with a big stick wasn't helping. That he might want to try another way of looking at things.

*Easy for him to say,* thought Will at the time. *He doesn't have to live in my head.*

But the psychologist's words stuck with him and, eventually, Will had found the courage to text Maddie.

*u ok sis?*

She'd texted back later that evening.

*yeah u?*

Will didn't answer her question, just said,

*dad told me*

There was a long gap before she replied.

*shit show huh?*

Will took a long time to select the correct emoji and settled for the face with the straight mouth.

*the biggest*

He hesitated for a moment longer, and on impulse, sent a green heart.

*xxx,* Maddie replied.

It takes another week and three more dates before Will tells Freya the truth about himself. About the drugs and what he did. He can't tell her in the crowded pubs and cafés, where sitting face to face across a table feels too confronting. What will he do if he sees disgust on her face? If she stands up and walks out, leaving him alone?

He tells her on a walk instead. They put on trainers and coats and walk out of Storrington one frosty February day until they reach the foot of the South Downs and start to climb. They are both puffing and rosy cheeked by the time they reach the top and stand looking out over the Sussex countryside rolling away to the north and the south. When they have captured their breath, they turn right onto the South Downs Way, which winds a westerly course for miles. Will wants to take Freya's hand – he kissed her for the first time the night before and has been able to think of little else – but he holds back, afraid she will snatch her hand away when she knows.

"I'm not here, living with Dad, because of what Mum did," says Will, fixing his eyes on the path ahead and skirting round the ruts of puddled ice underfoot.

Freya glances over at him and keeps walking.

"I'm here because of something I did. Something really stupid."

The sound of the wind whistling over the tops of the Downs fills the space between them.

"After lockdown," Will begins, "when I was in Chichester, I was in a bad place. I started smoking weed. Taking pills. Bunking off school..."

He risks a glance over at Freya but cannot read her.

"I found out about Mum, my dad..."

He glosses over Ros's place in the story. For now.

"I hated everything that I used to love."

Freya's gloved hand reaches for his, and Will's throat tightens.

"I didn't want to deal with all that shit anymore," he says, his voice tight. "So, I took a whole load of pills. An overdose. I almost died."

Freya squeezes his hand.

Tight.

She doesn't let go.

# Chapter 41

***John***

As the frozen brown and grey days of February merge one into another in their sluggish march towards spring, John's work picks up pace. His inbox fills up with queries from a mix of regular customers and word-of-mouth new names wanting to ready their gardens for the warmer days ahead. His diary is packed solid for the next six weeks at least, and he is struggling to keep up.

Normally this level of demand imbues John with satisfied well-being, his days marked out with the certainty of night following day. This year, he cannot grasp his usual quiet peace. He is not as young as he used to be for starters, and digging the solid ground invites an ache into his back and shoulders that never quite leaves him. But John knows this isn't the real reason for his disquiet. Each day of this new year takes him further and further away from the life that he knew just a few short months ago. For the first time since he was a boy, he feels utterly lost.

As he sits in his brother's conservatory in the early evening twilight, answering two new enquiries that have come in today, a deep sigh escapes him. Will is on his laptop in the corner of the room and looks up.

"Alright, Dad?" he asks.

Despite the heaviness which bows his head and shoulders, John smiles at his son. Will venturing out of Will's world long enough to engage with how John might be feeling is like a way marker for the adult relationship ahead of them.

"I'm OK," John replies, taking off his reading glasses and rubbing at his eyes. "Just busy with work. And tired."

He replaces the glasses and returns his attention to his inbox.

"I could help."

John looks up again and regards Will. He can see the little boy in his son's return gaze, a mix of defiance and determination. He considers Will's request for a moment, remembering all the times his son accompanied him to a job in the past few years, mute with adolescent outrage at the injustice of it.

"I could use an extra pair of hands," he replies slowly. "You'll have to work long days."

Will shrugs, like this is of no consequence to him.

"I need the money," he replies.

John stifles his smile as adolescent Will makes a return appearance.

"I'll pay you minimum wage," he offers.

Will considers this for a moment, then nods.

"Deal," he says.

"What about school?"

Will shrugs.

"I'm ahead with the work. And next week is half-term anyway."

John nods his head slowly.

"OK, then," he says. "Deal."

*

He takes Will with him the following week. He has a job in Amberley with the new neighbour of a long-standing client who has bought his picturesque thatched cottage on a whim but was quickly overwhelmed by the neglected garden. John gives a long whistle as they pass along the side of the cottage and emerge out back through an ancient wooden side gate, so low they both duck to pass through. He takes in the tangle of winter debris sprawling over borders and almost completely covering the crazy-paved path winding away into overgrown shrubbery. A post with an old bird's house atop it leans at an angle in a battle with gravity. John can just see the remnants of a bird's nest in its dark interior, its occupant long departed for warmer climes.

"Bloody hell," Will mutters as the garden's owner retreats into the warmth of the cottage to make tea. "What exactly are we supposed to do with this?"

John smiles at the familiar note of reluctance in Will's voice.

"It's a big job," he agrees, taking it in. "Enough to keep us busy all week."

Will sighs.

"What we're supposed to do," John adds, "is one small thing at a time."

Will throws him a look.

"Let's call an amnesty on empowering dad-talk," he says.

John smiles and nods as he tosses the keys of his van to Will. "We're going to need the big garden bags, spades, garden forks and shears," he says. "Think you can manage that?"

Will catches the keys.

"Please," he says, turning around and bending low back through the gate.

During the morning, John shows Will how to recognise and clear away last summer's growth, gently pulling away the brown-beige tangle of dead stems and seedheads to reveal small pockets of early spring colour where tiny snowdrops and yellow aconites emerge, heralding the change of season. He teaches him how to trim the side shoots from the old, twisted branches of wisteria winding their way up and over a rusted pergola, each to three buds from the base.

"Won't cutting off so much kill it?" Will asks, a crease of concentration across his face as he counts the tiny buds and fumbles with the small secateurs.

"No," John says, pointing him to the next clump of offshoots. "Just the opposite. Cutting it back encourages more flowers in spring. You'll see."

"Hmmmphh," Will mutters, leaning in and snipping away a long shoot. "Looks dead to me."

By the end of the morning, they have filled half a dozen big green gardening bags so full that they can only just lug them through the wooden gate and to the van. Once they have loaded everything into the back, they sit together in the front seats, eating the doorstop ham sandwiches Sue has prepared for their lunch. Warm air from the heater and music from the radio swill around them like comfort. The morning's exertions have replaced the winter pallor of Will's face with a ruddy flush of colour. Will senses John looking and turns towards him, smiling wide and clear in an unguarded moment.

John feels something hitch in his throat and looks down at his own lunch, gathering himself. How is it, he wonders, that in all those years when the fact of his fatherhood was never in question, the two of them struggled to connect, pushing one another away like the matching poles of a magnet? Now that being Will's dad is more privilege than given, it is like he has flipped, or Will has flipped, their opposite poles seeking one another out and connecting as naturally as physics.

"I'm thinking about what's next," John begins, looking ahead now through the windscreen starting to blur with fine rain.

Will nods thoughtfully beside him, squashing the foil sandwich packaging into a ball. He rolls it between his hands to smooth out its crumpled edges.

"I'm thinking it's probably time for me to find my own place," John continues. "To give Andy and Sue their house back."

Will is silent for a long moment, the foil ball growing smaller and more compact in his hands.

"So, you're not going to go home?" he asks at last. "Back to Mum?"

Now it is John's turn to be silent. Will's question gives shape to the wrestle that has been battling inside ever since he walked out their front door two and a half months ago.

"No," he replies slowly. As he says the words out loud, he knows this is the right decision. The sadness and regret over his split from Hope is an easier fit than the taut anxiety and watchfulness of returning to how things were before. "I don't think that I am."

He sees the crumple of Will's face, the little boy in him battling it out with the indifferent adolescent. The little boy wins and Will's voice is small. He tosses the foil ball into the footwell as he speaks.

"I thought you would go back," he says. "I thought… *we* would go back."

John reaches out and places his earth-covered hand over Will's. A man's hand, he thinks. Not a boy's hand anymore.

"You can go back, Will," he says gently. "It has never stopped being your home."

"But I don't want to go back without you."

A tear snakes its way down Will's cheek, and he swipes it away, wiping his nose with his fist like a child. John doesn't have an answer for this.

"I know," he says and squeezes Will's hand, his own heart contracting so tightly that it's hard to push the words out into the space between them. "I know."

It is late when the call from Ros comes later that night. John, normally fast asleep by this hour, is sitting alone in the darkened conservatory, nursing a single malt and staring quietly into the inky darkness through the window. Everyone else went to bed over an hour ago, and he is grateful for the quiet space. After talking to Will, they had returned to the jumble of the thatched cottage garden, working side by side until dusk. They cleared, cut and swept away the cumulation of months, probably years, of old growth, its only purpose now to insulate the tender shoots of a new spring. The reality of John's 'what's next' spoken out and painful as a new wound drove and accelerated their work. When the owner of the cottage came out, bearing the final tray of steaming mugs and a plateful of gingerbread as they finished, he could not contain his surprise at their progress. He was an older man, bird-like and hunched like a question mark, but his eyes held a lively sparkle.

"Well," he said, over and over, handing the tea to Will first and then John. "Who would have thought there was so much life hidden under all of that dead mess? Who would have thought it?"

The hard labour had a cathartic quality, and Will and John drove home in tired but easy silence. When John opened his browser later that evening after dinner, and found Rightmove and then Zoopla, scrolling through flats and bedsits for rent in the Chichester area, he felt, not peaceful exactly, but still. The back-and-forth shimmy of shock and indecision and wild, wordless rage had calmed. For the moment.

He starts when his phone rings. He hasn't switched the ringer to silent since the day Will overdosed, afraid of missing something vital, something urgent. Ros's name comes up on his screen and John frowns. It is 11.15pm, too late for a social call. He swipes the screen and lifts the phone to his ear.

"Ros?" he asks, feeling the slow beat of his heart gain pace as he sets his whisky on the side table.

"John!" Ros's voice is breathless. "You're in!"

"Yes..." he draws out the word, wondering what this is about.

"I know who it is," she says. It sounds like she is walking somewhere quickly.

"Who what is?" John is confused. "Ros, where are you?"

"In Brighton!" she answers impatiently, like it is obvious. "Who *he* is," she says. "The man who attacked Maddie."

John sits up straighter in his chair.

"Who?" he asks, fumbling his words, struggling to order his thoughts. "How? I mean, are you sure? What are you doing in Brighton? Why are you calling so late? Is Maddie OK?"

Ros cuts him off, hurrying him to the point.

"You need to come," she says.

"To Brighton?" John doesn't understand.

"Yes, to Brighton! John… I know who hurt Maddie and you and I are going to do something about it. Are you coming or not?"

Ros's words finally find their mark, landing in the painful place where dads are supposed to protect their little girls and keep them safe. In that place where dads make sure that bad things don't happen. He didn't, and they did. The decision, when he speaks it, comes easily.

"Yes," he says, voice steady. "When?"

# Chapter 42

**Me**

*The optimal age for playing with a doll's house is three to nine. By the time a child reaches three years old, they can create their own family stories, the more far-fetched the better. Between six and nine, their world-building reaches its peak, and Barbie and Ken might even make a guest appearance. Then come the pre-teen and teen years when doll's house play first dwindles, then goes underground before disappearing altogether.*

*When you are not privy to the freedom of childhood and pretending has always been more about survival than play, perhaps you can understand why you were 18 years old when you played with your first doll's house, 22 when your grown-up self told you to stop playing and grow up, and 30 when being grown up lost its shine. What do you do then? I'll tell you. You blow the dust away from your old doll's house and you make a life out of it.*

\*

After that awful 18th birthday party weekend, when Ros left our lives for good, or so I thought, and when that first flutter of life that was Will grew until I was no longer enough and he made his squalling appearance into the world, I gave centre-stage passes to the part of me that forgets. I buried my past and Will's start as deeply as they would go and threw myself into the invented role of John's wife and Will and Maddie's mother.

It worked for a while. It did. For a time, our Victorian terrace was filled with love and fights and shrieks of laughter. I made it my personal mission to give my children the childhood I'd been denied. Safe and protected. The way John always made me feel. As the years passed by, I could hardly believe this was my life.

*Because it isn't,* the parts of me inside had whispered, the ones who didn't forget and who guarded all my secrets and kept them in check. The parts who were getting tired of their thankless job and threatening to strike.

*You are just playing house.*

\*

The house is too quiet and empty, and I find myself pacing the ground floor most evenings, restlessly prowling from one quiet corner to another and feeling the absence of each member of my family even more keenly than I'd felt their presence. Even Ros with her meddling and mess would be better than this endless silence, now that the fiery energy of my anger has receded and cooled into something gentler. I find myself lingering longest in the loft bedroom that I shared with John for two decades. He has taken a lot of his stuff to his brother's place, slipping home while I am at work, separating further the detritus of our lives together with each quiet visit. I talk to Will and Maddie most days, forging tenuous new connections into their complicated lives with each conversation, but John is not answering my calls or texts, and his continued absence is shocking.

I reach into our shared wardrobe. John's summer clothes are still here between empty winter hangers, and I pull a light grey jumper towards me, holding it to my face and inhaling John's scent like an addict. I close my eyes and imagine it is him I am holding. The relief of secrets revealed which carried me through our first weeks of being apart has seeped away like water down a drain, leaving a chilled and empty space behind.

In the topsy-turvy reality of my life as it is now, the shop, which has always been my sanctuary, no longer has the power to pull me into its comforting fantasy world. Home has become the place that draws me and holds me, even without the main players in place. I have been going through the motions at work, delivering workshops, ordering stock, talking to customers and cashing up each evening, but for the first time in a decade my heart isn't in it. I have seen Fran noticing and have smiled my reassurance in her direction, but she isn't fooled and we both know it.

"Why don't you take some time out, Hope?" she asks one afternoon as weak winter sunshine arcs through the window from where it hangs low in the sky, like climbing any higher would be too much effort. I am going through a box of miniature fine china sets that need to go out onto the shop floor, but I keep losing track of what I am doing, and my hands haven't moved for a good five minutes, maybe ten. Fran lays her own hand, cool and papery soft over mine, and holds out a mug of Carlos' coffee with the other. The rich aroma swirls up and awakens the present me, so that I can focus on Fran for a moment and smile.

"Thanks," I say, taking the mug and bringing it gratefully to my mouth, inhaling and then sipping at the rich, hot coffee. "I'm fine."

I set the mug down and try to refocus on the box of china.

"You're not," says Fran. It is a statement. Fact.

I sigh deeply and turn my back on the task, picking up and cradling the coffee. I lean heavily on the shelf behind me.

"I'm not," I finally agree. "But what else am I supposed to do?"

"Go to your family," she says. "Be there for them."

I think of Fran's family. Her husband, who died five years ago. Her only son emigrated to Australia soon after and settled there. She is all alone.

"How do you do it?" I ask, ashamed that I have never really thought to ask before, too engrossed in my own family dramas, in holding all my secrets and demons at bay.

"Do what?" she asks.

"Do what you have to do. Live. Be at peace… You've lost so much, and I have never heard you complain. You are so brave. How do you do it?"

Fran smiles, her eyes crinkling along the edges as she considers my questions.

"I don't think of myself as brave," she says thoughtfully. "I just do what I have to do. Get up. Put one foot in front of the other. Find the things in life that bring me moments of joy and weave as many of those moments together as I can. Sometimes they are all around me – those are the good days. And sometimes they are nowhere to be found. But that is OK. I've been around long enough to know that nothing ever stays the same. Not the good times, but not the bad ones, either."

I think about her words as I look back and realise that even the very worst times, the times that I can hardly bear to glimpse, came to pass. Life carried me forward into my role of Hope the wife, the mother. I have been here, in this story, since everything that happened before, for more than 20 years and have almost sleep-walked through it. All my energy has been focused on holding my past at bay, like it is a wild animal ready to pounce and steal all that is good away. I feel a sudden rush of loss at how things could have been, how I could have been, the freedom I could have grasped and run with all this time.

"I'm not like you," I whisper to Fran, ashamed. "I think it might be too late."

"Hope."

I can't bring myself to look at Fran. I am so weak compared to her.

"The other thing I have learned is that it is never too late," she says. "Not while there is life. Your John… go to him. You can make that choice."

I nod, feeling the pull of her words, considering the prospect of having a choice and turning it over and over in my mind. It is a concept as tantalising as it is foreign. I realise that I have always considered myself to be helpless, a victim of circumstance tossed on the white-tipped waves of other people's choices.

*You can choose.*

\*

I take that thought to my counsellor later in the week. It is the fourth time we have met, and the tension that grips me whenever I arrive is lessening, settling around my edges like it is my last line of defense. Even so, I perch on the chair in her room, ramrod straight, hands clasped tightly on my lap as I try to present the together version of myself. It is harder than it sounds. As each fact of my previous existence bubbles to the surface and lands between us, the relief of release is quickly overpowered by the raw pain of the newly exposed space inside. All the parts of me that have found a way to keep me standing over the years have been quick to jump into the breach, redoubling their efforts to hold the pain at bay. After the first session, I retreated to my empty house and slept for 15 hours straight, only hauling myself out from the cocoon of my duvet because the cat needed to be fed and there was nobody else to do it. The urge to cut myself and open old scars that day had been almost intolerable. It took everything in me to drag myself back to the next session.

"It's making things worse!" I told my counsellor, Helen, in the next session. "I can't do this."

Helen regarded me for a moment, waiting. She was my age, short-haired and ordinary aside from kind grey eyes and an air of stillness that settled the buzzing inside me.

"Can't do…?" she prompted gently.

"This!" I swept my arm around the room, taking in its muted beige walls, the mindful nature prints and the box of tissues, carefully placed to remain unobtrusive. I pushed the box away and glared at it. "Talking about… everything. I thought this was supposed to help."

Helen took this in.

"It's not unusual," she said, "for things to feel harder before they feel better."

I nodded briskly, still angry, unsure I'd signed up for harder.

"Your system is responding exactly as it should," she said. "It is protecting you. Doing the amazing job it always has."

I frowned. Stuck in bed and cutting myself didn't sound all that amazing to me. Weak. That is how I would describe it. Crap. Failing.

"Let's see if we can get to know the parts of you that protect," Helen continued. "Would they be willing to let us try?"

It was an odd request, but something inside me felt curious, despite myself. Helen saw me in a whole different light, like I was good. Like the things I did were not bad. She acted like I was heroic. She actually used that word. *Heroic*. I felt sick when she first said it. I knew she was wrong. But slowly, slowly I began to talk, cautiously diving down beneath the surface of my story, testing the waters and the trustworthiness of this stranger.

Today I don't want to talk about my stuff, my past. I need a break from all that. It is one of the things I like about Helen. She isn't pushy. She lets me choose. Today I want to talk about John. About the day we met. How he is, or was, with me, and how he still is with Will and Maddie. Loss weighs heavily in my chest as I paint the picture of this man who has been a rock for us all. How have I messed it all up so badly? Helen lets me weep.

I am interrupted by the bleep of my phone. I fumble in my bag to find it and mute it, apologising and holding a damp tissue to my nose. I see a message from Maddie.

"Sorry," I say. "Can I just…?"

Helen nods and waves for me to continue.

*mum – herb says ros in brighton. gone off 2 find HIM. she has it all wrong. nt answering phone. dk what 2 do.*

I sit up straight in my chair and grapple with this jumble of information. Ros going after... *him?* I didn't realise we even knew who *he* was. Helen tips her head, concern on her face.

"Um..." I say, speaking at the same time as I quickly text a reply to Maddie. "I think I have to go."

# Chapter 43

**Ros**

Leaving the country and setting off to God knows where with just a backpack and no ties was better than any chemical high Ros had ever experienced. Nowhere to go. Nothing to do. Nobody to care about. Nobody to tell her everything she was doing wrong. She had never felt so free. If there was a heaven, then this was it. The high stayed with her for more than three years as she moved from one place to another, picking up casual work and even more casual hook-ups along the way, never settling for longer than a few weeks in any one spot.

After a summer spent partying in Ios, Ros decided to put down shallow roots, waiting tables at a British-run bar near Mylopotas beach, whiling away the months until Covid hit in March 2020 and Greece went into a strict, 42-day lockdown. Stuck in one place with a redundant job and the same people around her day in and day out filled Ros with a restless panic. As restrictions eased with the approach of summer, she fled the island like a cork released from a bottle, leaving behind half her belongings, an unmade hostel bed, and a bemused lover called Dimitris.

It wasn't the same after that, the sparkle of freedom dulled by time and the ever-looming threat of Covid. When Ros eventually made her way back to the UK, isolation nagging at her heels, she found herself googling Hope, finding local write ups about Teatime Miniatures, and checking that Hope still lived where she always had. An idea began to form, tugging this way then that by the mixture of love and hate Ros felt whenever she thought about her foster sister. She was not sure which side won out, but Ros had made up her mind. She would find Hope. And she would be a part of her life again. Whatever it took.

\*

Ros knows Warren's haunts. Knows what he likes to drink and which girls are his type. Blonde, leggy ones with straightened hair, over-plumped lips and look-at-me eyes framed with long, spidery lashes. Nothing like Maddie, but still. She knows when he goes out in the morning, and the shared flat near the station where he lives with Rob and the other knobs they call friends. She has been following him for days now, waiting for him to slip up and show his true colours. A bastard like him can't hold out forever. It is Saturday afternoon, and she feels in her gut that this weekend will be the one.

The call to John last night had been an impulse, a mustering of forces before advancing on the enemy. She is not quite sure how she feels about needing his help, but part of her, that 12-year-old who once upon a time could only freeze on the spot for the dickhead, is relieved to have backup. This dickhead is going nowhere.

Ros's hand reaches for the phone in her pocket, instinctively checking the screen which is blank and silent. After calling John last night, she switched it off, ignoring the missed calls and messages from Maddie, who knows she has been following Warren. Herb told her. Ros will talk to Maddie later. Not now. Maddie is frozen and scared, like Ros was once. She doesn't know what is best for her, what needs to happen, and she needs someone like Ros to take charge. Ros is doing this for Maddie.

She checks the time, prowling up and down the busying promenade to the west of the pier, impatiently waiting for John to arrive at their pre-arranged meeting spot. Half an hour later she is rewarded by the sight of his tall form navigating his way across the busy A259, clogged with stop-start traffic. His muddy work boots and heavy jacket look out of place amongst the weekend crowds, but the look on his face is determined.

He reaches her side, resting a hand lightly on her shoulder as he leans in to kiss the air by her ear. There is an energy about him that makes Ros take stock and reach out her own hand to lay it on his arm.

"OK?" she asks, scanning his face.

"Yes," John answers, falling into step beside Ros as they walk away from the pier, the shush of waves on the stony beach cushioning the sound of their steps.

"Talk to me, Ros," John says. "Tell me everything."

Ros does. She tells him about Herb's detective work, printing out the photos and going through them one by one with Maddie and Ella, talking and working out who it wasn't and who it could have been. She tells him about Warren, creepy and always hanging around Maddie's flat with that knobhead Rob and his girlfriend Kate.

"Kate is Maddie's friend," Ros explains. "Or at least she's meant to be. Personally, I think Maddie should kick her to the curb after bringing Warren into the picture."

John is taking it all in, brow furrowed as he examines the photo Ros hands him of Warren with Rob and Kate.

"But Ros," he asks after studying it for a moment and mulling over everything she has just said. "How do you know it is this guy, Warren?"

John hesitates before saying Warren's name, lip curling.

"Maddie just knows," says Ros. "A woman knows."

John looks like he is about to say something else, but Ros cuts him off. "I know where he is hanging out with his friends tonight," she says. "We don't have to do anything, OK? Just come with me and watch. You'll see what a dickhead he is, and we can decide our next steps then."

She holds her breath and thinks John will refuse, but he drops his gaze back to the picture in his hand, and something in his face hardens.

"OK," he says. "What time and where?"

*

They position themselves at the far end of the bar in Danny O'Toole's in the North Laine, an Irish pub popular with students. Herb told Ros that Warren and a load of his friends were meeting up there tonight for drinks. Kate was apparently pissed off because she wasn't invited.

Ros signals to the barman for another drink, struggling to capture his attention. Live music is starting in an hour or so and the place is already heaving. John has managed to make his pint last while they have been waiting, but Ros is too tense to sip slowly. *Where the hell are they?* Herb swore they would be here.

The pub continues to fill up, and just as Ros despairs of spotting Warren, she suddenly sees him pushing his way towards the bar with Rob, and, surprise, surprise, two girls trailing behind. Not Kate. One of them is

Warren's trademark blonde, laughing and talking loudly to the friend behind her who is darker, quieter. Ros wonders if they are students too.

She nudges John.

"There," she hisses, gesturing towards the four of them with a tip of her head. "That's him."

John's eyes narrow as he watches Warren flag down the barman and order a round of drinks. She feels a shiver at the look on his face, sizing up the man who hurt his daughter. Ros places a steadying hand on his arm. She has a feeling about tonight.

"Wait," she says.

So, they wait. And they watch, never taking their eyes off Warren and the blonde girl he is with as they quickly down the first round and order another. The band sets up and starts to play.

As the night wears on, Ros wonders if her radar is off. Warren is behaving like a plonker, that goes without saying. He is too handy with the blonde girl who is jigging to the music, leaning on him and laughing, shouting something into his ear. What does she see in him, Ros wonders, signaling for more drinks for her and John, never taking her eyes off Warren and his group. As she waits for the barman to fill their glasses, Ros notices Rob getting in another round and sees him glance furtively from side to side in the crowded space before reaching into his pocket and quickly cupping a hand over the cocktail. Ros leans forward and stares at him, forgetting for a moment that she is meant to be being subtle. John notices her sharpened attention.

"What is it?" he asks.

"Shhhhh..." she waves him off, concentrating. She watches Rob hand the drinks out. A pint for himself and Warren, the glass of red wine for the blonde girl, and the cocktail for the dark-haired girl who is with him. Ros has barely noticed her up until now. She is smaller and more reserved than her friend, and all Ros's attention has been focused on Warren.

"I think he's just slipped something into her drink," Ros says.

"Warren has put something in her drink?" John repeats.

"No! Not Warren. Rob..." Ros's voice trails off as she tries to make sense of this new information.

"Well, we need to go over there now," says John, putting down his drink and standing.

243

"No! Wait," Ros's mind is working furiously now. "Just wait for a minute."

She sees John's confusion, his need to act.

"She is safe for the moment," Ros says, reassuring him. "She's in here. With all of us. We won't let her go anywhere alone. Just wait. For half an hour. To be sure."

John takes in Ros's words and makes a visible effort to rein himself in. He nods once. Shortly.

"Half an hour," he says, sitting down, his gaze never leaving the dark-haired girl.

The band takes a break after their first set, the sudden drop in volume amplifying the buzz of voices and laughter all around them. The blonde girl is now sitting on Warren's lap, the two of them completely engrossed in one another.

"Get a room," Ros mutters under her breath, straining to see round them to where Rob and the dark-haired girl are sitting. The girl leans forward and rests her head on the bar before stumbling to her feet, wobbly and holding on to the back of her chair.

"Whoah..." Ros sees rather than hears Rob say as he stands with the girl and takes her by the arm. Ros's heart starts to yammer, a mix of rage and old fear coursing through her as the two of them walk unsteadily towards the ladies and the back exit. Rob supports the girl with one arm round her waist, the other gripping her arm.

She and John exchange glances.

"Now," he says, and Ros nods.

They get to their feet and push through the crowd as Rob and the girl disappear out the door.

"Get out of *the way*," Ros hisses, pushing past tightly packed groups of people crammed together buying drinks before the music starts again.

"Calm down, love!" a voice behind her says as she pushes past. She senses John's presence close behind her, equally impatient to reach Rob and the girl.

"She's not your *love*," he says, shoving the protester aside and clearing the pathway before them. "Come on."

He and Ros reach the exit and step into the corridor, empty and muted after the hubbub of the bar.

*Where are they?*

Ros looks frantically from side to side.

"I'll check the ladies," she says to John. "You check the gents."

Half a moment later, they are both back in the empty corridor.

"Not here!" Ros's voice scales high in panic.

"This way," John says, gesturing to the heavy back door beneath the glow of the green fire exit sign. He leads the way and pushes through the door and into the alleyway behind the pub. He looks first to the left, then to the right. Ros pushes impatiently behind him.

"There!" she cries at the same time as John runs suddenly to the right, barrelling into Rob and pulling him roughly away from the dark-haired girl, who slumps to the ground in slow motion. Ros hurries to the girl, crouching down beside her and wrapping her own coat around the girl's exposed shoulders. Her head is lolling, eyes vacant. Ros pulls her in, holding her tightly, and looks at John.

Gentle, steady John. Now towering over Rob, pinning him to the wall with one arm across his chest, the other holding his throat. She watches John lean in harder, breathing heavily until Rob's eyes bulge. Ros pulls herself to her feet, holding the girl against her, and reaches out a hand to grab John. He glances over at her, eyes wild and unfocused.

"John," Ros says. Then repeats herself, more urgently this time. "*John…*"

She sees the moment her voice and touch break through and watches the John she knows slide back into his shadowed features. He steps back, easing the pressure just enough for Rob to draw breath.

Ros watches as he leans in close, his face inches from Rob's.

"You worthless pile of shit!" John snarls, his voice low and dangerous. "You had better start talking."

# Chapter 44

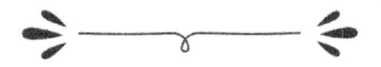

**_Maddie_**

Mum, Dad and Ros are all here. Maddie observes the strange tableau of the four of them, out of place in this trendy Brighton café. This whole place was supposed to launch her into a new life and adulthood, and held such promise six months ago. Today Maddie is grateful to be sitting in their warm close circle, sipping frothy hot drinks and peering through the fogged windows at the twisty lanes outside. She supposes she has been launched into adulthood. Just not the version she would have chosen.

"The police arrested him last night," Dad is saying after telling Maddie everything that they witnessed in Danny O'Toole's. "We called them from the pub."

The girl, Holly, was taken to hospital. They will have done tests, Maddie thinks, to see what Rob gave her. Maddie imagines Holly now, probably sick and confused, wondering what she did or didn't do to make all of this happen.

"I told the police what I saw that bastard do," says Ros, grim satisfaction on her face. "I can't believe I didn't realise it was him. The sick wanker."

Mum is quiet, sitting next to Maddie and holding her hand. Maddie leans her head on Mum's shoulder.

"With your evidence," Ros continues, "he won't stand a chance. That loser will be put away for years."

Maddie closes her eyes and takes a deep breath, leaning more closely into her mother. She doesn't open them as Ros keeps talking.

"Did you hear me, Maddie? With your evidence that..."

"I heard you." Maddie breaks in, cutting her off.

"So..."

"I'm not giving evidence," she says quietly.

At first, Ros doesn't hear, picturing out loud the justice due to be meted out to Rob, describing the rubble of his life when it is all over. But then Maddie's words land like the delayed crack of a gunshot.

"What?"

"I said, I'm not giving evidence," she repeats. "I'm not reporting."

"But... but we've already told the police. Me and your dad. We told them about you."

"I know," Maddie says, keeping her voice low, feeling Mum's hand squeeze hers more tightly and Dad's gaze on her. "I know *you* told them. But *I* am not going to press charges."

"Why? *Why?*"

Ros looks like she is going to jump to her feet and march Maddie to the police station herself.

"Why wouldn't you give evidence? For God's sake, Maddie, *we've got him!*"

Why isn't she giving evidence, Maddie wonders? Why, ever since she discovered it was Rob who spiked her drink, who raped her in her sleep, who left her pregnant and alone, has she known that she would not be pursuing a charge?

She reaches out a hand across the table to Ros, knowing at some level that it is Ros who is hurting and all alone. It is Ros who needs comfort and justice. More than Maddie. Ros snatches her hand away and glares at Maddie.

"Thank you, Ros," she says simply. "For everything you've done. For caring enough to... to... get to the truth. For saving Holly. I am truly grateful, and Rob won't get away with it."

"He didn't even do anything to Holly," Ros shouts. "We got there before he raped her! He'll probably get off with a bloody slap on the wrist!"

"Drink spiking carries a prison term of up to ten years," Dad says quietly, already aware of Maddie's decision after an earlier walk on the beach. "The police have all they need."

"It's not enough!" Ros shouts. "It's not enough!" She bangs the table with a clenched fist and their mugs rattle. Other customers glance quickly in their direction, then away again.

"I'm sorry, Ros," Maddie says, reaching out again. "But this is my choice. I have been thinking about it, and I don't want the rest of my time at uni or any more of my life to be linked to that man. Even if it gets to court, it could take years. And I can't prove what happened that night. He could still get off. Can you understand that?"

Ros doesn't speak, shaking her head and springing to her feet.

"He took away my choice," Maddie continues calmly. "But now I am taking it back."

*

Maddie is back on campus later that day, gathering books for a tutorial. She promised to meet up with Mum and Dad later. Ros has gone off somewhere, unable to get her head around Maddie's decision. Maddie is sad for her, understands even. But she doesn't have capacity to follow Ros down her rabbit hole right now. As Maddie closes her door behind her, hoisting her heavy bag higher on her shoulder, she passes Kate's closed door and pauses, wondering how the other girl is doing after all that transpired last night. She probably isn't even here. After a moment's hesitation, Maddie lifts her hand and raps once, twice, on Kate's door. She can hear voices inside.

"Kate?" she calls through the door. "It's Maddie. Are you... are you OK?"

There is a shuffling sound on the other side of the door, then Kate opens it a crack. Her eyes are red and puffy, face pale. Her usually immaculate long hair is pushed limply behind her ears.

"Kate?" Maddie is alarmed at the sight of her. "I just wanted to check if..."

"If I'm *OK?*" Kate interrupts bitterly. "After that crazy stunt your family pulled last night?"

Maddie opens her mouth to reply, but Kate keeps on talking.

"Accusing *my boyfriend* of spiking a girl's drink and... and *attacking her?*"

Maddie becomes aware of movement in the room, and then Kate's door swings open further. She sees Rob, standing just behind Kate, more disheveled than usual, but smug, his hand resting possessively on her back. Maddie takes an involuntary step back, crossing her arms over her chest.

"Surprised to see me?" Rob says, mouth curling into an arrogant smile.

Maddie's heart is hammering as she looks at him and imagines his hands on her, on Holly last night, and who knows how many other women in between. She thinks of his lies curling upwards, deadly as a snake. She drops her arms, steadying first her breathing and then her heart as she lifts her chin and holds his gaze. His snake charming won't work on her. Not now.

"I know what you did," she says softly.

He opens his eyes in exaggerated confusion, looking first at Kate and then back at Maddie.

"What I *did*?" he repeats, forehead wrinkled in feigned innocence.

"I know you raped me," says Maddie.

"Maddie, what the fu…" Kate starts to say, but Rob cuts her off.

"Raped you?" he sneers, stepping forward and getting into Maddie's space. "You wish, you lying bitch."

Kate gasps and cranes her neck to see round Rob, to take in the sight of Maddie, trembling but holding her ground.

"That night," she continues. "Fifth of October. You drugged me. You came to my room. You raped me. And then you told your girlfriend that I came on to you. That you had to fight *me* off."

Rob laughs now, draping an arm over Kate who is standing next to him now, speechless and stiff as a board.

"You are a fantasist," he says, pulling Kate close.

"Am I?" Maddie asks quietly.

"You have no proof."

Maddie smiles.

"Ah yes," she says. "Proof."

With exaggerated care, Maddie unbuttons her oversized coat, shifting the bag higher on her shoulder. Then she turns to the side and runs her hands slowly and deliberately over the now clearly visible swell of her stomach. She watches as Rob's smile slips. Understanding percolates through Kate's denial and she steps abruptly away from Rob.

"I have all the proof I need, you arrogant prick."

\*

It is a week later, and Mum and Dad are back in Brighton with Maddie, walking with her along the stony beach between the town centre and the marina. The frigid winter has given way to one unseasonable day of warmth, and Maddie is breathing hard and sweating as her feet sink into the stones with every step. She carries her long black coat over her arm, the lighter clothing she wears underneath clinging to her rounded belly. She stops walking, tired suddenly, and plonks herself down on the stones, facing the silvery blue glitter of the sea. A fresh breeze lifts her bobbed hair lightly off her neck, and Maddie closes her eyes and enjoys the cool refreshment it brings. Mum and Dad sit down too, one on each side of her. Maddie feels a wave of sadness at the distance between her parents. She can't believe they are not together.

"Thank you both for coming back," she says at last, the formality of her words feeling odd. But which part of this picture isn't odd, Maddie thinks? They are all of them in uncharted territory.

"I wanted to talk to you. Together. About my decision."

Dad nods, and Mum speaks.

"We know. About your decision not to report," says Mum. "And that's fine with us. Whatever is right for you. That's all we want," she adds.

Maddie shakes her head. This is not what she wants to talk about. As satisfying as it had been to see Rob squirm and wonder if she would play the trump card of DNA testing the baby in due course, it hadn't changed her mind about not pursuing a case against him.

*Truth and proof are two different things*, the police officer had told her when she'd made enquiries and found out exactly what would be involved if she reported, and how long it would take. It wouldn't matter how true her truth was. If there wasn't incontrovertible proof showing what actually happened that night, there would be no conviction. Just months and years taken away from her when all she wants to do is live her life. Rob has been suspended from uni while investigations into the drink spiking incident in Danny O'Toole's are underway. Holly's blood test showed high levels of Rohypnol, or 'roofies'. Somehow Herb had gleaned this information. Maddie doesn't know how. Herb had directed all her energies to digging up every last detail about Rob's suspension and police charge when she realised that Maddie would not report, and no amount of arguing would change her mind.

"I don't understand you," she'd said gruffly, pulling Maddie in tight while Ella smiled at her from the other side of the room. The rest of her flat had reacted to the news of her pregnancy and Rob's attack in different ways. Kate fled home the day of the revelation and hadn't returned. Maddie wasn't sure how they would move forward from this. Hannah, rarely around these days anyway, was in equal measure outraged and distracted by end of terms labs, promising to 'be there' for Maddie as she hurried from the flat to meet her course friends. Josh and Martin were quiet, shocked by the news, circling around her at a careful distance, eyes darting to her belly when they thought she wasn't looking.

"It's a baby, not an alien, you idiots," she said, breaking the ice and putting in an order for tea and cake. She may as well make the most of being pregnant while it lasted.

She has asked Mum and Dad here because of the baby. Because she has finally made her decision. About what's next. She watches a group of seagulls swirling and dipping above them, and follows the path of one particularly bold gull as it swoops down low towards a family walking along the beach with chips. The little girl, maybe five years old, screams and runs to her parents for cover. Maddie smiles as she watches the mum gather the little girl in tight, while the dad shouts and chases the seagull away, brandishing an invisible sword. That is what she wants for her child. To be that mother. And that father. The one who loves and protects.

But Maddie knows she can't be that right now. She is not ready to be a parent. She wants the freedom to live her life while she is young, and all her choices are her own. And just like she doesn't want *his* name and *his* presence woven forever around her name and her life through endless court proceedings, she doesn't want this baby to grow up in the shadow of a rape. She rests her hand gently on her abdomen, feeling for the now familiar stir and kick of the child inside. Everything is still, right now. The baby must be asleep.

"I am going to give the baby up for adoption," she tells her parents.

Dad reaches over and picks up her left hand and Mum holds tight to her right. Nobody speaks. All their eyes are fixed on the break of the waves, gentle and relentless, and the seagulls continuing their swirling quest to find hapless chip-bearing victims.

Maddie sees Dad's eyes widen as an old man, nude and wrinkled apart from battered old trainers, strides confidently past them, briskly waving the seagulls away like they are nothing.

"What the…" Dad can't finish his sentence, and Maddie and Mum hold back their laughter.

"What is he…" Dad is about to lurch to his feet but Maddie pulls him back.

"It's the nudist bit of the beach, Dad," she says, tears of mirth springing to her eyes. "We are the odd ones out here, not him."

Dad's eyes widen with understanding, and he pulls Maddie to her feet. Mum gets herself up off the ground, and the three of them turn back towards the pier.

"In that case," Dad says, wrapping a strong arm round Maddie's shoulders and drawing her close, "we'd best be heading back."

# Chapter 45

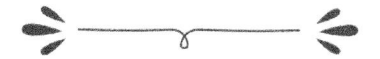

***Will***

There is an old red Ford Fiesta with one blue door on Uncle Andy's drive when Will arrives back after meeting Freya for a drink. It is the second Friday in March and dusk settles over the street like a shroud, broken only by the halogen glow of streetlamps blinking on like soldiers taking up their posts. Will pulls his coat more tightly around him as he walks up the drive to the front door, feeling the day's fragile warmth trumped by the last bite of winter.

As he fumbles for his keys to let himself in, the door opens, and there standing in the warm light spilling from the door is Sam, leaning on the door frame looking smug and dangling a set of car keys from his finger.

"Fancy a spin?" he says, grinning at Will as if it hasn't been nearly three months since they last stood face to face.

Will's eyes widen and he looks from Sam to the red car in the drive, and back again.

"In that?" he asks, eyeing the battered old car dubiously. "With you?"

Sam raises his eyebrows and shakes the keys in front of Will's face in invitation.

"Do you even know how to drive?"

"As of today," replies Sam, "the answer is yes. Are you coming or not?"

Will shrugs and follows him to the car, opening the blue passenger door and grimacing at its loud creak of protest. He pulls the seatbelt across his left shoulder and takes in the tape deck where the satnav should be.

"Mate..." he says to Sam. "What is *this*?"

Sam shrugs, unconcerned. "It's a relic," he says. "I'll give you that. But it's *my* relic. Get ready for the ride of your life."

Will rolls his eyes and suppresses a smile, the banter safe and familiar as an old friend.

They drive out of Storrington, winding along the narrow road until they reach the faster dual carriageway where Sam turns south towards Worthing. He puts his foot down and grins over at Will.

"Now we'll see what this baby can do," he says, and Will shakes his head, laughing.

Sam had messaged him regularly in those first days after Will's overdose, his words shocked and devoid of their usual casual insults.

*u ok?*

*m8?*

*wots going on?*

Will hadn't replied in the beginning, locked in his own wordless shock at what had happened. Shame and disbelief had wrapped themselves round him, holding him in that lonely space for weeks. When Sam had tried to see him in hospital, Will had simply shaken his head at Dad, refusing Sam entry. Sam finally retreated, messages dwindling and eventually stopping all together as school closed for the Christmas break and the old year gave way to the next. Gradually, Will began to feel again, and sadness at the painful loss of his oldest friend was first in line, clamouring for his attention.

When Will had finally reached out with a small and tentative *alright?*, Sam's response had been immediate.

*thot u'd never ask*

Sitting here now, together in Sam's battered old car which he'd bought with money he'd been saving for the day he passed his test, it seems all at once surreal and exactly right to be back in the same space as Sam. Will feels himself relax and exhale.

"Sorry, mate," he says quietly into the darkness of the car as Sam indicates to the right and overtakes a flash-looking BMW. "For everything."

Sam pulls back into the nearside lane and drops his speed.

"Nothing to apologise for," he replies.

"But..."

"We're mates," Sam says. "End of."

Will nods into the silence and stares at the road ahead of them, the black silhouettes of trees and lamp-lit green road signs flashing past in his periphery.

"Thanks," he says at last. "For sticking around."

Sam takes his eyes off the road, just for a moment, and says, "Just to be clear, though. If you ever feel like not sticking around again, you call me first."

Will's throat tightens. Why had he shut Sam out like that? Got so tight with Liam, who hasn't messaged him once? Word is that Liam is not even living at home now. He's disappeared off somewhere. Will feels a heaviness when he thinks of the other boy. It could so easily have been him. He hopes Liam will be OK.

"Yeah," he manages.

"I mean it," says Sam. "Pull that shit again and I'll set Josh on you."

Will laughs, an image of clueless, clean-cut Josh springing to mind.

"God help us all," he says.

*

Freya is sitting on Will's bed two weeks later, Jake's bed really, while Will gathers the last of his things and stuffs them into a duffel bag. Daniel is standing in the room drinking a can of Fanta, a frown creasing his forehead as he hops from one foot to the other.

"I don't see why you have to leave," he says. "I don't mind Jake staying in my room for a bit longer."

He tips his head back and swallows the last of his drink, setting the empty can on his desk and flopping down on the bed next to Freya.

"And anyway, Freya lives *here*, in Storrington," he continues, like this is the clincher.

Freya reaches out and tousles Daniel's dark hair. Daniel pulls away and glares at her. He is not taking Will's imminent departure well.

"I'll be just down the road mate," Will says. "Chichester's not that far away."

"It's *miles* away," says Daniel.

"I'll come back and visit," Will says, zipping up his bag and squeezing between Freya and Daniel on the bed.

"Visit *me*?" Daniel asks in a small voice. "Promise?"

Will shoves him gently on the shoulder.

"Promise."

Dad is taking him home tonight. Will finally decided to go after Sam's visit. Seeing his friend and hearing all the gossip from school triggered a longing for normality in Will that surprised him. He has had enough of online learning and is feeling restless. Plus, Dad has found a flat in the centre of Chichester and will be leaving Uncle Andy and Aunty Sue's early in April. Staying here without Dad doesn't feel right.

He and Freya have talked and talked about Will's next move, and she is cool with him going home. It is one of the things he likes about her. She knows who she is and what she wants and encourages Will to be the same.

"It's hardly the other side of the world," she'd said when Will tentatively raised the subject of leaving. "Finish your exams – you'll be done in three months – and then we'll see what's next."

She is comfortable with the unknowing, content to see where life takes them. Will envies her calm acceptance of the way things are. In hospital, the psychiatrist talked to him about the importance of learning to tolerate uncertainty, of finding the tools to keep himself well even while his external world spins away out of his control. Will didn't get it back then, but he thinks Freya does it naturally. He is drawn to her in ways that he struggles to articulate. They are talking about next year. Maybe saving up their money and going travelling together. Will finds it hard to grasp that this is one of his choices.

"What's stopping you?" Freya asked one evening when they were out together and Will discovered he couldn't answer her.

Now he pulls himself forward and up on to his feet, slinging the duffel bag over his shoulder and picking up his backpack. His sketchpad is sticking out. Will pulls it out and hands it to Daniel.

"Look after this, will you?" he asks, smiling as the younger boy grasps the notebook with both hands.

"Really?" Daniel asks, flicking through the pages of finished and half-finished drawings. Daniel's favourites are the super-hero sketches.

"Really," says Will. "Now, are you going to help me carry this lot down or leave me to do all the work?"

"You can do it," Daniel says, engrossed in the notebook. "I'm just a kid."

\*

His room is too neat. That's Mum for you. Lining everything up and finding out of sight places for stuff whose rightful place is on the floor or draped over his chair. But even the unfamiliar tidiness doesn't stop Will from feeling the relief of coming home. When he first left, his head was so messed up that all he could think about was getting away. He had no space to clock what he was leaving behind. Now he drops his bag on the floor and shrugs the backpack from his shoulders, tossing it on his desk and lowering himself onto his bed. The sheets smell clean and fresh.

Dad had dropped him off outside, not even switching off the engine before he drove off back to Storrington. He would talk to Mum later in the week, he told Will, once he'd moved into his new flat. He needed to get back tonight. He had a lot to do. Will knows this is not completely true, that Dad didn't want to come in and see Mum. But he can't think about that right now. The newfound hope and stillness inside feels fragile and fleeting, like a strong gust of wind might blow it away and leave him with nothing but the frightening emptiness from before. He can't risk that. Not yet. So he waved Dad off like it was no big deal, and turned to face the house that was the only real home he'd ever known.

Now Mum is standing at his bedroom door, tentative, like she is not sure she is welcome. She'd hugged him when he walked through the door, tight and wordless, and he'd hugged her back. It is complicated, how he feels about Mum. About what she did and what she hid from him. From all of them. He is not sure if he is ready to forgive her just yet, but also, he misses her. Misses being part of a whole family.

He glances over at her, nodding that she can come in if she wants. Mum gives a little smile and walks quickly over to his desk chair.

"I tidied up," she says, sitting down and gesturing at the orderly room like an offering.

"You don't say," Will answers. "Enjoy it while it lasts."

He kicks his shoes off to make his point, letting them lay where they drop. She smiles at him and leans back in the chair.

"Noted," she says, swiveling the desk chair from side to side, toe carving a dark arc in the pile of the carpet.

"I'm glad you're back," she says. "I missed you."

Will nods. He missed her too, but he is not ready to say the words out loud. He changes the subject.

"Mum," he begins, and she leans forward, elbows on knees. "I've been thinking... After school has finished, and I've earned a bit of money working with Dad, I'm thinking of maybe travelling a bit. Getting out of here."

Mum frowns as she thinks about this.

"I have been talking to Freya," he says. "She's great. Really amazing. She's saving up at the moment and well, we're thinking of going together."

Mum swallows and sits back.

"Just the two of you?" she asks.

"Yeah. Well, at first, anyway. You always meet other backpackers and stuff on the way. That's what Freya says."

Mum nods slowly. Will can tell that she is weighing up her words, talking carefully instead of just bundling in like she usually does, full of advice and direction.

"Where will you go?" she asks instead.

Will shrugs.

"I don't know any of that yet," he says. "I just know that I need to go. To do something… different."

"OK…" Mum says. "OK. Well. It sounds like you have a plan. Good for you, Will."

He looks at Mum. Smiles at her and realises that she is right. He does have a plan. It feels good.

"You'd better send me postcards," Mum says. "When you get to wherever you are going."

"Mum." Will shakes his head at her. "Have I taught you nothing? Postcards are for old people. If you want to get down with the kids, you are going to have to rethink."

Mum laughs.

"Maybe you can help me set up an Instagram account before you go. Or TikTok? Or that Snapchat thing?" she says as Will covers his face with his hands.

"Stick to the postcards, Mum," he says, laughing despite himself. "TikTok's not ready for you."

The next morning, Will wakes early. He is anxious about his first day back at school. He's met a lot of his tutor group online over the past few weeks and has spoken to most of his teachers about the work and assignments he's had to make up. But he hasn't seen anyone face to face and can't stand the thought of everyone looking at him and talking behind his back. He is nervous that the familiar environment will wake up the part of him that spiralled into self-destruct. He is still not sure exactly how he got to where he did. Maybe he'll talk to someone about it someday. But for now, he just wants to feel like his old self. His really old self. The one from before lockdown when his family was still whole and the world was normal.

As he stuffs a piece of toast and jam in his mouth, ignoring Mum telling him to clean up his crumbs, there is a knock at the door. Sam is outside, his red and blue car parked in the road outside the house.

"Taxi?" Sam asks.

Will looks at the car, considering his options.

"I don't know," he says. "I have a reputation to uphold you know."

Sam raises his eyebrows. "A reputation?"

Will nods. "Yup."

"Well," Sam replies carefully, "given that your transport choices are a tad limited, you may wish to reconsider. But, as I always say in situations just like this, your choice. You do you."

Will picks up his backpack, shutting the front door behind him and punching Sam on the shoulder.

"Fuck off, mate," he laughs.

Sam shoves him back and opens the blue door with a loud creak and a flourish.

"Not my style," Sam says as Will tosses his bag onto the back seat and climbs into Sam's car.

# Chapter 46

*John*

That first year with Hope was one of the happiest and most carefree of John's life. Apart from when he was a small boy, perhaps, his family intact and the world an exciting place full of adventure where he was allowed to be a child. During the first sun-kissed weeks of that Indian summer, they were rarely apart, each filling something in the other that had been lost along the way. Hope stayed at his caravan most nights, windows thrown open to let cooler air caress bare, entangled limbs. He spent days working at a local garden centre, she in a café in town, both willing the hours to pass more quickly so they could be together again. As the days grew shorter, nipped either end by first mist, then frost, John gathered Hope in his arms one day and held her close.

"Marry me," he murmured, breathing in the fresh air scent of untamed curls as she rested her head on his chest. "Let's never be apart."

He felt her smile and nod, the squeeze of her arms tightening around him.

"When?" she asked.

"Now."

Hope laughed. "I don't think it's that simple," she said.

"Tomorrow then, this weekend!" John shouted, lifting her chin to kiss her. "Soon."

They were married by Christmas, expecting Maddie by spring, and parents by the time the long days of their second summer drew to a close. John is not sure when Hope started to change. Was it that first spring when she learned she would be a mother, catapulting her into premature adulthood? Or later, when Maddie made her appearance as a mewling infant, and their nights moved from lovemaking to caretaking, their days from spontaneity to routine and responsibility. Parenthood unearthed an intense anxiety in Hope which shackled the free spirit he had first met, and introduced something more brittle and fragile into their marriage. But John never stopped loving her. If anything, responding to her vulnerability was like reconnecting with an old friend. He knew this life. Apart from the dark days around Will's conception, when John could not reach Hope through the darkness that engulfed her, there was comfort in this dynamic between them, its echo of harder, earlier times familiar and safe to them both. They made a life together, muddling through like families do until those halcyon early days became a dim memory, belonging to someone else.

*

John remembers them now as he surveys the small, two-bedroom flat he is renting in the centre of Chichester. It is situated on the top floor of a townhouse in mews just east of the cathedral. For the first time in his life, he has no garden. Just a wrought-iron balcony overlooking a small private car park. Standing there looking down, he can see shoppers, heads down and unaware of his gaze, intent on scurrying from A to B as quickly as possible. When he has settled in, he will fill the balcony with pots, carefully selecting perennials to bring life and colour to this small space every month of the year.

He imagines how the young Hope would have responded to this flat, hurrying in and doing a little dance, maybe even clapping her hands at this space that was all theirs. When he first met her, even the smallest, most inconsequential thing had brought her joy, like she was experiencing each pleasure for the very first time. He shakes this ghost of her away. There is work to be done, boxes to unpack.

Within days he has settled in and made as much of a home out of the cramped space as possible. He finishes the second bedroom first, painting the walls a soft blue. He hangs blinds and builds a small double bed next to a bedside table with a lamp that switches on with a tap and has two phone-charging ports. This is for Maddie or for Will when one of them wants to stay. They have both been to visit, to inspect this new space. Their enthusiastic words did not quite hide their discomfort at seeing their father living more permanently alone, away from home.

"Bit of a party pad," Will said, running a hand over the kitchen worktop, quiet at first as he took in the masculine surroundings. "May need to kick you out when I have the boys round."

John raised his eyebrows.

"That will need some further discussion."

Maddie was more direct, plumping down on his sofa after doing a recce of each room, each cupboard. She was like her mother. She rested her hands on her belly, sinking gratefully back into the cushions and lifting swollen ankles to rest on his coffee table.

"Don't you miss Mum?" she asked.

John didn't have to think about this. The answer to her question was as much a part of him as his own breath.

"Yes," he said.

Maddie pursed her lips and considered this.

"Then, why…?" Her voice trailed off.

"Sometimes, Maddie," he said thoughtfully, "missing someone is not enough."

He is not sure what would be enough. Not sure if anything will ever be enough. It is not just the betrayal, being left with the phantom pain of the severed biological connection with Will. It is the stepping away, the time outside the orb of all their marriage had become. Only within this outside space has John discovered how hard he has been working. How tired he is. He needs time to recover, to rehabilitate. It is the first time in his life that he has considered his own needs first. In the middle of the missing and the sadness, there is also a new peace, soothing as a warm bath after a hard day's work.

Hope comes to the flat for the first time a few weeks later. She has started texting him, at first on the pretext of sharing practical information and news about Maddie and Will, but more recently to ask after him. How is he doing? How is work? Would he like her to bring some of his summer things over? The warmer, drier weather is finally replacing the endless, damp spring. He agrees, wary of seeing her, but knowing that he must at some point.

Now she stands uneasily just inside the threshold of the flat, a suitcase and bulging box of his stuff resting either side of her like bookends propping her up.

She looks around, taking it all in.

"Never took you for a townie," she says at last.

He beckons her in.

"Neither did I," he says.

He has been surprised at how much this little space has felt like home. Not like the home of before. A new kind of home. He gestures out to the balcony, inviting Hope outside where clustered pots already sprout a riot of colour. Two honeybees dip, buzzing, from one flower to another.

"You can take the boy out of the countryside…" he says, and Hope smiles. A real smile that tugs at something deep inside John. The missing doesn't get any easier.

Hope rests her arms on the balcony, closing her eyes in the afternoon sunshine. Her hair lifts slightly in the soft breeze. John can see two strands of grey tucked behind her left ear and feels a rush of warmth towards her. The grey hairs are new, he thinks, a marker of the separate journeys they have walked these past six months. John wants to reach out and touch the silvery glint in her hair, but steps back instead.

"Thanks for bringing my stuff," he says, retreating to the living room and crouching down to rummage through the box. There are books, old CDs, some family photos, framed and frozen in time, a multi-tool that Hope bought for him on their tenth anniversary. He holds it lightly in his hand, then puts it back in the box, straightening and going into the kitchen as Hope comes back into the flat from the balcony.

"Cup of tea?" he asks.

Hope shakes her head.

"No," she replies, shifting the strap of her handbag on her shoulder and fidgeting with the clasp. "Thanks. I'd best be going. I've got to pick Maddie up soon," she adds. "For the appointment with the social worker at the hospital. About the adoption. She wants me to go with her."

John nods. He knows about the appointment, is glad Maddie has her mum with her.

"Let me know how it goes," he says as Hope walks towards the front door.

She nods, and opens it, lingering, her back still to him.

"John?" she says, his name soft and tentative on her lips.

"Yes?"

There is a pause, and Hope doesn't turn to face him.

"I was wondering. If…" she hesitates. "If you would think about coming home," she says in a rush. "Or if not coming home maybe going to counselling. Or…" She runs out of words. "I miss you, John."

*I miss you too.*

The thought is instant but he can't bring himself to say the words. The peace of the last few weeks has created a buffer around him, something different, and he doesn't want to lose it. To go back to how things were.

"The lease is for 12 months," he says instead. "So…"

Hope nods quickly.

"Yes," she says, gathering herself and turning back to face him with a too-bright smile. "OK then. Well. I'd better be off."

John lifts a hand.

"See you," he says.

"Yeah. See you."

And she is gone.

\*

He and Maddie meet up in Brighton that weekend and head for a quiet part of the seafront.

"Not the nudist bit, right?" he asks Maddie.

Maddie laughs. "No, Dad. Not the nudist bit. We'll spare the general public, shall we?"

John carries a small bag holding his swimming trunks, towel and flip flops. Maddie has her swimming gear already on underneath a long skirt and hoodie. Both sky and sea are slate grey, and a fresh breeze has kicked in from the southeast. The few people out walking in the blustery weather have jackets pulled tightly around themselves.

"Are you sure this is a good idea?" John asks, looking dubiously around and wondering where he will change into his trunks.

"Dad. It's called wild swimming for a reason. Come on, get changed."

"I thought it was called swimming in the sea. Which is normally reserved for hot days."

He shrugs off his coat and steps out of his boots. The stones on the beach are cold against his feet. Wrapping his towel around his middle, he slips off his trousers and boxers and pulls his trunks on. He is already shivering in the cool air.

Maddie is standing in a swimsuit, pregnancy clearly visible as she looks out at the white-tipped waves, dark hair whipping round her face with each gust of wind. Her cheeks are red and when she looks over at him, her eyes spark with challenge.

"Ready?" she asks.

"I'm not sure ready is the right word…"

"Come on, Dad," she says, slipping on her own flip flops and picking her way down to the water's edge. "It's good for you. Everybody is doing it."

"Everybody's doing it, are they?" John mutters, following her to the water's edge and dipping a toe in.

"Beat you in?" Maddie challenges, wading in without hesitation.

John watches his daughter, laughing as the water reaches first her knees, then her thighs, and finally her waist. She lifts her arms up and gasps, not stopping as she goes deeper and deeper. She amazes him. He starts forward, wading giant steps to reach her.

"No chance!" he calls out, not stopping until he passes Maddie, diving in headfirst.

The ice-cold water envelops him and, after the initial shock, he feels a rush of happiness and energy, like he has knocked back three strong cups of coffee. Just for a moment, painful past and uncertain future step away and all that remains is now. Now, in this place, with his daughter. Nothing else.

When his head breaks the surface, Maddie splashes him.

"See?" she shouts over to him, bobbing in the waves. "I told you!"

This wild swimming was Maddie's idea. She has been restless without her running and wanted to try something new. He came because she invited him, nothing more. But as the endorphins course through his bloodstream, and the peace of this present moment lingers on, he wonders if this day is also for him.

"Yes," he says, flipping over on his back and floating as grey clouds scud across the moody sky. "I think I do see."

# Chapter 47

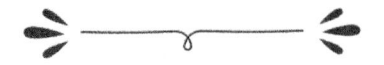

**Me**

*In your dream, you are at one end of a long corridor. It stretches so far into the distance that you cannot see the other side. There are no windows in the corridor, just open-shelved display cabinets lining both walls. The displays are filled with dolls' houses. Cottages, farmhouses, village shops, Victorian terraces, colonial mansions, Tudor barns, log cabins – even a converted lighthouse. You take one step. Then two. Gradually walking down the corridor, head turning from side to side so you don't miss one single detail. It is truly magical. Each doll's house is not only fully furnished, lit from the inside with tiny electrical circuits, but also filled with the detritus of daily life: discarded newspapers, tiny snow globes, an open biscuit tin, baby clothes on a washing line, a dog bowl. Dolls populate each house, arranged just so, their frozen features never changing. You walk from one house to the next, fingers trailing, taking in everything, adjusting one detail here, another there.*

*As you walk, a strange thing happens. The dolls' houses start to blur one into another. The miniature details become commonplace so that you no longer notice them in quite the same way. The fixed tableaux each capturing a moment in time begin to make you feel restless, agitated even. They are pretend. They are not real. You reach out and close the front of one house. You do the same thing to the next, and the next, shutting down each little miniature world as you pass. Your footsteps quicken. You raise your eyes to look beyond the dolls' houses, scanning the walls until finally you see it. There. The green glow of an exit sign, white stick figure running in the direction of the arrow. You hurry along until you reach it, still closing each house as you pass it, breathing quickly now.*

*Beneath the sign is a door. A real door. Your size. You stop and look back at the way you have just come. Back at all the closed houses, holding all those perfectly ordered miniature worlds. Then you turn to the real door and you open it. Sunlight streams in, beckoning you on. You step out and you lift your face, closing your eyes against the sudden brightness, the warmth. The door swings shut behind you and you start to walk, letting the messy, beautiful real world swallow you whole.*

\*

At first, I don't think of Ros. My world is full to capacity.

After talking to the social worker, Maddie has been put in touch with an adoption agency in Brighton and is meeting with them later this week. She has asked me to go with her. Her baby is due at the end of next month and everything is suddenly moving very quickly. When it is born, the baby will be placed with a temporary foster family until its new family is found. Maddie will have to wait six weeks before signing the baby away. Loss and respect mingle in my chest as I think of this final parting and wonder how Maddie will be. I want to kill that bastard Rob for putting her through this. I push him away. He is not worth the space in my head.

Will has been home since the end of March. His exams start on Wednesday and I hope he is ready. I find myself watching him when we are together. Subtly, so he doesn't notice. Gathering each word and change of expression like evidence, noting it and weighing it up to reassure myself that he is OK. I can't know, of course. I will never know for sure what is going on inside my son, whether he will stay upright, bending with the wind of life's cruelties and disappointments, or snap in two when faced with their force. Have my actions contributed to his vulnerability, or to his resilience? What have I given him in the end? I don't know. He is over six feet tall now. Just like his father. His real father in every way that matters. John.

My sadness about John is a constant companion. It greets me when I wake in the morning. Accompanies me downstairs as I pull back the curtains and open the blinds to each new day. Sits in the passenger seat of my car as I navigate the familiar route to my shop. Paves the way home again, sitting with me and Will and sometimes Sam, or Maddie and Herb as we chat together around the dinner table. Whispers a soft goodnight into my ear as I drift into exhausted sleep at the end of each day. I no longer hide from the sadness. Not the sadness of now nor the sadness of my past. I welcome it in as a part of me. Helen has taught me that. Introducing me to even the most shameful, deeply buried parts of myself that I never thought I would acknowledge myself, let alone share with another. It is a slow process, but we have time. There is no rush.

As the new shape of my life right now settles into place, the unknowing is all around me still. But it is held at bay by a new and growing sense of calm inside, and I find myself wondering about Ros. After that day in Brighton, when Maddie told Ros she would not report Rob to the police, Ros simply disappeared. Walked out of the café and out of our lives. Like she always does. I asked Maddie if she'd heard from her, but she hadn't. At first all I felt was relief, falling easily into my old narrative like water through smooth, eroded rock. Everything started with Ros. If she had never showed up in our lives, then maybe, maybe…

But since I'd started counselling, responding despite myself to Helen's compassionate re-ordering and framing of all the broken pieces of my life, I'd awakened my own internal observer. Which part of me blamed Ros for everything? And did that part of me hold the whole picture? Ros had stirred things up without question. But if I am honest, my life had been shaken to pieces long before Ros came onto the scene. And shaken again when she was simply a witness. A child as helpless as me. Sure, she colluded with the part of me that self-destructs when she fed me drugged brownies all those years ago, but that doesn't make her the villain. Just a messed-up kid like me.

So when my phone rings on a bright May afternoon, when Maddie is in Brighton and Will is out gardening with John, relief, rather than rage rises up as I hear Ros's voice on the other end of the line.

"Fancy a cup of coffee, sis?" she asks. "Or maybe something a bit stronger?"

I nod into the phone. "I have a bottle of Chardonnay in the fridge with your name on it," I say.

Ros is there half an hour later. She was already in Chichester when she called. Typical Ros. Leaving things until the last minute. We are sitting outside in the garden, chairs backing on to the summer house, chilled glasses of wine on the table before us. Ros is smoking a roll-up, inhaling deeply and blowing out little puffs like an ellipsis. We are quiet for a while, the silence soft and comfortable.

"That dickhead," she begins, and I know who she means without her saying his name. The dickhead of all dickheads. "He did it to me, too," she says.

The catch in her voice tugs at my heart. I am not surprised. A part of me has always known this to be true, but I have never given it a voice to speak the words. The rest of me couldn't face this last awful truth, and the part I played in it.

"I'm so sorry, Ros," I say now, bowing my head.

Ros gives a tired smile. "What are you sorry for?" she asks. "You weren't the dickhead."

"I left," I say. "I left you. With him."

Ros stubs out her roll-up on the arm of the chair and flicks the butt onto the grass. I nearly make a comment, point out the ashtray on the table, but stay silent instead.

She looks at me. "I would have left too," she says. "If I had been you."

"But..."

Ros cuts me off with a wave of her hand.

"Maybe," she says, "it's about time we stopped blaming each other. Maybe it is time to focus our energy on putting the blame right where it belongs."

I scrunch up my eyes as I consider her words. Swallow hard over the lump in my throat. She sounds like Helen.

"I think I'd like that," I say slowly.

"So, you're in?"

I look at Ros in confusion.

"In what?"

"Hope," she says. "That dickhead has got away with his crap for long enough. I think we should report him. Together."

"Report him?" My brain is lagging behind, still wrapped around the metaphorical re-laying of blame, not grasping at all what Ros is suggesting. "It's too late!" I say.

Ros sits forward now.

"Why is it, though?" she says. "*Why* is it too late?"

"Because... because..." I scout around for the reasons. "Well, for starters, it was 25 years ago!" I say. "We don't even know where he is. If he's still alive..."

"I know where he is," says Ros triumphantly. "And that dickhead is still alive and well. Unfortunately."

Of course she knows. I don't know why her tenacity surprises me. The thought of him, real in this present world, makes me feel nauseous.

"After Maddie," Ros continues. "After that day in the café, I was so wound up I thought I was going to explode. We had him. We had that bastard, and she was going to let him get away with it…"

I start to interrupt her to defend Maddie's decision, maternal instincts kicking in like a bodyguard. Ros waves impatiently for me to be quiet.

"I know, I know," she says. "It's Maddie's choice. I do get it. I just couldn't see it then. But after a few days, I couldn't get out of my head how it had felt being so close, *so close,* to getting justice. And I realised then… it's *me* who needs justice. And you. That's *our choice,* Hope. So I tracked him down. The dickhead. I tracked him down and I know where he is."

I am still fumbling to keep up with the direction this conversation has taken but feel an answering thump in my chest as I allow the possibility of putting the truth out there, after all these years, to filter through.

"But isn't it too late?" I ask, not trusting myself, the hope inside not yet fully formed.

"No!" Ros is grinning now, like she is holding the ultimate trump card. "I called the NSPCC and they told me it is never too late to report historic abuse. Never."

"But…" A part of me wants to follow her, to pick up the gauntlet and run with it. With Ros. But another part is sluggish and fearful.

"They won't believe us," I say. "We don't have proof."

"We have your story," says Ros, "and we have mine. It's a start."

I am quiet for a long moment, weighing it all up.

"Come on, Hope," she says. "Let's do this. For us. Even if it goes nowhere, we'll give that bastard some sleepless nights."

She is right. I think of all the sleepless nights that I endured, that Ros endured at his hands. When we were vulnerable. Without a grown-up in the world to take care of us. I think of the sleepless nights since, and the days and nights when all I could do to survive was sleep. The legacy of all that happened.

I reach across the gap between us and grab Ros's hand, feeling the cold, sharp edges of her rings as I squeeze, tight.

"OK," I say, and she smiles. "OK."

*

A week later, Ros and I stand outside the red brick building of Chichester police station, its double row of white-framed windows staring down at us like sentinels. Three concrete steps lead up to the double wooden doors. Ros looks over at me with a fierce grin, short hair pushed back into messy spikes. Just like Ros. Just like both of us.

"Ready?" she asks.

I look at the door, then back at Ros, breathing deeply like Helen has taught me to slow the racing of my heart, to access the grown-up part of me that is right at this moment holding tightly to the hand of the young girl inside.

"Ready," I say.

We walk up the steps together.

# EPILOGUE

## Ten months later

We've all come to the airport to see Will and Freya off. We arrive at Gatwick's South Terminal with plenty of time to spare – me, Maddie, Herb and Ros first. John in his car with Will, Freya and her mum half an hour later. The small delay tightens the knots in my stomach, forcing me to sit down and draw up my knees until the discomfort inside settles.

*traffic on a23*, Will taps back in response to my anxious message 20 minutes after our arrival. Ros, Maddie and Herb are buying coffees, unperturbed.

*chill mum*

I am chilled, I think, standing up again and pacing. This is as chilled as I get on the day I am saying goodbye to my youngest child for the next six months. They are flying to Barcelona on the 13.10 flight. It is 10.30 now. Freya has friends there, so they will stay with them before heading south. They have both been working for the past year or so, saving every penny for this trip, and finally they are ready to take the leap.

"But where will you go after that?" I asked Will as he packed up his things earlier this week, unable to imagine setting off with a passport and backpack and no clear idea of my destination.

*You've been doing that all your life.*

*Yes, I know.*

I responded to the voice inside with an edge of impatience, and I imagined it holding up its hands, *OK, OK!*

*That's metaphorical.* I lobbed the words after the voice as it retreated to the edge of my awareness. *It's different.*

I was talking to myself now.

*I just want him to be safe.*

"We don't know where we'll go," Will had explained to me in a voice that suggested I was acting very old right now. "That is kind of the point."

So here we are. John, Will, Freya and her mum are here now as well, walking together and laughing easily like it is any other day and check-in hasn't been open for nearly an hour already.

I feel Maddie link her arm through mine and lean into me.

"OK, Mum?" she asks.

I nod, not trusting myself to speak.

*I will not cry*, I tell myself.

"Liar," she says, smiling at me and squeezing.

I reach over and smooth my daughter's hair behind one ear. It has grown out from last year's bob and rests on her shoulders in messy waves. Red highlights run from root to tip like a bold statement. Herb's influence, I think.

The last year has been hard on Maddie. There were times when I wondered if she would make it through. The baby came two weeks late in the end, holding on inside Maddie like he knew the world wasn't all it was cracked up to be. He made his entrance on the first day of July. Maddie, exhausted after a two-day labour, reached out for him and held him close, pressing her face to his, whispering words and tears over this brand-new life that only he could hear. I couldn't watch as the nurse took him gently from her arms, leaving the room and our lives. I had gone to Maddie then. Holding my child as tightly as she had held hers. Later, John came. Gathering her up and covering her over like a wounded chick.

In the weeks following the birth, Maddie had drifted between my house and John's, silent and pale while we baked in record-breaking heat. Ros stayed with us for a bit, coaxing first a smile and sometimes even laughter from Maddie with her tales of outrageous behaviour from her travels. Will finally stopped circling round the edges of their conversations and joined in. Time and the anticipation of his own escape dulled and eventually laid to rest the shame he still carried from that disastrous night with Ros. Standing in the doorway one evening, watching them laugh and joke together, I realised I was grateful. For Ros. For Will, wrapped up in life now instead of fleeing from it. For Maddie. Quiet. More serious now. Older than her years. I wish she would talk to somebody. Somebody like Helen. But whenever I suggest it, she refuses.

"I don't want to go over everything again, Mum," she said. "I just want to get on with my life now."

"But..." I thought of how I had tried to do that. For so long. How burying things had left me.

"Mum," Maddie said gently. "I'm not you."

I swallowed. Hard.

"My story is not your story. I need to do this my way."

Maddie doesn't know my whole story. Maybe I will tell her one day. Maybe I won't. Helen is the only person who knows it all. Maybe that's enough. Watching Maddie confront what happened to her head-on and make her own hard choices in the aftermath has been humbling for me. She went back to uni in the autumn, sharing a flat in the centre of Brighton with Herb and Ella. She is stronger than I ever could be.

*What is strong, Hope?*

I hear Helen's voice in my head, gently challenging, and roll my eyes at her. It is crowded enough in here already.

"We're ready!"

The excitement in Will's voice is palpable. He has a bag slung over his shoulder, boarding pass in hand. He holds his arms open, inviting me in for a hug. My eyes widen. This is new. I smile, his happiness infectious, and walk into his arms, squeezing tight.

*Yes, you are.*

My throat is too tight to speak the words out loud. I watch as Will and Freya hug first John, then Freya's mum, who is openly weeping, and lastly Maddie.

"Have fun writing boring essays," Will calls back at her as he and Freya walk away. Maddie laughs, holding up two fingers to his departing back.

*

A week later, I am on my way to John's flat to pick up Maddie. It is reading week at Sussex Uni and she has come home, splitting her time between the two of us. She is out with friends and isn't back when I arrive. John offers me a coffee, and I accept. I have been to his flat a handful of times in the past year and have never been able to relax in this new space. I am not a part of it. Even two floors up, it smells and feels like John and the outdoors, patio doors thrown open even in the cool March air, early spring flowers making an appearance on the balcony.

Things between us are softer now. Gentler. He and Maddie have been wild swimming every week since she recovered from the birth and have taken to walking miles and miles together through the Sussex countryside. Will and his friends are regulars in the flat. I have seen a lightness in John that has surprised me. In all our time together, my own darkness always took precedence, an unspoken part of me assuming that his life was easy. Yes, his dad died when he was still a boy, but at least he had a dad. My disavowed bitterness at the injustice of my life had obliterated John along with everything and everyone else. Unwrapping and exploring each layer of my story with Helen has helped me to see that.

John's relaxed smile as he pours the coffee makes me happy and sad all at the same time. I want what is best for him. Want him to be happy. But I miss him too. Long for him. For the chance to love him as the grown-up me. Not as the angry, wounded child me.

"Sugar?" he asks.

I tilt my head at him.

"How long have you known me?" I ask, shaking my head as he holds the spoon up in question.

John smiles.

"A lifetime," he says simply.

"Exactly," I reply, standing up and taking the mug of coffee he holds out. "And when have I ever taken sugar?"

John is quiet, stirring his own coffee longer than necessary. Finally, he looks up at me.

"Maybe you've changed," he says quietly, and we both know that he is not talking about the coffee.

"Maybe we've both changed," I reply, holding his gaze. We stand like that for a long moment.

"I was wondering," he says softly, not taking his eyes from mine. "If you'd like dinner sometime."

I am nodding before I find the words.

"I'd like that," I say finally. "I'd like that very much."

Maddie arrives back and we drive home together. I am 19 years old again. A different kind of nineteen. Young and tanned and laughing and free. Properly free. And Maddie is twenty. Her 19th year growing smaller and smaller in the rear-view mirror. We pull into the drive, and before the engine has stopped, Ros opens the front door and comes flying down the path, phone in hand.

"Hope!" she cries, yanking open the driver's door and leaning into the car, face flushed and eyes sparkling. "The police called. They just called!"

I am holding my breath, and Maddie reaches out and squeezes my hand. Ros and I gave our statements nearly a year earlier, and the police have been investigating Jeremy ever since. Long months passed without us hearing anything. Part of me thinks that reporting was enough. It's all we could do. We have been warned that the Crown Prosecution Service won't pick up the case if the evidence isn't likely to lead to a guilty verdict. Most cases end up NFA – no further action.

"There are others," Ros is saying. "Lots of others!"

I nod, unable to fully take in what she is saying.

"The CPS. They have enough evidence," she says. "They're picking up the case…"

She waits.

"Hope!" she cries. "We're going to court! We're going to take that dickhead down."

Ros is laughing now, pulling me out of the car and hugging me tightly while her words unfurl inside me and take on meaning. A mix of emotions rise up. I will need to unpick those with Helen. For now, Maddie hurries round from her side of the car and wraps her arms around both of us.

The three of us stand like that for a long time, each of us thinking our own thoughts. A light rain begins to fall, and we turn, hurrying together through the front door and into the warmth and light of home.

**The End**

# ABOUT THE AUTHOR

L.N. Lenon is a journalist turned trauma therapist. As well as working with her own clients, she runs a local counselling centre supporting people from all walks of life. Her writing is inspired by those who have survived and touched freedom on the other side. Born in California, she moved to the UK as a child and now lives in West Sussex with her husband Ian, two cats and a head full of stories and characters from the perennial pile of books on her bedside table. Her lovely grown-up children and their partners live nearby. *Playing House* is L.N. Lenon's first novel.

# ACKNOWLEDGEMENTS

Thanks to my family for your unwavering support and encouragement. To my husband, Ian, for always believing in me. You are my rock. To my daughter, Meghann - a first, honest reader of this book and reflector of truth. And my son, Zac, a great supporter who warned unwary bystanders not to linger lest they be written into the story.

Thank you to my mother, who taught me to love books as soon as I was old enough to read and who read each chapter of this book as soon as it was written.

A final thanks to my own counsellor who helped me both to find and learn to accept all the parts of myself. Especially the badass ones.